Melissa H

NEBUCHADNEZZAR
KING OF BABYLON

MASCHLER
PUBLISHING

Donegal, Ireland

ISBN: 978-0-9955122-1-4
© 2016 by Melissa Riordan
Second edition
Published by Maschler Publishing
Cornaveigh
Lough Eske
Co. Donegal F94 W9Y0
Ireland
Contact: Timothy Maschler
tjmaschler@gmail.com
Cover: BorneOfDreamsDesign.com

To
Patti McKay Grewe
with love and gratitude

To the LORD be the glory!

From King Nebuchadnezzar

To all the peoples, nations, and languages
living throughout the earth

"Shalom rav! (Abundant peace!)"

PROLOGUE

Jerusalem, c. 3397 Anno Mundi (c. 600 BCE)

IT was spoken long ago, the wind blows wherever it pleases, and although we hear its sound, we cannot tell where it comes from or where it goes. Indeed, long long ago, a whirlwind blew wherever it pleased. Advancing like the clouds, it churned across the land crushing everything in its path. But it was so far away from Jerusalem, no one saw its brutal force or heard its roaring din. Yet, for three-year-old Aridatha, even though the leaves were not rustling and the flags on the Jerusalem wall were not fluttering, it was there, upon her, jolting her awake, its impact so startling she thought it must be her father grabbing her and telling her to get up because something important was happening today. But papa was in a distant land fighting Nebuchadnezzar's wars and there was no one in her nursery except Lazy Lamb sleeping at her feet. Still, she sensed papa wanted her to know something. What was it? Whom could she ask?

Hearing her mother's gentle breathing on the other side of the curtain, she rose quietly and peered into Zillah's room, more exquisite than any bed chamber in Jerusalem with its life-size marble sculptures of Sarah laughing and Ruth gleaning, the silver-framed mirrors reflecting her mother's jeweled capes, the silk-canopied bed stationed to get the breezes and, of course, Zillah, known throughout Jerusalem as a rare beauty, melting into the cushions like a young queen, her arm draped over the linen sheet.

Aridatha was tempted to creep over, take hold of her mother's eyelashes, open her eyes, and ask what was happening today. But Zillah had a sharp tongue whenever she was awakened, especially for what she called one of Aridatha's prattling questions. So the three-year-old crawled back into bed and, nuzzling into Lazy Lamb, immediately thought of the tall

man. He would know. All she had to do was go to the entrance gate and
wait for him to pass by. But she was not allowed to go out in the dark.
Besides, what would she say to him? She did not know his name or who
he was. Yet somehow she knew papa would want her to go. So, motioning her lamb to be quiet, she hitched on her wooden dagger, tip-toed
from the room, and sneaked out the front door.

The fastest route to the entrance was through the fig grove, and even
though it was dark, she took it, her feet crunching against the leaves
so loudly she thought she would wake the house. But no one shouted or came running, and thrilled by her daring, her three-year-old legs
pumped faster, racing through the grove, into the fountain courtyard,
and across the gravel path to Yosef ben-Moshe's massive wrought-iron
gate. Grabbing the bars, she hopped onto the bottom rung and peered
out at the road. The tall man was not there.

Nothing was there except night, the leaves of the sycamine trees no
longer sunlit green but a dusky moonlit silver. Startled by her sudden
arrival, a desert owl flew out of the towering branches, swooped onto the
bronze Star of David at the top of the gate, and stared down at her. Just
as unexpectedly, he flew away, his wings ruffling the silence. After that,
all was quiet; so quiet, her ears felt deaf. A rabbit and a fox dashed by but
no sign of the tall man.

So she waited and while she waited she remembered the first time
she saw him: a crisp spring morning when she was one year old and
strapped to her mother's back. High in her perch, she could observe
her entire world: the main house with its shady corridors and papa's
palms on the rooftop, Zillah's Ashtoreth banners lining the courtyards,
slaves and their children working the gardens, ancient weavers spinning
in front of squatty stone homes with bright red doors, and a flurry of
cooks at the outdoor ovens scaling fish, kneading breads, and chopping
onions. Looking down, she watched lambs capering, ewes chewing, and
a lonesome ram scratching his head against the rocks. Turning her attention beyond the wall, she gazed out at her favorite sight: the Temple of
Solomon. Not the whole Temple because papa's fig grove, the broadest
and most fruitful in Jerusalem, blocked most of its golden glory. Still, if
she looked hard enough, she could see the lily-shaped tops of the two
bronze pillars, and that was when she saw him: the tall man.

He was a fearsome presence striding down the road, tall like papa, but unlike papa bent in the shoulders as if weighed down by a heavy yoke. He wore a crimson pouch swaying at his heart and he looked so alone she reached out to grab him, kicking her legs and thrashing her arms so frantically, she threw her mother off balance and they both fell to the ground. Zillah scolded her sharply, but Aridatha did not hear because she was too overwhelmed by the joy of discovering the tall man and the grief of instantly losing him.

As soon as she was able to walk alone, she toddled out to the gate every morning just to get a glimpse of him, and now in the dark, his silhouette rose up in the distance, moving quickly. As usual he was alone and, as usual, he seemed to be in a great turmoil, his brow knotted and his lips moving as if talking to someone. Indeed, he was very early this morning.

"Shalom," she called.

Jolted from his reverie, he looked around, surprised to see a little girl hanging half-in and half-out of Yosef ben-Moshe's gate. She had rumpled chestnut hair falling below her shoulders, half braided, half loose; a miniature wooden dagger hanging at her waist; and the Stars of David embroidered in her tunic hem.

"You must be the daughter of Yosef ben-Moshe." Watching her chin jut out proudly and her head bob up and down, he probed further, "What is your name?"

"Aridatha," she replied, concentrating on making her three-year-old voice speak clearly. "What is your name?"

"Jeremiah," he said, leaning in low. "It is dark out here and you look cold. Is anything wrong?"

"Jeremiah!" she exclaimed, her eyes widening. "Are you the prophet of God?"

He nodded.

Staring at the small crimson pouch swaying at his heart, then up at his looming features, she stated matter-of-factly, "I come out here every morning and watch for you. But you never see me."

No, he had not seen her, but studying her closely, he wished he had. For even at her young age, her thoughtful expression revealed the same stubborn strength of her father. Her eyes, especially riveting, were like none he had ever seen, drawing one into a grave knowledge. "Your eyes," he said, "They shine like a light at the end of a tunnel. Like Jerusalem."

Without hesitation, she replied, "That is because I am Aridatha of Jerusalem." Normally, she would have rattled off a list of Jerusalem's high points, especially the Temple of Solomon and the Ark of the Covenant, but afraid he might move on, she blurted, "Something important is happening today. What is it?"

Now he understood why she was at the gate. Yosef ben-Moshe was away, and without her father to go to, she had been drawn out to him.

"A great battle is being fought today," he replied gravely. Seeing she wanted to know more, he picked up a stone and drew two large circles in the dirt, one above the other, and then a very small circle next to them. "Do you see this small circle?"

Slipping through the bars—for although papa's gates successfully kept in the horses and the sheep, Aridatha could easily squeeze through—she hunkered down to look. The prophet had drawn the two large circles like boulders and the small circle like a pebble.

"Today, far away to the north, this small circle—Nebuchadnezzar Crown Prince of Babylon—will fight against these two large circles—Assyria and Egypt."

"That small circle is Nebuchadnezzar?"

It was a difficult name to pronounce, but Jeremiah understood her tortured abridged version and nodded.

"But it cannot be! Papa has gone away to fight for him!"

Again he nodded.

"And these two big circles," she queried, outlining each boulder, "are they really that big?"

"Bigger."

Shaking her head, Aridatha sighed, "Such a small circle cannot win."

Knowing such a small circle was going to win, Jeremiah waited until she turned and met his eyes. "A voice is heard in Ramah, mourning and weeping."

It was as if he had entered into a conversation with someone else, but no one else was there and he was looking straight at her, so she listened.

"Rachel weeping for her children," he continued. "Refusing to be comforted because her children are no more." He glared keenly at her, as if searching to see if the strange message had landed on fertile soil.

Although she understood most of the words, the way he had combined them made no sense at all. Still, she nodded because something inside suddenly hurt as if she had been jabbed, almost wounded, bringing tears to her eyes. Tears filled his eyes also, and for a long moment, they stood silent in their shared grief. Soon he picked her up, and enunciating the name Nebuchadnezzar very slowly, he made her repeat it. When she could say it correctly, he turned her to face the horizon, and watching the sunrise together, he declared, "He advances like the clouds. His chariots come like a whirlwind and his horses are swifter than eagles."

PART I

THE HEAD OF GOLD

1

Carchemish

FAR away in Carchemish, the same sunrise brightened a cloudless sky. Yet, as Jeremiah had told Aridatha, clouds were advancing. Furthermore, the air was completely still, not one breeze tousling the leaves or rumpling the river mists. Yet a whirlwind was blowing over the land: Nebuchadnezzar Crown Prince of Babylon.

Careering his chariot across the back plateau of the Carchemish ridge, his thick black braids, having broken free from their eagle clasps, flew out behind him, his wet raven beard catching the gnats. His coat of polished bronze scale, a gift from the Chinese Emperor Kuangwang, rattled fiercely against his body; his leather armor, inscribed with the prayer, *To Marduk: With this victory I will cause your temple to shine like the sun*, tightened against his chest; and his double-edged swords and bronze daggers bumped and thumped against his sides. From his chest down, he was glistening wet because he and his charioteers, cavalries, and running infantry had sneaked across the Euphrates River just before dawn. To keep his surprise, he had led his men across the backside of the plateau, and now breaching the sunlight at the summit's edge, he whipped his horses over the crest with such fury, his chariot took to the air as if wanting to ascend to the heavens. But the heavenlies were not Nebuchadnezzar's goal today. Another day definitely, but not today. So crashing the cart back to the earth, he catapulted down the hill.

To his left, his chief commander Arioch led South Division, his huge dog Alcola barking wildly at the horses, keeping them at a thunderous pace. To Nebuchadnezzar's right, his other chief commander Yosef ben-Moshe led North Division. Assigned the most treacherous grade, Yosef ben-Moshe charged headlong into the crags, dodging thickets and vaulting over rocky troughs, determined to keep his men at the same thunderous gait. However, unlike Nebuchadnezzar and Arioch, he did not need a whip or a dog to urge his horses onward. Instead, he had a shield fixed to his chariot's front panel, and under its Star of David crest, his horses ran like the wind, all ease and brilliance.

Nebuchadnezzar did not have to ask what was happening today. He knew. Today was the Battle of Carchemish. Assigned to Babylon before the ancient past and ascribed to last beyond the distant future, it was a day reserved for him. Yes, it was his final blow against Jeremiah's large top circle, the crumbling Assyrian empire, but in his mind that carried no more weight than one small kingdom overthrowing an empire. However, when Egypt had entered the fray, marching north to ally with Assyria against Babylon, the battle had been upgraded to a watershed shakeout that would change the future of the world. Either Egypt would win and rule the world with all the future and glories of men stemming from Pharaoh, or Nebuchadnezzar would win and rule the world with all the future and glories of men stemming from him.

Well, not exactly from him, not while his father, Nabopolassar King of Babylon, was still alive. For as long as his father lived, Nebuchadnezzar was trapped in the role of Crown Prince which meant all his victories, along with all the power and glory that went with them, belonged to his father. Furthermore, his father might live for decades leaving Nebuchadnezzar, although a conquering hero, a complete nothing in the annals of history. Even worse, a complete nothing in the great Babylonian epic written and sung by Shining One. Indeed, that fate would be a bitter pill to swallow, but for now Nebuchadnezzar swallowed it because Babylon was all that mattered. So hurtling out onto the plain, followed by the deafening roar of boots, hooves, and chariot wheels, he shouted, "BA-BY-LON!"

The wild creatures on the plain knew the difference between a storm fueled by wind and fire and one fueled by cruelty that showed no mercy, and sensing the latter approaching, every deer, boar, mountain lion, fox, and hare ran for cover. Arioch, on the other hand, hearing Nebuchadnezzar's shout, turned and stared in awe because there was no other man like him. No other warrior, prince, or visionary. Certainly no other voice, a voice that shattered the dawn, for at Nebuchadnezzar's command, it was so.

Arioch had first heard that voice when he and Nebuchadnezzar were fifteen years old and complete strangers, each galloping from a different direction toward a burning bridge. Arioch had come to put out the fire, but young Nebuchadnezzar had come to cross the bridge because that was the direction he was traveling. Without slowing down, he shouted, "NOTHING CAN SHAKE ME," to all around: the sky, mountains, trees, grasses, and especially the fire before him, then galloped headlong onto the bridge. Spellbound, Arioch watched him disappear into the inferno and, after a gripping delay, blast out of the smoke and onto the other shore.

Having never seen anything like it, Arioch could not let the young man get away, so abandoning his mission to save the bridge, he charged after him. Racing onto the flaming timbers, he briskly dodged falling logs and burning floorboards, when a sudden wall of smoke blocked his vision. He could still see the shore behind him, but the young man was on the shore ahead of him. So choking on the fumes, he plunged into the darkness, ordering his horse to jump. Hooves catching on the crumbling planks, his mare leapt and, soaring into the blinding air, landed them safely on the riverbank just as the bridge collapsed.

The two boys checked their horses for burns, and grateful there were none, they burst into laughter, introduced themselves, and rode on together. Even during that first mile, Arioch stared in awe at Nebuchadnezzar, elegantly clad in sturdy leather breeches, knee-high boots, and a supple reindeer cloak, every garment and weapon tattooed with the royal seal of Babylon. His thick black braids, tied back in silver eagle clasps, magnified his angular face, not sharp angles but strong demonstrative features, and his eyes, roving the landscape, possessed a restless hunted look. His gait was easy in the saddle, his horse understanding his every shade of command, and suddenly Arioch wondered where the Crown Prince and his horse were going in such haste. To the river to fish? The mountains to hunt? Perhaps the next village to buy grain? Wherever it was, he hoped he could go with him, so he shouted over their galloping horses, "Where are you going?"

Nebuchadnezzar stopped. Could he trust this new acquaintance? Even more to the point, did he want him following him everywhere he went? By the look of him, he was probably a Scythian with his wheat-blonde hair shorn at the neck and his clear blue eyes sparkling, at least for now, with fresh exuberance. If he was a Scythian, one day those eyes would be as hard as a cold sea. Moreover, his tall, lanky frame would fill out to be broad and intimidating. He wore a pointed felt cap and a wool-tasseled felt jacket fitted to his torso. Both were dyed in mottled forest greens, enabling him to disappear into the forest. Clearly, someone of fine taste and a cultivator of rare wool must have made them, perhaps his mother, placing her as nobility. But the dagger in his belt was a common blade, so his father was surely a peasant. Even so, an unusual one because he had a noblewoman for a wife and he obviously knew horses. For although the youth's milking mare was a dowdy-looking, shaggy sorrel, she was of strong working stock, not to mention willing to gallop through fire for her master.

"I am going to the catacombs of the Far East. Want to come?" Without waiting for an answer, he galloped away.

"China?!" Arioch gasped, wondering how he could go to China and still hurry home to tell his father and mother. More importantly, what about his wedding day, his marriage to fifteen-year-old Soheil in two months? If he went directly to China and turned around on the same day, he would not make it back in time. Besides, if he just rode off, who would help his father build their new house? Were his seven younger siblings strong enough to dig out the rooms, install the timber panels, then cover the outside with thick sod? Could they corral the migrating reindeer and earmark their calves? What about the sheep and goats, the haying and timbering? Above all, what about Soheil, her warmth like the sunrise, her smile like the fox? The two had grown up together, and if he went away, his eyes would search for her everywhere: her laughter amidst the herds, her bronze arms cradling an injured goat, her scarf blowing in the wind when she waved goodbye to him at sunset. All these were his life.

Or was his life taking a turn? The young man galloping away was not just any young man. He was the Crown Prince of Babylon. Surely Soheil would understand, and if not, his mother would help her understand because his mother would want him to go. With her bloodline going back to Hammurabi, she had quietly imprinted her background into Arioch's life, steering him toward nobility. On the other hand, his father whom he loved and admired more than anyone would be angry at him, even worse, disappointed. After keeping the tribes from going to war against one another, he had been their chieftain for years. Moreover, he had been grooming Arioch to take his place. But the Crown Prince of Babylon was galloping farther down the road, and Arioch had to choose: should he go with Nebuchadnezzar to the Far East or return to a bridge that had already burned? Telling himself his siblings could manage without him for a year, he did what any normal fifteen-year-old would do: he raced after the Crown Prince of Babylon.

Soon he learned Nebuchadnezzar was headed to the Far East to search out the history behind Shining One's great Babylonian epic. The young Prince, having planned the journey to the last day, assured Arioch they would be gone no longer than three years. They were gone five.

That was over ten years ago, and ever since, Arioch had lived and breathed for this one man. Together they had gathered Babylon's mightiest men and trained them to be the greatest warriors on earth. Together they had defeated every Assyrian capital until they had the dying empire cornered at Carchemish. Now, with arrows sharpened and shields oiled, they were taking on Egypt. What might! What brilliance! What unadulterated joy!

So, Arioch returned the shout, "BA-BY-LON!"

Then, as if the two had already mastered the world, they burst into laughter.

Seeing Arioch laughing in the distance, Nebuchadnezzar remembered the day they had laughed together after crossing the burning bridge. He had made it across the bridge because nothing could shake him. But Arioch? He still did not know how Arioch had made it across. He should have caught fire or fallen through the floorboards into the rapids below. But because he had made it across, Nebuchadnezzar concluded the young Scythian had been sent to him by the gods and thus agreed to let him accompany him to China.

China...

Over the years, he had forgotten about China and its curious hold on him, but during the past week, the sleeping giant had risen up before him like a haunting muse. Starting with Arioch suggesting he bribe the Carchemish villages for their loyalty, to trying on his coat of polished bronze scale given to him by Emperor Kuangwang, to practicing the Chinese chariot grip on his reins, thoughts of China had interrupted his concentration at least once a day, especially the repeated image of the Chinese Emperor and his *Sangong:* the Three Grand

Dukes—Grand Guardian Li, Grand Preceptor Au Yang and Grand Mentor Tin—laughing at him. They had never laughed at him when he was in China, but he was sure they were laughing now, each declaring with winks and know-it-all grunts that his stay in China had been more important to his life than Carchemish. China more important than defeating Assyria and Egypt? A preposterous notion! Nothing was more important than Carchemish.

Still, he had to admit his years in China had influenced him, expanding his knowledge, widening his understanding, and perhaps even changing his life. So as he pounded across the plain, he let his mind drift back to those years, starting with his first day in the capital Luoyi, when just like today, he was wearing wet clothes and riding a wet horse.

2

Luoyi, *China's capital of the Third Dynasty, Zhou*

AFTER a night of swimming the banks of the Luo River, fifteen-year-old Nebuchadnezzar had planned to gallop boldly up to the gate of Emperor Kuangwang's walled palace and announce himself. However, before he could get near, he was blocked by a maze of giant bronze dragons obstructing the road with false switchbacks, blind alleys, and deadends. Arioch suggested they travel north and enter the city through the public gates, but young Nebuchadnezzar was not going to be detoured by dragon tails painted green and gold and red or razor-sharp tongues sticking out as if to devour the intruder, also painted green and gold and red. So the two moved slowly through the maze, crisscrossing in and out of tails and ducking under tongues, making their way toward the palace gate.

"I do not like the look of this," fifteen-year-old Arioch grumbled.

"Each dragon is probably inhabited by a different god," the Crown Prince explained, dropping his head to his horse's neck so the two could shimmy under a scowling scarlet tongue. "But Shining One is greater than all China's dragons."

"I am not talking about these monstrosities," replied Arioch. "I am talking about the entry before us."

Because Nebuchadnezzar now trusted Arioch as his watchman—for the young Scythian was ever-alert, expecting danger around every corner and behind every tree—he had not been studying the hazards ahead but thinking of Luoyi's fragmented wall left behind. Supposedly the wall, like all walls, was meant to protect and in this case meant to protect the capital. But the wall stopped at the Luo River as if expecting the river to be a continuation of the barrier and thus keep invaders out. Indeed, the river was a substantial deterrent, but last night, he, Arioch, and their two horses had inched along the riverbank around the wall—sometimes swimming, sometimes treading water, sometimes almost drowning—and sneaked into the emperor's city, proving the "river wall" useless and Luoyi's security weak.

So young Nebuchadnezzar, instead of fretting over present dangers, was fretting over how to build his wall for his future capital, Babylon. Learning from China's mistake, he decided his wall would not stop at the River Euphrates but surround the capital completely. Second, and this was the exciting part, he would re-route the River Euphrates into a canal around his wall, creating a double barrier to protect the capital. Third, because he planned to have secondary canals running throughout the city, they would be gated, grated, and guarded. Finally, he would build his wall not only tall and wide but reaching into the depths of the earth, so no invader could climb it, breach it, or dig under it.

It was a brilliant plan, but he knew it would be impossible to implement because Babylon raised warriors, not builders. As a result, no one in Babylon knew how to construct anything but rudimentary barricades, earthworks, siege ramps, and a hodge-podge of unleveled roads connecting a half dozen structures to the chieftains' tents. His father, King Nabopolassar, had refurbished some buildings and temples, but he had no overall plan. Even worse, he did not build anything to last. Of course, Nebuchadnezzar understood; Babylon was too busy fighting wars. So how was he, Nebuchadnezzar, going to build his Great City when his people only knew the art of destruction? Who would engineer his canals, roadways, and hydraulic systems? Who would map his drainage and waste systems? Who would construct his tunnels, bridges, and buildings, or oversee his ironworks, bronze works, and brick masonry?

"There must be eighty guards on that wall," Arioch said, shaking his head. "And look at that tower!"

His voice was so urgent, Nebuchadnezzar, still damp from his night-time river ride, tabled his thoughts for another time.

"Have you ever seen anything like it?"

Indeed, the tiered tower was mammoth, but more disconcerting was its ominous shape, not at all like Babylon's ziggurats with their tiers built in square or circular blocks. Instead, the eight tiers of this tower looked like eight boats: wide, heavy, settled sampans stacked one on top of the other, largest at the bottom, smallest at the top, with a red-glazed brick building in the middle of each. The ends of the boats—the actual corners of the building—were curved upward as if the tower could be steered in four different directions.

"A hundred archers could be hiding inside those nooks and crannies," Arioch cautioned. "Look at the archway we have to ride through. See how it narrows at the other end? It is a death trap."

Indeed, the archway was an intimidating hazard, especially the iron netting attached to the ceiling—most likely meant to drop on anyone entering uninvited. If anyone actually did make it through, four impalement poles stood ready in the courtyard beyond. Arioch, of course, regarded these as the serious threats, but not Nebuchadnezzar. To him, the real threat was the tower, a threat to all history because it was built to last. Built to last was the unstated message blaring from each ascending boat. From its heavy brick walls to its ethereal curved ends, the tower exuded a settled stability and generational permanence so great, so sure, and so real, perhaps China's fragmented wall and tongue-slavering bronze dragons were all she needed for protection. Moreover, any other effort at precaution might have been viewed not only as extraneous, but as a humiliating declaration of helplessness.

Arioch was rapidly mapping out multiple escape strategies, repeating his favorite: split up now, gallop away, and regroup in the mulberry trees down by the river. But Nebuchadnezzar barely heard, his every fiber glowering at the tower standing a bit too tall for his liking. Meanwhile, six stone-faced guards jumped into action. Contrary to Arioch's expectations, they were all smiles and fawning bows, waving the two foreigners toward the gate. Truly suspicious now, Arioch stopped. Nebuchadnezzar however kept his horse pacing forward, so Arioch grabbed him.

"What are you doing?" the Crown Prince protested, keeping his voice low.

"Don't you see? It is an ambush. They want us to come in. Once we get to the other side, they will surround us and chop off our heads. Or, if you like, impale us alive."

"They cannot kill me. Babylon must be built and I am going to build it."

"You know that and I know that, but do those smiling guards know it?"

"Arioch," the Crown Prince chided, "don't you remember the bridge?"

"The what?"

"The burning bridge. Don't you remember what I said?"

"Of course, I do. You said, 'Nothing can shake me.'"

"Exactly."

His tone was so matter of fact, Arioch stared dumbfounded. He had thought Nebuchadnezzar's declaration *nothing can shake me* followed by his ride across the burning bridge a boyish prank. Furthermore, a stupid one. Then, as he had chased the Crown Prince across the flaming floorboards, he had thought himself a foolish young man, especially if the fire injured his trusting horse. Now, in a foreign land and facing China's might, his companion was rallying to the same principle? Thinking China could not shake him? It was certainly a novel idea and his father would heartily disapprove, yet because it had worked once before or perhaps because Arioch still had some foolishness in him, he straightened to his full height and, spurring his horse into the archway, placed one hand on his sword and the other on his dagger.

Of course, there was no ambush. In fact, the two were quickly ensconced in a small pagoda in the center of Emperor Kuangwang's garden. Stepping onto the gleaming elm wood floor, young Nebuchadnezzar marveled at the clean simplicity of the rooms and their furnishings: mahogany chests, art tables laid out with inks, brushes and parchments, low wooden beds with firm silk pillows. He was so impressed by the heated rocks steaming in the lavatory, he ordered Arioch to come and see. But Arioch, stomping from one room to another, was in a frown because there were no doors or curtains, grumbling they were probably being watched from all sides.

Indeed, they were being watched. But as the platters of poached fish, lentils, rice, and honeyed breads arrived regularly, and the different tutors came and went, teaching them three hundred words of Chinese, the elements of Chinese protocol, and the insignias of the Chinese leaders and military, Arioch soon forgot his worries and enjoyed the pleasantries of being in a foreign land. In contrast, Nebuchadnezzar grew impatient. Glaring out at the guards, he reminded them daily he was the Crown Prince of Babylon and wanted to meet the emperor. Finally, after three weeks, he and Arioch were summoned into the presence of Kuangwang Emperor of China.

Escorted by Chinese warriors wearing crescent shaped swords, the two were marched into a courtyard of lily gardens, fish pools, and one shimmering stone walkway leading to a marble platform where Emperor Kuangwang sat in a gilded chair. Shaded by elm trees, he was robed in silk, his royal train sweeping down the steps. His crown was braided gold with eight miniature gold arrows aiming at the heavens, and his eight jade rings, weighing heavily on his bony fingers, were decorated with the Eight Immortals. Red silk fans swayed overhead, silver bells hung like raindrops from the trees, and doves, their heads bobbing up and down, quietly pecked in pairs on the lawns. It was a masterly combination of understated power and controlled beauty, and it certainly left its impact on Nebuchadnezzar.

However, he was most impressed by how the Emperor spoke, not loudly and demanding like his father, but softly so everyone had to lean in to catch his words. One young man on the platform listened as if his life depended on it, his head bowed in fierce concentration, his orange silk trousers quivering unnaturally. He was the interpreter.

Even so, when the emperor went silent, he did not race over to Nebuchadnezzar to relay the message before forgetting it. Instead, he floated down the steps, tread silently over the stones, bowed slowly to the foreigners and, in the same soft-tones, repeated the question. Nebuchadnezzar answered as best he could and the interpreter, after bowing again to the foreigners, tiptoed over the stone pathway, glided back up the steps, bowed calmly before the emperor, and quietly repeated the answer. Hearing it, the emperor grunted his disapproval, asked another question, and the ritual began all over again, punctuated by the emperor's tightening frown and snappish harrumphs.

Poor fifteen-year-old Nebuchadnezzar. If the emperor had asked about swords, hunting, or the mind of a horse, about sparring techniques, surviving in the wilderness, or Shining One's great Babylonian epic, he would have proven stellar in his responses. But the emperor's questions came from another world, the world of the Far East, questions about wars to be fought in the future using war plans of the past, the South-pointer with its twelve terrestrial branches and ten celestial stems, and the characters, or logograms, used in Chinese writing. He then wanted to know if the Crown Prince of Babylon knew anything about the significance of the star pictures once seen in the sky or the conjunction of Jupiter and Saturn in Pisces. Well, he surely must know one specific about Fohi, the Patriarch of the Sea and Founder of China. No? Then perhaps he had been taught the basics of bronze works or engineering: bridge building, road building, canal building?

Question after question wafted down the steps so serenely, young Nebuchadnezzar was about to explode with impatience. Why couldn't the emperor just volley his questions at him? Why did everything have to be drawn out into a painstaking crawl, each eye blink and nose twitch measured and calm, as if no one had anything better to do than bake in the afternoon sun? However, he did not explode, because although he had come to China to learn about Shining One's epic, by some amazing good fortune, he had found something else he was looking for: knowledge.

China had not been idle over the past thousands of years, but had built up storehouses of knowledge, not only about wars, geography, stars, and history, but more importantly, engineering: road building, canal building, city and bridge building. Here was the knowledge he needed to build Babylon, not as a temporary stronghold or a fleeting ideal, but as a permanent presence: the glory of kingdoms throughout the ages, built to last!

Emperor Kuangwang was having similar thoughts about Nebuchadnezzar's need for knowledge. Watching the young man grasping clumsily for answers, he had countered with angry grunts to cover his chuckling. Clearly, the boy was meant for great destiny, but although intuitively brilliant and a striking visionary, when it came to the finer matters of power, he was pathetically unlettered, and without someone's intervention, he would never reach his aspirations for Babylon. Hence, the Emperor appointed his *Sangong*, the three Grand Dukes— Grand Guardian Li, Grand Preceptor Au Yang and Grand Mentor Tin—to open all of China's doors of knowledge to him in order to prepare him for his golden era.

3

THEIR first year in China, the young Babylonians were assigned to the Grand Guardian Li. Chief over all military matters, he was not only protector of the Emperor, but ruler over China's armies and feudal lords. Hence, his countenance was like an iron shield as he measured the young Babylonians' performances. Finding them well-trained in bow, javelin, horsemanship, and infantry, he assigned them to the emperor's personal army. Finding them inadequate in mobile warfare—cavalry and chariots—he had no qualms relegating them to the nursery: China's twelve-year-olds.

At the end of each day, he instructed them in his private war room lined with spears, axes, shields, bows, and fire darts. Speaking to them in a murmur, as if he did not want the walls to hear, he outlined offensive and defensive strategies for court intrigues and civil wars including bribery, spying, and bestowing favors, strategies important to China because of her vast feudal system, adding with cool eyes, if a bribe or intrigue could win a subject or an enemy's lands, the king was obliged to use them instead of going to war because war decimated the strength of a nation: its fields, forests, and men.

Nebuchadnezzar straightaway disagreed, declaring he would never allow court intrigues or feudal favors to defile his kingdom. Furthermore, he would never use bribery or spying. Instead, he would deal forthrightly with all his subjects, and under such an enlightened code, Babylon would flourish. Subject closed, he marched for the door, but the Grand Guardian Li with springing swiftness latched onto his shoulders and swung him around.

"Babylon," the Grand Guardian glared, breathing fire into Nebuchadnezzar's face, "waxes and wanes with the moon, rising up in full fury and disappearing just as fast."

"Babylon will not disappear under me!"

"On the other hand," Li smiled, pleased to put Babylon in its place, "China is as steady as the sun, outshining the moon and the stars for thousands of years and will continue to outshine them for thousands more. To do so, she must not wax and wane with every passion, nor invade or invite invasion at the sound of every trumpet, nor kill off every feudal lord who does not bow. We survive using intrigues and counter intrigues, favors and counter favors, bribes and counter bribes and, if necessary, wars. Thus our emperors are prepared for all emergencies and thus China remains." Drawing his dagger, he slammed it on the table. "Now shut your mouth and listen."

It was a clear challenge and, eyeing the dagger set before him, then glancing at its twin ready for action in Li's other sheath, Nebuchadnezzar would have liked to ask how many men the Grand Guardian had felled in this simple way. But instead, he shut his mouth and listened.

The second year, the Emperor split the two up. Arioch stayed with the Grand Guardian to learn China's defensive and offensive strategies for protecting and destroying moats, citadels, and fortifications, while Nebuchadnezzar was placed under the Grand Preceptor Au Yang to learn engineering and mathematics for constructing moats, citadels, and fortifications—built to last!

Although the Grand Preceptor Au Yang, a nephew of the emperor, was in control of building China, he knew nothing of mathematics or engineering, nor did he want to. He regarded the office of the Grand Preceptor as a stepping stone toward seizing the throne and the Crown Prince of Babylon as a potential ally in reaching that goal. Consequently, unlike the emperor and the Grand Guardian Li, Au Yang's manner was pleasant, in fact ingratiating, as he asked Nebuchadnezzar questions about his father and the successes of Babylon's wars. But the Crown Prince, although just as pleasant, was exceptionally close-mouthed. So the squat, smiling Au Yang, after placing Nebuchadnezzar under the guidance of his first lieutenant, the one who actually ran the Preceptor's office, rode off for a month of hunting and falconry with China's wealthiest landowners and warlords.

The third year, in great pomp, Arioch was promoted to the Palace Elite Corps, while Nebuchadnezzar received a hasty note ordering him to report to the Grand Mentor Tin to learn the language of the stars. The assignment infuriated him. After a year of learning how to build cities for the glory of Babylon, he had no intention of squandering his time learning China's folklore about the stars. Babylon already knew everything about the starry hosts, so packing his engineering scrolls into his saddlebag, he told Arioch they were leaving in the morning.

Arioch, busily preparing for the next day's chariot march to the northern kingdoms, was humming so brightly he did not hear, scrubbing oil on his shield, looking at his reflection—Soheil would not even recognize him, he had grown so—and scrubbing again.

"Arioch, we leave for Babylon in the morning!"

This time he heard and almost dropped his shield. "Leave? What are you talking about?"

"I am talking about Shining One and his epic! Every year I have humbly asked the emperor to see his archives and every year I hear nothing. My guess is he is trying to teach me Chinese patience, which I have no patience for. I already know about the stars. More than most stargazers do. Probably more than the Grand Mentor Tin does. So start packing."

Arioch, not wanting to give up his new assignment, argued that leaving so abruptly would insult the emperor. Then, in order to save face, he would have to seek vengeance on Babylon. However, if the Crown Prince stayed another month or two, they could contrive an excuse for leaving which would honor the emperor. Nebuchadnezzar scoffed at Arioch's blindness. Hadn't he seen that China had been insulting Nebuchadnezzar all along? Ignoring all his requests to see her archives and now this petty commission to study the stars were only a few of a long list of slights! Therefore, he, the Crown Prince of Babylon, had more justification to seek vengeance on China than the other way around. But Arioch, in his plodding way, pressed for staying, and although the Crown Prince groaned and grumbled, the next morning he reported to China's Grand Mentor Tin.

The Grand Mentor Tin wore stiff black silks, matched by a stiff black three-pronged cap teetering like a crow on the top of his head. Without saying a word, he lit two torches, handed one to Nebuchadnezzar, and with eyes as bright as spring and every step as slow as winter, he led him down a dank stairwell into a maze of tunnels under the earth. There they zigzagged and switchbacked mile upon mile in silence, Tin's silks swaying like a pendulum, Nebuchadnezzar's boots

marching like the tide. As the hours wasted away, the young Crown
Prince wished he had never listened to Arioch. Naturally, Arioch wanted to stay in China, galloping all over the kingdom with the Palace
Elite Corps, but why should he, Nebuchadnezzar, fade into the bowels
of the earth to supposedly learn about the stars in the heavens? And
what about Tin's listing three-pronged hat? With every step, it teetered
further back on his head until Nebuchadnezzar's hand shot up invol-
untarily to catch it before it fell. But it did not fall, leaving Nebuchadnezzar's hand casting a claw-like shadow on the wall trailing behind a
crow-like shadow on Tin's head.

Young Nebuchadnezzar thought the cap a disgraceful representation
of the Grand Mentor's high position. Caps, hats, turbans, and crowns
identified the man and his power. Thus, Babylon's wise men, sorcerers,
astrologers, enchanters, and magicians were going to wear something
impressive to fit their rank and, just as importantly, their heads. Turbans
perhaps. Yes, high turbans. High scarlet turbans fitting so securely, a gale
could not blow them off.

Suddenly, the Grand Mentor stopped, his hat stopped, Nebuchadnezzar stopped, and everything went silent. So silent, one could almost
hear the voices of the past echoing through the tunnels. Not Nebuchadnezzar. All he could hear was his own voice raging in his head, ordering
Arioch to think of a quick emperor-honoring exit strategy because after
today's goose chase, they were leaving in the morning.

However, as Tin lit the torches, Nebuchadnezzar forgot his impatience, intrigued by a massive marble chair planted in the middle of the
cedar-lined room. Straightaway, he knew it was a judgment seat, but
unlike any he had ever seen, sitting inside a huge marble doorframe, the
posts shaped like palm trunks, the lintel like palm fronds. The chair's
legs, reflected in the glossy elm wood floor, looked like thick white pillars shining into the deeps, and its arm rests, flat heavy squares with bird
claws carved at the ends, reminded Nebuchadnezzar of war.

He wanted to get close to it, touch it, and think about it, but Tin
waved him over to one of two matching gold doors—one to the left of the
seat and one to the right. Each door had a dragon's head in its center, and
in the dragon's mouth was a spherical lock, the most amazing lock he had
ever seen. Certainly more impressive than Egypt's pin lock. Nebuchadnezzar leaned in to study it, but Tin ordered him to step aside as he disengaged

the three-dimensional puzzle. Then, opening the door, he motioned the Crown Prince to cross the threshold.

The room dazzled! On one side, mounds of gold and silver glittered like sand dunes. On the other, rubies, emeralds, jasper, jade, and topaz, sparkling like stars, spilled out of carved ivory vats. The next room was filled with floor-to-ceiling shelves stacked with the very thing Nebuchadnezzar had come to find: Shining One's epic and the description of what happened the day he wrote it, not only in Chinese, but written in many languages, including Babylonian.

But Tin would not let Nebuchadnezzar tarry, tugging him into another room where eight life-size silver statues of Chinese warriors guarded eight cedar boxes. Opening a box, the Grand Mentor pulled out a silk painting and lifted it to a torch so Nebuchadnezzar could see the man in the painting. Attached by thin ropes to a wide canopy overhead, the man was floating in the air amidst mountains. Flabbergasted, Nebuchadnezzar stared. Could it be that here in China, men could actually fly? He turned to Tin for an explanation, but the Grand Mentor, his stiff hat quivering excitedly, was lifting out another painting. Again Nebuchadnezzar stared in wonder, this time at archers shooting bamboo tubes with fiery tips. Of course, fiery tips, designed to set targets on fire, were not unusual. However, in this painting, wherever the bamboo tubes hit—whether trees, huts, or soldiers—great fiery explosions erupted. Nebuchadnezzar wanted to see more, but Tin motioned for him to follow.

Mind reeling, the Crown Prince hurried after the Grand Mentor, out the gold door, across the elm wood floor, past the judgment seat, and on to the other gold door. Eager to see the treasures behind that door, he rushed inside; but to his disappointment, the room was empty. Just four stone walls and an entrance into a musty tunnel.

Anxious to return to the dazzling jewels, Shining One's texts, and the extraordinary paintings, Nebuchadnezzar headed for the door. Apparently, the Grand Mentor did not notice because he was venturing into the tunnel, slowly lighting more torches. Of course, Nebuchadnezzar had to follow, so together they slogged in and out of small inlets laden with racks of dried plants with lists of their healing components written on silk, mounted fish and sea creatures with similar lists, mounted animals and their descriptions, different kinds of woods and metals, salt, charcoal, and fragrances.

Stepping past a cave, Nebuchadnezzar caught a glimpse of a massive unhewn rock deep inside. It had a lambskin draped over the top and the word *yi* written on the front, probably in blood and probably from the lamb whose skin was on the top. It was an ancient altar, a solid grey mass with no beauty to recommend it. However, the four silk banners hanging beside it, just as ancient, were elegantly adorned with jewels and pearls. Each had a different message embroidered with gold thread, each message in a different language: Chinese, Hebrew, Babylonian, and Egyptian. After the past two years, Nebuchadnezzar could read the Chinese:

"Of old in the beginning, there was the great chaos, without form and dark. The five planets had not begun to revolve, nor the two lights to shine. You, O Spiritual Sovereign, ShangDi, Ruler of Heaven, first did separate the impure from the pure. You made heaven. You made earth. You made man. All things became alive with reproducing power..."

Enough of this! The young Prince wanted to get back to Shining One's texts, but when he turned to leave, Tin grabbed his arm, and pulling him into one more dusty cavern smelling of eucalyptus and myrrh, he ordered him to light the torches. Relieved not to have to wait for the slow-moving Grand Mentor, Nebuchadnezzar quickly lit the first row, but he never lit the second because as light filtered through the room, he was distracted by the vast star map sculpted into the wall before him. Glittering like the night sky, the stars were represented by precious gems: rubies, sapphires, emeralds, and topaz. Each star shot out beams represented by gold or silver threads which connected to other star beams, creating the pictures of the Signs and Constellations of the Zodiac. Astounded, he stepped back so he could view the entire heavenly equator and ecliptic.

Tin had been aware of the young man's impatience throughout the day, and because of it he had decided not to say a word about the map. But seeing wonder light up the boy's face, he changed his mind, explaining that China's founder, Fohi—the one who built the boat that saved the Eight and all the animals two by two from the worldwide Deluge—carved the map into the wall.

"It is the most amazing star map I have ever seen," stammered the Crown Prince.

"It is also the most reliable star map you have ever seen," replied Tin, "because Fohi studied the sky for six hundred years before the Deluge, learning the star names from his grandfather Methuselah, who learned them from Adam. This map shows what Fohi saw before the Deluge. If it is not," he hastened to add, "then it is what Adam saw before the Fall, and Adam told Methuselah, and Methuselah told Fohi. As you can see, it is not the same sky we look at every night."

No, it was not the same. The map before him displayed at least a third more stars than the sky above. Even more intriguing were the gold and silver star beams threaded together to create the pictures of the Signs and Constellations: *Orion, Argo, Ursa Major, Pisces, Leo…* These pictures were in every stargazer's notebook, charted over and over in Babylon's astronomical masterpiece *The Illumination of Bel* with its seventy astrological tablets, but in the stargazers' notebooks the pen created the pictures, not the star beams, because there were no star beams in the sky outlining *Orion* The Glorious One, *Argo* the Ship, *Ursa Major* the Great Bear, *Pisces* the Fishes, *Leo* the Lion… In fact, there were no pictures in the sky at all.

Consequently, Babylon's stargazers thought the ancients had attached random pictures, which everyone agreed on, to clusters of random stars, which everyone agreed on, so when a father said to his son, "Look up at the Great Bear," his son would excitedly look up at eight individual disconnected stars, and imagining they connected to make a picture of a pan with a handle, he would nod as if he was looking at a picture of a Great Bear.

Yes, it was nonsensical, but it was all they had had to go on, whereas the map before him was an explanation that did make sense: the pictures, all forty-eight of them, and the story they told had been in the sky, the heavens pouring forth knowledge day and night. The men of old went to bed under that knowledge, staring up at the silver star beams outlining the Great Bear's head, body, tail, and legs, and the gold star beams outlining the Lion, with a myriad of glimmering gold stars filling in his mane.

Living hundreds of years, the ancients had had time to study the pictures in the sky and copy them down. But the pictures were no longer in the sky. Why? What had happened to them? Had they fallen during the forty days of cataclysmic worldwide rains known as the Deluge? If they had, then when Fohi disembarked from his boat and looked up, he did not see the glittering regalia he had been studying for six hundred years: the actual pictures of the Twelve Signs and their Constellations starting with *Bethulah* the Virgin and ending with *Arieh* the Lion hunting down his prey. Instead, he saw great black holes where the pictures had been, the heavenly story erased forever leaving only a remnant of starry splendor. Not only had the earth been razed, but the sky and its heavenly message also. No wonder he planted a vineyard and got drunk.

On the other hand, perhaps it was another event that had caused the darkening of the stars, or worse, cast them down, leaving only their memory on tablets, parchments, and an earthen wall like the one before him.

Tin left Nebuchadnezzar alone to read Shining One's epic and the narrative telling about the day he wrote it. He also kept the door open to the tunnel leading to Fohi's star map room. Thus, Nebuchadnezzar forgot all about his timetable for leaving China. During the day, he studied the narratives about Shining One, and at night, he shadowed Tin from one observatory to another studying his calculations and personal notes, writing the Babylonian translation beside them.

Even Arioch joined in, his sudden interest in the stars stemming from the moment he saw Tin's fifteen-year-old granddaughter, Chenguang, working in her grandfather's office. Captivated by her delicate form, her plaited raven hair, and her fragrance of peonies, he kept darting his eyes her way until finally her eyes responded. Normally, their budding ardor would have been quickly noticed and forbidden by both Nebuchadnezzar and Tin because Chenguang was intended for the Grand Preceptor Au Yang. But the Crown Prince and the Grand Mentor were too engrossed in checking, re-checking, and arguing over Tin's calculations to observe such mundane matters as Arioch and Chenguang's star-crossed infatuation. In fact, Nebuchadnezzar and Tin argued more and more as the years went by, especially when Tin asserted the stars were indicators for many nations—Babylon, Israel, Egypt, China, and nations yet to be born.

Annoyed by Tin's penchant for seeking historical purpose for every nation, young Nebuchadnezzar reminded him repeatedly that Babylon was the center of history and whatever the stars had to say about other nations—if anything—was irrelevant. Tin would rummage through his purple sack, a beautiful silk sack with the Signs and Constellations embroidered in gold, and pull out scroll after scroll to prove his point.

But Nebuchadnezzar, citing Shining One's epic, argued that the glory of Babylon was the sole purpose for all history. Their verbal sparring was certainly lively and oftentimes heated, but it was always amicable until the day Tin showed the Crown Prince his calculations for the conjunction of Jupiter and Saturn in Pisces, insisting the conjunction was a sign that marked historical events for Israel.

Nebuchadnezzar exploded. Stamping his boots as if he was kicking the dust off his feet, he challenged Tin as never before, arguing there was no relationship between any conjunction and Israel. Babylon was the world, the Grand Mentor was wrong, his evidence faulty and his sums inaccurate. Then, with hands clenching and unclenching, he marched out the door, and from that day on, the tension between them, although buried, grew.

Finally, after three years of sharing the discoveries of eclipses, comets, and conjunctions, and the mysteries of light, time, and space, Tin once again brought up the Jupiter, Saturn, Pisces conjunction. At first Nebuchadnezzar said nothing, but when the Grand Mentor referred to three such conjunctions occurring in one year in six hundred years, the Crown Prince slammed his fists on the work table with such fury, he broke it.

Looking at the shattered boards on the floor, Tin shook his head. "It is time for you to go home."

Nebuchadnezzar was certainly ready to go home but to have the Grand Mentor dismiss him because he did not agree with his faulty calculations was not only insulting, but a national affront. "Who are you to tell me when it is time to go home?"

"Come," Tin commanded, far from calmly, marching out of Fohi's star map room, up through the tunnel, and into the central room with the massive marble chair. There he soundlessly shut the two matching gold doors, locked the two spherical locks, and motioned to the chair. "Sit."

The twenty-year-old Crown Prince had been waiting to take the judgment seat since the first day he saw it. Back then his youthful frame would have been overwhelmed by the wide marble seat and high rigid back, but now he filled them out, and feeling like a king already, he slapped his hands on his knees and glowered at Tin.

"You, Crown Prince Nebuchadnezzar," Tin announced formally, "after all these years in China continue to see everything as if it belongs to

Babylon. Or more specifically, as if everything belongs to you. From the
heavens above to the earth below, everything." Raising his arms outward
like angry wings, motioning first to one gold door and then the other, he
dropped his voice to a whisper, forcing the Crown Prince to lean in to
hear. "But you, Nebuchadnezzar, cannot have everything."

Folding his arms, the Crown Prince settled back in the chair. He
liked the chair, its cold strength, its weighty arms and back. How many
Chinese emperors had sat in this chair? Perhaps even Fohi had sat here.
Now he was sitting in judgment. "I will have everything," he said, easy
and confident to all the exalted who once possessed the chair. "I will have
everything because I am Babylon."

Shaking his head, Tin muttered under his breath, "Where have I
gone wrong? Why does he not understand?"

But Nebuchadnezzar heard, and enjoying his momentary brush
with power, he replied smugly, "No, Tin, you are the one who does not
understand."

"I?"

"You heard me. You do not understand because you are China, and
China does not live in the present. I do understand because I am Babylon. I do live in the present. Do not interrupt. You told me to sit. Now
you must listen to me.

"China hangs suspended between its great and remote past with
Fohi, and a great and remote future so far away not even the setting
sun can reach it. Everywhere I go, it is the same. A sense of permanence
settled in the past, yet also settled in some distant future. Walling yourself away from the world of today for thousands of years, invading
none and being invaded by none, cultivating patience as most men
cultivate crops. For if patience is the fruit of life, then your waiting
seems more palatable.

"But what are you waiting for? Another worldwide Deluge? Another
Fohi? Perhaps something greater than the Deluge. Perhaps a deliverer
greater than Fohi. Waiting for something or someone who will once
again set China apart from all other nations.

"Tin, you are the one who does not understand. But how could you,
when you must slow down every part of life to a crawl because your wait
is so long? How could you understand that yes, I want everything? And

yes, I must have it now. Today. In the present. Which demands a dedicated and ruthless impatience."

Tin stared at the youth, no longer a fifteen-year-old gangler but a solid young man of twenty, ready to take on the world and win. He had spoken from the judgment seat and he had spoken correctly. Yes, China had to wait and Tin understood that. He also understood that China's wait would be worthwhile. But Nebuchadnezzar, even after five years under China's care, had not understood his point, for the Crown Prince still believed everything belonged to Babylon. So heaving a beaten sigh, the Grand Mentor said without rancor, "You think nothing can shake you? We will see. I will meet you in the future, and at that time, I will measure your success."

"*You?* Measure *my...*?!" Nebuchadnezzar leapt off the seat, his eyes blinded by rage. "Who are *you* to measure *my...*"

But Tin, no longer his mentor, disappeared into the tunnel.

———

A month-long celebration was given in honor of the Crown Prince, and on the last day, Emperor Kuangwang awarded him a white stallion and twenty mares, a coat of polished bronze scale descending to the knees, an engraved silver sword with matching silver sheath, and a rare treasure for Babylon: Tin's purple silk sack with all his star maps, notes, calculations, and conclusions inside. Finally, the day came, and after five years of living inside the sleeping giant China, Nebuchadnezzar and Arioch left for home.

4

SPEEDING across the Carchemish plain with Tin's words ringing in his ears, Nebuchadnezzar remembered why he had not given China another thought since the day he left. The Grand Mentor Tin was the reason. How dare he think he could measure his success? The ordeal still rankled him. So forgetting China once and for all, he turned his attention to his chief commander on his right, the calculating and forceful Yosef ben-Moshe leading his men as lightning leads thunder.

He was a formidable presence, not just because he was tall and broad, but because he had a prematurely white beard, a dagger-scar bisecting his forehead, and rope burns seared into his arms, wrists, and neck. At the very sight of him, most men stepped back. There were many whisperings about his past, but no one actually knew how he had acquired his scars or his great wealth. Certainly, no one knew how he, a Hebrew, had risen so quickly to be third in command over Nebuchadnezzar's military might. Even Nebuchadnezzar mused over his decision to promote him so swiftly to such extensive power. Indeed, the Hebrew's calm, taciturn, and incisive nature had instilled trust. Furthermore, ben-Moshe was his most faithful ally against Egypt, vital in war plans, and indispensable in training men in endurance and armor. But most importantly, unbeknownst to anyone, Nebuchadnezzar had not had one horrific dream or vision since Yosef ben-Moshe's arrival, a deliverance far more meaningful to him than all the gods of Babylon.

Yosef ben-Moshe could feel Nebuchadnezzar's eyes drilling into him, but he did not turn or shout Babylon. For unlike Arioch, he did not live or breathe for the Crown Prince. Instead, he lived and breathed for Jerusalem. Why he was even in this war was beyond him. Yet he knew he was supposed to be here, so calculating the remaining distance, he waited ten seconds, then thrust his fist into the air.

Seeing the signal, Nebuchadnezzar tightened with excitement. This was it. This was the day and this was the moment. Was surprise still on his side? Or was he riding into an ambush? Early yesterday morning he had ordered his spies into the surrounding villages to bribe the locals for their loyalty, adding the threat of annihilation if they revealed Babylon's whereabouts. At dusk, leaving a skeleton army behind with fires blazing and food cooking, he had spirited his chariots, cavalry, and foot soldiers away from the Euphrates and traveled south to the shallow part of the river. There they had waited through the night, eating curds and dried fish, replenishing water bags and keeping the horses calm. Then, under the bright morning star, he, Arioch, and Yosef ben-Moshe had silently led the first wave across the river. His fourth commander Nergal had just come ashore leading the second wave, and the third wave was still crossing over. Meticulously planned to the minute, it appeared surprise was still in his favor. So, turning to Yosef ben-Moshe, he nodded.

Ben-Moshe, like Nebuchadnezzar, knew surprise was important. But equally important was maximum saturation of arrows on the first salvo. To insure that success, he had crossed the river three days before to study the terrain and scout for landmarks. Now, as he and his archers passed the ravine, he was on the lookout for two shittah trees. If they could get beyond those trees, Babylon's arrows would not only be a surprise, but the beginning of a complete rout. But where were the trees? With each hoofbeat he wondered if darkness had deceived him and he had seen only shadows. If so, should he order his archers to shoot now? As he searched the horizon, his apprehension grew. Should he wait or shoot? Shoot or wait? Suddenly, there they were. Two lone silhouettes splitting the horizon in half.

Shoving his feet into the floorboard straps and gripping the reins in one hand, he raised a blue flag. At his signal, the appointed charioteers along the front line raised their blue flags, and at their signal, the archers sped into formation. It was a sight that took one's breath away. Even ben-Moshe, who had orchestrated this same attack several times before, could not help staring at the sheer numbers: thousands of armored men sitting ramrod straight on thousands of armored horses, all galloping in precision time across the plain. Snapping the blue flag down, the other charioteers followed suit, and thousands of bows bolted upright with arrows ready to launch.

As he counted off the seconds before giving the signal, Yosef ben-Moshe uttered the prayer he always prayed before battle, "Lead me in the way everlasting."

Then he raised the red flag.

In contrast to Babylon's turbulent advance, the Egyptian and Assyrian encampment was calm. In fact, most of the camp, emboldened by the arrival of Egypt's fresh armies, still slept. Even Pharaoh Necho's disciplined Egyptian commander Apis Knem decided to wait for the sun to warm his tent before facing the dawn. But drifting in and out of sleep, he kept dreaming of far-away rumblings trembling through the earth. Indeed, they seemed to be getting closer, even stronger, and if Nebuchadnezzar's armies had not been camped on the other side of the river the night before, he might have thought the tremors were the harbinger of one thousand war chariots, five thousand galloping archers, ten thousand cavalry, and twenty thousand running infantry. But that was ridiculous because Nebuchadnezzar's armies had been camped on the other side of the river and it would have been impossible to...

Apis Knem's eyes snapped open. This was no dream! Leaping up, he bolted out of his tent and yelled, "To arms!"

The warriors slowly dressing for sparring drills, the archers chomping leisurely on seared fish, and the tribal chiefs betting on which day Nebuchadnezzar was going to attack stared warily at the shrieking figure, his arms flailing and feet hopping, each wondering if Pharaoh had been caught napping, sending a tippler to defend his empire.

"Nebuchadnezzar!" Knem bawled again and again, then bellowed, "His chariots! They are coming!"

"Now, now..." cajoled an Assyrian commander, approaching cautiously. "Don't you remember? Nebuchadnezzar's armies were on the other side of the river last night."

"No wonder you Assyrians have lost your empire!" Knem grabbed him and pointed to the sky.

The Assyrian played along and as expected saw nothing. But the Egyptian held him fast until he did see something: a mile-wide shimmering glow. Then everyone saw it, thousands of gleaming arrows soaring straight at them, and the camp lunged for cover.

—⁓⁓⁓—

Back on the plain, Yosef ben-Moshe raised the red flag over and over, quickly now for rapid fire, wondering once again why he was here. Not many, including his wife, Zillah, had agreed with his decision to fight for Nebuchadnezzar. He had explained to the men of Jerusalem that if he fought, he might gain Nebuchadnezzar's favor, and if Babylon won the war, he could use that favor to protect Jerusalem. Of course, such reasoning was faulty because kings and princes notoriously gave way to whim and dissipation rather than war-time loyalties. Besides, what if Assyria or Egypt won? That would be his execution for sure. More practically, he could have been killed in any of Babylon's previous battles or could be killed in combat today.

Indeed, the explanation was riddled with holes, but he had never wavered from it because the true explanation was so extraordinary—or so delusional—he did not want anyone to know. One night when he was alone in his garden, someone hit him on the back, felling him. Immediately drawing his dagger, he swung around ready to kill. But there was no one to kill. Instead, there was a huge angel glowering down at him. He had never seen an angel, but it certainly was not a man, so what else could it have been?

Without any introduction, the blinding figure told him to be strong and courageous—a bit insulting because he had always been strong and courageous. Then came the surprise. The angel told him to go and fight for Nebuchadnezzar and, without another word, disappeared into the night. Who would have believed that?! Even he had been flooded with doubts, because he was not a priest or a prophet that the Lord would send his messenger to him. But in the end he knew the vision was true, so he had come to fight for Nebuchadnezzar.

Again he hoisted the flag and whipped it down. Again thousands of arrows shot up into the air, sailing confidently across the plain.

—⁓⁓⁓—

Under Apis Knem's commands, the Assyrian and Egyptian archers scrambled for bows and arrows. When half were armed, he ordered them to shoot—and keep shooting!

But their belated defense did not have the same lethal impact as Babylon's offense. Without flinching, Nebuchadnezzar's warriors simply raised their shields and hurtled closer until stretching farther than the eye could see and thundering louder than the ear could hear, their scythed chariot wheels crashed full speed into the astonished empires of Assyria and Egypt—and the Battle of Carchemish began.

5

AFTER watching Jeremiah disappear down the road, Aridatha squeezed back through the wrought iron gate, raced to the house, and slipped inside. Hopping into bed, she snuggled her feet into Lazy Lamb's fleece and tried to go back to sleep. But how could anyone sleep on a day like this, the day Nebuchadnezzar was advancing like the clouds, his horses swifter than eagles? Even her mother was asleep, her face still flattened on the pillow, her arm still draped over the linen sheet. Perhaps she did not know there was a great battle going on today and that papa was a part of it. Papa! Aridatha could certainly envision him with his white beard and scarred forehead advancing like the clouds, his horses swifter than eagles. Suddenly, she wondered if he was safe. Of course, he was safe. He was papa. Once that was settled, her thoughts flew to Nebuchadnezzar. What did he look like? What weapons was he wearing? Did he have a shield like papa's? Was he really going to conquer the two large circles? With so much going on, she again wondered how anyone in Jerusalem could sleep.

Knowing the Battle of Carchemish was imminent, most of Jerusalem slept better that night than any other night throughout the past year. Before that, they had slept safely and securely in their everyday predictable world governed by the great powers of Assyria and Egypt. In those days, the city had not given much thought to Babylon because everyone knew Babylon was a sprawling mass of in-fighting tribes going up against a military empire. Hence, the accepted wisdom of the day—bandied about at all the city gates, watering holes, marketplaces, and even the Temple of Solomon—was that Babylon would be vanquished quickly.

Still, there had been a bit of apprehension regarding Nebuchadnezzar's repeated victories because, according to Jeremiah, Nebuchadnezzar was going to destroy Jerusalem. However, when it came to Jeremiah, the accepted wisdom of the day—also bandied about widely—was that he was a troublemaker and not to be believed. Therefore, if no one took Jeremiah seriously, no one had to take Babylon seriously, hence Jerusalem's confidence, although strained, prevailed.

But as Assyria kept losing and Babylon's wings kept spreading, Jerusalem sank into an uneasy year of sleepless nights followed by churlish days where no one dared mention the names Nebuchadnezzar and Babylon, as if by not speaking them the threat did not exist. Then the miracle came: Egypt rose up out of the Nile like an angry crocodile and marched north. Instant euphoria! The names of Nebuchadnezzar and Babylon were on everyone's lips, happily deriding the Crown Prince for even thinking he could conquer such mighty powers as Assyria and Egypt. In fact, Jerusalem was so certain of Egypt's soon-to-be victory over Babylon, the city took to the streets drinking and dancing.

Spirits also soared at the Temple of Solomon, all the priests, prophets, and noblemen gushing over Egypt's forthcoming victory and Jerusalem's future of peace. If they had been anywhere else in the city, they too would have been drinking and dancing, but not at the Temple because Jeremiah was standing on the Temple steps, an ever-present specter of gloom and doom, always severe and weeping. In fact, he was weeping as they celebrated, so the murmur spread that he was a traitor.

Jeremiah was the son of Hilkiah, one of the priests of Anathoth in the territory of Benjamin. Before Jeremiah was born, the Lord appointed him as a prophet to the nations, making him an iron pillar and a bronze wall to stand against the whole land. But he took his task so literally, no one liked him at all. In fact, he was a man with whom the whole land contended and with good reason: he had been terrorizing Jerusalem for twenty-two years, threatening if the city did not reject evil and return to the Lord, the Lord would destroy it by sword, famine, and plague.

Naturally, nothing had happened. Yet he was so arrogant, he never once recanted but instead railed on further, putting an actual name on Jerusalem's so-called destroyer: Nebuchadnezzar King of Babylon. Such a wild and irresponsible assertion became instant fodder for the city's jokes and, like all jokes, was soon forgotten until reports of the Crown Prince's victories started trickling in. But with Egypt headed north to destroy Babylon, Jerusalem was more confident than ever, eagerly reviewing all the well-worn reasons why the City of David was not in danger.

First, Jerusalem was not a military or economic power, so there was no motive to squander Babylon's armies destroying her. Second, a hundred years before, when Assyria's armies marched against Jerusalem, they had been destroyed by the hand of the Lord. That intervention had become the evidence for the third reason: it was impossible to destroy Jerusalem because the Lord Almighty had set the city apart to house the Temple of Solomon which bore his Name and housed the Ark of the Covenant. No other city in the world had such favor. Consequently, no one in the world—well, almost no one—believed Jerusalem could be destroyed, at least not by such banal implements as sword, famine, or plague, and certainly not by Babylon.

There was also a fourth reason, a reason rarely mentioned because it rarely surfaced from the depths of the heart into the words of the mind. However, it was there, powerful and active: the unspoken conviction that the God of Abraham, Isaac and Jacob could threaten and rattle his swords all he wanted, but ultimately, if he really was the Most High God, he would never tear down Jerusalem, but build it up. Never pour out his wrath on his Chosen, but his mercy. Never destroy his Temple, but save it.

Thus, as the Battle of Carchemish began, Jerusalem slept... and slept well.

6

As Jerusalem slept, the morning sun cast a friendly warmth on Babylon's armies, drying their river-soaked bodies. However, by mid-day it was an enemy to all, baking the Egyptians, Assyrians, and Babylonians alike with its relentless heat, and Yosef ben-Moshe, his weapons blood-caked and dull, yearned for shade. Normally, he would have left the field to sharpen his weapons and replenish his vinegar drink, but today something held him back. He did not know what it was, but it kept him close to the Crown Prince, making it impossible for him to leave until he left.

But, Nebuchadnezzar, thrusting and clanging his sword against an Egyptian, was not about to leave. After slaughtering Egyptians and Assyrians all morning, instead of growing faint he seemed to be enjoying the rigors of the day, oblivious to such commonplace hazards as heat exhaustion, dull weapons, hunger, thirst, even death. Moreover, it was the same for his men, as if each bloodletting was nourishing them into a greater will to destroy, while the Egyptian and Assyrian armies, mere mortals as they were, flagged shamelessly under the sun's heat.

Even the Egyptian commander Apis Knem had to stop and rest. Never before had a battle sapped him of so much strength. Each strike, iron against iron, jarred his bones. Each thrust of his sword through armor and sinew, coupled with the grinding effort of yanking it out again, left his arms and legs trembling uncontrollably. Now, staring out at the battle, his eyes stinging from sweat, he saw it was the same for his warriors. Weakening rapidly, they were thrashing their weapons in confusion, dropping to the ground, crying out for mercy and running away.

Something had to be done. Pharaoh Necho had ordered him to decimate Babylon and seize the Assyrian empire. But how? Yes, his elite warriors were being slaughtered like sheep, but to retreat would be reprehensible. Better to die like a warrior than to run like a rabbit.

Then came a vision of hope. In the distance, the Crown Prince of Babylon was wide open and in full view. Grabbing a bow from a fallen archer, Knem quickly loaded an arrow and pulled the bowstring. At least, he thought he pulled it, but the string still stood upright. So he pulled again. Again, the string did not move because his arms had no strength left in them.

"No!" he bellowed.

Hearing the outcry, Yosef ben-Moshe turned to see an arrow aimed at the Crown Prince. Even more alarming, the Crown Prince was wide open. In that brief moment, Yosef ben-Moshe, Arioch, and Nebuchadnezzar's elite guard, caught up in the heat of combat, had been lured away. Ben-Moshe shouted to Nebuchadnezzar, telling him to take cover, but the battle drowned him out. So, dropping his sword and shield, he ran toward him.

Apis Knem, focusing all his anger—the only strength he had left—into his deadened arms, finally wrenched the bowstring back and shot. It was a perfect shot, and he was about to yell the long-awaited victory cry when he saw a white-bearded warrior leaping through the air onto Nebuchadnezzar's back, his perfect shot sinking into him instead of the Crown Prince of Babylon.

Nebuchadnezzar wrestled the man off, then seeing it was Yosef ben-Moshe with an arrow in his back, he quickly scanned the field. Spotting another arrow spinning toward him, he raised his shield and in one seamless motion blocked the oncoming arrow, grabbed up a javelin, and hurled it at the Egyptian. Knowing no one could throw a javelin that far, Apis Knem calmly reloaded. Nevertheless, before he shot, Nebuchadnezzar's spear slammed into his chest. Flying backward, Apis Knem once again ordered his arm to shoot, a pitiful gesture because he was pinned to the earth staring at vultures swarming overhead.

When the Egyptian army learned Pharaoh Necho's commander would no longer be giving orders, one enlightened chief yelled retreat, and without balking, both armies lunged pell-mell for their horses and fled.

After Nebuchadnezzar ordered his men to follow, he stared down at Yosef ben-Moshe. He had sensed the Hebrew's hovering instincts throughout the day. In fact, ben-Moshe's pesky protectiveness had started to irritate him because Arioch and Babylon's elite guard were there to defend him. But now, looking back, he had to wonder why it was Yosef ben-Moshe who had been so watchful, why he had been the only one to see the threat and, more importantly, why he had saved his life.

"Yosef, can you hear me?"

Yosef ben-Moshe could not hear a thing except the thrum of the earth calling him home, and it startled him because he did not want to return to the dust. Nevertheless, with each breath the arrow scored deeper so he readied himself, uttering, "Hear, O Israel: the Lord our God, the Lord is one." As he spoke, he knew he was sinking fast because he could not hear his own voice. Yet curiously, he heard another voice deep inside trying to get out, too faint to understand.

Nebuchadnezzar's foot pressed hard against his back, and feeling the Crown Prince take hold of the arrow, ben-Moshe braced himself for the probing: that long drawn-out agony from many small calculated tugs. Soon they both knew the arrow was caught between his ribs, and if Nebuchadnezzar did not dislodge it before pulling, it would catch on the ribcage and break. But Nebuchadnezzar knew his business, tapped the arrow forward and with a deft twist yanked it free, ripping it through ben-Moshe's sinew and out of his flesh.

Through it all, Yosef ben-Moshe did not make a sound. His eyes simply flared bright and closed. Then his body, after one explosive convulsion, slowly sagged to the ground. The sight shocked Nebuchadnezzar. Never before had he seen the Hebrew downed. In fact, he could not remember seeing him recline, not even to eat or stretch out on the earth to rest. He had certainly never seen him in the most vulnerable position of sleep. Instead, he had always seen him upright, striding through his men or going sword to sword in battle. The last to retire and the first to rise, he was like a guardian at the gate. Yet more. In fact, Nebuchadnezzar had studied him long enough to discover just how much more, concluding that Yosef ben-Moshe carried inside him not only the stature of leadership, the rank of wealth, and the distinction of a secret violent past, but imprinted in his very being were two conflicting virtues every man coveted: power and rest.

So to see him flattened on the ground like a sack of meal rattled Nebuchadnezzar more than he would have liked because the grip of death, like the grip of old age, made strong men look weak and inconsequential. Moreover, the bloodied arrow in his hand had been aimed at him, which meant the helpless lump on the ground should have been him.

Not wanting to think about it—after all, he had done all he could—he hurried away. But what about his dreams? If Yosef ben-Moshe died, would his dreams return? Swinging around, he called out to him. When the Hebrew did nothing, he lunged back to his side.

"Wake up!"

It took all ben-Moshe's strength to peel his eyes open. Even then, they kept rolling back, causing his head to spin.

"You must live," commanded Nebuchadnezzar.

Dry heaving, the Hebrew would have liked to obey, but some things even Babylon could not control.

"Keep your eyes open!" Digging into his honey pouch, Nebuchadnezzar dripped the golden syrup into his wound. "Look at the sky."

Ben-Moshe moved his eyes dully toward the peaceful canopy overhead.

Nebuchadnezzar's eyes also moved upward, traveling north to south, east to west. "It looks innocent, doesn't it? Especially at night with its pristine moon and faraway stars. But it is not innocent. Not innocent at all. It is a mask." Although the afternoon sun seared the battlefield, the Crown Prince shivered with cold, his teeth chattering. "Did you know that? A deceiving mask. Keep your eyes open! A vast veneer built to hide all that is beyond it. Open them!"

Yosef ben-Moshe's eyes were open. But instead of looking at the sky, he was staring at Nebuchadnezzar's hands clenching and unclenching.

"I wager you do not know what is on the other side of that mask," he said, glancing over one shoulder and then the other. "But I know. I know because the moment I am the most vulnerable, the moment I fall asleep, howling winds rip the sky open and I see…"

Suddenly, he stopped. He had had shocking dreams since childhood, and because he was the Crown Prince, almost everyone in Babylon knew about them. Even so, he had not gone so far as to confide in anyone. Arioch's outlook on life was so simplistic, he would never understand. But with all of Yosef ben-Moshe's torments: the dagger scar on his forehead, the rope burn on his neck, his vast wealth, and especially his link to the God of Abraham, Isaac and Jacob, surely he would understand. So, leaning in close to his ear, he uttered, "I see winged creatures and chains… storehouses and keys… messengers and images… all pretending they are dreams and visions, but I know they are real because they fly at me and battle with me until I think I will go mad. Why me? Tell me, ben-Moshe, you saved my life. Why me?" Once again his eyes roved the heavens, then quickly darted back to the lump on the ground. "I will tell you something else you do not know. Since the day you arrived, I have not had one dream or vision. So you must live!"

"I know about dreams and visions," murmured Yosef ben-Moshe, barely able to breathe. He could not yet taste blood in his mouth, but knowing he would soon, he cracked an ironic grin. "A vision told me to come and fight for you. Absurd, isn't it? A Hebrew fighting for a Babylonian. I thought an angel of the Lord was speaking to me, but look at me now. I am going to die and lose everything: my home, my wealth, my daughter. For what?"

"You must live. I command you."

"I would like to live," he gulped, still tasting no blood.

Not knowing what to do, Nebuchadnezzar tugged his royal ring off his finger and jammed it onto Yosef ben-Moshe's. Then, locking his fearsome eyes onto the Hebrew's fearsome eyes, he solemnly pronounced, "For saving my life."

"I had to," welled up from deep inside.

"You had to?" demanded Nebuchadnezzar. "Why? Was it part of your vision?"

Pain searing through his back, Yosef ben-Moshe tried to find the answer. Certainly, he had not planned on saving Nebuchadnezzar's life, yet he had stayed close to him throughout the battle, something he had never done before because Arioch and the elite guard were his appointed watchmen. So why had he posted himself nearby today? He had no idea why and was about to say so, when the voice deep inside came into focus. It was the voice of Jeremiah crying out at Jerusalem's city gates, shouting before the Temple of Solomon, and speaking in the king's palace, saying, "This is what the Lord Almighty, the God of Israel says: 'I will hand all your countries over to my servant Nebuchadnezzar King of Babylon.'"

Over the years, Jeremiah had cried out so many threats, Jerusalem had learned to roll her eyes at the prospect of the Lord Almighty handing her over to the King of Babylon. But calling Nebuchadnezzar the servant of the Lord Almighty was so close to blasphemy, the city had exploded with righteous indignation. For how could an uncircumcised Babylonian be anywhere near the Lord, let alone be his servant?

Nonetheless, because Jeremiah was the prophet of God, Yosef ben-Moshe had forced himself to accept his appalling words—at least conceptually. But here on the battlefield, to think he had come all this way to die because Nebuchadnezzar was the servant of the Lord Almighty? No, that was too close to home, bringing it out of the conceptual into his personal life, and he would not have it. Nebuchadnezzar was Babylon and because he was Babylon, it was impossible for him to be the servant of the Lord Almighty. Even so, he heard his voice say, "I saved your life because you are the servant of the Lord Almighty."

He was so weak, the words barely whispered out of his parched lips, yet they struck Nebuchadnezzar with such force, he jerked back and, for an eternity, said nothing.

During his silence, Yosef ben-Moshe had time to reflect on why he believed the prophet's words enough to repeat them. Curiously, it had to do with his wealth and violent past. As a young man going out into the desert to find his future with nothing more than his donkey and bare feet, he had cried out to the name of the Lord asking for protection and success. Within five years, he returned to Jerusalem not only alive, but with his health intact and richer than any other man. The bountiful kindnesses he had received during those years of torment—from one lonely cloud raining down water for him to drink, to the rope on his neck suddenly unraveling as he dropped from the hanging tree—instilled in him a fear of the Lord far greater than if the Lord had crushed him. So in the end, no matter how incredulous and repugnant it was to say Nebuchadnezzar was the servant of the Lord Almighty, he knew he could not bury or thwart the word of the Lord spoken by his prophet.

The Crown Prince thought the statement just as incredulous and repugnant as ben-Moshe. However, before he could object, all the words he had ever known abruptly disappeared, leaving his mind and tongue empty. He was as aware and alert as ever, perhaps more so, his nose twitching at every scent and his hair prickling at every sound, but without words he had no way to formulate thoughts or identify the world around him, no tools to remember the past or think about the present or future. Thus, suspended in a strange wordless world, he had no way of even knowing it. Then, after seven long minutes, he heaved a breath and all his words came rushing back.

It would seem that because he had lost his words, he would not remember the experience, as one does not remember unconsciousness or sleep. But that was not the case. He remembered every detail: the strangeness of the unidentified clumps on the battlefield, a quick movement in the sky, the startling sounds of hacking, clanging, and running. At the sound of running, he wanted to run also, his heart racing, his eyes darting here and there. When the sounds calmed, he calmed. Indeed, it was as if his mind for those seven minutes had been changed into a different mind, his awareness heightened to his immediate surroundings—danger, hunger, thirst, heat, and cold—and now with his words and thoughts returned, the urgent visceral awareness was gone.

"I serve no one," he stated.

It was a nondescript statement, calmly spoken, yet the brutality in his voice ignited such foreboding, Yosef ben-Moshe immediately thought of his daughter, Aridatha. Lurching himself out of his pain-soaked oblivion, he grabbed the Crown Prince and said, "I have a daughter in Jerusalem."

"Yosef, you are not going to die," Nebuchadnezzar declared, irritated because he needed him to live.

"Her name is Aridatha. Protect her."

"Yes, yes, I will protect her. Whether you live or die, I will protect her, your household, and your wealth. But you must live. Think of your daughter. Think of me!"

Yosef ben-Moshe's head spun. Aridatha was safe. Her future secure. Perhaps that was the reason the angel of the Lord had sent him here, not to save Nebuchadnezzar's life, but to save his daughter's. Flooded with happiness, he collapsed.

Watching the Hebrew's chest sink, the Crown Prince felt a rush of relief. After divulging his nightmarish dreams to him and confessing he needed him to live, he suddenly wanted him to die and take all his confidences with him, to die and never call him a servant again. But if he wanted him to die, why was he groaning, his eyes brimming with tears? Why was he holding his gut to keep himself standing upright? How could another life bleeding into the earth, bleed him? How could the death of one man leave such a void in his soul?

His soul... That was it! The presence of Yosef ben-Moshe, with his strange ability to be powerful while at the same time at rest, had fed and eased his soul. Of course, at times it had torn at it, rankled it, and set it on edge, but most often, it had strengthened and calmed it. Power and rest. How frequently he had considered the two intangibles.

The day Yosef ben-Moshe first stepped into his tent, without one weapon on him yet armed with fearless straightforwardness, Nebuchadnezzar instantly recognized his power: the authority to draw not only men to oneself, but men willing to obey one's commands. However, power was not unique. With enough cunning and might, it was easily acquired by the most inadequate of men. No, something else had set him apart as he announced he had come to fight for the Crown Prince and then, as if he had already taken command, suggesting endurance training for Babylon's elite and mandatory metal toothpicks for the entire army in order to save the men's teeth and cure their rank breath. Indeed, the man was like no other.

At first, Nebuchadnezzar had thought he was different because he was a Hebrew. But other Hebrews, although different, were not like the warrior standing before him, his white beard sculpted to his jawline and the Star of David etched into his bronze armband. Perhaps because Nebuchadnezzar had never known rest, it took him five months before he considered the idea and even then he believed the notion absurd. Absurd because power needed to be watched over and guarded day and night. If a man rested, even for a moment, his power, even for that moment, would disappear. In fact, his very self would disappear. Yet in Yosef ben-Moshe's case, no matter what the burden of power was, he always seemed to be at rest. Even more puzzling, he seemed to grow more powerful. Thus, the Crown Prince began to suspect that rest complemented power. Even more intriguing, perhaps rest was actually foundational to power, and if it was he must have it.

So Nebuchadnezzar set out to have rest: sitting quietly during the day, bathing in lavender after hunting, staring at the sunrise, riding alone by tranquil streams… The list went on and on, each boring him to death. He even wasted three whole hours getting his feet massaged. In fact, it was when his toes were being brutally kneaded, it dawned on him that rest, unlike power, was impossible to acquire. After all, he had tried everything and the more he had tried the more it had eluded him. Nonetheless, since the arrival of Yosef ben-Moshe, he had experienced some rest: rest from his nightmarish dreams. So was he going to let such an asset die?

"Get his shield," he ordered, and sweeping the Hebrew up into his arms, the victor of the Battle of Carchemish strode toward the tents.

7

As Yosef ben-Moshe trembled with cold, images from his life swirled inside his feverish mind. At first, he was a young man alone in the Dead Lands under a blistering sun, his mule dead, food stolen, side stabbed, and head slashed. Suddenly, he was in a cave clawing at its walls, searching for rocks he could polish into rare gems, gems to build his future so Jerusalem would once again revere the house of Moshe as it did before the Egyptians burned his father's caravans. Time jumped and he was the wealthy owner of the coveted Pillar of Salt Caravan. In the distance, the young beauty Zillah came running toward him, but he was distracted by a child, three-year-old Aridatha sitting outside Jerusalem's East Gate throwing handfuls of dirt in the air. A cloud of dust fell onto her face, but she did not see it because her concentration, as always, was fixed on some fine point of thought. Standing nearby was the boy Baruch ben-Zadok watching over her, while in the east, Nebuchadnezzar shot up like an enormous tree overshadowing the land.

As the images of Aridatha and Baruch and Nebuchadnezzar swam inside his head, three-year-old Aridatha was in fact outside Jerusalem's East Gate throwing a handful of dirt in the air. And, just like in his feverish thoughts, eight-year-old Baruch ben-Zadok was watching over her because it was his job to take her away from the house when the astrologers came to meet with her mother. This arrangement had started when she was an infant and screamed every time they visited. Even if they tiptoed out onto the terrace or met in the garden, she would shriek the entire double hour. So Baruch's mother offered to take her, and when she could walk safely on her own, Baruch took charge of her.

"Ari, you follow behind," he said as if talking to a peer, for she always did exactly what he told her without asking silly questions or whining. "If one of the goats starts to stray, just raise your arm slowly and direct it back to the herd."

Aridatha nodded confidently. She knew how to herd any number of goats and today, wearing her miniature leather belt with its miniature wooden dagger, she was prepared to protect them all. Her papa had made the dagger for her, and she was so proud of it, she stomped up the hillside just to feel it slap against her leg.

When the goats were settled, the two children did what they always did: Aridatha studying the world around her and Baruch reciting from Yosef ben-Moshe's scrolls. The commander had entrusted the scrolls to the boy, ordering him to read them daily to his daughter. Naturally, Baruch thought reading Moses and the Prophets to a three-year-old girl a silly notion, but he did it because no one ever disobeyed Yosef ben-Moshe, possibly because of the ever-present rope burn around his neck or the equally inspiring dagger scar across his forehead.

Whatever the reason, it was Baruch's opportunity to memorize the scrolls so he could grow up and be like his brother's best friend, Daniel. Under Jeremiah, Daniel had already memorized many of the scrolls—Moses, Judges, Kings, the Songs of David—reasoning he could go anywhere without them and still have them with him. Daniel was also the best swordsman and mathematician in Jerusalem, and if Baruch was going to grow up and be like him, he still had a long way to go, so he read aloud, "'Lift up your heads, O you gates. Lift up your heads, so the King of glory may come in.'"

"Who is this King of glory?" murmured softly through the air.

"What?"

She had not meant for Baruch to hear, but now that he had, she carefully moved her lips like grown-ups and said, "Is the King of glory the Crown Prince of the small circle?"

Sometimes Aridatha's three-year-old questions were a challenge, like the night she quizzed him about the pictures made by the stars or the morning she demanded to know who was guarding the Ark of the Covenant. But today she did not even make sense.

"What small circle?"

"The one Jeremiah showed me."

"Jeremiah? You mean the prophet of God?"

Sifting dirt into her palm, she nodded. "He said the Lord says, 'A voice is heard in Ramah, mourning and weeping...'"

"He said what?"

"'Rachel weeping for her children and refusing to be comforted because her children are no more.' Who is Rachel?"

"Jeremiah told you all that?!"

Nodding, she added, "He said Nebuchadnezzar's chariots come like a whirlwind and his horses are swifter than eagles."

Anger broiling in his chest, Baruch could barely breathe. His brother Hananiah and his three friends Daniel, Azariah, and Mishael talked often with the prophet, but they were fourteen years old and Jeremiah was training them in the Law of Moses. Even so, every time they walked off to study with him, Baruch beat his fists in the air, yelling they were not being fair and that he should be able to go with them. Waving him off, they would swagger away saying he was too young to meet with the prophet, even calling Baruch a baby. So, hearing that three-year-old Aridatha had discussed small circles, crown princes, Rachel weeping, and Nebuchadnezzar's chariots with the prophet of God was a bit much for the eight-year-old to handle maturely.

"Is he, Baruch? Is the King of glory the Crown Prince of the small circle?"

"Of course, not," he huffed, hot tears brimming. "The King of glory is *not* a small circle or a crown prince. He is…" Looking at the scroll, he read through blurred eyes, "'The Lord strong and mighty, the Lord mighty in battle. The Lord Almighty, he is the King of glory!'"

Reflecting on the peculiar words, she pitched another handful of dirt in the air.

"Stop it, Ari!" he yelled, stamping his foot. "You are getting dirt in my face."

"I am not, Baruch!" To prove it, she shot another blast upward, oblivious to the dust cloud powdering his face and the haze wafting toward the Temple of Solomon because she was watching the few particles of Jerusalem dirt countering all natural laws. They were rising upward. Going higher… and higher… and higher…

Watching those specks she whispered, not to Baruch or even to herself, but to all the mysteries surrounding her, "The dirt is going to heaven."

8

AFTER defeating Assyria and routing Egypt, Babylon's warriors mended chariots and sharpened swords under the hawkish eyes of Nebuchadnezzar and Arioch tramping across the Carchemish battlefield. Arioch, like everyone else, had a bounce in his step describing in bloody detail how Alcola saved his life by tearing an Assyrian's throat apart. But Nebuchadnezzar, convinced his dreams were going to return, barely heard. In fact, he felt them hunting him down at that very moment, so he whipped around to face them. But there were no keys or chains or storehouses blasting out of the sky, only the moon and stars hanging serenely in their places. Even so, he was not fooled. Whether he saw the nightmarish visions or not, he knew they were there. So changing course, he marched to the triage to see how Yosef ben-Moshe was fairing.

Seeing him in the same crumpled heap, he exploded, "Why haven't you done anything?"

Huddled over the mangled legs of a commander nearby, two royal physicians jerked to attention. "My prince?"

"Ben-Moshe," he said, jabbing his finger toward the Hebrew. "Why haven't you done anything?"

"There is no hope for him."

"No hope?" the Crown Prince almost shrieked. "I will tell you about no hope. If he dies, you die."

"We die?" they gasped, more incredulous than frightened because after their splendid feats of healing during the Assyrian campaign—re-attaching severed arms, irrigating and packing poisonous wounds, even drilling into a skull or two—it was impossible to believe they were going to die if some Jew died. "He has lost too much blood. There is nothing we can do for him."

"He will live."

Staring at fire blazing out of the Crown Prince's eyes, the two physicians suddenly understood that their splendid feats, even their very lives, meant nothing to him. So they gulped, "Yes, my lord."

"Keep his shield beside him at all times," he glowered, then hurried away.

Feeling the rope tightening around their necks, the two healers frantically searched for ben-Moshe's pulse. When they found nothing, they put their hands on his chest and their ears to his mouth trying to find breath. Unfortunately for them, their diagnosis was correct. It was hopeless. And yet… What about his shield? Nebuchadnezzar had studied the bloodied, dented Star of David for a long time before commanding them to keep it beside their patient. Perhaps it carried some magical power from the land of the Hebrews. If it did, why not use its magic to bring ben-Moshe's half-dead body back to life and save their own? Stunned by such improbable good fortune, they wondered how it worked. Both having the same thought at the same time, they placed their hands on the shield and, pressing down hard, waited for the transfer of power.

Nebuchadnezzar forced himself to stop thinking about his dreams and start thinking about Egypt. His scouts had reported that her fleeing armies had stopped at dusk. But the sons of the Nile had been so terrified, to the point of trampling one another, they would surely be on the run again before dawn. To lose Egypt now would be irresponsible. Even worse, humiliating. So he swung around and shouted, "Babylon!"

Immediately, his warriors stopped everything: separating the battlefield loot, fixing chariot wheels and floorboards, repairing tack and saddles, chasing down horses.

"Egypt's armies fled from the battlefield," he roared. "But they will not find refuge in the reeds of the Nile. Babylon will crush them out of existence before they reach Hamath!"

His men leapt to their feet, shouting and pounding their spears.

"Feed and water your horses before you feed and water yourselves," the Crown Prince bawled, rapping out each word to the cadence of their drumming spears. "Sharpen your weapons before you sleep. We ride before dawn and after that…" Suddenly, he paused. Such a complete demonstrative pause, the shouts and the spears paused too. What was he thinking? What was he going to say next? Every man strained to hear, climbing atop chariots, standing on horseback, stretching on tiptoes.

But Nebuchadnezzar had paused not for emphasis, but because he had sunk into a world of gloom. Yes, he was the victor of the Battle of Carchemish—Assyria vanquished and Egypt on the run—but he was the defeated one. Defeated because Shining One's epic was not about a Crown Prince, but about the King of Babylon: '*The King of Babylon. All nations bow before him. The king of kings. Nothing can shake him... Nothing can shake him...*'

Nothing can shake him, nothing can shake him echoed round and round in his head. Yes, the words had applied to every endeavor he had ever attempted—except being king! For no matter what he did, he was always the Crown Prince. Nations were not going to bow to a Crown Prince. *Crown Prince, Crown Prince* taunted him, mocked him, laughed at him like crows laughing from the heights until blinded by rage he raised both arms blood-streaked from battle and shouted:

"NOTHING CAN SHAKE ME!"

It was like magic: a shock wave of power, awesome and wild, upsetting the air and igniting his men, not with rage or defiance, but triumph. Jumping up and down, they punched their fists into the air, shouting, "BA-BY-LON! BA-BY-LON! BA-BY-LON!"

"My prince," Arioch called over the din, pointing to a dust-covered messenger galloping in.

Jumping from his horse, the messenger handed Nebuchadnezzar a small scroll. "News from the capital."

"Probably your father wanting to know how the battle is going," grinned Arioch, eager to tell Polassar the battle was won and Assyria was now his.

But Nebuchadnezzar, moving toward the torchlight and breaking open the seal, had no such eagerness, not while *Crown Prince, Crown Prince* was throbbing through his head. However, as he read the message—a short missive pelting him from every side—all the taunting, mocking, and laughing stopped. In fact, everything stopped.

Stopped. So history could turn to a new page.

"BA-BY-LON!!! BA-BY-LON!!! BA-BY-LON!!!"

During that blink of time which only comes to a handful of men, Nebuchadnezzar, through no effort of his own, was placed on the threshold of glory. A glory which would wing him into a future so remote, he no longer cared what was at the end of China's patient waiting. A glory which would carry him to such heights, he no longer cared if Yosef ben-Moshe lived or died. He did not even care if his horrific dreams returned.

"Arioch," he said, rolling up the parchment and placing it securely in his chest pocket, "you will take charge of the Hamath campaign."

Arioch wondered if he had heard correctly. Next to building Babylon, Nebuchadnezzar's foremost ambition was defeating Egypt, so he should be leading the campaign.

"Once you have the victory, you will send our armies into every city and town from here to Egypt and take captives. Only the finest and brightest."

"But, my prince, this is your battle."

"I must return to Babylon."

"Babylon?" Arioch protested. "Fighting Egypt is more important than anything going on in Babylon."

"Is it?"

Arioch studied Nebuchadnezzar's settled, scheming eyes. Only moments before, they had been consumed by his restless hunted look. What had changed?

"My father," Nebuchadnezzar spoke slowly, as if treading cautiously on newly plowed soil, "is dead."

"What?"

Pulling the scroll from his pocket, he handed it to Arioch. Opening it, Arioch read aloud, "Nabopolassar King of Babylon is dead."

Arioch's stomach lurched so violently, he thought he was going to be sick. For years, they—Nabopolassar, Nebuchadnezzar, and Arioch—had planned for this day. So, yes, he had expected it. In fact, he had dreamed about it, even play-acted it out in his mind, but now that it was here, on the very day Nebuchadnezzar conquered Assyria and had Egypt on the run, he was not prepared for it. How could anyone be prepared?

"Then that means…" he stammered. "That means…" Hesitant to say it, he stopped.

But, the Crown Prince was not hesitant, stating emphatically, "Yes, Arioch. That means I am now Nebuchadnezzar King of Babylon."

"King of Babylon." Their eyes met. Although Arioch was not ready for the drastic changeover, it was obvious Nebuchadnezzar was, filling Arioch with the confidence he needed. Even so, his eyes misted over, not with the sudden thrill of standing before his new king, but with the sudden realization that gone were the days of walking side by side: the days of riding together, hunting together, eating, laughing, and drinking together. From now on, Nebuchadnezzar would walk alone and he, Arioch, would be one step behind. With the passing away of Polassar, their friendship had also passed away; so yes, Arioch's throat was somewhat tight and his eyes somewhat watery because he knew he would miss his friend.

In fact, he missed him already, feeling like an outsider, as Nebuchadnezzar narrated his plans for building his Northern and Southern Palaces, his temples to Marduk and Ishtar, and his canals and walls around the city. But when the King of Babylon started rapping out timetables for replenishing swords, daggers, bows, chariots, and armies in order to fight Egypt and win, Arioch finally saw what Nebuchadnezzar saw: absolute power falling into their hands. Yes, their boyhood friendship was gone, but in exchange, Nebuchadnezzar would now rule the world and he, Nebuchadnezzar's chief commander, would lead the armies of Babylon into unconquered lands and win. So, throwing off the past, he eagerly stepped into the future, exclaiming, "Now you can build Babylon to the ends of the earth!"

"I will build Babylon further than that," the new king chided from his new lofty clime.

"Further than the ends of the earth? How can anyone build further than…"

"Arioch," Nebuchadnezzar tutted. "Why did I go to China?"

"China?" A long-forgotten ember in Arioch's heart flared: the sudden fragrance of peonies, the floating image of plaited raven hair, the sparkle of a small silver ring. And it startled him. On his last day in China, he had resolved to forget Chenguang because back then he had been committed to the Crown Prince of Babylon. Now he was committed to the King of Babylon. Nothing in the world was more important. So quickly forgetting her again, he sucked in the stench of the battlefield and replied, "You went to China to learn more about Shining One's epic, *I Will Sit Enthroned…*"

"…*on the Mount*," Nebuchadnezzar interrupted, his mind flashing to thousands upon thousands of angels flying across the heavens to the Fountains of the Deep and singing under the jeweled wings of the great and mighty Shining One. "My whole life," he whispered, his breath steaming into the cool night air, "I have hoped I was the man in the epic.

Now I know I am. Shining One's words—*'I will ascend to the heights. I will raise my throne above the stars of God. I will sit enthroned on the Mount'*—will live through me, Nebuchadnezzar King of Babylon."

Staring at his king, Arioch felt fifteen years old all over again watching the young Crown Prince charge across the burning bridge, shouting, "NOTHING CAN SHAKE ME!" It had been a moment of youth and brilliance, future and glory, all headed for this one day. Just as eager to follow him now as then, Arioch bowed humbly before his new king.

"But first," Nebuchadnezzar said, slapping him on the shoulder, "I must go to Babylon, receive the royal pendant, and sign the documents." Striding toward the tents, he called back, "Remember, only the finest and the brightest to build Babylon." Catching a glimpse of ben-Moshe still in a heap, he added, "And when you get to Jerusalem…"

He paused to stare at his two royal physicians thumping ben-Moshe's shield, then backing away and glaring at it. When they did it again, thumping, then glaring at the shield as if expecting it to come alive, he shook his head. "Those two have been working too hard."

"When I get to Jerusalem?" Arioch queried.

"When you get to Jerusalem, protect Yosef ben-Moshe's wealth, his household, and his family. Especially his daughter. Her name is Aridatha."

As he disappeared into his tent, the victory chant, "BA-BY-LON!!! BA-BY-LON!!! BA-BY-LON!!!" was still going strong, ushering in a new era.

9

Arioch pursued the Egyptian army and wiped it out at Hamath. He then sent his armies into every city, town, and village north of the Egyptian border claiming all the land and crops, fish and animals, gold and silver, and the bodies and souls of men for Nebuchadnezzar King of Babylon.

Because Jerusalem was north of Egypt, it was inevitable Babylon would soon be galloping through her gates, so the City of David, still reeling because Egypt had been routed, prepared for the invader. Pregnant women and newborns were hurried out of the city, flocks and horses hidden in the wastelands, and gold and silver stashed inside the walls. Men buried oil in caves, women lowered jewels into cisterns, and children concealed sacks of spices high up in the trees. After three-quarters of the wealth was safely hidden away, a glow of pride fell upon the city because it had outwitted its conquerors before they had even arrived.

Then one morning at sunrise, Babylon came. Not in the usual conquering fashion, all ceremony and parade, but like lions charging out of the forest, and Jerusalem panicked. Nobles and priests swarmed to the king's palace for safety. Merchants and craftsmen, after locking their doors, hid behind water jars and wall hangings. The poor, who had no water jars or wall hangings, took cover under moldy tarps and inside thickets.

However, not everyone lost his nerve. Baruch's brother Hananiah and his three friends Daniel, Azariah, and Mishael were too curious about the foreigners to run and hide. So, at Daniel's suggestion, they hurried to the top of the Jerusalem wall to see their new conquerors.

Zillah's foyer was jammed with astrologers frantically coordinating Babylon's demise with the stars overhead, so she ordered Baruch to take charge of Aridatha, expecting him to hide her at his home. But Baruch wanted to see Babylon just as much as his brother, so tugging Aridatha along, he hurried after the four older boys. Aridatha, equally determined to see Babylon, still fixed in her mind as the small circle, tried to keep up, but the stairs were steep and the Stars of David in her hem kept catching on the sharp-edged stones. Even so, she climbed as fast as she could, frowning at the Jerusalem men racing down pushing and shoving the children out of their way.

"Baruch," she called over the clamor. "They look afraid."

"They are." Losing pace with the older boys, he picked her up and carried her.

"Are you?" she asked.

"Am I what?"

"Afraid."

"No," he stated matter-of-factly, regretting bringing her because she was getting heavier by the moment. "Are you?"

"No."

His eyes flashed with pride, and stopping on the landing, he looked at her. "Do you know why you are not afraid?"

Tapping the scrolls jutting out of his knapsack, she nodded. "'Though an army besiege me, my heart will not fear. Though war break out against me...'" She stopped, letting him finish the words of King David.

"'Even then will I be confident,'" he declared. Their eyes met, Aridatha's filled with the glory of being in Baruch's arms, Baruch's brimming with the glory of King David. He was a handsome boy with a winning smile, his curly black hair cropped short, his brown eyes solid like the earth. He had a boyish temper exploding at every frustration, yet he was patient with her, spending hours teaching her about the world around them: the goats, the breeding and the feeding; the grapes, the pruning and the harvesting; the wheat, the planting and the threshing. Although he was demanding, expecting her to run faster and work harder than her years allowed, he pushed himself just as hard and, when it came to memorizing the scrolls, even harder.

"Whatever happens to us, Baruch," she said, pronouncing each word carefully, determined to make herself understood. "I love you." Without warning, she planted her lips on his, surprising them both.

It was an artless awkward gift, so naturally the boy wanted to laugh at her. But looking from her solemn dust-covered face down to her toes peeking out of her Stars of David hem, his heart that loved the scrolls was seized with a fierce protectiveness for her. "Nothing is going to happen to us, Ari," he promised, then hurried on up the steps.

Except for the four youths, the top of the wall was deserted. Apparently, the men of Jerusalem had come, taken one look and fled. And no wonder! Never before had they seen war in the flesh, rivers of armor marching straight at them, no longer a concept or a prophet's threat, but immediate and real.

Baruch's older brother, Hananiah, stared in disbelief at the countless horsemen, warriors, spears, swords, banners, flags, and war chariots. "War chariots?" he gasped. "They brought war chariots, too?" Grabbing Daniel's arm, he demanded, "What happened? Why didn't Pharaoh fight?"

"They will make us eunuchs and slaves!" shrieked Azariah. "They will feed us to their lions."

All looking to Daniel, they waited for an explanation but he said nothing. For unlike the others, his iron grey eyes were not staring at armies advancing because armies were made of men, and he and his friends could fight men. Instead, after twenty-two years of Jeremiah's warnings, he was staring at judgment advancing and who could fight judgment? Who could face the Avenger of Justice and say, 'Stop, go no further or I will vanquish you?'

Daniel's unusual silence was so rattling, Mishael nervously took charge. "Nothing is going to happen to Jerusalem," he declared, punching both fists in the air. His silver armbands and gold rings, all trophies from sparring contests, reminded his friends he was a winner. "Jerusalem cannot be destroyed because it houses the Temple of Solomon."

"Mishael is right," Azariah agreed, suddenly full of fight. "The Temple of Solomon bears the Name of the Lord and houses the Ark of the Covenant. As long as we have the Ark of the Covenant, no one can harm us."

"'But if you turn away and forsake my commands and go off to serve other gods,'" interjected a warm steady voice, startling them all, "'I will uproot Israel from my land, which I have given them, and reject this Temple I have consecrated in my Name.'" It was Aridatha, pointing to the Temple of Solomon. "'When Solomon finished praying, fire came down from heaven and the glory of the Lord filled the Temple.'"

All the boys, except Baruch, stared at her in surprise.

"How do you know that?" demanded Daniel, his eyes boring into hers.

"She knows everything," answered Baruch. "When I take care of her, I memorize the scrolls." Motioning to ben-Moshe's scrolls in his knapsack, he identified each one, "Moses, Chronicles, Judges, Kings, Prophets. Now she knows them, too."

Daniel gazed at the Temple. In her simple recitation, Aridatha had reminded them of the day it was dedicated and of a day when it might be rejected. Was this that day? Or was today the beginning, leading up to that day? Whichever it was, he did not know. But one thing was certain: Nebuchadnezzar had come as Jeremiah had warned, his armies were at the gate and his merciless yoke was about to fall. Furthermore, it was about to fall on them, not on the old but on the young: on him and the five standing before him. Whereas their parents had lived rich full lives, buying and selling, eating and drinking, if he and his friends were captured, they would not grow up under the blessings of Jerusalem. Instead, they would be the firstfruits for Babylon, caught and shackled to serve a foreign nation far away from their Temple and their Promised Land.

"Give her to me," he ordered Baruch, and taking Aridatha in his arms, he turned to the others. "We will hide in Hezekiah's tunnel."

Without a second to lose, the five boys ran for the stairs.

10

It was a short but strange journey for Aridatha. Wrapped in Daniel's arms and sheltered close to his chest, she felt as if she was in both the formidable grasp of her father and the sorrowful turmoil of the prophet Jeremiah. For unlike the other boys hurtling down the steps with their eyes fixed on escape, Daniel's vision was fixed on establishing a promise, his lips whispering, "I will keep the Law of Moses. Whatever happens, I will keep the Law of Moses." As he spoke, a mysterious fragrance perfumed the air, unlike any she had ever known, rich like frankincense and warm like flowing wine. She had no idea where it was coming from, certainly not from the musty walls of the stairwell, but it encircled Daniel's head like a helmet worn in combat, and because of it, she knew his whispered promise would keep them safe.

Reaching ground level, they ran into a cobblestone tunnel leading toward the marketplace when suddenly they heard Babylonian boots thundering after them.

"If we are caught," Daniel yelled to the others, "we must keep the Law of Moses!"

Hananiah heard but could not believe Daniel really meant it, just as he could not believe he was being hunted down by Babylonian warriors. Only that morning, he and Baruch had been awakened by their mother's voice singing one of King David's songs, "Where can I go from your Spirit? Where can I flee from your presence? If I rise on the wings of the dawn, if I settle on the far side of the sea, even there your hand will guide me; your right hand will hold me fast."

Not planning to rise on the wings of the dawn or settle on the far side of the sea, Hananiah had paid little attention. Then when she reminded him to hide in the family cistern if Babylon came, he paid even less attention because he was in a hurry to get to his friends. Now he wished he had listened to his mother and stayed home.

"Keep the Law of Moses?" he objected. "Impossible!"

"We must," commanded Daniel, his grip tightening around Aridatha.

"They will kill us if we do!" protested Mishael.

"Then we will be with our Father Abraham!" Daniel blasted back. Charging out of the tunnel into the marketplace, he grabbed Baruch, planted Aridatha at his side, put her hand in his, and said, "Get her home. They want us, not you."

"Go, Baruch!" Hananiah shouted as he hurried by, motioning his little brother to get away.

But Baruch and Aridatha, transfixed by the terror around them, stayed where they were, gaping at old men helping old women take cover behind vendors' stalls, mothers with babes in arms ducking behind water jars, fathers clinging to four, five, and six children escaping into the clogged alleyways, and lost children circling round and round searching for their families. Aridatha's mother, Zillah, was somewhere in the crowd crying out for her, but Aridatha did not hear because leather-armored warriors were hurtling by, racing after Jerusalem's finest and brightest.

As if in a dream, the two children watched a hulk pounce on Azariah's back. But Azariah, although stringy, had wrestled bull calves since he was seven, so he easily flipped him over and onto the ground. Aridatha and Baruch were about to cheer, when another warrior with a toothy grin clubbed Azariah into the dirt. Drawing his dagger, Daniel scrambled back to Azariah but was kicked in the stomach. Mishael tried to help Azariah; Azariah motioned him to go on. Daniel shouted he would bring Azariah, ordering Mishael to get to Hezekiah's tunnel. But it was impossible. Hulks were everywhere, jumping on all three, driving them to the ground and roping their arms. Baruch's brother, Hananiah, the fastest of the four, had taken the lead. Now, racing back to find his friends, he vaulted onto the toothy warrior, wrapped his arms around his neck, and was well on his way to choking him to death when another warrior clubbed him on the back.

"Hananiah!" yelped Baruch, throwing Aridatha's hand aside and running after him.

Aridatha followed but her three-year-old legs, as fast as they were, could not keep up. So, she stopped in the center of the frenzy, and without warning, two bloodied hands reached down and grabbed her.

"Baruch!" she cried.

Baruch turned. A huge red-bearded warrior, cursing in a thick slobbering tongue, was holding Aridatha high above the crowd. Bowling his way toward a swordfight on the other side of the well, he was not even thinking about the little girl screaming overhead. Apparently, she had been in his way, he had picked her up and now... Baruch's heart froze. Now he was going to throw her out of his way. Horrified, the boy yelled for him to stop, but it was too late. Red-Beard, with the ease of tossing a sack of meal, thrust her forward and let her go.

Voiceless, Aridatha spun through the air watching white billowy clouds blend with the Temple, the Temple blur into the shackled ankles of Daniel and Hananiah, a distant image of her mother, and a crimson pouch swaying back and forth. Then suddenly slamming into a wall, she gasped for air that was not there and crashed down onto the lilies below.

Heart in his throat, Baruch ran to her. Dodging soldiers and punching his way through wailing families, he quickly reached the lily bed. "Ari!" he cried.

When she did not move, he burst into tears. It was his fault! He had let go of her hand and now blood was streaming from her forehead into her chestnut hair. Horrified, he started shaking uncontrollably, when someone pushed him aside. It was Jeremiah scrambling in next to him, taking Aridatha in his arms, Zillah lunging in beside him, crying, "You are the prophet of God! Help her! My baby. My only baby."

Jeremiah studied the open wound on the child's brow, considered her limp body and still limbs, then gently pressing his thumb to her eyelid, opened her eye. It was vacant and unreceptive, yet the distant glimmer he had seen on the morning of the Battle of Carchemish, like a light at the end of a tunnel, was still there. Quickly yanking off his crimson pouch, he scraped up some dirt and started sifting it into it.

"What are you doing?!" shrieked Zillah. "Her chest is not moving. Help her!"

But the prophet had trained his heart to follow absolute purposes and fixed boundaries, not the urgent demands of man or woman, so he continued filling the pouch. When he was finished, he put it on Aridatha, clasped his enormous hand on her small brow, and said, "This is what the Lord Almighty, the God of Israel..."

Instantly, her chest rose into full breath, but immediately sank.

Zillah and Baruch, thinking they had witnessed her last gasp for life, stared at the motionless chest in sickening disbelief. But Jeremiah was undaunted and, leaning in close to her heart, repeated, "This is what the Lord Almighty, the God of Israel, says..."

Again Aridatha's chest heaved, sucking in a great bath of air. This time her small ribs did not collapse. They sank slowly, rested and rose again, over and over until her lungs breathed calmly and she fell into a deep sleep.

"My baby," cried Zillah, covering her with kisses. "My baby!"

Baruch had never been so happy. Yes, he had let go of her hand, but Babylon had not destroyed her. She was alive! Nevertheless, because he had lost her, even for those few moments, he did not want to lose her again. So he resolved he would never let go of her hand again, but always protect her. He would even teach her more about the world around them, read the scrolls happily to her, and search eagerly for the answers to her strange questions.

Yet, something bothered him: the crimson pouch. It had never bothered him when Jeremiah wore it. But laying so fixedly over Aridatha's heart, it seemed as if the prophet had placed a wall between her heart and his heart. He told himself he was being silly. It was only Jerusalem dirt and Jerusalem could never be a wall between them. Jerusalem united them. So, dismissing the notion, he listened to the prophet.

"This is what the Lord Almighty, the God of Israel says, to all he carries away into exile from Jerusalem to Babylon..."

"Exile?" gasped Zillah.

"Babylon?" objected Baruch.

"Build houses and settle down..." commanded Jeremiah.

"No!" Zillah exploded. "Aridatha is not going to Babylon."

Keeping his massive hand clutching the child's brow, the prophet continued, "Plant gardens and eat what they produce."

"Get away!" Zillah screeched, yanking her daughter out of his arms. "I know what you are. Everyone knows. You are an enemy to Jerusalem!" Hurrying off, she kept screeching, "Enemy! You want us to serve Babylon. Traitor!"

Baruch stared in disbelief. He had never seen anyone yell at the prophet or call him a traitor. He had only seen his brother and his brother's friends speak reverently to the man of God. His brother? What had happened to his brother?!

Frantically, he looked out at the marketplace but no one was there. Babylon's warriors, Jerusalem's fathers, mothers and children, and the finest and brightest were gone. Only he and the prophet were left, along with one old man helping one old woman creep away from a vendor's stall and one little girl, about Ari's age, turning round and round looking for her family. The little girl's father came running and, whisking her up in his arms, raced away.

Certainly, Hananiah, just like the father of the little girl, would come running. He always came running. With the sun setting behind him, he would race home from Daniel's house, rumple Baruch's Sabbath-combed hair and tell him he was a baby. So Baruch watched for his brother, looking from the well to the cobblestone alleyway, from the battered jewelry store to the empty road. But his brother did not come. No one came. Even the old man and the old woman were gone now and all was as silent as stone.

Fear crept into Baruch's heart, telling him Hananiah was never going to come. Telling him Daniel, Mishael, and Azariah would not come either. Telling him they had been taken away by the brutal hands of Babylon, and Jeremiah had done nothing. Worse than nothing, Jeremiah had condemned them to Babylon year after year, which meant Zillah was right: it was Jeremiah's fault!

Furious, Baruch turned on the prophet, beating his eight-year-old fists against Jeremiah's legs, yelling, "Traitor! You are an enemy to Jerusalem!"

To Jeremiah, Baruch's pelting fists were a balm compared to the anguish of seeing his four scholars shackled and herded away. He had known Daniel, Hananiah, Mishael, and Azariah since they were children, watched them grow up and trained them in the Word of God. So more than anything, he wanted to rescue them from sorrow, degradation, suffering, and violent deaths. But he refused to indulge himself because they were no longer boys but young men, and just as the Lord had appointed him to his task, the Lord had appointed them to theirs. It was up to them to fulfill or reject those tasks, not up to him to wrench them away from the Lord's calling. Furthermore, he was confident they would do well. Of course, that did not make it easier, for they were still so very young.

Instead of pounding on the prophet's legs, Baruch was now clinging to them because when he looked up to really shout his fury, he met such anguish in Jeremiah's eyes he had thrown his arms around his legs and was now begging for forgiveness.

The prophet loved the boy and, wrapping his arm around him, tried to comfort him. And Baruch was comforted. After all, Jeremiah was as distraught as he was, so how could he be Jerusalem's enemy? It was not his fault he was the messenger for the Lord Almighty, he just was. Furthermore, it was not his message, it was the Lord Almighty's message. So if Baruch was going to call anyone an enemy, it would have to be...

No! He would not let himself think it!

Yet, in the secret rooms of his heart, he did think it. The enemy had to be the Lord Almighty. Destroying Jerusalem by famine, plague, and sword was the Lord's message, not Jeremiah's. Exiling Hananiah and Aridatha was the Lord's work, not Jeremiah's. Only an enemy would say and do such things. On the other hand, perhaps the Lord had good reasons for destroying Jerusalem and exiling Hananiah and Aridatha to Babylon. No, there were no good reasons. To prove it—to himself, Jeremiah, and the Lord Almighty—he yanked away from the prophet and, stamping his foot, demanded, "Why! Why is the Lord doing this?"

Jeremiah was tired. For years the men and women of Jerusalem had been demanding *why,* and whenever he gave an answer, they disregarded it. Moreover, with Babylon rampaging through Jerusalem's streets because no one had listened to him, he was sorely tempted to ask why he should ever answer the question *why* again. But perhaps the boy—who might also end up wearing Babylon's chains—would embrace his answer. So waiting for him to calm down, he said, "Who knows the mind of the Lord? His judgments are unsearchable. His paths beyond tracing out. He speaks the truth. He declares what is right."

A nothing answer! Nothing about Hananiah, nothing about Aridatha, nothing about Jerusalem, nothing about Babylon, and Baruch was about to kick the dust off his feet and run away. But instead, perhaps because he had lived under Hananiah and Daniel all his life, he stayed where he was, forcing himself to accept the answer as they would: accepting it as an answer that answered everything. So with lips tight and jaw grinding, he nodded, agreeing he did not know the mind, judgments or paths of the Lord, agreeing the Lord spoke the truth and declared what was right. Therefore, Jeremiah's answer was the true answer. End of argument.

Curiously, as he nodded his agreement, he saw for the first time it was his question, not Jeremiah's answer, which was flawed: demanding from his limited mind, his limited experience, and his limited heart the accounting of the whys and wherefores of a limitless God. No wonder Hananiah had always called him a baby. Just because he, eight-year-old Baruch ben-Zadok, did not understand the ways of the Lord Almighty, that did not make his eight-year-old ways right and the Lord's eternal ways wrong. Nor did it make him, Baruch ben-Zadok, a great friend to Jerusalem and the Lord her enemy. Furthermore, what a relief! Yes, what a relief to know that the Lord spoke the truth and declared what was right. Indeed, it was the end of the argument.

So the young boy, Baruch ben-Zadok, standing tall in the certain knowledge he did not understand the Lord's mind, judgments and paths, moved on to something he did understand: Babylon. Thus, he trained his anger and hatred in that direction, especially at Red-Beard who had thrown Aridatha against the wall and Nebuchadnezzar King of Babylon who was taking his brother away. Furthermore, knowing the Lord was merciful and often relented from his judgments, he decided not to tell Aridatha what Jeremiah had said about her exile to Babylon. For, if the Lord was going to relent, what was the point of telling her?

11

Leaving in the dead of night and following the River Euphrates, Nebuchadnezzar galloped from Carchemish to Babylon. Exchanging his horse at relay stations, he rode day and night passing small fishing villages, newly-sprouted barley fields, flocks of sheep, herds of donkeys, bustling ports, and rain-soaked grasslands. As king, all of this was now his, but he did not see it. Nor was he aware of the sudden surging winds, the bone-chilling fogs, or the drenching showers. He had even forgotten his fatigue from the Assyrian wars, because his thoughts and concerns were in a new world: the world of Nebuchadnezzar King of Babylon enthroned in his Great City.

However, first he had to build it. So the long hours on horseback were a welcome opportunity to review his timetables for rerouting the Euphrates, the man-hours for constructing the city wall, the different courses for the Lebanon canal, and the multiple irrigation systems for the wastelands. On his last night before entering the city, he shelved his construction plans so he could reflect on the essence of Babylon—its meaning, purpose, destiny, and glory—as mapped out in Shining One's epic, "*I Will Sit Enthroned on the Mount.*"

Longer than the entirety of King David's psalms, Shining One's epic, riddled with poetic mysteries and elaborate puzzles, was a path into the deeps, into the light, and into the supernatural. Most importantly, at least to Nebuchadnezzar, it was a path into the secrets of the glory of kingdoms. In fact, it was as if Shining One created the glory of kingdoms on the day he sang his epic, not long after the Lord laid the earth's foundations.

Not much was known about that day, so at the age of ten, Nebuchadnezzar decided to find out. Searching the archives of Chaldea, he discovered fourteen copies of the entire poem but only one incomplete narrative about the day. At thirteen, he journeyed to the temples of Egypt and, at fifteen, to the catacombs of China. Everywhere he went he found Shining One's masterpiece recorded in all the local languages, but the narratives about the events of the day, although splendorous, were sketchy, fragmented, and sometimes contradictory.

The different versions did agree that Shining One was one of the most brilliant, most powerful, and most light-filled of all the angels. They also agreed he had two other titles: Son of Dawn and Prince of the Power of the Air. As Son of Dawn, his birthright was formidable and widespread, inheriting the dawn of time and all subsequent dawns. As Prince of the Power of the Air, his dominion was equally formidable and widespread, covering the regions of light and sound, the starry splendors and the heavens.

Determined to fill those regions with his lighted beauty, he composed a musical masterpiece of praise to the Lord Almighty, ordering all the angels to report to the Fountains of the Deep to sing it. Because he was a Prince they instantly obeyed, swooping in from all the heavenly ranges, taking their positions and awaiting his signal. After a great silence, he slowly raised his arm and half the angels breathed a simple melody into the air. Before long, the other half surrounded the melody with a multidimensional harmony. Never before had such majestic praise flooded the heavenly realms, yet Shining One was not satisfied.

So he introduced his own voice into the melody, his own light into the harmonies, and his own power into the rhythms. Using his command over the dawn and his power over the air, he formed pearl-white images looking like angels flying, angels singing, and angels dancing. He produced sapphire-blue sounds swirling out of their mouths and glittering streamers pouring out of their wings. Then, by some seraphic brilliance, he cast his own light-filled image into the air, repeating it again and again and again, always transforming and ever fleeting, until all his images, voices, and sounds completely surrounded the highest house in the heavenly realms, the House with the Seven Hewn Pillars. For the climax of his composition, he had planned for all the angels to cast their images into the heavens. But suddenly and without warning, the angelic host abandoned his score, each going his own way, crying out his own spontaneous praise to the Lord Almighty.

Young Nebuchadnezzar was appalled, actually in a fury, because the angels had disobeyed their Prince. Not wanting to hear another word about how beautiful and joyful the renegades' songs were, he was about to throw the Chaldean tablet to the floor, but curious to know Shining One's response, he kept reading.

Instead of showing anger, Shining One simply stood at attention, appearing as if he was listening to the angels, when in fact he was calculating how he could retrieve their allegiance and keep it forever. He knew whatever he did, he had to stay within his realm, so he considered his entitlements. As Son of Dawn, his birthright applied not just to one dawn, like the Dawn of Time, but to all Beginnings. As Prince of the Power of the Air, he practically owned the air! Considering these titles and calculating the combined powers and authorities that went with them, along with his ultimate destiny based on his birthright and royal domain, he smiled a slow cunning grin, leapt into the air—his air—and took off like an eagle taking flight.

Everyone had to scramble to get out of his way, for he was the Prince of the Power of the Air, governing all its pathways and byways, light waves and dark waves, images and sounds, even its entrances and exits. So, clearing a path for the Prince, the heavenly hosts watched him wing upward through layers and layers of emerald air, sardonyx air, chrysolite air, amethyst air, and finally the rarified gold air at the top, gleaming like ice. There, next to the Great River, always clear as crystal, he planted his feet. Two angels stood nearby, equally powerful angels, yet they did nothing when Shining One stepped out onto the Mount of God.

The Mount of God! The very thought sent chills up and down Nebuchadnezzar's spine. But wait, there was more. Standing on the Mount of God, Shining One extended his jeweled wings and, opening his golden mouth, sang an even greater song of praise to fill the air: his great Babylonian epic, beginning with the words, *"I will ascend to the heights..."*

At this point, no two descriptions were alike. The Egyptian account said Shining One's words shot through the heavens like rivers of gold at flood stage. China's version, buried in Tin's subterranean room, disagreed, contending the words flashed out like fiery swords from dragons' mouths. The Chaldean records identified them as sheet-lightning transforming into the glory of kingdoms. Whatever the visions, they stunned the angelic multitudes into silence. Never before had they seen such radiance, never before such pomp. Even the shadows under Shining One's wings were spellbinding, a fearsome darkness rumbling like a thousand tambours and glowing like a thousand crowns pealing, *"I will ascend to*

KING OF BABYLON 77

the heights. I will raise my throne above the stars of God. I will sit enthroned on the mount of assembly…"

Apparently, God could do nothing about it because as Shining One filled the firmament with his dizzying delights, no one interrupted or stopped him. More significantly, no one ordered him off the mount. Thus, a multitude of angels soared in under his wings and joined him, singing his choruses and trumpeting his verses over land and sea until they became so popular, they found their way into the hearts and souls of newly created man.

Since that day, every man had shared in the glory of the epic, but history was still awaiting the one man who could actually claim it for his own. All his life, Nebuchadnezzar had suspected he was that one and only man, and if he was, he was determined not to miss it. Consequently, he had spent his childhood immersed in Shining One's epic, a mystery to the ordinary mind but to him the key to power. Then at the age of eleven, while fighting alongside his father, he was proven right when Shining One's words living in his heart quickened in his hands, giving him the strength to kill warriors twice his size. He never told anyone about this power, but when he took command of Babylon's armies, he used the epic's secrets to train his legions to be the mightiest warriors on earth, leading them into his quest: Babylon, glory of kingdoms.

Thus, on his final night before entering Babylon and taking the crown, Nebuchadnezzar sang the entire epic, its choruses and verses, secrets and mysteries, starting with, *"I will ascend to the heights. I will raise my throne above the stars of God. I will sit enthroned on the mount of assembly…"* His voice rose and fell as he chanted the chapters, but when he reached his favorite section—the part about himself—he cried out with his voice that shattered the dawn:

"There comes a Man!
"There comes a Man! The King of Babylon!
All nations bow before him: the king of kings.
Nothing can shake him.
"There comes a Man! He builds Babylon
by his mighty power: the Glory of Kingdoms to last forever.
Nothing can shake him.
"Envious of the Man, the Heavens and Nations
wage war against him. But the Man overcomes them.

Nothing can shake him.
"At the End of the Age, the Heavens and Nations
wage a Great Final War against him.
Nothing can shake him.
"There comes a Man! The King of Babylon!
He ascends to the heights. He sets his throne on the Mount of God.
Nothing can shake him."

"Nothing can shake ME…" Nebuchadnezzar trilled to the warbling doves and laughing crows. "Nothing can shake ME…" he guffawed to the rising sun. Sucking in the aromas of breakfasts cooking over open fires, he was suddenly hungry for grilled fish and warm bread, lentils and lamb, grapes and pomegranates, hungry for anything and everything good in his kingdom. Even so, he decided to wait and eat when he entered the Great City, no longer his father's domain, but his.

However, when he rode into Babylon, his appetite sank at the sight of the ragged tents lining the rutted roads, the crumbling temples, and blank-eyed children. Looking down at a young woman old before her time, flies begetting flies in her matted hair, then looking at her three children languishing beside her, he thought of the pyramid of Cheops. It had taken over one hundred thousand men working nonstop for ten years just to get ready to build it. Another twenty to construct it. But he was not going to have this woman and her children wait thirty years for Babylon to comfort and enrich her. He, Nebuchadnezzar King of Babylon, was going to build his Great City in seven years' time into such pomp, splendor, and wealth, it was going to be the envy of all the earth. Why else had he ordered Arioch to bring him the finest and brightest from all his conquered nations? For the glory of Babylon.

12

ALTHOUGH the glory of Babylon was an old friend to Nebuchadnezzar, it was a new and unwelcome stranger to Jerusalem. So naturally, Jerusalem's elders, chief priests, noblemen, and city leaders believed Babylon had made a mistake singling out and capturing the sons and daughters of noble families, choosing only the best looking, the most well-informed, and those who had the highest aptitude for learning. Clearly, Chief Commander Arioch had misunderstood his role as benign conqueror, so someone had to tell him. But who? Who was going to walk out the city gates, march across the valley through Babylon's armies, hike up the mount to Babylon's command post, and meet with the brutal Scythian? Each group believed they were the only ones with the wits and boldness to go up against the commander and succeed, arguing heatedly that with their stature and the king's sanction, they would outshine all the others' lackluster capabilities. So, in the end, the palace sent one man from each group.

Because a stiff south wind was silting the outside scribes' tables, Arioch had gone inside to review the inventories of confiscated property: gold, silver, wine, oil, horses, oxen, and captives. Once again, the captive count was off by three bodies, so he ordered another numbering of the Hebrews—the seventh! The commander of the captives was a scrupulous, hardened warrior who rarely erred, so Arioch suspected the Hebrews. What mischief were they up to? How could three men be counted and then not counted, counted again and then not...? Only a few months ago, he would have shrugged it off and galloped to the river for a swim, but now as second in command over Babylon, he no longer shrugged anything off. In fact, he had become as exacting as his father and Nebuchadnezzar. Consequently, no bodies were ever going to fall through the cracks on his watch. Even so, he was considering an afternoon ride, possibly to the river, when his guard announced representatives from Jerusalem requesting an audience.

Every city, town, and village had requested an audience for the sole purpose of begging him to return their children, so knowing this would not interfere with his afternoon ride or possible swim, he nodded. When he heard them rustle into the tent, he lifted a bored finger signaling them to speak and kept working.

The chief priest, chosen by lot, stepped forward, cleared his throat and waited for the commander to look up. But Arioch just wagged his finger more vigorously, as if to say get on with it. So with honeyed subservience, the high priest praised Babylon for its impressive victory over Assyria and Egypt, adding because the wars were over, Jerusalem was confident Babylon would treat the city justly and in that light return their sons and daughters. When the commander still did not look up, the city leader pushed the chief priest aside, stepped forward, and brightly suggested that, in exchange, Jerusalem would give Babylon her finest and brightest servants and slaves.

Arioch raised his eyes. No one had ever proposed a swap before, and looking fierce with his gold amulets dripping from his wheat-blonde beard and his clear blue eyes flashing like a cold hard sea, he did not know whether to rage at their temerity or laugh at their stupidity. Leaning back, he studied the Elder. His hair was shorn in sorrow, his leathery feet covered with ashes. He was the only one who had his head bowed, not because he was afraid, but because he was humble. Arioch had seen men like him standing before his father many times, and always his father welcomed and listened to them. Arioch had also seen men like the other three standing before his father: a narrow face, a ruddy face with fat cheeks, and a stern face with a grey pallor, all afraid, yet their veiled eyes revealed rebelliousness and arrogance to the core. If the city had sent only the Elder, Arioch would have welcomed and listened to him. Obviously, he would not have rescinded Nebuchadnezzar's orders, but he would have perceived that the city was wise. Instead, the city had sent the other three, outnumbering the Elder, revealing more about Jerusalem than sheaves of reports.

"Go home," he said, waving them out.

When the four returned to the palace empty-handed, Jerusalem reeled. What had gone wrong? Only months before their young men and maidens had been dancing in the streets celebrating Egypt's soon-to-be victory over Babylon. Now their children were being herded through the streets like cattle, heads shaved, arms branded, no personal property—no extra tunic or extra pair of sandals, not even a bag of water—because as Chief Commander Arioch said, the finest and the brightest no longer owned property. Instead, they were the property, owned by Nebuchadnezzar King of Babylon.

Thus, when Nebuchadnezzar's property marched out of the city gates and Nebuchadnezzar's warriors slammed those gates shut locking the rest of the city inside, Jerusalem's fathers and mothers, with no other recourse, hurtled to the top of the wall and stretching their arms toward the valley below, ordered their children to escape or at least beg Babylon to let them go. The uproar was so horrific, like animals shrieking when being clawed to death, anyone would have turned to look. Yet, although tears were in their eyes, the sons and daughters of Jerusalem did not turn because they had quickly learned that Babylon had whips and used them on those who did not march face forward.

So the throngs on the top of the wall bellowed louder, crying out their children's names, shouting blessings, and screaming advice: keep warm, eat well, be good, remember papa and mama, run away, fight, pray! But all their last-minute entreaties did not change a thing. The long doleful line did not stop or slow down. Instead, it kept its brisk pace crossing the valley below and an even brisker pace climbing up the opposite hillside, taking the thousands of newly shaved heads and freshly-branded wounds farther and farther away.

As the front of the line reached the summit, a hush fell over the wall, all eyes straining to see what was going to happen next. Was the line going to travel across the top of the summit? Or, mercifully, turn around and come back? It took some minutes to discern it was not traveling across or turning back, but shrinking. Their children were marching over the top and disappearing down the other side. Swiftly now, as a snake gets shorter when it slides into a hole, the line grew shorter until Jerusalem's finest and brightest were gone.

A staggering moment! Similar to when someone dies and the one left behind, always caught by surprise, stares at the body wondering if the loved one is really gone or still there. Likewise, everyone on the wall stared at the horizon wondering if their children were gone or still there.

Of course, their children had to be there because the Lord Almighty, the God of Israel, protected Jerusalem and her children. Consequently, no one moved.

For three hours, no one moved, each heart watching, waiting, hoping. Meanwhile, the sun slowly set, dusk blew in on a hot wind, and darkness stole the light away. About to be engulfed by night, hesitant whispers suggested that their children might not return in the dark, but perhaps at sunrise. Yes, that was it. Babylon would send them back at sunrise. Still, no one moved because no one knew where to go. Certainly, not home. Who could face a son's empty workbench or a daughter's empty bed? Who could gather for a meal with half the family knowing the other half had nothing to eat? Who could sleep in comfort when one's own flesh and blood was sleeping in chains in the wilderness?

"To the Temple!" shouted a lone voice.

Of course! The Temple! Without a moment to lose, Jerusalem hurtled down the stairwells and stampeded to the House of the Lord.

When Zillah heard everyone was going to the Temple, she could not dress fast enough. After all, Aridatha had almost died, which meant Zillah had suffered just as much as anyone. So donning her most elegant mourning clothes—fine Egyptian linen dyed a deep purple which almost looked black—and wearing three scarves: a purple, blue, and grey mantling her head in staggered tiers, she hurried out onto the road. Not surprisingly, it was jammed. In fact, every road, passageway, footpath, and trail was jammed. So keeping to the main road, she pushed through the city streets along with everyone else until she reached the Temple courtyard. After another hour of pressing through crowds, she found her friends, noblewomen like herself, and plunged into their grieving arms.

It was a night like no other, multitudes of men, women and children wailing uncontrollably for their lost. Someone shouted the Lord Almighty was going to bring their children back, and wild exaltation erupted, arms reaching to the heavens, everyone crying out praises and thanksgivings to the Lord. Another voice yelled the God of Israel had forsaken them, and the throngs fell to the ground, screaming and tearing their clothes. As the city flooded into the courtyard, the frenzy grew. Women caught up in the surge fainted; children crushed between robes and boots could not breathe; fathers trying to get their children out came to blows; and old men wrestling with their last racing heartbeats slumped to the tiles. The priests and the prophets on the Temple steps shouted louder ordering everyone to be calm because the God of Abraham, Isaac and Jacob was going to return their children at sunrise, and once again, Jerusalem would be at peace.

Of course, the crowds believed them. No one was going to exchange the hope of their children returning and living in Jerusalem for the horrors of living in Babylon. So listening to the prophets, they began to breathe easier. However, when the priests took charge and raged against the injustices done to Jerusalem, a sudden need to blame someone for the monstrous calamity swept through the courtyard.

Babylon was first on the list, but there was no satisfaction in swinging one's arms at air. The second target was the Lord Almighty because he had all the power to do something yet had done nothing. But to rail against the Lord would be imprudent because they were relying on him to save their children. They certainly could not blame themselves; they were the victims! Furthermore, it was absurd to blame anyone who wanted hope and prayed for peace. Consequently, there was only one person left to blame: the traitor, Jeremiah.

Jeremiah had never offered hope or peace, only destruction, yelling it over and over from the Temple steps. Where was he now? Certainly, his absence proved his despicable nature, because if he really cared about Jerusalem, he would be standing with Jerusalem's priests and prophets and, along with them, begging the Lord to bring their children back. Indeed, where was he when they needed him most?

Jeremiah was not far away. After watching Daniel, Hananiah, Mishael, and Azariah disappear over the ridge, he had quietly slipped into the city's most splendid park, Flowering Field. Now, standing in its center, he stared at a tall thicket of thorny acanthus and prickly junipers mantled by trumpet vines. The thicket had been there so long not many knew an ancient stele, a stone marker with a message written on it, stood deep inside its tangled branches. But Jeremiah knew. He also knew the message written on it, inscribed by a prophet from another time, the prophet Isaiah, and tonight he needed its consolation. Not only because of the sorrows of the day, but because of Jerusalem's oncoming future sorrows, knowledge he had cried out many times: "Zion, stretches out her hands, but there is no one to comfort her." As always, the city had shouted threats and insults at him, but the Lord like a mighty warrior had been with him, so he had pressed on: "The Lord determined to tear down the wall around the Daughter of Zion." Today, he had repeatedly proclaimed the full warning, and now bones aching and strength gone, he was hungry for the other prophet's words: "All men are like grass and all their glory is like the flowers of the…"

Suddenly, his arms were grabbed by four men, their faces wrapped, their rough swearing voices muffled. Without explanation, they lifted him from his feet, hurried him out of the park and, dropping him onto the road, dragged him up the hill to the Temple. They had planned to make a spectacle of him on the Temple steps, but when they reached the courtyard entrance, it was blocked by men and women crushed so tightly together there was no room for one man to squeeze through, let alone five. Yet, by some uncanny prescience, a path opened before them. So they rammed the prophet through, all the way to the Temple steps, then posted him at his usual corner, forcing him to face the assembly and its desperate chant: "Pray for our children! Ask the Lord to bring them home! Pray for our children! Ask the Lord to bring them home!"

In a flash, Jeremiah lifted his captors up and tossed them down like Samson tossing down Gaza's city gate. Seizing their necks, he yanked off their masks and ordered them out of the Temple courtyard. Astonished by his sudden raw power, the four scattered, stumbling down the steps as if being chased. But Jeremiah was not chasing them, in fact he had turned his back on them and the crowd.

Angry because he had turned his back on them, the crowd shouted louder, "Pray for our children! Ask the Lord to bring them home!" But Jeremiah just stood there, so silent another idea spread: perhaps the prophet had turned his back on them not to insult them, but to face the Temple and actually pray for them. Thus, his silence silenced them, and because he kept facing the Temple, they faced the Temple too.

No one knew what to expect, but as they waited once again their grief turned to hope, a powerful, tangible hope, because it was a hope they could see: the Temple of Solomon. Some remembered it bore the Name of the Lord. Some remembered it housed the Ark of the Covenant. Others remembered fire came down from heaven the day it was dedicated. Still others remembered it took Solomon seven years to build it. But one frightened heart, perhaps because Jeremiah's head kept bowing lower and lower, remembered the two stone tablets inside the Ark of the Covenant and the words written on them. In fact, it was as if the words on the tablets were bleeding out from the depths of the Temple, and the frightened heart, not wanting the words to get away, shouted them for all to hear, familiar to some, unfamiliar to most: the words known as the Testimony.

Long ago, the Testimony was spoken to Moses and the Israelites not by ordinary means, but out of the fire by the Lord, and written on two stone tablets, again not by ordinary means, but by the finger of God, striking an unprecedented blow into history: the finger of God writing the Word of God on stone tablets and giving it to man. Then again, two blows because Moses broke the first tablets and the finger of God wrote it on two more stone tablets. Ever since, the Hebrews had been in charge of the Testimony, yet amazingly, most of Jerusalem did not know the words written on the two stone tablets or had forgotten them. But hearing the lone voice, those who had forgotten opened their mouths and stammered along, filling in a phrase here and a sentence there until bit by bit the long-neglected words spoken out of the fire and written by the finger of God chorused through the hushed night air. Hence, those who had never heard the Testimony heard it for the first time: "I the Lord am your God who brought you out of the land of Egypt, the house of bondage: You shall have no other gods before Me."

Other commands followed, ordering the Israelites not to make carved images or bow down to them, not to use the Lord's name lightly and to set Shabbat apart for God. There were Ten Commands in all, and as they straggled into the air, a much-needed serenity warmed the Israelites' hearts, filling them with the quiet confidence that yes, they were God's Chosen People; and no, they were not like any other nation because they had been given the Testimony by the finger of God.

In fact, the courtyard grew so serene and so quiet, when Jeremiah finally did turn to speak, there was no doubt as to what he said and what they heard when he shouted, "The Lord said to me..."

Every eye brightened, every hand reached out to hold another hand, every heart soared in anticipation. The other prophets had promised peace, prosperity, and security, but if Jeremiah said they had suffered enough, they knew it would be true. He had been praying the entire time, so surely he had won the Lord's favor. They had recited the Lord's Testimony, so surely they had won his favor.

"Do not pray for the well-being of this people!" flew out of Jeremiah's mouth like a master's whip.

The shock was so absolute, no one moved. So staggering, no one breathed. Yet every man, woman, and child stood secure because even though the words pounded against their heads and pummeled their ears, they could not get through because no one would let them through. Why should they? Everyone knew the Lord Almighty would never say not to pray for his Chosen People. He might tell his prophet not to pray for Jerusalem's enemies, but he would never tell his prophet not to pray for Jerusalem. Therefore, the words were referring to someone else. Jeremiah was not condemning their flesh and blood. He was probably just warming up with a prophecy about a future people who did not deserve prayer. Yes, that was it. So again they listened, their hands gripping other hands so hard bones began to crack.

"Although they fast, I will not listen to their cry! Though they offer burnt offerings and grain offerings, I will not accept them. I will destroy them with sword, famine, and plague!'"

No longer in doubt as to whom he was talking about, chests rumbled, limbs shook, and blood began to boil.

"The Lord said to me!" Jeremiah continued, "'Even if Moses and Samuel were to stand before me, my heart would not go out to this people. Send them away from my presence! Let them go. And if they ask, where shall we go? Tell them, this is what the Lord says: Those destined for death, to death; those for the sword, to the sword; those for starvation, to starvation; those for captivity, to captivity.'" Staring out at thousands of coal-red eyes, it was obvious Jerusalem had traded her grief over her children for the greater satisfaction of killing the traitor, so Jeremiah braced himself, waiting for the onslaught.

Strangely, no one moved. Instead, once again by some uncanny prescience, a path opened before him. As he stepped onto it, the crowd found its voice, yelling, "You must die!" With every step, they yelled it: "You must die! You must die!" Nevertheless, no one touched him as he walked the long distance from the Temple, across the courtyard, and out the gate. When he disappeared, the path closed and the mob shouted to the heavens with even greater fervor, begging the God of Abraham, Isaac and Jacob to return their children by sunrise, thereby proving Jeremiah wrong.

When the sun rose and the children of Israel did not return, Jerusalem waited. When the sun rose higher—and higher—and their children still did not return, instead of conceding Jeremiah might have been right, the crowd simply decided it had not done enough for the God of Abraham, Isaac and Jacob. Therefore, each household promised to offer burnt offerings and grain offerings, reject wine, feasting, singing, and dancing, pray in sackcloth and fast in ashes until the God of Israel saw their good intentions, had pity on them, and brought their children back.

Thus reassured, Jerusalem went home.

13

JERUSALEM was like a city razed. Yes, her roads, buildings, and fields still stood, but the heart of the city, her finest and brightest striding through her streets, praying on the rooftops, and singing in the pastures, had been leveled, leaving old and young wandering about in sickening bewilderment, unable to work, eat, or sleep. Every sunset, Daniel's father expected to hear his son's footsteps bounding up the stairs, late as usual for the evening meal, and as usual, he waited for him. He waited and waited kneading his hands raw, then without warning, he rose and left, never eating or saying a word. Every night, when Baruch slipped into bed, his feet stayed cold because Hananiah was not there. So, hiding his face in his hands, he muffled his sobs, hoping his father and mother would not hear because it would break their hearts even more. Every morning, Mishael's mother started to clean her son's room, but there was nothing to clean: no clothes to put away, no new trophies from sparring contests to polish, no ink wells to fill. Standing there alone, she would stare out at nothing for hours. Day after day, parents labored up the steep stairwells to the top of the wall and, searching the ridge, waited for their children to reappear. Day after day, grandparents assembled at the palace wanting to see the king, but the king was not seeing anyone. Day after day, the elders, chief priests, noblemen, and city leaders argued over what to do next, but there was nothing to do next. Day after day, merchants came into the city and set up their wares in the marketplaces, but there were no shoppers. Yes, Jerusalem still stood looking as it always did, but it had lost its core, leaving nothing behind except the haunting nightmares of loved ones being starved, beaten, raped, mutilated, and then left to die in some ditch. Moreover, if that was not enough misery, there was always the chilling remorse that their children's agony might be Jerusalem's fault. For if the city had listened to Jeremiah…

Yosef ben-Moshe's wife, Zillah, had no such nightmares or remorse. No nightmares, because she was incapable of attaching herself to anyone else's sufferings, even in her dreams. No remorse, because self-reproach was not in her character. So for her, this was an exciting time with much to do. Her jewelry had to be put away, new sackcloth tunics had to be sewn because she was not going to look dowdy while fasting and praying, drink offerings had to be mixed, and hankies had to be washed for the steady stream of noblewomen who came to share their troubles. Of course, Zillah listened with sad sympathetic eyes and wept streams of tears, but it was difficult to get over how awful her friends looked.

Only the week before, they had been sitting together on mosaic-tiled benches under lacy palms, all elegantly attired in gauzy veils, brightly embroidered tunics, nose rings and bangles, all sharing merrily how they had hidden their valuables from Babylon. Leah had sown her gilded cloaks inside her goose-down bedding; Tirzah, after spending days carving holes in rocks, had crammed her jewels inside, then stashed the rocks in the sheepcote; and Marah had buried her marble statues in the family tomb.

Now, a week later, under the same lacy palms and sitting on the same mosaic benches, they were all wearing heavy black veils and robes, their laughter turned to mourning, their eyelash powder smearing their cheeks. Leah's rosy complexion was almost yellow; Tirzah's smooth supple forehead was scored with wrinkles, her mouth drawn down in sharp lines; and Marah's glossy black hair was turning white right before their eyes. Worse than that, none of them seemed to care. It was so shocking, Zillah wanted to hasten to the nearest mirror—for she had at least one in every room—to see if she had succumbed to any such horrors.

But knowing a dash to the mirror might appear unseemly, she stayed put, lighting incense to her Queen of Heaven statue and opening her astrological books. Zillah's mother had raised her in astrology and upon her marriage to Yosef ben-Moshe had given her an Egyptian calendar, a bronze Egyptian Zodiac, and an ancient Queen of Heaven statue seated in marble. Using these tools, along with her charts and knowledge, Zillah had developed a faithful following, but after the past harrowing week, her friends were starting to doubt her powers because Zillah—like the other Jerusalem astrologers who refused to believe Jeremiah's gloom and doom predictions—continued to promise a future full of hope. And why not? The worst was probably over.

So reviewing her friends' birth charts, charts she knew well, she started with the planet movements in the current month, then looked into her friends' pasts for a positive experience. If a positive experience could be found under similar planet movements, then it could be applied to the current circumstance. It took some searching, but she finally found one for each of them: for Leah, *hopeful news was on the way*; for Tirzah, *peace will follow turmoil*; and for Marah, *happiness will supplant tears*.

The three gushed over Zillah's prescience because they could already see her predictions coming true. The city leaders had sent a petition to Nebuchadnezzar which might match her forecast for hopeful news on the way. In addition, the men who had secretly followed the captured children had not found any abandoned or dead along the road which definitely brought some peace of mind. But what about Marah? What would bring happiness to her? Suddenly, they barraged Zillah with questions about her husband, Yosef ben-Moshe.

Thinking they were angry at him for fighting with Babylon, she was eager to share her anger too. But they were not angry, they were excited. Pressing their faces into hers, they wanted to know if he really had saved Nebuchadnezzar's life and, if he had, couldn't he intervene for their children? That would bring happiness to Marah. In fact, it would bring happiness to all Jerusalem.

So that was it! They had not come to see her, but to find out if her husband had saved the Crown Prince's life. For the rest of the afternoon, they quizzed her: had he written to her, when would he be home, would he be willing to meet with the city elders, would he come and dine with each of their families and friends? Then, before leaving, they made her promise she would let them know the moment—yes, the very moment—he returned from Carchemish.

From that day on, Zillah's friends only wanted to talk about two things: their personal sufferings and the long awaited arrival of Yosef ben-Moshe, two very dull and irritating topics to Zillah. However, she maintained a sincere sorrowful mien, for what else could she do?

When Yosef ben-Moshe did return, Zillah said nothing to her friends, but straightaway told him about Aridatha's near-death experience, the horrific words Jeremiah spoke over her, and how she, as her mother, had suffered unfathomable grief because of it. But, instead of commiserating with her, he was angry, ripping down the shrouds of black, ordering the wailing in the household stopped, and calling for the fattened calf.

"We should be rejoicing," he said. "Aridatha is alive. She was not taken."

"But the prophet, Jeremiah…"

"Silence, woman!" Pouring wine, he gulped it down, trying to steady his shaken nerves. "Are you sure you heard Jeremiah correctly?" he probed one more time.

"'Exiled from Jerusalem to Babylon… Settle down… Build houses… Plant gardens.' Do you think I made that up?"

"But did he know she is my daughter? Perhaps he thought she was someone else's."

"He knew."

"Did Aridatha hear him?"

"She was half dead. How could she hear him?"

"She must never know," he muttered to himself. Then, looking her in the eye, he ordered, "You must never tell her."

Having no intention of telling her, Zillah sought out her reflection in the mirror. "Jeremiah does this all the time," she huffed, secretly pleased she could wear her jewelry again. She had such exquisite jewelry and she looked so attractive when she wore it. "He shows up at every festival, every meeting, and every banquet, not to be pleasant or enjoy the company, but to threaten us with brutal images of the Lord ROARING at us from on high, disaster SPREADING from nation to nation, a storm RISING from the ends of the earth. He is all judgment and wrath, Yosef. It is shameful. Those kinds of superstitions belong back in the time of Noah, not now. We are God's Chosen People. This is the Promised Land. Jerusalem houses the Temple of Solomon which houses the Ark of the… "

As she rapped out the well-worn harangue to the mirror, Yosef ben-Moshe wondered why a beautiful woman like her, who worked so hard to keep her beauty, made no effort to protect herself from the brutal facial lines of scorn and contempt.

"If you had been at the Temple that night, with ALL Jerusalem weeping, you would know how HORRIBLE he is," she proclaimed to the mirror, thinking how pretty she was and how convincing her argu-

ment. Even so, she decided not to tell him she had called Jeremiah a traitor, at least not until she knew he agreed with her. "Everyone was there!
Except you-know-who. They had to DRAG him in. Parents begged him.
Begged him! Screaming at him, pleading with him to ask the Lord to
bring our children back. Do you know what he said?"

"I have no idea," he replied disinterestedly, trying to end the
conversation.

"He said no."

"He said what?" The blow was so unexpected, the blood drained
from his face.

"He said the Lord said NOT to pray for us. You know as well as I do
the Lord would never say that."

The hole in his back began to throb. If he accepted that the Lord Almighty commanded the prophet not to pray for Jerusalem, then he had
to accept all was lost. But how could anyone accept all was lost? How
could anyone live in absolute despair? Suddenly, he was very weary. "Are
you calling Jeremiah a liar?"

"What if I am?" she rebounded, whipping around to face him. Obviously he did not agree with her about Jeremiah, but why should she
be surprised? On important matters, he never agreed with her. "What
is worse?" she challenged. "Being a liar or a traitor? Because everyone
knows he is a traitor!"

"Now you listen to me." He grabbed her before she could turn back
to the mirror. "You will never speak about the prophet like that again."
He paused to measure her flashing eyes, her jeweled hair flowing to her
waist, her lips of scarlet. She was as beautiful as the day he met her, yet
she had no beauty at all. "In fact, you will never speak his name again.
Not to me, not to Aridatha, not to your astrologers, not to anyone.
Ever."

Wrenching out of his grip, all she could think was she hated him.
Before he went to fight for Nebuchadnezzar, she told him it would be
the ruin of him. But it did not ruin him. Instead, he had garnered Nebuchadnezzar's confidence and now the whole city wanted to be his friend.
She had even lost her own friends to him. But those were not the only
reasons she hated him.

Zillah had a long list of reasons going back to the first day she saw
him: the day he returned to Jerusalem, the new owner of the Pillar of

Salt Caravan. When she overheard he was going to be the richest man in Jerusalem, she determined to be the first to meet him at the city gate. Waking up hours before dawn to dress to look her loveliest, she had to run fast to overtake the other Daughters of Jerusalem.

Lined up at the city gate, the maidens looked like a pretty parade of frolicking hair and colorful tunics lit up by the glowing sun. Chattering and laughing, their eyes squinted toward Yosef ben-Moshe's faraway caravan slowly approaching inside a mountain of dust. Suddenly, a camel broke away, steadily outpacing the line, sending the girls into giggling excitement. Zillah, on the other hand, simply steadied her sunlit eyes on the rider with his cloak billowing out behind him. Watching him lope up the hillside radiating ease and confidence, she knew what she had to do to catch such a man. Yes, she thought, let the other girls giggle, but she would not look so foolish. She would radiate the same ease and confidence, and she would win him.

Then, as he drew closer and she saw his face, she hated him. Hated him, because she was going to have to live the rest of her life looking at his scarred forehead and prematurely-white beard, so repulsive she thought she was going to be sick, not to mention the hideous rope-burn scars winding down his arms and wrapping around his neck. Those she discovered later! It had taken all her effort to conceal her repugnance, but she did, smiling with ease and confidence for him and him alone. From the turn of her head to the folds of the linen at her breasts, from complimenting him not too much and not too little to only speaking when spoken to, she directed her every movement to please the richest man in Jerusalem so he would marry her. Finally, after weeks of being painstakingly pleasant and adoring, while at the same time aloof and controlled, she got her way: he married her. And nine months later, Aridatha was born.

Zillah had expected a man to be excited over his firstborn son, but when she saw how her husband gazed at the screaming baby girl in his arms, his eyes overflowing with a warmth and devotion he had never given to her, she turned to stone. Without doing anything except showing up and bawling, Aridatha had won his heart, the heart she had worked for day and night, especially night, sacrificing herself to the pleasures of a scarred man. Yes, she hated him and always would.

"As you command," she replied with a mocking bow. "I will never mention the prophet's name again. But remember this, Yosef ben-Moshe, you have deceived this city, but you cannot fool me. I know why you fought for Nebuchadnezzar. You fought so Babylon would take away our children. You fought so Babylon would destroy us. That makes you just as much a traitor as that prophet." When he said nothing, she knew she had won and, turning on her heel, marched from the room.

Yosef ben-Moshe stared at the lavish luxury surrounding him: mosaic sofas decked with embroidered pillows, cedar shelves lined with gold cups and chargers, wine jars brimming with rare wines, Egyptian linen shading out the day and rippling in the breezes at night. It was everything a man could want, except peace and comfort. Once he had looked to Zillah for such virtues, but when Aridatha was born, his wife turned on him, yelling and thrashing and snarling. Thinking it was a temporary season after giving birth, he waited and watched for the day she would return to her former self. Soon, he realized from her snappish irritation with Aridatha, her sharp tongue with the servants, and her quick irritable judgments of friends and foes alike, Zillah had returned to her former self: the self she was before their marriage. Even so, it took him months to admit he had been duped by her wiles, a hard lesson to learn, not only because it was a blow to his pride but because Yosef ben-Moshe was still a young man and would have liked to share the joys of life with his wife.

But with or without Zillah, he had a special place in his heart for his little girl, Aridatha. It was he who had ordered the Stars of David to be embroidered in the ankle hems of all her tunics. Then, dressing her in her first baby tunic, he trotted her through Jerusalem with a pride most men reserved for their firstborn son. Before she was one year old, he put her on her first horse and walked alongside holding her up. When she was two, he placed a miniature bow and arrow in her hands, and before going off to fight for Babylon, he carved a wooden dagger for her. Then at Carchemish, he procured the greatest gift of all: Nebuchadnezzar's promise to protect her.

Now, surrounded by his hard-earned luxury, he wanted to lie down and rest his back, but the room still churned with Zillah's hostility, so he stepped out into the night. He could not have asked for a more restful evening, his vineyards glimmering in the moonlight and his sheep dotting the pastures, yet he was uneasy. Jeremiah's words about Aridatha could not be dismissed. Already, one Babylonian had tried to kill her, hence it was up to him to plan for every situation and so he would.

First, he would try to keep her from falling into Babylon's hands. Since exile seemed to be the Lord's idea, he would work on changing the Lord's mind by giving to the poor and obeying the Law. Perhaps after seeing ben-Moshe's good works, the Lord would reconsider and spare her. If that failed and she was exiled, he could ensure her safety by continuing to be an asset to Nebuchadnezzar, the new King of Babylon. Most importantly, he would prepare Aridatha by teaching her how to fight, speak the tongues of the times, read, write, add, multiply, even plant gardens and build houses. He would do everything he could to carve a way out for her, because if there was one thing he had learned in life, there was always a way out.

Satisfied with his plan, he found his feet moving in the direction of peace and comfort: Aridatha's new nursery, far away from Zillah's room.

14

It was long into the night and four-year-old Aridatha was supposed to be asleep. But to her way of thinking she had been asleep since the day Babylon threw her across the marketplace, casting her into a world without words. Without words, she had not been able to define her experiences: sitting up in bed, hearing rain, placing her feet on the floor, searching through her cedar chest, pulling out her wooden dagger. Furthermore, she had not been able to assess time, unable to remember one hour to the next. Nevertheless, whether the sun was shining or the stars sparkling, she had clung to her crimson pouch because her mother kept trying to take it away from her.

Then yesterday, papa galloped through the entrance gate on his lathered horse, and seeing him for the first time in over a year, she cried out one explosive "Papa," and all her words flooded back to her. Suddenly, her experiences were no longer shapeless, time no longer a vacant crossing. Now she could separate sitting up in bed from listening to the rain. She could identify her feet, the floor, her cedar chest, and her wooden dagger. Most importantly, she could think, and with so much to think about, instead of being in bed she was staring into an ivory-framed mirror, studying the scar on her forehead and wondering about Babylon. Without words, she had not been able to think about the small circle and Nebuchadnezzar, but now they were very much on her mind. Furthermore, Jeremiah's crimson pouch settled at her heart, its leather cord doubled-tied at the back of her neck, troubled her. Just that morning, she had quizzed Baruch about it, asking why Jeremiah had given her the pouch, but he had just shrugged. Then when she asked why her mother had tried to take it from her, he mumbled something about Jeremiah filling it with dirt before putting it on her.

"You are not asleep."

Turning, she saw her father at the door, handsome in every way, for unlike Zillah, Aridatha saw his scars as a record of suffering and his white beard a hallmark of wisdom. Many times while he was away, she had imagined him standing as he was now at her door while at the same time charging across the plain in his chariot. But he had been gone so long, it was hard to believe he was really here.

"Into bed," he said.

She wanted to obey but she could not move.

Seeing her stiffen, Yosef ben-Moshe wondered what ideas Zillah had been planting in her heart about men while he was away. He knew the ideas Aridatha formed now would someday flower into her own woman-ly beauty. He also knew Zillah would do everything to shape his daugh-ter into her ideal of womanhood: supple skin, alluring form, and jeweled hair, all paraded out at whim to snare the quarry. But Aridatha was his daughter too, and knowing her future was at stake, along with the future of his grandchildren and great grandchildren, he had his own plans to shape her into the woman he thought she should be.

Still she did not move, so he picked her up and carried her to bed, but instead of snuggling in, she tossed and turned. Aware she had been unable to speak for a month, he wondered if some other injury lay hid-den inside. Then, when she took his hand and brought it to the light, he smiled. Nebuchadnezzar's ring had caught her attention, and watching her outline each gem of the Babylonian insignia and the gold wings etched in the background, he knew her faculties were not only intact, but better than ever.

Looking him in the eye, she said, "Who is Rachel?"

Expecting a question about the ring, he again wondered if she was all right. "Aridatha, you know who Rachel is. She is Baruch's mother."

"I know. But Jeremiah said, 'A voice is heard in Ramah, Rachel weeping for her children.'"

"You talked to Jeremiah?"

"Early one morning when he was passing by."

So... Not only did Jeremiah know Aridatha was his daughter, but he had already spoken to her and, considering his words, spoken to her not as a child, but as a Daughter of Zion. "Rachel," he replied, "was Jacob's wife. She is buried near Bethlehem."

"You mean she is dead?"

He nodded.

"Then how can she be weeping?"

"Cain's brother Abel is dead and his blood cries out from the ground."

She did not know about Cain or his brother or how his blood could cry out from the ground, but if papa said so, it must be true. "Who are Rachel's children? The ones she is weeping for?"

Rachel's children were Joseph and Benjamin, but they lived so long ago, it seemed unlikely the prophet would be talking about them. So perhaps Jeremiah had been talking about the northern tribes of Israel slaughtered by the Assyrians. However, for the prophet to stop and tell Aridatha a riddle about a well-known past event was just as unlikely. So, guessing the message, like most of his messages, was about the future, he simply said, "Rachel had two children, Joseph and Benjamin."

Again she looked at his ring. "They say he will be the most powerful king of all time."

"Yes, Aridatha, I believe he will."

"You fought for him."

"I fought for him."

"Babylon attacked me."

"Nebuchadnezzar ordered his soldiers to protect you. Those who attacked you did not know who you were."

"They say you fought for him to win favors for Jerusalem."

"I know what they say. But that is not why I fought." He could see she believed him, and grateful for her trust, he wondered if he should tell her about his vision, but quickly decided no. After all, he still questioned if he had seen an angel of the Lord. Moreover, he did not want to encourage her to read too much into visions and signs. Zillah found prophetic meaning in every blink of a star and death of a cat. Better for Aridatha to trust Jeremiah's strange words than to run after visions.

"I fought for him, Aridatha, because…" With great sadness, he touched the scar on her brow hoping she would never endure another. "I fought for him because sometimes everything in your life leads to a decision that does not make sense, is at odds with everything you are, and most people do not agree with, yet you have to do it because it is right. Do you understand?"

"No."

He smiled. Of course, she did not understand. He had spoken around the truth instead of directly from it. "Someday you will."

"Yes, someday I will," she replied, then with equal certainty added, "Someday I will meet him."

"Meet whom?"

"Nebuchadnezzar."

The thought of his daughter meeting the King of Babylon hit him like a wailing wall. "No, Aridatha," he said, looking from her scar to the crimson pouch laying at her heart. "You will never meet him. Never." Subject closed, he placed his hand on her brow and whispered, "May the Lord bless you and keep you and shine his face upon you." Kissing her good night, he moved to the door. "Get some sleep."

"They say he cannot sleep. They say he has dreams that are bigger than dreams."

"Yes, I know what they say," he replied as if it was idle chatter, his mind flashing to the aftermath of the Battle of Carchemish, the earth calling him home, Nebuchadnezzar frantically ordering him to keep his eyes open, telling him, "I see winged creatures and chains... Storehouses and keys... Messengers and images... All pretending they are dreams and visions, but I know they are real because they fly at me and battle with me, until I think I will go mad!"

"They say he has..."

"Shalom, Aridatha," he stated firmly, blowing out the lamp.

"Nightmares..." she breathed into the dark.

15

Babylon, *two years later.*

ALTHOUGH Nebuchadnezzar was asleep, his eyes were staring at the most amazing thing: heavenly gates ripping open and a tidal wave of darkness spewing out into the Babylonian sky. Not an ordinary darkness like in a cave or on a cloud-covered night, but a thick lightless mass not intended for man's sight or knowledge but meant to be locked in storehouses outside of man's grasp. Yet there it was, flooding the firmament, swallowing up every bit of starlight, moonlight, and sunlight. Finished with its repast and hungry for more, it plunged to the earth ready to swallow it too, but it jerked to a halt as if on a leash.

So the mass settled where it was, a thick darkness covering the earth. Or wait. Was it settled? Or was its center turning? Indeed, it was turning, sending out spirals so rhythmic and soothing, Nebuchadnezzar sank into a warm tranquility. In fact, he was about to drift out of the picture altogether when without warning its center exploded, shooting gold, silver, and iron into the firmament, followed by volleys of bronze and clay. Spinning round and round, they crashed into each other, crunching and grating so shrilly, Nebuchadnezzar put his hands over his ears. But the din was still there, pounding against his skull and raking into his nerves until he thought he would go mad, and then the noise stopped. Keeping his hands over his ears, he waited. When nothing happened, he slowly looked up.

What a sight he saw! A dazzling, splendorous statue of a man, so great and so vast it towered over the whole earth.

Nebuchadnezzar was still asleep, but he took in every detail. The feet were made of iron and baked clay; the legs, iron; the thighs and belly, bronze; the chest and arms, silver; and the head was solid gold. The gold face was its most striking feature, knowledge carved into its brow, power into its jawline, glory into its eyes. It was a perfect face and Nebuchadnezzar was in perfect bliss because it looked exactly like his own. Moreover, he would have stared at it forever, except somewhere in the distance, a rock was being cut out of a mountain, but not by human hands. It was a simple and nondescript rock yet frightening in every way, and within moments, it was hurtling toward the statue.

Nebuchadnezzar clamped his eyes shut, but it made no difference. Eyes open or shut, he could still see it coming. However the statue, too enamored with itself, did not. So Nebuchadnezzar yelled, ordering it to run. But how could its gold ears hear and its iron legs run? Thrashing his own legs back and forth in his bed, Nebuchadnezzar tried to reach the statue, but the harder he tried the farther away it got. Instantly, the rock hit the statue's iron-and-clay feet, and instantly the entire statue shattered into millions of tiny shards, sending a glittering cloudburst of gold, silver, bronze, iron, and clay blowing away like chaff on the wind. Nothing was left behind, not one sparkle. In fact, it was as if the statue had never been there because now the rock was there. But unlike the statue, the rock grew. It grew and grew and grew until it was a huge mountain filling the earth.

Nebuchadnezzar, his eyes still closed in sleep, stared in horror because the rock was growing so fast it was almost in his bed. Thinking he could stop the rock if he found the remains of the gold head, he leapt and lunged, searching inside linen cupboards that only exist in dreams and under giant chairs that rattle about in visions. But the gold was gone. The clay, the iron, the bronze, the silver... Gone. Frantic, he roared for the gold to come back and unexpectedly woke himself up.

Even so, the dream was still there, floating over his bed. Trying to escape, he bolted for the farthest corner of the room and, cringing like a trapped animal, fixed his eyes on tangible things like cedar tables, gold lampstands, parchments and pens.

"Time?" he yelled.

"First watch, my king," shouted the guard from outside the door.

"Only the first...?" gagged Nebuchadnezzar, wondering if he was ever going to have a full night's sleep again.

"Does the king want a woman to help him sleep?" called the guard.

"I have got a woman!" he blasted, glaring at the quivering female in his bed. "Out!"

The hapless beauty, after enduring an eternity of terror watching the sleeping King of Babylon shout, kick, sweat, and flail, grabbed a sheet for cover and fled.

After she was gone, Nebuchadnezzar pounded his head against the wall, trying to pound the dream out and Babylon back in. But the dream was everywhere, lining the shelves, reclining on his bed, bouncing off the ceiling, down to the floor and back up again. So, throwing his shoulders back and standing to his full height, he shouted, "NOTHING CAN SHAKE ME!"

To prove it, he poured wine with a steady hand, sipped it calmly, marched back to his bed, and laid down. But when he closed his eyes, the vision was still there. In fact, it was starting all over again, the heavenly gates ripping open, darkness rushing into the Babylonian sky...

Vaulting from his bed, he yelled, "Get my sorcerers and astrologers!"

16

NEBUCHADNEZZAR's three-hundred-and-sixty sorcerers, astrologers, enchanters, and magicians huddled together as far away from the king as possible. A vain effort because although the throne room was vast—built to accommodate ten thousand subjects, five hundred warriors, and one hundred cavalry on horseback—there was no place to hide. Of course, there were many shadowy jambs and alcoves, but stone-faced men the size of Gog and Magog wearing leather armor and double-edged swords stood guard over every jamb and alcove, nook and cranny, entrance and exit.

The throne room had been designed to intimidate and indeed it did. Even more so tonight, because the room was unfinished. The incomplete sky-high frescoes of Nebuchadnezzar in violent battle exuded a coarse primitive power; the skeletal frames of twelve onyx pillars encircling the room created the illusion of a specter-like haunting; the oil lamps hanging from the scaffolding swayed eerily without a breeze; and the Signs and Constellations outlined in chalk over the gold double-door entrance looked as if even the stars were erasable before the glory of Babylon. The rows and rows of stacked tile, piles and piles of broken tile, and the smell of dank mortar choking the air reminded one of death, and the King of Babylon sitting on a rickety workbench on his half-finished throne platform, glaring down at the sages like a famished vulture, reminded one of a torturous death.

Not long ago, the king's summons to interpret a dream had been no cause for alarm. In fact, nothing had been more rewarding than listening to his dreams, dissecting them down to their basic words and images, then searching through the ancient Dream Books—fragile parchments copied over and over since Hammurabi—and the *Illumination of Bel* to determine if the dreams were about harvests or famines, rain or drought, health or plague, or most intriguing, Nebuchadnezzar's personal future. The wise men spent days, sometimes weeks, arguing over a correct interpretation, and as one might expect, the different departments never agreed. So they each brought their own interpretation to the king.

Then, six months ago, the king stormed into the throne room and demanded they stop his dreams. Of course, they tried everything: placing him in different temples for dream incubation, plying him with bread and herbs sprinkled with beer while he recited incantations to Ishtar, rubbing aromatic oils on his forehead, reading the entrails of an owl, even changing his diet. But as luck would have it, nothing worked. So now every time he had a dream, it was their pound of flesh.

Tonight, however, he had added a new wrinkle. Instead of *him* telling *them* his dream, he had ordered *them* to tell *him* his dream. Tell him his dream?! Surely, he knew no one could go back in time to see what the king saw, whereas going into the future… Well, that was different. Any wise man could look into the unknown future and make a reasonable prediction that was so far away, they would all be dead before it came to pass. That is, if it did come to pass. But who would know the difference?

"Answer me," the King of Babylon barked. "Tell me my dream."

His voice certainly sent their scarlet turbans to joggling and robes to rustling, but it was not enough to convince anyone to speak up. What would he say? Who could possibly know the bizarre visions that had danced through the king's head during the night? So the woebegone wise cringed closer together.

Unlike the sages, Arioch stood confident and strong behind the king's workbench, actually grateful for the midnight summons. His wife, Soheil, had come for her yearly three-week visit, and because she was leaving in the morning, she had targeted this last night to strongly suggest that because Nebuchadnezzar was at peace with the world, Arioch quit the capital and come home to help his father rule over the tribes and, furthermore, start raising their four sons. Arioch had stood silent under her barrage, his mind blank and emotions empty. After all, she was right. He should occasionally return home, but if he left the capital and something happened to the king, he would never forgive himself. It was a reasonable excuse and he had used it so often, he believed it. Still, if he had ventured beyond the compartments of his mind into the quarries of his heart, he would have found another reason, a burning ember: his love for fifteen-year-old Chenguang.

Because he was the noble man he thought he was, he had assumed he had extinguished every trace of the lovely Chenguang from his heart, but how could one extinguish love? Of course, one could not. Thus the ember still glowed, going back to the day he first laid eyes on her.

Bursting into the Grand Mentor Tin's library, he had been in a hurry to get to the ax-throwing contest between the Grand Preceptor Au Yang's champion and the Grand Guardian Li's. Intent on convincing the Crown Prince to accompany him, he did not notice the slight figure in the narrow passageway reaching up for scrolls and tablets. But when she stepped quietly past Nebuchadnezzar, her peony fragrance caught his attention, and for a long moment he stared at her plaited raven hair wrapped in carved ivory tusks, then at her small waist encircled by embroidered peonies. She was the granddaughter of the Grand Mentor Tin, and when Arioch discovered she worked every day with her grandfather, he developed a passion for studying the stars in Tin's library.

Like all girls of nobility, Chenguang was forbidden to speak to any man except those in her immediate family, so as the months passed, Arioch and Chenguang found other—more interesting—ways of communicating. Hence, when Nebuchadnezzar told Arioch it was time to leave China, Arioch declared he was staying in Luoyi and marrying Chenguang. Nebuchadnezzar exploded, telling him Chenguang was intended to marry the Grand Preceptor Au Yang. Moreover, Arioch was destined to marry Soheil, so he ordered him to return to the mountains and marry her. Arioch argued and sulked, but in the end, he left China and married Soheil. Then, after two weeks of marital discovery, he waved goodbye to his new bride and galloped to Babylon, putting both women out of his mind. Not a hard thing to do because his life was dedicated to his king, a mission demanding constant vigilance.

Even now in the throne room, a singular disturbance caught his eye, someone shoving his way through the pack trying to break through, his voice demanding and strident. Arioch's hand went to his dagger, then signaling surreptitiously to his guards, his eyes moved to his warriors quietly closing the doors, to the open pathway leading to his king, and back to the troublemaker thrashing through layers of robes, tripping on an enchanter's wand, and thudding to the floor. Watching him clumsily right himself, up on one foot and then the other, Arioch's hand sagged. This man was no threat. His tight turban, still garishly scarlet, said it all: he was new to Babylon, a young astrologer, so skinny the wind could blow him away. So what was he up to? Surely, he was not going to pretend to know the dream.

Indeed, the Damascan was new to Babylon. However, he was also eager to work and thus, like Nebuchadnezzar, had no patience with the cowering sheep surrounding him. So seizing the moment to prove himself, he bowed with a flourish and then shouted for all to hear, "Mighty King of Babylon, what you ask is impossible. No one can tell anyone the dream he has had."

Without a sound, the other three-hundred-and-fifty-nine turbans took two steps back, quickly disconnecting themselves from the harrowing echo that had just relegated Nebuchadnezzar to the category of *anyone*. Arioch, feeling the full heat of the king's disapproval, could not help pitying the stupid young man. Why hadn't someone tried to stop him?

But the Damascan, although clever in the art of predicting the future, could not read the faces of the present, and assuming Nebuchadnezzar's silence reflected slow Babylonian thinking, he took up the gauntlet again. This time, however, he enunciated his words more slowly, as if talking to a child, "Great King Nebuchadnezzar, you must first tell us the dream you had, then we can interpret it for you."

Normally, the king would have berated the fool in order to rouse the others into action, but tonight, head exploding, he simply lifted his finger and the young astrologer, after being escorted to the door, was never seen or heard from again. After he was gone, the King of Babylon stared out in a gloomy silence, far more intimidating than any of his tirades, especially because it gave the remaining three-hundred-and-fifty-nine an eon to digest the sky-high fresco behind him: a larger-than-life portrayal of their king in ferocious battle, his arms massive, his sword bloody, his victim not yet filled in. Wasn't anyone going to speak up?

Finally, Nebuchadnezzar spoke. "If you really possess the Seeing Eye, whatever that is," he breathed quietly, forcing them all to lean in closer, "Then your Seeing Eye should be able to see my dream."

They knew he had a point, a very good point. But suffice it to say, no one was as foolish as the young man from Damascus. Besides, if they all stuck together, what could the king do?

"Arioch."

"Yes, my lord?"

"Cut them all to pieces and turn their houses into piles of rubble."

The wise men of Babylon could not believe their ears. Surely, he did not mean it. But if the king did not mean it, why was he leaving the room? Looking for help, their communal head, as if drawn by a string, turned to Arioch. But Arioch's eyes were honed in on the sentries, his hand raised and spinning in a circle, signaling the stone-faced guards to round them up.

It did not take wisdom to know the pack was no longer safe, it only took instinct, and instinct cried scatter. But those who had found refuge in the center could not move because those on the perimeter, trying to dodge Arioch's quick-marching warriors, were rearing into them, when suddenly the king's name was shouted from the other side of the room. Wondering who had risked his life to call out the royal name, everyone turned to see four men striding boldly through the massive gold double-doors, the one in the lead, calling out, "King Nebuchadnezzar!"

When Nebuchadnezzar heard the first shout, he ignored it. Weakened by sleepless nights and the long grueling days of building Babylon, along with the prospect of never knowing the meaning of his dream while being plagued by the conviction he must know, he was determined to get back to his room, down a cup of wine, and try for an hour of sleep. But when he heard his name shouted a second time all his frustrations erupted, and drawing his sword, he swung around ready to cut the agitator to pieces. However, instead of one, there were four and all four were approaching fast. They wore simple tunics and stout leather sandals instead of scarlet turbans, blue robes, and dainty shoes, and Arioch was doing nothing about it except glowering at them. So, with his sword poised for action, Nebuchadnezzar bawled, "Who are you?"

"Belteshezzar, my lord," replied Daniel, using his Babylonian name. With the same assuredness, he introduced his friends, Hananiah, Mishael, and Azariah, using their Babylonian names: Shadrach, Meshach, and Abedneggo. "We are Hebrews, nobility from Jerusalem."

Arioch's braided beard trembled with anger. Daniel, Shadrach, Meshach, and Abedneggo were the wisest and most trusted men in the kingdom, and not wanting to lose them to the king's caprice over some dream, he had ordered them stay home tonight. But instead, here they were.

Quickly speaking up for them, he said, "Daniel interprets dreams and visions of all kinds, sire."

Studying them carefully, Nebuchadnezzar remembered meeting them once before. The one called Belteshezzar, with his iron grey eyes and hard-set jaw, had stood up to him face to face as he was doing now. The other three, lacking his boldness, had kept back as they were doing now. He also remembered there was something different about them, reminding him of someone else. But who was it?

"We have met," he said, returning his sword to his sheath.

"Yes, my king," Daniel replied.

"You are the four who refused to eat my royal food."

"That is true, my lord," interjected Arioch. "They requested to eat according to their Law as prescribed by Moses. It was a ten day trial to prove they would not weaken on their own food of vegetables and water."

The astrologers, magicians, enchanters, and sorcerers, still trapped by the king's sentries, were encouraged by the king's amicable tone. Perhaps after speaking to Daniel, he would reconsider his harsh judgment and let them go.

"At the end of those ten days," inquired Nebuchadnezzar, "weren't you stronger and healthier than any of the other young men eating my royal food?"

"Yes, sire," answered Arioch. "They were."

Now he remembered! They had reminded him of Yosef ben-Moshe, for they also possessed that rare blend of power and rest. Again, he marveled at the paradox. Power demanded complete watchful control, whereas rest demanded... Well, he did not know what rest demanded. How could he? He had never found it. Furthermore, he did not want to think about it, so glaring at the four, he probed further. "After your training, didn't I question you in every matter of wisdom and understanding? And didn't I find you ten times brighter than all the magicians and enchanters in my kingdom?"

"Yes, my lord," replied Daniel.

"So! You can tell me what I dreamt? You can tell me the meaning of my dream?"

"No wise man, enchanter, or magician can explain these mysteries to the king."

"Hah!" he scoffed. "You may dress differently and eat differently, but you are no different from the others."

"However," Daniel added, looking him in the eye, "there is a God in heaven who reveals mysteries."

Waving him off, the king headed for the door.

"You saw an enormous statue with a head of gold!"

Nebuchadnezzar spun around so fast and fixed such dangerous eyes on Daniel, the wise men gasped in horror. Clearly, the Hebrew was not even close to the dream, and watching the king marching straight at him, they wondered what savage execution he was plotting.

"You, Nebuchadnezzar King of Babylon," proclaimed Daniel, "are the head of gold. You are the king of kings."

There it was: power and rest shooting out of Daniel's mouth, sending tremors through Nebuchadnezzar's soul and awe into his heart. What kind of man was this: fearless and exuding splendor, unaware of anything except the message he was speaking? Furthermore, how did he, a mere mortal, have access to a dream he had never seen or heard? And, because he had access to the dream, he must also have access to its interpretation.

"The interpretation is this," Daniel continued, "the God of heaven has given you wealth, power, and glory. The Lord God has placed..."

"Silence!" blasted so fiercely out of Nebuchadnezzar's mouth, his head spun.

The room went deathly pale. Not only the wise men and the sentries, but the sky-high frescoes, the gold icons of Marduk, the silver images of Ishtar, and the oil lamps overhead suddenly seemed drained of color, all staring at the King of Babylon jutting his face into Daniel's.

"Nobody gave me my wealth. Nobody gave me my power. Nobody gave me my glory. I, Nebuchadnezzar, took it. It is mine, from beginning to end."

Digging his heels in, Daniel jutted his face right back. "The Lord God has placed mankind, the beasts of the field, and the birds of the air in your hands. He has made you ruler over them all."

"He? Made me?" shuddered Nebuchadnezzar, his hands clenching and unclenching. "I fought the battles. I won the wars. From Babylon to the Great Sea, from north to south, east to west, I conquered everything. I, Nebuchadnezzar, made me ruler over..."

But Daniel, swept away by the dream, simply cut him off, saying, "My king, you saw a rock."

The King of Babylon stopped breathing, his eyes bulged, and his face grew red. More than anything he wanted to know about the rock, yet more than anything he did not. For the rock smashed the statue and nothing good could come from that.

"You saw a rock cut out of a mountain, but not by human hands."

"Enough!" exploded Nebuchadnezzar, saliva foaming at his mouth. "I will not hear it!" Moreover, he did not want anyone else to hear it. No one must know about the rock. Why else had he not told Babylon's wise men his dream? He did not want them to know about the rock, unless they knew about the rock! Now before him was a man who did know and he was shouting so loudly everyone could hear.

"The rock is a kingdom set up by the God of heaven," Daniel shouted, not so everyone could hear, but from wild-eyed excitement. In fact, he was so excited, his body was crouched low, his fists pelting the air. "This kingdom will never be destroyed. It will crush the other kingdoms and bring them to an end, but it will endure forever."

"You just told me, I am the king of kings! Therefore, there can be no greater kingdom than mine."

"But this is about the future, my lord. The God of Heaven has shown King Nebuchadnezzar what will happen in days to come."

"Days to come," he sneered, his eyes flashing to the three-hundred-and-fifty-nine cringing turbans. "Anyone can say anything about the unknown and unknowable days to come."

"After your kingdom, another kingdom will rise, inferior to yours. Next a third kingdom, one of bronze, will rule over the whole earth. Finally…"

As Daniel hammered out the details of kingdoms rising and falling, leading up to some future kingdom never to be destroyed, Nebuchadnezzar started assessing Daniel's future. The Hebrew had proven to be ten times wiser than all the wise men of Babylon, and right now he was proving himself to be wiser than any man ought to be. So why not use his talents for the glory of Babylon? By promoting him to rule over the province of Babylon, he would not only be advancing his own cause, but gaining the favor of Daniel's God.

Pleased with the notion, he turned to Arioch. "Prepare an offering for Daniel and present incense to him." Then, falling prostrate before the Hebrew, he shouted, "Surely your God is the God of gods, the Lord of kings, and a revealer of mysteries, for you were able to reveal this mystery."

After paying homage, Nebuchadnezzar felt every bit the head of gold, and striding to the doorway, he gazed out at his capital, awakening with the dawn. After only two years, he was well on his way to completing his royal palace, Procession Way, and the canals redirecting the Euphrates River. The children of Babylon had clean water to drink, flies no longer reigned supreme, and most importantly, Babylon's finest and brightest captives, after learning the literature of Babylon, Hammurabi's Laws, mathematics, engineering, and astronomy, were now building Babylon beyond the splendor of any kingdom, past, present or future. Even so, after hearing Daniel's interpretation, Nebuchadnezzar knew he had to do more: something to prove that he and no one else was the king of kings, something to ensure that Babylon and not some rock would endure forever.

Suddenly, the sunrise shot out one glorious ray bathing Nebuchadnezzar in a golden glow, not just his head but his entire body, and instantly a plan that had been brewing in his mind for years took shape: the way to unite all the nations of the world under Babylon, once and for all.

17

NEBUCHADNEZZAR had no qualms about going to war to conquer the world. War was his specialty and he was not afraid to use it. However, as the Grand Guardian Li once said, if a bribe or an intrigue could win a subject or an enemy's lands, the king was obliged to use them instead of going to war because war decimated the strength of a nation: its fields, forests, and men. War also squandered Nebuchadnezzar's most precious commodity: time. So if he could conquer the world off the battlefield, he could use all that time to build Babylon.

The customary way to unite nations without going to war was to establish a League of Mutual Assistance where nations, small and large, promised to assist each other during times of war, plague, famine, and drought. It was a method which may have satisfied most kings, emperors, and pharaohs, but to Nebuchadnezzar it was abhorrent. Babylon was not in league with other nations, Babylon conquered them. Babylon had no mutuality with other nations, Babylon was separate and above. Babylon did not assist other nations, Babylon ruled over them. But alas, what could he do? It was either fight wars endlessly as his father had done or establish some kind of compromise.

Consequently, he had been thinking more and more about creating a League of Mutual Assistance. However, in his League of Mutual Assistance, Babylon would be supreme ruler which meant all the other nations were going to have to do more than merely sign a treaty. But what? It was then, as Daniel was rattling off the rise and fall of future kingdoms, that the sunrise lit Nebuchadnezzar's body in a golden glow and instantly he knew the answer: a spectacular gold image of himself! Not just a gold head but the entire body with the whole world bowing down to it. All nations united in one Grand Bow to Babylon! An historic public display of subservience, a bloodless victory where Babylon was the conqueror, and all the nations, in one fell swoop, the conquered.

Furthermore, in order to have the maximum hours of sunlight shining on his great gold edifice, he would have his Grand Bow at the summer solstice. Daniel would oversee the project from beginning to end, and when the time was right, Nebuchadnezzar would order all the nations to the plain of Dura to bow to his image.

The plan was so perfect, he was suddenly grateful he had had the dream, murmuring not only to himself but to all the mysteries surrounding him, "Then we will see what the rock not cut out by human hands can do about that."

It was three years before the mandate went out, but when it did, the smaller nations, seeing the Grand Bow as an opportunity to ingratiate themselves to Babylon, quickly accepted the invitation. However, the empires of China and Egypt were so outraged by Babylon's effrontery that after months of sending emissaries galloping back and forth from the River Luo to the River Nile, they created their own alliance, both agreeing if Nebuchadnezzar attacked them for not attending the Grand Bow, they would go to war against him, plunging him into a two-front war he could not win. Naturally, there were those who did not want to go to war, arguing that bowing to a ridiculous image was less costly, adding forcefully if this was Nebuchadnezzar's hour in history, they could not stop him no matter how great their armies. So in the end, Egypt and China in great pomp and riches headed to the plain of Dura to bow to Nebuchadnezzar's gold image.

When Arioch heard that the *Sangong*, the Three Grand Dukes of China, were coming to Babylon, his stomach churned with the nervousness of a fifteen-year-old boy because one of the *Sangong*, the Grand Mentor Tin, never went anywhere without his granddaughter Chenguang.

Chenguang... He had not thought about her for years. After all, he had gone on to marry Soheil and they had had five sons together. So, of course, he had not thought about Chenguang. But now he could see her delicate form rising up in Tin's office reaching for scrolls and tablets, then floating past Nebuchadnezzar on her way to her grandfather. Her arms full of scrolls, she always took the same route—passing Nebuchadnezzar—until one day, for whatever lovely reason, she took the longer route to her grandfather, crisscrossing through a tangle of scribes' benches and drawing tables in order to float by him. In fact, she floated so near, it was as if she wanted him to see the wayward strand of hair falling across her cheek, daring him to reach out and brush it away from her lily soft skin, as if willing her perfume of peonies to rush into his mouth and haunt him forever. Indeed, he could taste it now: lemon and allspice.

Of course, it was foolish to think Tin would bring Chenguang to Babylon. After all these years, she was probably married, and most likely to the scheming Grand Preceptor Au Yang. Even if she was not married and Tin did bring her, would she be in love with him as he was today, or would she still be in love with the Arioch she once knew? Would she even recognize him? Turning to the mirror, he studied his face. It was not a bad face. But the man in the mirror was no longer fifteen or even twenty. His clear blue eyes, once wide and trusting, had narrowed with the burdens of knowledge and experience. His youthful lanky frame was now as thick as an oak. And his wheat blonde beard, cropped shorter than most, certainly added maturity to his years. No, he did not look like the handsome young man he once was. He looked better!

"What are you doing?" barked from the doorway.

Knowing it was Nebuchadnezzar, Arioch jolted away from the mirror, face burning. "Nothing."

"I was thinking..." the king announced, stepping freely into the room. "You have not been home since you married Soheil, and because I do not need you here for the Grand Bow, I have decided you will go home for the summer months and help your father govern the tribes."

Arioch's mouth dropped. Nebuchadnezzar had ordered him to marry Soheil, so he would never return to Chenguang, thus never fight the Grand Preceptor Au Yang. Now, because Au Yang was coming to the capital, he wanted him to run like a thieving dog? "I am not afraid of Au Yang."

Nebuchadnezzar waved him off and, stepping over to the window, looked out at the plain of Dura lit with thousands of torches so his thousands of slaves could work non-stop building his Grand Square for his Grand Bow only three weeks away. In the center of the mad dash, his ninety-foot icon rose up like a gleaming black pearl silhouetted in the dying sunset, and not far away, his newest addition was rapidly taking shape: a brick building housing a giant underground furnace. There the hammers rang out more fiercely, the foremen shouted more urgently, and the passersby gaped more solemnly.

"I expected Egypt to come sniveling to my Grand Bow," he said, pouring a fine pale wine. "Pharaoh would do anything to avoid a war with me. But why is China coming? To bow to my image? Not likely!" Gulping the wine without pleasure, he glared at Arioch. "If the Grand Preceptor Au Yang has any inkling that you and Chenguang fell in love, he could use this visit to trap the two of you together and demand your execution. If I say yes to his demand, then I lose my chief commander. If I say no, I could have a war with China on my hands."

"You mean Chenguang is coming?"

"Certainly, she is coming."

Quickly returning to the mirror, he said, "Do you think she will recognize me?"

"Arioch! Au Yang could use the two of you to start a war against me."

"We can win a war against China."

"I do not want a war against China!" Seeing he was getting nowhere, he said, "Do not let this woman ruin your life. Chenguang is Chinese."

"I know she is Chinese."

"Are you aware the Chinese are different?"

"Of course, I am."

"No, you are not! Babylon's roots are in Hammurabi. Your mother is a descendant of Hammurabi. Very impressive! The Hebrews go back to Abraham. Daniel, Shadrach, Meshach, Abedneggo, and Yosef ben-Moshe are descendants of Abraham. Very impressive! The Egyptians are rooted in their pharaohs. Very impressive! But the Chinese go back to Fohi!"

"Fohi?"

"Noah!"

"We all go back to Noah."

"Not as the Chinese do! Noah founded China. He was the first emperor of the Chinese monarchy."

"What does that matter?"

"What does that matter?!" Nebuchadnezzar always knew Arioch had a dull streak or perhaps more accurately pretended to be obtuse when needed. "Didn't you notice their icons when we were there? Their silk paintings and murals? Most of them portrayed the Eight in the boat. The Immortal Eight, they call them. However, amongst the Immortal Eight, there is always the Elder, the ancient white-bearded one: Fohi. He is the Elder, Arioch. The Elder over us all."

The thought of Fohi whisked Nebuchadnezzar back to the altar in the cave in Tin's subterranean tunnel. Every day on his way to Fohi's star map room, he had stopped at the cave wanting to enter and study the altar, to run his fingers along the rough edges, and smell the lambskin on top. But he never did. More than once, he had wanted to ask Tin who wrote the word *yi* on the altar. Was it Fohi? But he never asked. Even more, he had wanted to ask if the word, *yi*, on the altar had any connection to the heavenly Sign *Taleh* the *lamb*, also known as *Baraziggar* meaning *altar of right-making*. But he never got around to it.

"*Yi*, Arioch. Do you know what the Chinese word *yi* means?"

Arioch shook his head.

"It means righteousness. To write it, the Chinese characters are *hand, dagger, lamb*." Their eyes met; Arioch's were as unreceptive as if he had told him *yi* meant culvert or copper piping. So, heaving a frustrated sigh, Nebuchadnezzar explained, "I could have gone to war against my father and easily taken his throne. But to go to war against my father would not have been *yi*, Arioch. So, although I hated waiting, I waited. Now I have the throne. Likewise, I will never go to war against China because Fohi, who is father to us all, is the Founder of China."

Arioch disagreed. In his mind, fighting a war against China was not the same as fighting a war against one's own father. Still, he did not object because he knew Nebuchadnezzar saw the world through different eyes. So, possibly in some grander scheme, when one considered such profundities as righteousness and unrighteousness, patriarchs of nations and progenies of nations, the gods, the stars, and Shining One, then perhaps going to war against China was the same as going to war against one's own father. Either way, it did not matter to him. What mattered to him was he was not afraid of Au Yang, and he wanted to fight him.

Again, he went to the mirror, searching for the youth he once was. But this time he saw himself more clearly: a face ravaged by the brutalities of war, two eyes darkened by the weight of conquest, and a jawline hardened by the responsibility of Nebuchadnezzar's well-being. In fact, he looked like a stranger to himself, so cold and detached it saddened him because the man in the mirror had nothing to offer Chenguang. And, because he had nothing to offer her, he believed this time it would be easier to forget her. Instead, it was harder.

"I will not go near her," he stated simply and without rancor. "I will not be the cause of a war between you and China."

———⟨⟩———

Eight days before the Grand Bow, China arrived in Babylon, a breathtaking mile-long parade of regal disposition and ancient roots, so grand that her gala of flags—the emperor's royal seal catching the sunlight, fire-breathing dragons snapping in the wind, and the Immortal Eight sailing closer and closer to Nebuchadnezzar's gold image—could be seen from all horizons. The *Sangong*—Grand Guardian Li, Grand Preceptor Au Yang, and Grand Mentor Tin—led the procession driving gold-plated chariots decorated with silver serpents wrapped around jade bamboo and ruby-fruited plum trees. Wearing leather capes with gold fanned epaulettes and crescent-shaped swords crisscrossed at their waists, their beardless faces were set like stone, their mustaches hanging straight down on either side of their scowling lips, their hair fastened in a tight knot at the back of their heads. The cavalry and infantry followed in soft-stepped rhythm escorting sixty-four silk-covered sedan chairs with curtains tied shut, a retinue of royal princes in one-horse chariots, and hundreds of ambassadors on horseback. Next, came a mile-long column of reindeer-drawn wagons brimming with gifts, caged falcons, fodder, food, and Chinese boys throwing bronze coins embossed with the Immortal Eight. From beginning to end, China's grandeur challenged Babylon's not just in simplicity and beauty, but in her very existence. For, without even trying, she displayed the soul of superiority over the nations.

Chenguang rode inside the first sedan chair on a small cushioned plank enclosed by wood siding, its outside covered with heavy embroidered silks. At the base of the litter were two horizontal poles carried by four silent guards walking in a smooth gait so as not to jostle her. Whenever the procession was safely out of the villages and towns, she was allowed to open her curtains. So, veiling her face, she would open all three, grateful to breathe in the fresh air. Throughout the long hot journey, she worked on a small tapestry, embroidering picture-stories of Au Yang's plans for power: uniting China's feudal lords against the emperor, overthrowing the Zhou throne, conquering Babylon, and claiming the world for China. From listening around corners and behind thin walls, she had discovered that Au Yang was looking for an ally in Babylon, someone with enough power to overthrow Nebuchadnezzar, yet weak enough to be overthrown by Au Yang. So, with every stitch she hoped for the opportunity to give the tapestry as a gift to Nebuchadnezzar. Confident he would quickly understand its meaning, she believed he would just as quickly assign guards to watch Au Yang's every move.

18

The Plain of Dura

TEN-YEAR-OLD Aridatha stared up at the ninety-foot gold statue looming larger and larger before her. At sunrise, when she and her father were racing their camels toward the Dura plain, it had only been a glittering shard sparkling in the distance. He had explained it was probably an obelisk built as a landmark for travelers journeying to the Grand Bow. But as they drew near, instead of an obelisk, she found herself staring up at a dazzling sky-high gold statue of a man, the glare so blinding, her eyes hurt.

"It is him," she gasped.

Yosef ben-Moshe turned to see his ten-year-old daughter not looking down toward the marketplace but up, craning back so far she was about to fall from her camel. "Be careful," he said.

"It is, isn't it, papa? King Nebuchadnezzar."

Ben-Moshe had seen hundreds of Babylonian statues, so he had ignored this one. But now, squinting through the glare, he could not believe his eyes. It was him! A ninety-foot gold replica of Nebuchadnezzar frozen in battle, his sinewy hands clenching his Babylonian-scripted sword, his resolute arms suspended in mid-swing. The artisan had certainly captured his fierce will, even his merciless mouth and glory-driven eyes. Of course, the massive eagle's wings growing out of his back were a bit excessive, but other than that the likeness was so stunning, he could not help wondering if Nebuchadnezzar—not lacking in personal vanity—was somewhere close by admiring the image too. Normally, he would have been amused by the thought, but today he was seized with alarm.

What if Nebuchadnezzar was close by? What if he rode around the corner and saw Aridatha? What if upon seeing her, he seized her for Babylon, fulfilling Jeremiah's prophecy? What if he hurt her? What if…?

No! He refused to be influenced by the follies of *what ifs*! *What ifs* were not based on reason, but on imagined menacing events that might occur in the next hour or the next year. Once a man started fearing what might happen, he became so lost in its snare, he could no longer grasp reality. And the reality was Nebuchadnezzar was not going to ride around the corner and see Aridatha.

Before he had come to Babylon, Zillah had hounded him with *what ifs*, demanding, "*What if* Aridatha comes face to face with King Nebuchadnezzar?" His reasoning to her then was just as valid now: no one ever came face to face with a king unless the king invited him. Therefore, it was impossible for their ten-year-old daughter to meet the King of Babylon. What he did not tell her was that he would rather risk having Aridatha with him in Babylon than at home with her, subtly training her to use her beauty to trap royalty for marriage. Having thus been trapped himself, he was against manipulating matters of the heart, believing what Solomon wrote, "Daughters of Jerusalem, I charge you, do not arouse or awaken love, until it so desires."

So, forgetting his *what ifs*, he addressed his daughter's question with another question, "How do you know it looks like King Nebuchadnezzar?"

"What do you mean?"

"Aridatha, you have never seen him."

"I know," she replied, aiming her disappointment straight at him. "But it does look like him, doesn't it?"

Not wanting to encourage her, he shrugged.

"Except for the wings," she grinned. Again, he shrugged as if he did not care. But she was not fooled. She saw the twinkle in his eyes. Then, throwing her head back, she continued staring at the gold face.

Meanwhile, Yosef ben-Moshe stared at the gold wings. They were an odd addition, not because they were wings, but because they were arched and pointed high like an eagle dropping down for its quarry. He had no idea why Nebuchadnezzar had added the predator's touch, although it certainly fit. There he was, the King of Babylon, swooping down on all the nations, using their gold to make an image of himself, then ordering them to bow to it.

"Why can't I meet him?"

"Hm?"

"Why can't I meet King Nebuchadnezzar?"

"Aridatha," he warned, not wanting to hear it again. Her fascination for Nebuchadnezzar had never waned causing him much anxiety, but also some relief. Anxiety, not because Nebuchadnezzar was a man or a king, but because he was King of Babylon. Babylon had been identified by the prophet Isaiah as the "glory of kingdoms" to be overthrown by God like Sodom and Gomorrah, whereas Jerusalem had been identified by the prophet Jeremiah as the "Throne of the Lord" where all nations would assemble in the name of the Lord. With such different identities, *glory of kingdoms* and *Throne of the Lord*, leading to such different outcomes in history, it was obvious the two were at odds. Moreover, he had lectured on it many times to Aridatha.

He had also wanted to warn her that Nebuchadnezzar would never give up the *glory of kingdoms* for Jerusalem, and therefore she must be on her guard and never give up the *Throne of the Lord* for Nebuchadnezzar. But on this, he had held his tongue because he had not wanted to appear too heavy-handed and thus drive her away, perhaps driving her into Zillah's world. Besides, he had hoped she had enough sense to draw the same conclusion. No wonder he was anxious.

On the other hand, he was relieved by her eagerness to know about Nebuchadnezzar because if the Lord did exile her to Babylon, he could use his ring to get her to the king, and if she already had a place for him in her heart, then perhaps exile would be less grievous.

"Did you see his official decree?" she asked.

Wanting to get off the ever-present topic of the King of Babylon, he turned his attention to the plain of Dura, a sprawling temporary city of tents, corrals, slaughtering pens, and tax-free marketplaces where thousands of merchants hawked their wares—sheep, cheese, wine, and beer, hoes, harnesses, water bags, and ropes, veils, necklaces, tiaras, and tattoos—to thousands of shoppers searching for something unique to buy for a nothing price. As they drew closer to the Grand Square, the festival atmosphere heightened: Scythians prancing along the roads on glossy-coated warhorses, Vitalians on donkeys, Franks on mules, and crowds and more crowds on foot, in sedan chairs, litters, and carts, all drinking, eating, laughing, and shouting. Even so, there was a sense of order and security with sentries everywhere, lavatories nearby, magicians for the children, shaded benches for the elderly, and the sudden appearance of an animal-waste-removal cart with slaves quickly cleaning up and just as quickly disappearing. Yet, in all this cornucopia of color, noise, and multinational wonder, the masses—just like Aridatha—were interested in only one thing: Nebuchadnezzar's towering image, the throngs happily waiting in line for hours at King's Market just to buy silver, iron, or clay replicas sold in large, medium, and small sizes.

"It says when the music starts to play all the nations must bow to King Nebuchadnezzar's image or they will be thrown into a fiery furnace." She knew she was trying his patience, but the decree was so astounding. "Did you hear me, papa? They will be roasted alive if they do not bow." Looking up at the lifeless gold statue with its lifeless gold wings, she shouted to its lifeless gold head, "I would never bow down!"

"That is why you are never going to meet him."

Their eyes locked. He could not imagine a more beautiful child. Even the hair on her head, a glossy chestnut mane, thick and rippling down her back, was more dazzling than Nebuchadnezzar's gold icon. Indeed, her name suited her perfectly, Aridatha, *a flowering field*. For like a flowering field, once one rested one's eyes upon her, it was unbearable to turn away.

Music blasted into the air, the signal for all the nations inside the Grand Square to bow before Nebuchadnezzar's image. Hearing it, Yosef ben-Moshe remembered with bitterness the original decree assuring everyone that bowing to the image was a mere formality, an outward sign meant to show unification under Babylon's new League of Mutual Assistance. According to Nebuchadnezzar, the League was going to have far-reaching and glorious benefits because as nations promised to work together, wars would cease, and with no wars, there would be peace. Furthermore, as nations opened their doors to trade with other nations, there would be prosperity. So with stars in their eyes, governors, prefects, treasurers, judges, and top-ranking emissaries from all nations flocked to Dura. It was not until after they had been feasting at Nebuchadnezzar's royal table for a week that his new edict was posted: bow to the statue when the music plays or be thrown into a blazing furnace. In other words, complete national surrender or complete national annihilation.

Listening to the horns, flutes, and tambours, Aridatha's thoughts rushed back to Jerusalem and Baruch ben-Zadok. If Baruch was inside the Grand Square, he would not bow to the winged image because the

Law of Moses commanded man not to make, bow down to, or worship images. Man was to worship the Lord and the Lord alone. Therefore, if one bowed to the gold image, it would be more than just renouncing the sovereignty of one's nation for the sovereignty of Babylon, it would be renouncing the sovereignty of the Lord Almighty for the sovereignty of a winged statue that could not see, hear, think, breathe, or move. Knowing how incredibly ridiculous that was, she was sure most of the men in the Grand Square, like she and Baruch, would not bow down.

The men in the Grand Square, however, reasoned differently. Knowing their gods were sovereign, they also knew it would not make them any less sovereign if they bowed or stood. Therefore, they decided to obey the decree, planning to ask their sovereign gods for forgiveness when they returned to their homeland. The important thing was to stay alive, because if they did not stay alive, their nations would be destroyed. Thus, when the music played, all the governors, prefects, treasurers, judges, and top-ranking emissaries dropped to the ground and ate dirt. All, that is, except five. Nebuchadnezzar's son, fourteen-year-old Crown Prince Gaspar, and his friend Zorpo, with great satisfaction, did not move a muscle. Hence, they were able to see, with even greater satisfaction, three men in the shadowy sidelines still standing.

19

THREE hours later the blaring music, the incense choking the air, and the heat reflecting off the gold icon were so oppressive, Aridatha, who had not eaten since dawn, felt like throwing up. However, instead of asking her father to take her back to camp, she kept silent and alert, watching for the thousands who had not bowed down. No one had yet appeared on the road leading to the furnace building, so she wondered if Nebuchadnezzar was going to burn the multitude in the Grand Square.

Suddenly, the music stopped and a wide-eyed hush fell upon the land, everyone turning to look at the Square. Aridatha, heart in her throat, stared at the sky above it, watching for plumes of smoke and listening for tortured shrieks. But there were no plumes or shrieks, only horns, tambours, and choruses blasting into the air again, breaking the silence with such startling force, the birds in the dung heaps flew to the sky for safety. Watching them circle over the Square, she wondered what they could see. Bonfires being built? Men being roped in twos and threes? Which men? Who had not bowed down? China? Egypt? Lydia? What if no one had bowed to the image? What if Athens, Media, Vitalia, Macedon, and all the countries, islands, and maritime nations from far and wide were still standing? Was Nebuchadnezzar going to burn the whole world?

"Into the fire!" cried out behind her.

Swinging around, she saw a mob hurtling toward a detachment of stern-faced soldiers marching out of the Square. Again, she felt like throwing up, but this time from excitement. And leaping to her feet, she readied to cheer.

"Sit back down on that camel!" ordered ben-Moshe.

"I can only see three."

"Aridatha!"

Plopping back down, she tried to find more turbans inside the blockade of soldiers, but she was not high enough. "Can you see the rest of them, papa? There must be more!" When he did not answer, she turned to ask again, but seeing tears welling in his raging eyes, she stopped.

"Papa, what is it?"

Because no one had been summoned from Jerusalem, Yosef ben-Moshe had assumed with great relief that Nebuchadnezzar had exempted Hebrews from the Grand Bow. But now he had to admit, he too had come to Dura with stars in his eyes. "Don't you recognize the one on the right?"

Craning her neck, Aridatha looked closer and gasped. "Baruch's brother?"

"And his two friends, Mishael and Azariah. Looking just like their fathers when they were that age."

"I knew it! I knew we would not bow down."

Yosef ben-Moshe had to act fast, but what about Aridatha?

"Papa, you must do something," she said.

Why hadn't he left her back at the camp? Or at least brought one of his servants to look after her?

"Your ring, papa. You can use it to get to Nebuchadnezzar. He will listen to you."

He was having the same thoughts, but he could not take her with him, not to Nebuchadnezzar, not with Jeremiah's prophecy hanging over her head.

"Papa!" she pleaded.

"Go back to camp."

"What?"

"You heard me."

"But I want to go with you."

Shooting her a glare that melted armies, he drove his camel into the crowd.

Aridatha, however, was not one of his warriors, so she did not always melt as they did. Instead, she responded as the willful beloved daughter she was, crying out pathetically "Paaa-pa!" When he did not turn, she tried another tack, shouting, "You are not being fair!" When he still did not turn, she yelled something about never ever wanting to travel with him again, EVER! Naturally, he did not turn for that, so shrugging good-naturedly at his win and her loss, she bought some fish cakes and headed back to camp.

20

MARCHING across the Ishtar Colonnade toward the furnace arena, Arioch on his left and his son Gaspar on his right, Nebuchadnezzar, gilded from head to toe, looked like an angry replica of his ninety-foot gold icon. Clenching and unclenching the hilt of his sword, he silently congratulated himself for having the foresight to build the fiery furnace because the sword was too merciful for the three who had just ruined his day. Ruined his week! Ruined his entire celebration!

The morning had started out with such promise. Sun bright breezes, birds singing, doves cooing. Not a quarrel in sight. In fact, the entire week had been a balm to his soul, starting with the Grand Mentor Tin asking for a private meeting to present his granddaughter, Chenguang. Of course, with Tin's final words still seared in his mind, "I will meet you in the future, and at that time, I will measure your success," Nebuchadnezzar had initially been on his guard. But because the Grand Mentor had been so respectful, almost humble, when he presented Chenguang, Nebuchadnezzar assumed he had measured his successes and been impressed. So to honor the Grand Mentor, he continued on with China's traditional long drawn-out greetings: the slow tedious questions and answers about one's health, prosperity, families, and future.

Tin, however, quickly terminated the formalities, yanking a small tapestry from Chenguang's hand and placing it into Nebuchadnezzar's. The king was not surprised when he saw the miniature pictures of a squat man with a forced smile wielding a dagger before the Chinese and Babylonian thrones. He had always known Au Yang was ambitious. But when he saw the picture of the smiling Grand Preceptor bribing Babylon's royalty with gold, he immediately saw Chenguang in a new light. Not as a threat because of Arioch's yearning attentions, but as an ally. And he wanted to reward her.

On the other hand, where was her husband? She was wearing a veil, so she must be married. Moreover, if she was married to Au Yang, why was she betraying him?

"Chenguang, where is your husband?"

"Chenguang has never married," responded Tin.

Surprised, Nebuchadnezzar turned to the Grand Mentor. "Why is she wearing a veil?"

"She had a falcon accident," he explained. "It made her face displeasing."

A falcon accident? As far as Nebuchadnezzar knew, Chenguang was not a falconer or a hunter. When he was in China, she had worked in her grandfather's library, tended herbs in the emperor's garden, and embroidered in the cloister. Wanting to know more, he looked to Tin, but the Grand Mentor remained silent, his eyes glassy and uncommunicative. So he motioned for Chenguang to remove the veil. Anticipating the king's command, she let the shroud fall from her face, revealing three jagged scars raked across her cheek and down her neck.

Staring at the brutal disfigurement, Nebuchadnezzar immediately knew this was not the work of a bird, but the work of a man, an expert with the talon glove. Again, he looked at Tin. Again, the Grand Mentor said nothing, but now, his eyes were ablaze with the answer: Au Yang had done this to her. Using a talon glove, he had torn Chenguang's flesh and beauty away, destroying her life yet keeping her alive.

Nebuchadnezzar's face knotted in anger as he stated calmly, "I want to reward you, Chenguang, for this beautiful tapestry."

"If it pleases King Nebuchadnezzar," Tin bowed solemnly, "Chenguang would like to be your wife."

Nebuchadnezzar quickly understood the request. As King of Babylon he could not marry Chenguang or have her as a concubine because of her mangled face, so Tin was hoping he would keep her as his guarded property. "Chenguang is beautiful and gracious," he responded. "I am humbled."

Meeting her eyes, he hoped she understood that if Au Yang was in the room, he, Nebuchadnezzar, would kill him with his own hand, whereas he, the King of Babylon, would not. She did not move, not a tremor in her hand or a blink in her eyes, yet her face shone with gratitude to both Nebuchadnezzar and the King of Babylon. Indeed, she was an ally. Studying the rest of her face, her lily soft skin and one smooth cheek bounded by rich raven hair, he understood why Arioch had been attracted to her. Still, the way Arioch had pined over her had been a disappointment because women were a weakness no man could afford. Certainly a weakness no king could afford. In fact, when it came to women, Nebuchadnezzar used them as he used everything else: to build Babylon. After that, he forgot about them.

Looking at Tin, he said, "To reward the granddaughter of the Grand Mentor Tin for her loyalty to the Zhou throne and her valuable assistance to the Babylonian throne, she will be mine, not as a wife or as a concubine, but as a sister. If there comes a time and she wants to marry, she will marry a man from her own house in China." Relief spread across Tin's face. "Meanwhile, she will remain here in Babylon and she will be safe. The King of Babylon will protect Chenguang and her servants as his own."

As he spoke, he knew Arioch would demand Chenguang for himself, even challenge him for her. So he arranged for the two to meet in his royal garden, reasoning that once Arioch saw her face, he would be grateful to forget about her.

⫷⫷⫷

Later that day, Arioch paced back and forth in Nebuchadnezzar's winter greenhouse. Frustrated because he did not have a gift for Chenguang, he was thinking about giving her his gold earrings or his leather belt engraved with Marduk's war song. Stopping abruptly, he asked if it was time to meet her. When Nebuchadnezzar shook his head, he resumed pacing. Straightening the pleats of his black silk trousers, then gulping for breath and belching, he thanked the king over and over for this blessing, jabbering about how he had thought Chenguang had been lost to him forever but now... Now he had no words for his happiness!

It was embarrassing watching the blonde-bearded giant gushing with gratitude and trembling like a leaf. It was also annoying because Chenguang's face was ruined and Arioch was expecting perfection that only lived in memories. Finally, it was time to meet her. So, opening the door, Nebuchadnezzar pushed him out.

Looking to his left at the empty marble seats, to his right at the empty gardens, and straight ahead at the fountain, Arioch's heart sank. Nebuchadnezzar had said it was time, but where was she? Scanning the lily beds, the pomegranate and apple groves, he finally saw movement in the distant fig grove. Yes, there inside the dappled shadows, a slender figure waited: Chenguang! At the mere sight of her, Arioch's cheeks flushed with a booming radiance. No, he would not give her his earrings or his leather belt. How crude. How banal. Instead, he would give her something beautiful, something made by the gods. He would give her lilies. Quickly moving into the garden, into the blended fragrance of earth and flowers, he picked only the perfect ones, and when his hands were full, he sucked in a breath and stepped onto the pebbled path.

The breeze was so soft and the birdsong so sweet, he felt as if he was floating back to his youth, to those dreamlike days when she came early in the morning to the emperor's garden and worked under his window. Because their love had to be kept a secret, she had never looked up at him whereas he, hidden in the shadows of his room, stole glances at her as she harvested gan cao roots, dug narcissus bulbs, collected peony seeds for medicines and petals for teas. Each day before she left, she drew a picture in the dirt. One day, it was birds flying. The next, rain falling on the fields. A tearful face, a smiling face, the moon and stars. Since he had to leave early every morning to report to the Grand Guardian Li, he never saw the pictures until he returned at the end of the day. Then he would go into the garden alone and, thinking of her, add something to her picture: feathers, a bundle of wheat, a handkerchief, a tiny sack of tea, a small silver ring.

Now, after all these years, he was so close to her, he could see the small silver ring on her finger, the sun brightening it like a beacon, and his heart burst with joy. Looking up from the ring to meet her eyes, he met her face and stared at it. He stared and stared, his pulse galloping, his mouth gone dry, the lilies dropping one by one from his hand. Finally, he dared to meet her eyes. They had never spoken to each other but they had learned to read each other's thoughts, and turning on his heel, he marched back to Nebuchadnezzar's winter greenhouse.

Lunging inside, he panted for air, his face so white it was almost blue. "Obviously, Chenguang and I are no longer fifteen years old. Thank you, my lord." Without stopping, he moved toward the door.

"Where are you going?"

"To kill Au Yang."

"Don't you want to know how she got those scars?"

"I know how she got them!" He grabbed the door handle, his arm shaking uncontrollably. "He tied a talon-glove on his hand and attacked her. I saw it in her eyes."

"You saw nothing in her eyes!" Nebuchadnezzar grabbed him. "Tin said she was injured in a falcon accident."

"A falcon accident?! No falcon would do a thing like that. Tin is lying."

"Whether he is lying or not, we will never know. It does not matter."

"It matters to me." Arioch ripped his arm loose and threw open the door.

"Chenguang is mine," declared the King of Babylon.

His words hit Arioch so hard his knees gave way. "Yours?" All he could see was Nebuchadnezzar lying with her.

"Not as a concubine, you fool! Not even as a wife! She will be a sister to me, and as a sister, I will protect her."

Arioch staggered, circling round and round like a dying bull. When he was about to drop, Nebuchadnezzar caught him and dragged him to a chair. "She will be safe here. No one will ever have her. Not me. Not you. Not Au Yang. Now sit down."

Arioch sank into the cushions, a huge crumbling figure.

"Tin brought her cook, her perfumer, her hair dresser, seamstress, jeweler, and servants. He brought everything she will need, and I am going to build a special village for her. All in Chinese architecture. With a moon gate in the wall. I will put it near the river and grow peonies and orange trees for her. What do you think?"

Arioch could barely breathe, let alone think. Nevertheless, he nodded. What else could he do? Two or three lifetimes ago, he and Chenguang had fallen in love. One afternoon, during his fifth year in China, she had used her hands to make shadow-pictures on Tin's sunlit wall telling him a story about a smiling Grand Duke with a double-edged sword ready to kill a young foreigner because the Duke's intended had fallen in love with him. But Arioch, staring at the sash of embroidered peonies cinched around her small waist, had not cared if the Grand Preceptor Au Yang wanted to kill him. All he could think was her waist was so small, he could surely hold it in one hand, but when he reached out to try, Nebuchadnezzar unexpectedly appeared, grabbed his arm with viselike fury and escorted him away. Biding his time, the Grand Preceptor Au Yang had waited until Arioch left the country, then sliced Chenguang's face to ribbons with hooked talons so no one would marry her. Now she was in Nebuchadnezzar's hands.

Arioch pushed himself off the chair and straightened to his full height. "After you build this village for her," he murmured more to himself than to the king, "I will go up to the mountains and build a home for Soheil and my family."

Nebuchadnezzar felt like telling him it was about time, but instead he simply nodded.

Indeed, the past week had been filled with pleasant surprises. The Grand Mentor Tin had obviously been impressed by his successes or he would not have entrusted Chenguang to him. Because of Chenguang's tapestry, he had doubled his surveillance of Au Yang. Furthermore, Arioch was no longer torn between Soheil and Chenguang because Chenguang was his. In fact, everything had gone so smoothly, he had interpreted it as a positive omen for his Grand Bow.

Then this morning another surprise, but not a pleasant one. His three Hebrew judges did not bow down. Shadrach, Meshach, and Abednego, three men he had listened to, depended on, and trusted, had disobeyed his royal order. Not just in private, but before the whole world! How dare they?! Certainly, Babylon had done them no harm. They were well-fed, clothed in royal linens, and were living in the most elegant part of the city: Marduk Plaza! Yes, they were his finest and brightest judges, but he could find other judges. Or did they consider themselves exempt because he had ordered Daniel to stay in the capital?

Of course, Nebuchadnezzar had not always intended for Daniel to remain in the capital. During the planning stages of the ceremony, he had honored him by appointing him to lead the Grand Bow. But Daniel, always chafing at his every good idea, immediately proclaimed he would never bow to any image. Enraged, Nebuchadnezzar threatened to throw him into fire if he did not bow, stating any man would rather bow to gold than burn to death. Amazingly, Daniel had agreed. Hence, to insure that everyone bowed, especially Daniel, Nebuchadnezzar ordered a special furnace built near the Grand Square. However, as the months passed, Daniel never let up, declaring he would not bow. Knowing he was a man of his word, and worn down by his mule-headed logic, Nebuchadnezzar, after slamming his fists on his desk and kicking the dust off his boots, banished Daniel from the entire celebration, ordering him to stay in the capital. What else could he do? Lose his most trusted administrator because he would not plant his face in the dirt? Reduce the man behind his Great Calendar to fuel for the flames?

The Great Calendar was everything to Nebuchadnezzar. Ever since studying with the Grand Mentor Tin, he had puzzled over why in such an orderly lunisolar system, the yearly calendar always ended up skewed and had to be adjusted, adding a day here or a month there. When he approached Daniel on the subject, as always the Hebrew shrugged, saying nothing. But Nebuchadnezzar knew Daniel had something on his mind, so he pressed the issue.

Daniel did have something on his mind: he wanted a commission to study the stars. Knowing his indifference would push the king into probing further, and perhaps result in a commission, he calmly stated that Nebuchadnezzar's calendar had to be adjusted because his priests wanted to keep the holy days in the same seasons of spring, summer, autumn, and winter.

"What is wrong with that?" glowered Nebuchadnezzar. "The holy days are supposed to coincide with spring, summer, autumn, and winter: new life, growth, harvest, and death. It is the full cycle completed in one year."

"Nothing is wrong with it. We Hebrews do the same, adjusting our calendar to keep the holy days of Pesach in early spring and Rosh HaShana at summer's end." Like a cat toying with a mouse, he returned to his notes on the expansion of the King's Highway, then quietly needled, "But you said it yourself. It does not work. The calendar has to be adjusted."

"I suppose you know better?"

"I know the holy days and the seasons of spring, summer, autumn, and winter, although constant, are not the true signs."

"True signs?" scoffed Nebuchadnezzar. "Daniel, what are you talking about?"

"I am talking about the sun, moon, and stars. The Lord God made them to serve as the true signs to mark the seasons, days, and years."

"Hah! We do use the sun, moon, and stars," rejoined Nebuchadnezzar, storming over to the window and looking up at the night sky. "Yet, you are saying we abandon them in order to keep our holy days in spring, summer, autumn, and winter!"

"I am saying there is another calendar which needs no adjusting."

Nebuchadnezzar swung around. "Another calendar?"

By now Daniel was so excited, he could feign indifference no longer. "Yes, my lord. A calendar using only the sun, moon, and stars to mark the years. It is the true calendar marching on in resolute order and will remain in timely congruence until the fulfillment of the ages."

Resolute order? Timely congruence? Fulfillment of the ages? Nebuchadnezzar rubbed his hands together like an excited boy. He had never heard of a calendar that did not adjust to the holy days and their specific seasons. Nor had he heard of a calendar that tracked time in resolute order until the fulfillment of the ages. Moreover, what was the fulfillment of the ages? Could it be the End of the Age as cited in Shining One's epic when the Heavens and the Nations wage one Great Final War against the King of Babylon? Or could it be when the King of Babylon ascends to the heights and sets his throne on the Mount of God? Yes! That was it. It must be! Quickly, he ordered Daniel to search everything and make another calendar, a Great Calendar, using only the heavenly markers so all of Babylon would know when the fulfillment of the ages was near.

Daniel simply nodded, but inside, he was whooping for joy! He was going to study the stars! He was going to search for the fulfillment of the ages! He was going to search and search, documenting everything he learned, and someday he would take it all back to Jerusalem. From then on, he managed Babylon's government by day, and by night, delving into Babylon's astronomy charts and chronologies, Hebrew documents and histories, and the contents of Tin's purple sack bequeathed to Nebuchadnezzar by Emperor Kuangwang, he worked on the Great Calendar.

Nebuchadnezzar ordered the brilliant youth Zoroaster to assist Daniel and report his progress daily. Even so, the king could not stay away because, for him, divining the mysteries of the heavens and locking them into time and reason was more exhilarating than conquest. Thus, before long, he was working shoulder to shoulder with Daniel, plowing through histories, star maps, and Tin's calculations. Of course, Daniel had his shortcomings, much too outspoken when he disagreed with the king, but his insight into the heavenly courses of the past, present, and future was greater than any wisdom Nebuchadnezzar had ever encountered, even in himself!

So to lose a man like Daniel to a forced show of obeisance would have been a foolish vanity. Therefore, he had chosen the three timid ones to represent Jerusalem, believing that without Daniel to shore them up, they would have dropped to the ground before the music even started.

"You expected the three Hebrews to bow, didn't you, father?" challenged Gaspar, matching stride for stride across the walkway.

Gaspar's fourteen-year-old cocksure voice was a festering sore to Arioch, and if the king had not ordered hands off, he would have crunched his fist into the youth's face, dropping him permanently to the ground.

Knowing Arioch had no authority over him, Gaspar shot him a smug grin, then turned back to his father. "But you knew Daniel would never bow, so you ordered him to stay in the capital."

"Daniel is in the capital because that is where he belongs," the king replied disinterestedly. Unlike Arioch, he did not concern himself with his son. Yes, he was ambitious, but the daggers tattooed on the outsides of each of his forearms, always bare to the world, were just pictures, nothing more.

"When I am king," the Crown Prince declared, "I will never put foreigners in high positions." To prove his words and the power behind them, he *accidently* bumped his shoulder against the king.

Arioch drew his sword, but not as fast as Nebuchadnezzar's arm shot out and slammed the boy against a pillar. Then, eye to eye and as calm as death, he whispered, "I only put those who serve me in high positions. If they are wise, they will bring wisdom to Babylon. If they are strong, strength. If they are good, goodness."

Gaspar reached for his dagger, but the king grabbed his wrist, clenching it to the breaking point. "Those, Gaspar, who do not serve me and my purpose..." he enunciated pointedly, "Those who are stupid, cowardly and vile..." He waited for Gaspar's dagger to clatter to the floor. "... I destroy."

"You will never destroy me."

"Just remember, boy. Nothing can shake me." Driving Gaspar against the pillar one last time, Nebuchadnezzar continued striding toward the roar of the fire.

On the other side of the park, hiding in the shadows of Ishtar's shrine, Chenguang watched Nebuchadnezzar and Arioch marching like warships toward their destination. Years ago when the two arrived in China, she barely noticed Arioch because she instantly fell in love with Nebuchadnezzar. Everything about him—his quick decisive manner when he spoke to the emperor, the tightening of his jaw when he argued with her grandfather, his looming presence when he walked into a room—swept her into a wonderful new world of trembling knees, blushing cheeks, and racing heart. But no matter how many times she passed by him, he never noticed her.

So she decided to make him jealous by raising her eyes to Arioch. When that gave no results—except Arioch staring at her—she determined to throw herself at Arioch because if he married her, she could spend the rest of her life in the proximity of the great Nebuchadnezzar. She was forbidden to speak to any man outside her immediate family, so throwing herself at Arioch meant placing herself somewhere where they could communicate without speaking. Hence, when she worked in the emperor's garden, she contrived reasons to work under his window, and each morning before leaving, she drew a picture in the dirt where no one could find it.

Her first drawing was of a three-legged golden crow, known as a suncrow, inspired by the crows flying overhead. When she returned the next morning, three single-eyed peacock feathers were jabbed into the earth next to the crow. The peacock was considered the guardian to royalty, and impressed by his insightful response, she kept the feathers. Finding another hiding place, she drew a second picture: rain falling on the fields. The following morning she found the fruit of the field beside it: a miniature shock of wheat tied together with cedar bark twine. He left a silk orchid handkerchief alongside her drawing of a tearful face, a gold-rimmed teacup with a tiny sack of tea next to the smiling face, and below her picture of the moon and stars, she found a small silver ring with the moon and stars engraved on it.

As the months slipped by and her collection grew, her mornings in the garden became paramount in her thoughts. What picture was she going to draw today? What gift would be his answer? Of course, Nebuchadnezzar still remained a mighty presence in her life, but young Arioch had quietly won her heart, and the Grand Preceptor Au Yang found out. Hence, when the two foreigners left China, the stout grinning Au Yang trapped her in a hallway, and wearing a talon glove—not actually a glove but three iron talons strapped to the fingers, normally used for punishing slaves and criminals—he thrust it into her cheek and, dragging it from her cheekbone down across her neck, ripped her flesh away; not fatal, but a ghastly disfigurement, so no one would ever have her.

Now, standing in the shadows of Ishtar's shrine, she watched Nebuchadnezzar with grateful eyes because he had agreed to protect her and Arioch with devoted eyes because she still loved him. As the two disappeared around the corner, she turned to leave, but the Grand Preceptor Au Yang materialized in her path. Quickly, she hid inside the shrine, but she did not need to worry. The squat smiling man had not given her a thought since the satisfaction of tearing off her flesh. Besides, he was now courting the emperor's niece, hoping to use her to reach his goals of overthrowing the Zhou and Babylonian thrones.

With these goals in mind, Au Yang was now striding across the field toward the young man with the daggers tattooed on his forearms, standing against a pillar and muttering to himself. When the youth noticed the Grand Preceptor approaching, he scowled, trying to drive him away. But Au Yang simply opened his palms, shrugged amiably and moved in. Whatever he said, the two walked off side by side as if they were old friends, and Chenguang hurried back to her room to start another tapestry.

21

CHARTING her course, Aridatha rode steadily toward her father's camp. Traveling alone in a faraway land, she felt very grown up and could hardly wait to tell Baruch ben-Zadok how she was navigating her way along the Basin Road with the Euphrates to her left and Hammurabi's ancient battlements etched in the horizon ahead. More than that, she wanted to tell him about seeing his brother Hananiah and his friends, Mishael and Azariah. Completely confident her father was going rescue them, she wished he had let her stay to watch him win Nebuchadnezzar over and then invite everyone to celebrate. Everyone, that is, except her, because she had been ordered back to camp. The more she thought about it, the more she slowed down, and the more she slowed down, the more she thought about it until she stopped.

If she continued on, she would be obeying her father, but she would never see Nebuchadnezzar. If she went back, she might see Nebuchadnezzar, but her father would never trust her again and that would be worse than anything. So heaving a very disappointed sigh, she urged her camel into motion, steering him toward the camp. But the normally docile beast suddenly had a mind of his own, wheeling around and racing back toward the teeming plain. Yelling for him to stop, she yanked on the reins, even beat him with her whip, but there was no stopping him. Going full speed toward the icon, Aridatha burst into laughter. Papa was never going to believe this!

<hr/>

Dura was no longer a bastion of harmony with nations shopping together, eating together, and drinking together. Instead, it was a wide-open frenzy with crowds shouting "Into the fire." Battling their way toward the furnace building, they trampled over fallen tents, broke through vendors' stalls, even flooded across Nebuchadnezzar's formal gardens. Sentries took formation blocking their progress with swords and whips, while warriors on horseback charged into them pressing them back. From high on her camel, Aridatha saw the hazards, but like the crowds, she was determined to get to the brick building with the three chimneys belching black smoke.

Thinking she could move faster on foot, she dismounted and immediately regretted it. On top of her camel, she was able to see the streets and landmarks; now she could only see robed bellies, sandaled feet, and the smoky gleam of Nebuchadnezzar's gold image far above. So, aiming toward that gleam, she pushed into the throng, passing vendors who had just been robbed, boys and girls carrying miniature replicas of Nebuchadnezzar's icon, sentries chasing after looters, and warriors rounding up brawling tribesmen. Ending up at a canal with no way to get to the other side, she retraced her steps, then started in another direction through parks and squares, scrambling down one path and up another, all dead-ends. Realizing it could be hours before she found the main road, she was about to give up, when she was swept into a fast-moving crowd of the nations' dignitaries.

Pounding her arms against their jeweled capes and gold-braided cloaks, she tried to get out, but everyone was bashing against one another so no one noticed her small limbs. This, of course, did not bother her, because her father had taught her there was always a way out and the first thing to do was to get one's bearings. However, when she looked up, all her bearings were gone: Nebuchadnezzar's towering image, the plume of smoke, even the sky was turning into a torch-lit ceiling inside a huge tunnel. Still she did not worry, for he had also taught her never to panic. However, crushed in from all sides and descending into the bowels of the earth, she did wonder if she would ever see papa or Jerusalem again. And suddenly feeling very alone, she was about to cry out for help when she realized the chant, "Into the fire," was no longer blaring from behind but coming from somewhere down in the tunnel.

Could it be she was headed toward the furnace? Was she almost there? Were papa and Nebuchadnezzar already there? If so, she certainly did not want anyone to notice her now. So pulling her arms close and keeping in the shadows, she let the crowd drive her deeper into the earth. Soon, they were entering a vast hot arena, and as the dignitaries surged onto wooden bleachers, she quickly slipped underneath. There, hidden in the darkness, she crawled over to the middle benches, and finding a crack between two silk robes, she peered out and there it was.

Nebuchadnezzar's fiery furnace.

Enclosed by three huge stone walls and a fourth wall made of iron bars—so everyone could see inside—it held the biggest indoor fire she had ever seen. In fact, it was so big it shot a giant fireball into the air sending the dignitaries shrieking and lurching back, pulling in their robes and holding onto their turbans. Obviously, there was no danger because the flames were confined to the furnace. So to cover their embarrassment, they resumed their chant with even greater fury, thrusting their fists at the three tragic-looking figures standing center-stage.

With all eyes fixed on the three Hebrews, no one spotted a young girl stealing out from under the bleachers and ducking behind the royal curtain. Nor did anyone observe the curtain flutter as she moved behind it. Certainly, no one noticed her eyes peering around the gold-bordered edge and widening with astonishment at the sight of King Nebuchadnezzar seated on his throne. Covered from head to foot in glittering gold and wearing his royal pendant, he looked like his ninety-foot gold image sprung to life, and he was arguing with her father!

"They are Hebrews!" Yosef ben-Moshe shouted over the roar.

"Hebrews or not, they disobeyed the law!" Nebuchadnezzar shouted back.

"Your law!"

"Is there any other law?!"

"You know there is!" blasted Yosef ben-Moshe. "Furthermore, I am warning you, King Nebuchadnezzar," he proclaimed for all to hear, if anyone could hear over the din, "Those who walk in pride, those who build huge monoliths and order every nation to bow to them, He..." Yosef ben-Moshe brandished his finger toward the heavens, "He is able to humble!"

Nebuchadnezzar was so pleased to see his friend again, it was hard not to smile. Even so, Yosef ben-Moshe's sudden appearance was suspicious. "Did you come all this way to tell these three not to bow to my image?"

"No, I did not! I came all this way to bring goods for your celebration."

"A magnificent celebration, is it not?"

Glaring at the fiery furnace, Yosef ben-Moshe said nothing.

Nebuchadnezzar leaned in closer. "Come to my banquet tonight, Yosef. We will talk then."

"There will be nothing to talk about!"

Nebuchadnezzar sighed. If a king's subjects would just obey his commands for one day, how simple kingship would be. How much more he could build and expand. How much more fruitful his fields. How much more pleasant the land. No wonder he could not find rest when he was surrounded by rebellion and disciplinary matters instead of obedient subjects ready to serve him.

Indeed, the crowd was ready, but not to serve him. It was ready for the Hebrews' blood. His three Hebrew judges were ready for a reprieve. And the Grand Mentor Tin, occupying the best seat in the arena—front row center—his three-pronged hat tightened like a crown atop his head, was ready to continue measuring his success. Was there not one person in the whole room ready to simply serve him?

Aridatha watched Nebuchadnezzar's keen eyes probing the room. She could tell he was searching for something and she hoped it was she. So, like her father, she stood tall and proud so he would find her. But when his eyes came to her, he did not see her. In fact, no one in the room saw her. Being a child and often overlooked because of the greater matters at hand, she understood sight was often blinded by vision. No one saw her standing tall and proud by the royal curtain because no one was looking for her. Their sight was blinded by the anticipated vision of the three Hebrews burning in the fire.

22

Studying his three Hebrew judges pale from fear, Nebuchadnezzar had to admit they had caught him off guard. Daniel had been the outspoken one. But Shadrach, Meshach, and Abedneggo had never said a word about not bowing, not even during his five-hour meeting with them when he described his plans for the day: all the nations parading in and standing at their appointed positions in absolute silence; the horns, flutes, zithers, pipes, and choruses bursting forth the first note of the Grand Bow; all the nations falling to the ground; their delegates, one by one, stepping up to the twelve marble podiums; each signing the Treaty; each returning to his place for the Grand Silence; the music exploding again for the second Grand Bow, only this time bowing to him, Nebuchadnezzar, galloping in on his stallion, both man and beast covered with gold, his royal pendant dazzling, his twenty-foot silk train blowing like a sail in the wind. A glorious spectacle, and during all that time his three unassuming Hebrew judges did not bow. Indeed, they had surprised him.

But why, he wondered, why had they remained standing? There was nothing to gain from it. Surely they did not think he was going to let them go. If he did let them go, he would be bowing to their demands, the complete opposite of the purpose of the Grand Bow: to subdue all nations under him. On the other hand, he really did not want to burn his three finest and brightest judges, and because a show of mercy was never without merit, he decided to show mercy.

"Shadrach, Meshach, and Abedneggo," King Nebuchadnezzar began, "you are my worthy judges. You are my interpreters of dreams along with my esteemed counselor Daniel. Because of the plea of your countryman, the honored and brave commander Yosef ben-Moshe..."

Aridatha's heart leapt. The King of Babylon had just singled out her father before all the nations, and now because of her father's plea, he was going to let the Hebrews go.

"I, Nebuchadnezzar, will allow you…" he paused, distracted by the thought of his gold image. When he first saw its wings, he ordered the execution of every artisan who had worked on them. The fools! He had wanted the wings to make him look as if he was *ascending*, not descending. Who in the world would want to bow to a downward flight? Even now he shuddered at the thought. No wonder Shadrach, Meshach, and Abedneggo were standing tall.

"I, Nebuchadnezzar…" he repeated with a flourish, then dropped his voice so all had to lean in to hear, "… will allow you another opportunity to obey me and bow before my image."

"No!" exploded from the bleachers, followed by "Into the fire! Into the fire," clear proof the nations' dignitaries were not ready to serve him. Even so, when he motioned for silence, silence he got, and turning to the Three, more worthy than any of the bloodthirsty sycophants before him, he continued, "If you do not bow immediately, I will throw you into my blazing furnace." Seeing terror flash through their eyes, he knew he had them. So, he added congenially, "Then what god can save you from my hand?"

Shadrach, once known as Hananiah, knew the king's question had only one answer: his God, the Lord Almighty, the God of Abraham, Isaac and Jacob was the only God who could save them. But just because his God could save them, did not mean He was going to save them, and with the flame's deafening roar demanding his flesh, everything in Shadrach was ready to bow down.

⌐═══⟨⟩═══⌐

At the same time Daniel, known as Belteshezzar, stood alone by the River Euphrates. Knowing if Hananiah, Mishael, and Azariah did not bow, they would soon be thrown into Nebuchadnezzar's fiery furnace, he had sought out the poplar grove where he and his three friends first stepped onto Babylonian soil. There their captors had demanded they sing songs of joy, taunting boisterously, "Sing us the songs of Zion!" But how could anyone sing the songs of the Lord while in a foreign land?

Yet Hananiah, frightened as he was, sang. With his thirst-dried tongue stuck to the roof of his mouth, he filled the sky not with songs of joy, but defiance, crying out, "If I forget you, O Jerusalem, may my right hand forget its skill. May my tongue cling to the roof of my mouth if I do not consider Jerusalem my highest joy."

Now, standing under the same poplars so many years later, Daniel wept for his friends and their plight. He wanted to be with them and help them, but Nebuchadnezzar had ordered him to stay in the capital. Even so, he was not completely powerless. He could bring their case before the Mighty One, the God of Abraham, Isaac and Jacob. So Daniel, without knowing why, sang Hananiah's song as a prayer for his three friends, "If I forget you, O Jerusalem, may my right hand forget its skill. May my tongue cling to the roof of my mouth if I do not consider Jerusalem my highest joy."

——

As Daniel sang by the River, Shadrach's tongue clung to the roof of his mouth, reminding him of his first day in Babylon. Back then his tongue clung to his palate because of thirst, yet he had pried it loose to sing out against his brutal masters. And why not? After months of agony and deprivation, there was nothing to lose except pain, whereas now he was a powerful judge in the most powerful kingdom on earth who, in a moment of boldness, had gone along with his friends and not bowed down. If he stayed on this course, the agony would be unbearable. Furthermore, he knew he did not have the strength to bear it and yet...

"If I forget you, O Jerusalem" kept welling up in his heart, "Jerusalem my highest joy, Jerusalem my highest joy" singing within him. He had no idea where the words were coming from, but suddenly his tongue was loosed, and he knew if he did not speak now, he would be betraying his highest joy: Jerusalem. It was only a momentary flash, but in that moment, remembering the Temple of Solomon, the Ark of the Covenant, and the Testimony inside the Ark of the Covenant, he immediately knew what he must do. For the Testimony spoken out of the fire by the Lord and written by the finger of God instilled a fear in him far greater than his fear of Nebuchadnezzar's fire. So, clamping his eyes shut, he gasped, "Our God is able to save us."

It was barely a whisper, but everyone heard it, and as Aridatha soared and Yosef ben-Moshe sank, Nebuchadnezzar's hand clenched the royal pendant of Babylon hanging at his heart.

Shadrach knew he could do better than a cautious murmur, so with eyes still shut, he took a deep breath and shouted, "Our God, the God of Abraham, Isaac and Jacob, is able to save us!" When nothing happened, he popped his eyes open to see the king and the fire spinning. In fact, everything was spinning, and if it had not been for his two friends leaning against him, he would have dropped to the floor.

Emboldened by Shadrach, Meshach raised his linen-draped arms, once dressed with silver armbands from sparring championships, and declared, "But whether our God saves us or not, we will not serve your gods!"

"You are serving me when you bow down!" bawled Nebuchadnezzar, shiny gold specks dripping from his sweaty face. "I am the king of kings. You said so. Remember my dream?" Leveling violent eyes on Abedneggo, the only one who had not yet spoken, he said, "Obey me at once."

Abedneggo did not want to die in a fiery furnace, yet he shook his head. "We will not bow down."

"Hotter!" Nebuchadnezzar yelled. "Seven times hotter!"

"Seven times hotter?" chortled through the crowd. Certainly, this was going to be a day to remember.

Pain shot through Nebuchadnezzar's temples, shards of light flashing before his eyes, a sure sign he had stopped breathing, and in truth, he had stopped breathing because he was too furious to breathe. Red-faced and eyes bulging, he glared at the Grand Mentor Tin. He was not chortling. Nor had he once shouted "Into the fire." He was just sitting there in his irritatingly patient manner waiting—always waiting.

"Throw them in!" ordered Nebuchadnezzar.

As the arena cheered, tears of regret sprang into Yosef ben-Moshe's eyes. He had risked his life to save Nebuchadnezzar and now Nebuchadnezzar was executing the Sons of Jerusalem. Yet, even in his regret, he burst with pride. For under the threat of death, the three Hebrews had refused to relinquish God's command for King Nebuchadnezzar's, and Yosef ben-Moshe rejoiced for Israel.

Facing the reality of being consumed by the tortures of fire, Hananiah, Mishael, and Azariah felt no such rejoicing. However, unlike Yosef ben-Moshe, they had no regrets. For although they were terrified, they each possessed for the first time in their lives a complete peace springing from the song Hananiah's mother sang the morning Babylon came to take them away: "Where can I go from your Spirit? Where can I flee from your presence? If I rise on the wings of the dawn, if I settle on the far side of the sea, even there your hand will guide me; your right hand will hold me fast."

They had always believed the words, but not until they told Nebuchadnezzar they would not bow down, did they know the words were true. Indeed, his Spirit would be with them—even in the fire.

23

"THROW them in!" bellowed Nebuchadnezzar, his breath fully recovered.

Six warriors converged on the Hebrews, blocking Aridatha's view. Faced with the prospect of either staying safely behind the curtain and seeing nothing or changing her position at the risk of exposing herself, she darted toward a shadowy corner at the side of the king's dais. Now she could see everything. Most of all she could see the judges' faces, especially Hananiah's, white from shock, terror in his eyes, resolve in his jaw. Quickly, she prayed someone would come forth and rescue them. But the only one who could rescue them now was Nebuchadnezzar, and because he had ordered them into the fire, he was not going order them out unless someone changed his mind.

The nations' dignitaries shouting "Into the fire" were not going to intervene, and her father had tried and failed. So Aridatha decided it was up to her. She would offer her life in exchange for the three Hebrews' lives explaining to the king if she died, he would lose nothing, whereas if they died, he would lose his three worthy judges. To her it was a sound plan, yet something held her back. It was not fear or timidity or even being a child, but something greater, an inner knowledge having to do with her father's words: "Daughters of Jerusalem, I charge you, do not arouse or awaken love, until it so desires." Of course, the message made no sense for this occasion, but because he had said it so often, explaining when it came to men she must wait, perhaps it did apply.

So, with his words thrumming through her head, she waited for someone else to save them, hoping it would be soon because the Babylonians were binding Hananiah, Mishael, and Azariah's legs and arms, and lugging them up the steps toward the platform above the fire. But no one did a thing. Then, when they reached the platform and threw the Hebrews down on it like slabs of meat, and still no one did anything, a sudden burst of music shook the air.

Startled, Aridatha turned to look, but she could not see any singers, musicians, horns, harps, or tambours. Scanning the bleachers more carefully, then the tunnel entrances, the royal platform, even the ceiling, she still found nothing. Finally, as absurd as it seemed, she moved her eyes toward the raging fire, and there it was. Inside the furnace. Not singers or musicians. Not horns, harps, or tambours. But music! Resplendent sounds living amidst the flames, each sound a different color, each wrapped in a pillar of light, all swirling inside massive gold wings. Strange beautiful voices, rumbling like chariots riding on the clouds, chorused, "The Mighty One, God the Lord, speaks and summons the earth." Underpinning the chorus, a tormented agony howled, "A fire devours before him," while flashing overhead, spangled lights called out, "The heavens proclaim his righteousness." It was a language she had never heard, yet she understood it, and caught up in the marvel, she wondered if anyone else saw and heard the sounds, but was too enthralled to look.

If she had looked, she would have seen terror all around, for Babylon's elite had not counted on Nebuchadnezzar's seven-times-hotter fire igniting a world of sounds and visions beyond their ken. So, with throats gone dry, they stared at the king, hoping for an explanation. Naturally, Nebuchadnezzar had one. The seven-times-hotter heat had sucked the air out of the arena producing a momentary illusion, making the fire look like ethereal lights and its roar sound like voices. So, ordering all the doors thrown open, he turned to his six warriors on the platform and yelled, "Throw them in!"

The king's wrath jolted the warriors back to their duties and the dignitaries back to their chant. However, no one was as enthusiastic as before, because even with the doors open, the chorus was still going strong.

The Grand Mentor Tin, his body braced against the heated gusts, stared at Nebuchadnezzar. The king's eyes, usually driven by a restless hunted look, now brimmed with a wild desperation. Indeed, the government on his shoulders was a massive yoke no man could carry, yet he had to do it, for he was Babylon.

Tin had recognized that yoke when he first met Nebuchadnezzar, because he too knew Shining One's Babylonian epic. However, Tin also knew the stars and the knowledge the heavens poured forth. Consequently, he expected far greater glories from Nebuchadnezzar than

Shining One's paltry offerings. Thus, when Nebuchadnezzar ordered the whole world to come and bow to his image, Tin had seen it as an opportunity to come and witness whatever those greater glories were. So far, he had not seen any, but sitting in the fiery furnace arena with "The Mighty One" blasting him to the core, he knew something was near. So, while many of the dignitaries seized the opportunity to slip out the open doors, the Grand Mentor Tin, along with the Grand Guardian Li, stayed put.

Meanwhile, for the warriors the only way out of the horrific music was to obey the king and throw the Hebrews into the fire. But as they reached out to grab them, three giant flames exploded upward. Unlike earlier when the flames fell back into the furnace, these spiraled toward the platform, fastened onto three warriors and, wrapping them in a fiery glow, ignited their hair, faces, arms, legs, and feet. It happened so fast, no one could do a thing except stare at Babylon's Gogs and Magogs tearing at their armor, racing down the steps, tumbling over one another, and crying out for help as they burned to death on the floor.

Even the King of Babylon was taken aback. While his warriors were being brutalized by fire, the Hebrews were still on the platform untouched. Looking to Yosef ben-Moshe for an explanation, he saw that he too was mystified. However, he also observed he was not unhappy. In fact, he looked downright pleased. Enraged, Nebuchadnezzar was about to order him into the blaze, but was sidetracked by another chorus of "A fire devours before Him" accompanied by a second flaming salvo flying upward and spinning overhead.

Trying to escape, the three remaining warriors leapt for the bleachers, but the fire engulfed them in midair, and the living torches landed on top of the crowd. No longer just spectators but participants in the horror, it was now every man for himself, pushing and shoving toward the tunnel exits.

The flames were so grotesque and so snarling, Arioch knew it had to be magic. The Three Hebrews flattened on the platform above, with their legs and arms roped, were probably reciting incantations ordering the fire to burn Babylon's warriors, possibly even burn the king. Appalled by the thought, he grabbed Nebuchadnezzar's arm and shouted, "My lord, you must get out of here!"

"Not now, Arioch!" Nebuchadnezzar yanked his arm away. Sometimes he did not understand his commander. Who would want to leave at a time like this?

Certainly not Aridatha, still standing in full view. Gaping from Nebuchadnezzar's burning warriors to the escaping dignitaries, she suddenly saw one flaming ambassador charging straight at her. With nowhere else to go, she scrambled up onto the king's dais for safety. Still no one noticed her, and not surprisingly, no one even noticed the Hebrew judges anymore except Nebuchadnezzar, pounding his fists and yelling to the three guards at the bottom of the steps, "Get up there and throw them in!"

Because the warriors had lived their lives dependent on sword and might, and knowing sword and might were a sad defense against seven-times-hotter fire, they ascended slowly.

"Now!!!" the king blared.

The three warriors, begging their gods for protection, hurried up the steps. One yelled something about the Hebrews causing the deaths of their comrades and how it was their duty to avenge them, so together they dove for the Three and pushed. Incredibly, Meshach's legs slipped over the lip, his weight pulled him down, and he plummeted into the belly of the flames. Likewise, with barely a shove, Shadrach and Abedneggo fell in after him, leaving the three warriors standing safely on the platform. They were exceedingly proud, and as they congratulated themselves for a job well done, three more columns jumped out of the inferno and swallowed them up.

The confusion on the floor was so great, no one noticed the last three guards' fiery transference to death, certainly not Nebuchadnezzar. Yes, his warriors had burned and his subjects had fled to the exits trampling one another, but all had ended well because his three rebellious judges were burning in his furnace. So, with his task completed, he turned to leave. However, on second thought and for no reason in the world, he turned back and looked at the fire.

If anyone had ever dangled between man's glory and the glory of the Lord, it was Nebuchadnezzar staring into his fiery furnace because... Well, the Three Hebrews were not screaming in agony. Nor were they dying. In fact, they were not even burning. Instead, his once staid and sad-faced judges, Shadrach, Meshach, and Abedneggo, were jumping up and down, punching their fists in the air, and laughing like boys in his seven-times-hotter exploding flames. Then, mustering their wits and straightening their chests like the oaks of old, they bowed to the ground before another man in the fire: a fourth man. However, unable to contain themselves, they instantly leapt to their feet and broke into excited conversation with him.

It would have been a singular moment for anyone, but for Nebuchadnezzar, it was an impossible moment. He was King of Babylon burning three Hebrews because they had not bowed to his image. Contrarily, the Three Hebrews were alive in his fire and bowing, not to an image, but to a fourth man who shone, not like gold, but like the sun. Everything about it was impossible, so there was only one explanation: he was having a nightmare! To prove it, he calmly queried, "Arioch, am I dreaming?"

"If you are," Arioch heaved a sickening sigh, "we both are." He too was staring at the Three Hebrews and the fourth man. In fact, the entire arena was slowly tiptoeing back to stare, including two new faces, the Grand Preceptor Au Yang and Crown Prince Gaspar. Having seen the exodus out of the tunnels—ambassadors slapping their smoking robes, satraps gulping for air, and wide-eyed governors gone pale—then watching the renegades race back inside, they had slipped in.

Nebuchadnezzar did not see them, nor did he see any of the returning escapees because his eyes were fixed on the other man in the furnace, the Fourth Man, the words "not cut out by human hands" driving through his skull. Then again, perhaps he was imagining the Fourth Man.

"Arioch, how many men did we tie up and throw into that fire?"

"Three, my lord."

"I see four."

Arioch nodded, a dismal beaten nod. Then, just to make sure they were both seeing the same thing, he broached, "And all four are alive and walking in the fire?"

"Yes, you idiot!" the king erupted. "All four are alive and all are walking in my fire!"

The Grand Mentor Tin along with the Grand Guardian Li did not move. Who would want to? Nebuchadnezzar had been outmatched and it was wonderful. Clearly, this was why the Grand Mentor had come to

Babylon. In fact, this was the moment he had been waiting for all his life, and heart bursting, he whispered the song of the ancients embroidered on the Chinese banner hanging next to the stone altar in Luoyi's subterranean cave. "*Of old in the beginning, there was the great chaos, without form and dark. The five planets had not begun to revolve, nor the two lights to shine. You, O Spiritual Sovereign, ShangDi, Ruler of Heaven, first did separate the impure from the pure. You made heaven. You made earth. You made man. All things became alive with reproducing power...*"

Ten-year-old Aridatha had not been waiting all her life for this moment. She had only been waiting since she prayed someone would rescue Hananiah, Mishael, and Azariah. So to her, it was the most natural thing in the world to see a man with a face as bright as the sun rescuing them. What she had not expected was he seemed so familiar, as if she knew him. But how could she know him? She did not know his name, where he came from, or anything about him. Perhaps, upon thought, it was he who knew her. But that did not make sense.

"That Fourth Man," said Nebuchadnezzar, tugging at his gold glittered beard, "He looks like a son of the gods."

Aridatha's soul leapt. That was exactly what he looked like. And turning to the King of Babylon to share his awe, she was surprised to see his face fixed in grim hard lines, his eyes battling terror. He looked so alone in his torment, her heart cried out to him. Of course, he did not hear her heart, so stepping quietly over to him, she slipped her hand into his.

Facing the immediate reality of the Fourth Man living in his fire while using that same fire to incinerate his Babylonian warriors, Nebuchadnezzar was not prepared for the touch of unexpected warmth slithering into his hand. Certain it must be another flaming leviathan about to creep up his arm and coil around his neck, he jerked away, drew his sword, and turned to slay it. But it was only a little girl. Impossible! A little girl could not just walk into his arena and appear at his side. She must have come with the Fourth Man, and if he brought her, she must be the hand of death. Perhaps only moments before, she had been a column of fire consuming one of his warriors and now, in a different form, had come to consume him.

"Where did you come from?" he demanded.

Normally, Aridatha would have answered but the explanation was so long, and not wanting to move her eyes away from the Fourth Man, she motioned for the king to look at him.

Watching her finger point to the furnace, he knew he was right. She was with the Fourth Man. But why hadn't she brought fire? Or a sword? Why had she taken his hand gently, not forcefully? Why were her eyes full of wonder, not destruction? Then it dawned on him. She had been sent to protect, not harm. That was it! He was King of Babylon, so the Fourth Man had provided her as protection from the fire, like a shield. So pulling her in close, he called to the furnace, "Shadrach. Meshach. Abedneggo. Come out."

Arioch could not believe it. Unbeknownst to anyone, he had just spent harrowing moments staring at Babylon's nine warriors dead on the ground, yet by some ghastly oversight still alive and shrieking for help while being locked into fiery metal cages and lowered into the earth. If the Three had received that kind of power from the Fourth Man, certainly the king did not want them stepping back onto Babylonian soil. "My king, are you sure you want them to come out?"

"If I did not want them out," barked Nebuchadnezzar, "I would not have ordered them out."

"What if the Fourth Man has transferred his powers to them?"

"Impossible," the king declared. "They are my servants. Not his." With a firm grip on the girl, he raised his fist and shouted, "Servants of the Most High God, I said come out."

Arioch felt like countering, "If they are your servants, then why are you calling them servants of the Most High God?" Of course, he knew the answer. If the Hebrews obeyed the king instead of remaining with the Fourth Man, it would prove they were subservient to Nebuchadnezzar's command, establishing Nebuchadnezzar as the reigning authority. Furthermore, five minutes earlier that kind of reasoning would have made sense to him. But after seeing the Hebrews alive in the fire and his Babylonian warriors dead but alive in fiery metal cages, nothing made sense anymore.

Hananiah, Mishael, and Azariah were equally shaken by Nebuchadnezzar's command. After facing trial after trial throughout the day, they had thought their trials were over because they were with the Fourth Man. But now, they were facing their greatest trial of all: leaving him. Hence, for the first time that day, they collapsed into tears, sobbing inconsolably.

Watching the Fourth Man bless Hananiah, the Grand Mentor Tin broke into a clammy sweat. He had come to Babylon hoping to find something great and he had found it: the Fourth Man and the three Hebrews living in fire. It was a greatness he had not expected. Beyond comprehension, beyond measure, clearly beyond attaining, and yet he could have had it. If he had not bowed to Nebuchadnezzar's image, he would be in the furnace with the Three Hebrews bowing to the Fourth Man and receiving his blessing. Now it was too late. He could never bow to the Fourth Man because he had already bowed to gold and his loyalty could not be rescinded. He had signed Nebuchadnezzar's treaty and his signature could never be erased. By bowing to gold and signing the treaty, he had shamed himself and shamed China. Now there was only one thing to do. He learned it when he was a boy studying the teachings in the caves where the dragons dwelt. There, with other boys from noble families, he learned the thirteen Doctrines of Destiny. The sixth doctrine said the only way to erase shame and restore righteousness was for a man to sacrifice himself and no other. So, gripping his crescent-shaped dagger, he yanked it from its sheath and aimed it at his heart.

No one noticed. Too enthralled with the Fourth Man living in fire, no one was looking at Tin, not even the Grand Guardian Li standing beside him. Even Tin, while his honor demanded he plunge his dagger into his heart, had paused to stare at the Fourth Man. When he did, he remembered another teaching hidden in another cave, the one near Fohi's star map room. Four banners with ancient readings lined the walls, but he was remembering the word written on the stone altar. Made up of three Chinese characters, *hand, dagger* and *lamb*, the first two characters, *hand* and *dagger,* blended to create a new word, *me*. The third character, *lamb,* hovered over the word *me*, resulting in *me* under the *lamb*. It was the word *yi*, meaning righteousness.

Of course, the Grand Mentor already knew all this. Once a year, the emperor led a lamb into Luoyi's subterranean tunnels, entered the cave and, after reading the inscriptions on all four banners, sacrificed the lamb on the altar to atone for unrighteousness. Undoubtedly, the sacrificial lifeblood of a lamb was enough for the peasants and feudal lords of China, but Tin was the Grand Mentor, the Stargazer, the Wise

One, the Pathfinder to Truth. No lamb could possibly restore his honor! So, with his hand poised and his heart waiting to be gutted, he ripped open his silk jacket and bared his chest, when suddenly he remembered another lamb—written in the stars: the Sign *Taleh*, meaning the *lamb*, also known as *Baraziggar*, meaning the *altar of right-making*.

How could he have missed it? His whole life he had studied the stars and their names. His whole life he had passed the altar with the word *yi* written on it. His whole life! Yet he had never realized that *Taleh* and *yi* were the same teaching: *Taleh* was the *lamb* and the altar of right-making; *yi* was *me* under the *lamb*, the word for righteousness. Now he could see it as clear as day. Unlike the Doctrines of Destiny, handed down on parchments from sage to sage, these were two established witnesses, one in the heavens, *Taleh*, and one in China's written word, *yi*, both teaching the Chinese from generation to generation that the way to righteousness or right-making was not through *me*, but through the *lamb*.

So the Grand Mentor Tin, throwing his dagger to the ground, prayed for the lamb to cover him and make him right, so he could bow to the Fourth Man.

As Tin prayed, and as the other dignitaries sorted through similar thoughts about bowing to the image of gold and thus forfeiting living in the fire with the Fourth Man, Shadrach, in obedience to the King of Babylon, opened the iron-barred door, and the Three Hebrews left the fire behind. As they stepped into the arena, a strange stillness accompanied them. Soft as rose petals and tasting like honey, it saturated the air until no one moved except to bow his head to the living who had come back, not from the dead, but from the living. Indeed, the nations' dignitaries stood helpless before the Three Hebrews. Yet in their helplessness, there was a mysterious strength. Perhaps it was joy. Perhaps peace. Or, if one wanted to look deeper, perhaps it was truth. Whatever it was, no one wanted the moment to end, because everyone knew when it did, they would all be back in the wonderful world of Babylon with all her wealth and happiness, power and glory. However, it would also be a world without the Fourth Man. A fearsome thought to more than one.

"The Lord be praised!" cried Yosef ben-Moshe, racing to Hananiah, Mishael, and Azariah. "I will tell all Jerusalem about this day!"

His jubilation ignited the crowd. Clamoring off the bleachers and hurtling in from the tunnels, the world's dignitaries talked and laughed

to anyone and everyone, eagerly reaching out to touch the judges' clothing, exclaiming: "Not a hair singed!" "Not a thread scorched!" "They do
not even smell of smoke!"

24

ARIDATHA was also eager to get to the judges. Even more, she wanted to get to her father, crowded behind two pillars on the other side of the room, crushed in conversation with Azariah. He had been so engrossed in Hananiah, Mishael, and Azariah's plight, Nebuchadnezzar's warriors burning, the Three Hebrews not burning, and the amazing presence of the Fourth Man, she knew he had not yet seen her. So, looking up at the king, she started to ask him to let her go, but seeing his eyes wincing as if some unbearable pain was attacking them from within, she thought it probably not a good time.

She was right. It was not a good time. Nebuchadnezzar's subjects were slipping away to new gods and new heroes, and yes, he was wincing, but not from pain. He was furious! Here he had constructed hundreds of temples and shrines to his gods Marduk, Ninmah, and Ishtar and for what?! Where were they now?! Hiding in their temples? Gorging themselves on his sacrifices? Sleeping? No matter! If the gods of Babylon were hiding, gorging, or sleeping, the King of Babylon was not.

"Praise be to the God of Shadrach, Meshach, and Abedneggo," he shouted, "For he has sent his angel and rescued his servants."

Stunned, the dignitaries turned to listen.

"They trusted in their God," he continued, "defying the king's command, willing to give up their lives rather than serve or worship any god except their own."

Cheers shook the rafters, not for the Hebrews, but for the King of Babylon who had just credited the Hebrews with courage. Thus, Nebuchadnezzar won his wayward sheep back and, determined to protect himself and Babylon from any more fiery outbursts from the Hebrews' God, added, "Therefore I decree that the people of any nation or language who say anything against the God of Shadrach, Meshach, and

Abedneggo be cut into pieces and their houses turned into piles of rubble, for no other god can save in this way."

Relieved he was commanding honor for the God who lived in fire, the dignitaries burst into foot-stomping applause.

Knowing they would foot-stomp at anything, Nebuchadnezzar was not impressed. Besides, he had more urgent matters at hand: the girl in his grip. Turning her around to face him, he motioned to the furnace. "You came with him, didn't you?"

The idea was so absurd, Aridatha just stared at him.

"You did," he declared. "You came with the Fourth Man."

Looking back at the fire, her shoulders sagged. "He is gone."

The king rose to get a better view. He was gone. The light, the power, the music gone. Even the flames, only moments before a raging inferno, drooped and hugged the floor leaving Nebuchadnezzar with a sickening dread, as if history had once again stopped to turn to a new page, leaving him freefalling forevermore. Foolishness! The Fourth Man was gone. The fire was gone. Even the young girl was gone. But nothing had happened to him or his kingdom.

Suddenly, he heard a child's voice deep inside the crowd calling, "Papa!" Hoping it was she calling to the Fourth Man, he searched for his sun-bright face and radiant clothing. Unable to find him, he kept his eyes on her, jumping into the arms of a man behind two pillars. The man's face broke into astonishment, then joy, then a flash of horror as he turned to face the throne. It was Yosef ben-Moshe.

Immediately, Nebuchadnezzar's mind laughed at him for thinking she was a shield when she was only Yosef ben-Moshe's daughter. But his heart instantly said no, arguing she had been sent to protect him from the flames as Yosef ben-Moshe had been sent to protect him from the Egyptian's arrow. She had brought him good luck like Yosef ben-Moshe and Daniel. It was always the Hebrews, and not wanting his luck to change—or their God to interfere again—he said, "Arioch, promote Shadrach, Meshach, and Abedneggo."

"Yes, my lord."

"I thought nothing can shake you," scoffed from behind.

Knowing it was Gaspar, the king ignored him.

"They have the whole world running after them," the Crown Prince smirked, motioning to the whole world standing in line to talk to the Hebrews, "and you are promoting them?"

"They have served Babylon better than most," the king replied drily, certainly better than his dignitaries who only five hours ago were groveling to his gold image and now were groveling to the empty furnace, then sneering at Babylon's dead warriors. Something had to be done about that! Tearing them limb from limb and ripping their houses to pieces would be satisfying, but everyone would be talking about it for generations. No, he had to do something to make them forget, something to drive the memory of today out of their minds. Forever! Thus, marching over to his scribes, he yanked the scrolls from their hands and declared for all to hear, "Today never happened!"

However, all did not hear. In fact, no one heard.

Appalled, Nebuchadnezzar gaped at the scene. For the first time in his life, he was standing in a room and no one was paying attention to him. His fat jeweled dignitaries whom he fed and bestowed largesse upon had completely forgotten him, talking and laughing freely about the events of the day. His warriors, no longer standing at attention but shambling here to there staring at their dead brothers-in-arms, had no idea he was even in the room. The Three Hebrews had certainly forgotten his all-powerful presence. Never again would they tremble before him as they did when he said so glibly, "Then what god can save you from my hand?" Even Yosef ben-Moshe and the girl had forgotten him. So, he roared with his voice that shattered the dawn, "TODAY NEVER HAPPENED!"

Startled out of their reveries, all turned to see what was going on. Shockingly, the King of Babylon was ripping apart the scribes' scrolls, throwing them to the floor, and stamping on them. "I, Nebuchadnezzar King of Babylon," he bellowed, "proclaim today never existed!"

Wrapped in her father's arms, Aridatha watched Nebuchadnezzar rage. She had never seen a man in such torment, wondering if the young warrior with the daggers tattooed on his arms had incited the outburst. But it was hard to believe any one man could be the cause of such turmoil. Even so, she frowned at the tattoos, then glancing back at the king, she was surprised to see he was looking directly at her, eye to eye and soul to soul, as if in a bitter wrangle with her.

"I forbid anyone to speak about this day or write about it. Ever!" Scanning the hundreds of eyes gawking at him, he roared, "Out!"

No one moved.

"Now," he whispered through bared teeth.

Everyone bolted for the exits except the Grand Mentor Tin and the Grand Guardian Li because Tin had hunkered down to the ground to write three Chinese characters: *hand, dagger, lamb*. He blended *hand* and *dagger* to make the word *me*, placing *me* under the *lamb*. Then, with all the majesty and patience of China, he and the Grand Guardian Li withdrew.

In contrast, Yosef ben-Moshe, not wanting to draw any more attention to Aridatha, was eager to escape, trying to stay hidden in the crowd while hurrying toward the nearest tunnel.

"Not Aridatha," Nebuchadnezzar ordered.

Amazed he had remembered her name, ben-Moshe pulled Aridatha in tighter, but she tugged away, dropped to the floor, and walked to the king.

25

AFTER the arena emptied, Nebuchadnezzar paced. Going from one stinking dead warrior to the next, he scowled at their charred remains and molten swords, the mocking proof of a disastrous day. Starting with the descending wings on his ninety-foot gold image to his warriors burning outside his fire and the Hebrews living inside his fire, the day had been one unprecedented disaster. All because of one unprecedented dream. If he had not had the dream of the statue with the head of gold and the rock crushing all the kingdoms, he never would have thought of building a gold statue and ordering the world to bow to it.

Then again, he had gods too! Marduk, Ninmah, and Ishtar! Where were they when the Fourth Man was trespassing into his fire, invading his kingdom, overruling his judgments, and burning his men? Even more exasperating, what about Shining One Son of Dawn, Prince of the Power of the Air?! Where had he been?! At the very least, he could have mentioned this day in his epic. But not one word about a rock crushing kingdoms or a Fourth Man living in fire. Yes, Shining One's presence had definitely been lacking. But not China's! The Grand Mentor Tin had shown up, sitting dead center, wearing a silk jacket embroidered with the conjunction of Jupiter and Saturn in Pisces. The conjunction they had argued over repeatedly.

"I said it does not smell like smoke in here."

Almost leaping out of his skin, he swung around. It was Yosef ben-Moshe's daughter twirling in his furnace. He had completely forgotten about her.

"Come in and smell."

Not wanting to go near the furnace, he stomped up the dais steps, sat on his throne, and said, "Why did you take my hand?" This he had to know because her answer would reveal if she was just another child running loose, disobedient to her father, recklessly in and out of people's affairs or if she was a child of sense, her paths governed by destiny, each step placed purposely in and out of people's affairs. Apparently, she did not hear, because instead of answering, she kept dancing round and round in the furnace.

"You took my hand when we saw the Fourth Man," he pronounced loudly so she would stop. "Why?"

"You said he looked like a son of the gods."

"I?" he huffed.

"Yes, you."

The light streaming in through the vents rested on the Stars of David in her hem, reminding him of her father's shield. "You took my hand," he said, "to protect me, as your father protected me."

"I took your hand because you were afraid."

"You do not have to shout it."

"I did not shout it. It echoes in here."

"Then get out," he ordered.

Stepping back into the arena, she said, "You can feel the air in there. Sparkling all around. Like the fragrance of apple blossoms misting on your face."

"Such prattle. It smells like smoke and is as black as death. Furthermore," he continued, as if speaking to a large crowd, "I was not afraid. I was thinking." Before she could object, he jutted his face into hers and charged, "You were afraid."

"I? Why should I be afraid? Your warriors are the ones who burned." To prove her point, she motioned to his nine warriors still smoldering on the ground, then moved to the evidence of the pristine furnace.

"You are very bright, Aridatha," he said, sagging onto a bleacher seat. "But there are some things you do not understand."

"I do not claim to understand even some things, King Nebuchadnezzar. But I do know when someone is scared."

Nebuchadnezzar barely heard because he was sitting in Tin's seat, staring down at a word written in the dirt. The characters were a *hand* and a *dagger* written side by side, meaning *me*, under the character for a *lamb*. Startled, he jumped up. "I was not scared," he snapped, scuffing the word *yi* out with his boot. "I was thinking. Thinking if Jerusalem ever defies me, I will attack and destroy her."

"With the Fourth Man there to protect us?"

"I agree we saw nine warriors burn to death outside the fire and three judges live inside the fire. But what about me? I am still here, am I not? Babylon is still here, is it not? The Fourth Man sent you…"

"You almost killed me once," she interrupted, pointing to the scar on her forehead.

"The Fourth Man sent you," he continued firmly, "to protect me. That is why you took my hand."

"You promised papa you would protect me, so how can I protect you?" she reasoned. Stepping up to him, she carefully searched his eyes. "Papa says you are the servant of the Lord Almighty."

"I serve no one!"

She turned away. If he was going to shout, she was finished with him.

Naturally, he did not care. But after some moments, the silence all around—the cavernous mouths of his dead warriors, the cold grey furnace, and the muted bleachers—unnerved him. If only she would say something to fill the air that not long ago had soared with his glory-bound power, then exploded with the appearance of the Fourth Man. It had been exhilarating, then threatening, but now… Now there was nothing. But how could there be nothing? Why didn't she say something? Why didn't she admit the Fourth Man had sent her to be his shield? Of course, he was being absurd. He did not need her to speak to him or shield him. Besides, there was no such thing as nothing. Irritated, not because of the girl, but because of his misjudgment of the Three Hebrews, he waved her off and marched toward the exit tunnel. On second thought, he spun around and declared, "Aridatha, you will stay here. In Babylon."

"Impossible."

"Impossible?" He had had enough rebellion for one day, especially from the Hebrews, so with shoulders hunched, he stalked back to her, whispering, "What do you mean, impossible?"

"I am going to marry Baruch ben-Zadok when I grow up."

He burst out laughing. Laughing and laughing. She was not a threat, she was a child.

"It is not funny," she stated simply. "Baruch and I grew up together. We are both from Jerusalem and we both love the Hebrew scrolls: Moses, King David, King Solomon, Isaiah… Baruch has read the scrolls to me all my life. Do you want to hear?" Before he could object, she launched into the first thing that came to mind. "'This is what the Lord says—Israel's King and Redeemer, the Lord Almighty—'"

"Enough!"

Bounding up to the highest bleacher, she raised her voice, "'I am the first and I am the last, apart from me there is no God. Who then is like me? Let him proclaim it! Let him declare...'"

"I will bring the boy Baruch ben-Zadok to Babylon," he shouted over her railing, silencing her. "He can read the Hebrew scrolls to you here."

"He would never come."

"He will do as I command," the king stated flatly, motioning her off the bleachers, for he never spoke to anyone higher than his head.

Obediently, she hopped back down and, stopping on the last bleacher, met him face to face. "I cannot stay."

"I will give you anything you want," he coaxed.

"I already have everything I want. I am a Daughter of Zion."

"Daughter of Zion," he scoffed. "Zion is nothing. No one knows where it is or what it is. But everyone knows where Babylon is and what it is. And I, King of Babylon, am offering you anything you want from my entire kingdom, an offer I make to no man, woman, or child." When she still shook her head, he decided to have her whipped. On the other hand, perhaps he should banish her to an isolated prison away from everyone, especially the boy Baruch ben-Zadok. That would teach her who her king was! But looking into her eyes, already burgeoning with power and rest, he had no desire to possess or rule over her. She was too much like a deer on the grasslands whose freedom was far more beautiful than any caged animal. Of course, one had to kill a deer from time to time but never capture it.

"You are a foolish girl, Aridatha," he said, striding into the tunnel. "No one at your age has everything he wants."

But the foolish girl, sensing she had won a victory, felt a bit guilty. So, hurrying alongside, she pulled off her crimson pouch and offered it to him. When he ignored it, she explained, "Jeremiah the prophet of the Most High gave it to me."

He stopped so abruptly, he almost stumbled, because it was Jeremiah who called him the servant of the Lord Almighty. An irresponsible statement! However, Jeremiah also said he was going to rule over all the land. A trustworthy statement but not remarkable. Anyone with a thumbnail of sense could have deduced that.

"What is it?" he demanded.

"Jerusalem dirt."

"Hah!" he sneered. "Does your prophet give dirt to all Jerusalem's children?"

Shaking her head, she pointed to the scar on her temple. "Only me." Pressing the pouch into his hand, she whispered solemnly, "To remember me by."

He almost laughed. Why would he want to remember her? Yet, it was such a simple, fragile gesture, unlike any he had ever received, certainly not from his sycophants at court, his wives, his children, or the women in his bed. However, with the events of the day weighing heavily upon him, he was reluctant to accept because coming from the prophet perhaps sorcery lay inside.

So, he challenged, "Will it bless or curse?"

Studying the pouch, she said, "I do not know."

A grave purity emanated from her heart, a steady and serious trust, and because the Hebrews brought him good luck, he bowed his head so she could put it on him.

She was so pleased, she trembled as she hoisted the leather strap over his head, her smile widening as she watched the pouch bounce off his gold glittered beard, slide across his pearl sash and land beside his royal pendant. A proud moment for both: Aridatha admiring her pouch because it held Jerusalem dirt and Nebuchadnezzar admiring his pendant because it held Babylon's power. Moreover, to insure she understood just how much power the pendant held, he tapped it and said, "Babylon."

With equal pride, she tapped the crimson pouch. "Jerusalem."

Nodding, he stated, "Two cities."

"More than just cities," she rebutted.

Impressed by her insight, he decided to give her a little history lesson, announcing grandly, "At war since the dawn of time."

"And their war will continue," she rattled off coolly, confirming she understood his little lesson, "affecting all kings, all men, all women, and all children in every generation. Then, at the end of the age, out of all the cities in all the world, these two cities will clash in one final war."

"I see you know all about this," he commended. "Do you also know who will be the victor?"

"I do."

"Babylon." He thumped his pendant. "Glory of kingdoms."

"No, King Nebuchadnezzar," she stated calmly although her chestnut hair and Stars of David hem certainly snapped excitedly in the tunnel breezes. "Jerusalem will be the final victor. Throne of the Lord."

She was only ten years old, yet startling, staring at him like a judge in a courtroom. Clearly, those eyes of hers, glowing like a lamp on a cold dark night, had no intention of backing down, reminding him of Daniel and Yosef ben-Moshe. Of course, she was wrong—also like Daniel and Yosef ben-Moshe. However, because she was young, perhaps she was someone he could influence and use. Perhaps even use to influence Daniel and Yosef ben-Moshe.

Meanwhile, it was time to move on to the business of Babylon, yet he could not move. In fact, he did not want to move. Neither did she. So they both just stood there, staring at the pendant and the pouch, when suddenly a tempest rose up inside the tunnel. Blowing out the torches, it howled and raged like a cracking thunderstorm with flashes of lightning and pelting hail. They both felt it, heard it, and saw it. But how could thunder, lightning, and hail be inside a tunnel? Or was it something else hammering at their hearts and swirling around their souls? Was it the Fourth Man? Was it Babylon? Or was it Jerusalem? Whatever it was, they both knew their lives, although completely opposed, were being sown together. They had no idea what that meant, but they knew there was no turning back. Moreover, they did not mind. In fact, they almost felt safe.

Thus, as the tumult waned, Nebuchadnezzar King of Babylon leaned down and, kissing the top of her head, said, "I will remember you, Aridatha of Jerusalem."

26

NEBUCHADNEZZAR of Babylon and Aridatha of Jerusalem stepped out of the tunnel into a brilliant sunset, marred only by the vast shadow of the king's towering image. Unlike that morning when Aridatha stared and stared at the ninety-foot gold icon, now she barely glanced at it because she could look at the king himself. Taller than most men with a face chiseled to perfection and thick braids rippling down his back, his chest was broad, his legs long, his hands mammoth. There was much more to drink in, but she was not interested in his outward appearance. Instead, she was drawn to his inner turmoil: that restless hunted look dominating his eyes and the bleak desperation ruling over his every breath, as if with each glance and word he was battling through some great Babylonian epic.

"You decreed today never happened," she said quietly, for even the air should not hear such things. "But I will not forget. I will always remember the Fourth Man."

When he said nothing, she asked, "Will you remember him?"

"I? Remember the Fourth Man?" The question wearied him, and staring out, he locked his eyes on an eagle riding on the north wind.

He was quiet for so long, she had time to regret her hasty refusal to stay in Babylon. She knew she was Aridatha of Jerusalem, yet all her life she had yearned for what she had now: sitting beside Nebuchadnezzar, privy to his thoughts and heart. Why return to Jerusalem if it meant leaving him? Of course, there was papa and Baruch, but they would understand. Then there was Jerusalem itself, but...

"While you are growing up, Aridatha..."

Yes, this is what she wanted. Not just to be sitting at his side, but to think with him and to think against him. To listen to his voice and to make him listen to hers. To walk together and to walk separately. Babylon and Jerusalem.

"I will secure my border on the Egyptian frontier and..." Moving his arm across the horizon, he whispered, "...create my vision of Babylon."

As he spoke, she decided he must have forgotten her question because he said nothing about remembering the Fourth Man. Instead, he talked in detail about his plans to build Babylon, defeat Egypt, and implement his League of Mutual Assistance. Then, without warning, he interrupted himself, muttering, "Gaspar." Drumming his fingers, he looked at her. "What will I do with Gaspar while you are growing up, eh?"

She had no idea who Gaspar was, but judging from his disdain, she did not like him.

"I know," he said, reaching into his pocket and pulling out a handful of dates. He offered her some and, seeing her eyes light up, gave her the whole handful. "I will send him to my eastern frontier. There he and his weak-minded collaborator Zorpo will plot against me. Pay attention, Aridatha, this is the world you live in. Bribing the ignorant and inciting the rebellious, he will build a great and secret army. His archers will yap like wolves as they train their arrows against me and his warriors will bray like donkeys as they boast about the day Gaspar overthrows my kingdom." Laughing at the thought, he plucked a date from her hand, popped it into his mouth, and said, "Are you staying in Babylon or not?"

Happily stunned because he brought it up again, she was about to say yes, but he was looking at her with such confident command, she blurted, "No. I am not staying. I am Aridatha of Jerusalem."

Curiously, he seemed to understand, even approve. Then a cloud fell over his face, a dangerous, lightless cloud, and taking her hand in his, he said, "Listen to me, Aridatha. In ten years, a new generation of Hebrew warriors will have grown up and they will want to fight."

She knew he was telling her something he did not want to speak, a warning that came from a full heart, a heart beyond his, causing her own heart to pound so furiously, it reminded her of chariots coming like a whirlwind.

"And you, Aridatha, will grow into a beautiful and desired young woman."

That gave her no solace because Jeremiah's words, "Rachel, weeping for her children because they are no more," were rising up inside her, causing tears to tumble down her cheeks.

"At that time," he stated flatly, pulling out a handkerchief and hand-ing it to her, "the King of Jerusalem will break away from my League of Mutual Assistance and ally with Egypt. But..." Looking up at his ninety-foot gold statue, he paused. The sun had set so the gold no longer glittered, leaving the fixture dull black, a looming silhouette of darkness overlapping darkness and shadows creeping into shadows creating a new, perhaps even more profound image: an enormous raven plummeting down from the highest tiers to devour the world. "I will have no oppo-nent from horizon to sky."

"Papa will never let Jerusalem ally with Egypt against you, you know that."

"Then Aridatha..." he said with such finality, she buried her face in his chest and shook her head, trying to make him stop because now she did not want him to answer her question. But unable to bend, unable to comfort, and unable to rescind what he was going to have to do, the King of Babylon said, "You and I will both remember the Fourth Man."

PART II

THE SERVANT
OF THE LORD ALMIGHTY

27

Jerusalem, *nine years later*

NEBUCHADNEZZAR had been right about his future. Since his talk with Ari-datha, he had gone on to secure his border at the Egyptian frontier and create his vision of Babylon. Under his finest and brightest architects and engineers, he built resplendent cities, vast thoroughfares, canals, and his great wall around his capital—or rather two walls: an outer wall and an inner wall with gold temples and fortresses embedded into it. Fifty-six miles long, they were three hundred feet high, and so wide, he ran yearly chariot races along the top. Under Shadrach, Meshach, and Abedneggo, absolute order prevailed because everyone knew, although the day of the fiery furnace never existed, the Three Hebrews had lived in the fiery furnace while Babylon's warriors died. Hence, every satrap, administrator, and governor towed the line when any of the Three entered a room. Under the direction of the two physicians who worked on Yosef ben-Moshe, Babylon's School of Medicine was now the most trusted medical center in the land because any doctor who botched an operation had his hand cut off. Under Arioch, war cities and training camps were now in full operation throughout the land, preparing for the day when Babylon would march against Egypt. Under Nebuchadnezzar's League of Mutual Assistance, nations were united in trade and, more importantly, increasingly dependent on Babylon. Chenguang continued to send tapestries outlining Au Yang's activities: marrying the emperor's niece, stealing half of the Chinese army out from under the Grand Guardian Li, bestowing lands to China's feudal lords, and supporting Gaspar's armies with vast amounts of gold, silver, and armor. In addition, a new marvel was taking shape: Nebuchadnezzar's Mountain! Not a lifeless stone mountain as the Egyptians built for their dead, but a living mountain with a huge hidden hydraulic system watering its trees, shrubs, gardens, streams and ponds.

Nebuchadnezzar had also been right about Aridatha. She had grown up to be a beautiful and desired young woman. At the age of nineteen, it had been sixteen years since she received her scar from Babylon and nine since she witnessed the Fourth Man and met King Nebuchadnezzar. After her return from Babylon when she was ten, she spent every moment thinking about the Fourth Man and Nebuchadnezzar. But as her mother threw her into the whirlwind obligations for Hebrew girls blossoming into womanhood, she was too busy to think about anything except girl-friends' weddings, weeklong stays with Jerusalem nobility, New Moon festivals, royal celebrations, and the annual King Solomon Pageant. Her list of activities never ceased, yet no matter how busy she was, her father relentlessly trained her in warfare, languages, building, and planting, and Zillah, with equal fervor, instructed her in running a household, enhancing her beauty, and attracting a husband. Aridatha continued to travel with her father but never again to Babylon. In fact since her return, the words Babylon and Nebuchadnezzar had been banished from the estate. Hence, as the years slipped away, thoughts about her scar, the Fourth Man, and Nebuchadnezzar also slipped away until they were out of reach, buried in a childhood which no longer existed.

Similarly, Jerusalem's well-meant promises made so many years ago—promises to reject wine, feasting, singing, and dancing until their children returned—had fallen out of reach until the city once again delighted in her master chefs and vintners far more than in the works and the word of the Lord. Naturally, their hearts still bled for their children and beat for their return, but with the passing of time, it became impossible to even remember their faces. Hence, to keep their memories alive, the city gathered once a year in Jerusalem's largest park, Flowering Field, to give speeches about sons who were ruling in Babylon's highest courts and daughters who were married and living in luxury in the most splendid city on earth. Speeches were also given about sons and daughters who were shackled and starving, building, digging, timbering, and excavating under brutish masters. Those were the speeches no one wanted to hear except the immediate family because there was nothing anyone could do about it except go to war against Babylon, which was out of the question because Babylon was the mightiest kingdom on earth.

Still, there was a growing desire to fight the mightiest kingdom on earth, and in this, Nebuchadnezzar had also been right. For since he had spoken to Aridatha, a new generation of Hebrew warriors had grown up and was now champing at the bit to throw off Babylon's yoke. At first, their impassioned speeches were regarded as irresponsible and childish. But as the months passed and their youthful determination broiled hotter, a newfound hope blazed throughout Judah. Perhaps these young men, like Gideon, Samson, and David, were Jerusalem's new deliverers. And before long, because everyone hoped they were, everyone believed they were.

Everyone, that is, except Jeremiah the prophet of the Most High.

Jeremiah had never wavered from his warnings about the imminent destruction of Jerusalem by Nebuchadnezzar. But after thirty-eight years of threats without any results, he had become a laughingstock. Especially so, because all the other prophets, promising peace and security, had been right: Jerusalem was at peace and Jerusalem was secure. Furthermore, the other prophets, in order to keep Jeremiah the laughingstock, never tired of reminding the city that it was Jeremiah, not Nebuchadnezzar, who threatened "if a nation does not bow to Babylon, the Lord will punish that nation with sword, famine, and plague until he destroys it by Nebuchadnezzar's hand," quickly adding that Nebuchadnezzar was far too busy building palaces and canals to go off to war. If he did go to war, it would be against Egypt, not against a land he had already conquered, especially one with no military or economic value. Finally and most importantly, the God of Israel would never use mere mortal men, especially Babylonian men, to destroy his city. *If* the Lord Almighty was going to destroy his city, which he was not going to do, but *if* he was, he would use angelic hosts or fire coming down from heaven or some other supernatural sign to prove it was his work and, thus, to his glory. The God of Israel would never use an uncircumcised dog to trample his Most Holy Place to the dog's glory. This last line was the prophets' favorite, bringing on an explosion of cheers and, even better, a shower of coins.

Zedekiah King of Jerusalem agreed with all the other prophets. Hence, he took it upon himself to defy the mightiest kingdom on earth. He had not always been so defiant. In fact, in the beginning of his reign, he was grateful Nebuchadnezzar had appointed him king. So much so, he eagerly joined Babylon's much-touted League of Mutual Assistance. As a League member, Jerusalem could trade throughout Babylon's empire, adding to Jerusalem's wealth and stature. But Zedekiah soon discovered

Jerusalem had nothing to trade because Babylon took it all. Riding into the city at will, Babylon's warriors ravaged the palace, stripped the temple, plundered the fields, and took captives. In other words, Jerusalem received nothing while Babylon took everything, and King Zedekiah was unwilling to bow his neck any longer.

So, one bright sunny morning, after months of listening to the city elders telling him to be a prudent king and submit to Babylon, and months of listening to his peers demanding he be a real king and fight, King Zedekiah ascended the stairs of the Jerusalem wall followed by fifty young, eager, and completely inexperienced Hebrew soldiers carrying fiery torches. For Zedekiah, it did not matter that they were wearing only frayed tunics and ragged sandals. Nor did it matter that they were armed with mere butcher knives and hoes. What mattered was that each young man wore a blue sash, the uniform of Jerusalem's infant army, and he, the King of Jerusalem, was wearing his heavy gold crown and new shiny bronze armor.

Watching his men fan out across the top of the wall, King Zedekiah reviewed his plan. First, his soldiers were going to burn the Babylonian flags flapping robustly along the wall, then raise the Stars of David. Next, he and his men would advance on Babylon's command post and execute the guards assigned to watch the city. After that, he would celebrate. As to the future, he had no plan because Nebuchadnezzar was not going to come all this way to fight a war against one small city. Furthermore, if he did, the God of Abraham, Isaac and Jacob would protect Jerusalem by destroying Babylon as he destroyed the Assyrian army a hundred years before.

For the first time in Zedekiah's life, he could feel his jewel-like eyes gleaming with power, because for the first time in his life, he was doing something kingly: reclaiming the sovereignty of Jerusalem. Moreover, by doing so, he would establish his position forever alongside kings like David and Solomon. He had never felt this way before, destiny throbbing in his chest, exhilarating yet horrifying, as if he was standing on a precipice waiting to jump. King David must have felt this way often. King Solomon too. Certainly Nebuchadnezzar. This was what real kings did, not decorate a throne, but defend their kingdoms.

So King Zedekiah, raising his sword triumphantly, shouted, "Remove Babylon's flags!"

"Halt!" blasted into the air.

Every soldier recognized the voice of Yosef ben-Moshe and obediently jerked to attention. Zedekiah also recognized the voice and, swinging around, saw not only Yosef ben-Moshe hurtling toward him from the stairwell, but Baruch ben-Zadok and Jeremiah as well.

"I said remove those flags!" Zedekiah yelled.

The soldiers pretended not to hear because the presence of Jerusalem's chief commander along with Baruch ben-Zadok, the finest of all warriors, and Jeremiah, the prophet of the Most High, carried far more weight than the flailing arms of their king demanding a dangerous insurrection.

Furious, Zedekiah was about to repeat his command, but Yosef ben-Moshe grabbed him and pulled him in close. "You are getting us into a war we cannot win," he whispered so his men could not hear.

"I rule Jerusalem, not that uncircumcised Babylonian dog," countered Zedekiah, surprised he was talking so forcefully to the veteran commander. Usually, he was intimidated by his jagged scar and rope burns, but not today. Why should he be? He was the king.

"What about our men?" demanded Yosef ben-Moshe, keeping his voice low. "Not one of them has body armor. Only one out of three has a sword. Their shields are made of wicker."

"Wicker, ben-Moshe?" the king challenged. "The Lord Almighty is our shield!" Ignited by the thrill of having the Lord Almighty at his fingertips, he yanked away and was about to repeat his command, but this time Jeremiah cut him off.

"If you do this, King Zedekiah, the Lord Almighty will send his servant Nebuchadnezzar and destroy Jerusalem."

"Nebuchadnezzar is not the Lord's servant! I am King of Jerusalem! Therefore, I am the Lord's servant! And I say, the Lord will defend us." He waited for his warriors to cheer, but no one made a sound. Nevertheless, he was not giving up. He had swallowed his first kingly morsel and had no intention of spitting it out because of some defunct prophet. So he continued, "Do you forget the Lord's glory and His Name dwell in our Temple? No man can destroy it. And anyone who tries..."

"The Lord," interjected Jeremiah, "has sent his prophets to warn Jerusalem to obey him. But instead of listening to them or responding to the Lord's discipline..."

"The Lord is not against Jerusalem!" Zedekiah blared back, trying to stop him. "The Lord is for Jerusalem!"

But Jeremiah had no intention of stopping, shouting to the young faces up and down the line, "The men of Judah and the people of Jerusalem have turned their backs on the Lord following the stubbornness of their evil hearts…"

"No!"

"…setting their eyes on dishonest gain, shedding innocent blood…"

"No! No!"

"…placing their abominations in the House that bears His Name, building shrines to the Baals in the Valley of Ben Hinnom…"

"No! No! No!" Zedekiah cranked his head to the left, glaring at his soldiers along the wall, then cranked it to the right, shouting for all fifty to hear, "If you, Jeremiah, are a true prophet of God, explain this! You say I will be taken to Babylon? Well, what about the prophet Ezekiel? He also claims to speak the word of the Lord, and he says I will never see Babylon. Which is it?!" After making sure his men understood the glaring contradiction, he turned to Baruch ben-Zadok. "Arrest this traitor."

Baruch did not move.

"Baruch ben-Zadok," threatened Zedekiah, despising him because he had been trained by Yosef ben-Moshe and looked as fierce as any Babylonian warrior, especially in his leather armor. Zedekiah suddenly wished he had worn leather instead of bronze. He also wished he had Baruch's curly black hair instead of his own lank braids, and Baruch's brown eyes, solid like the earth, instead of his own glittery emerald eyes.

"My king, I will burn every Babylonian flag here," stated Baruch, "but I will never arrest the prophet of God."

"Then burn them," Zedekiah dared.

"No!" ordered Yosef ben-Moshe.

Baruch wanted to obey Aridatha's father because he admired him more than any other man except his brother Hananiah and the prophet Jeremiah. In fact, Baruch had convinced his three friends, Ishri, Reuben, and Eli, not to participate in today's insurrection because Yosef ben-Moshe had not approved of it. But ever since the day Babylon took his brother and almost killed Aridatha, he had prayed for an opportunity to fight back. Burning a few flags was not much, but with the choices set before him: arresting Jeremiah, going to prison for disobeying the king, or setting off a war against Babylon, it was a start. So Baruch ben-Zadok grabbed a torch from a soldier, yanked down a Babylonian flag, plunged the flame into it, and watched the proud wings of Babylon burn.

Up and down the line, Zedekiah's soldiers followed Baruch's lead, burning the flags of Babylon, then raising the flags of Jerusalem. As the Stars of David ascended, King Zedekiah motioned for his men to take Jeremiah away. After the prophet's footsteps could no longer be heard, Zedekiah King of Jerusalem swaggered to the edge of the wall, looked out at the distant horizon, and declared for all of history to hear, "Now let the servant of the Lord Almighty come."

28

Ten-year-old Michael ben-Ram stood on top of the Jerusalem wall staring out at a faraway dust cloud. It was up to him to decide if Babylon was stirring up that haze or if it was just another windstorm blasting across the land. As he examined the growing yellow stain, his blood pounded hard against his temples because it took fierce concentration to search through long distances for something as small as a spearhead, banner, or torch. Besides, after ten days of watching, his gifted eyes were growing weary. But Michael ben-Ram was not about to give in to weariness or strained eyes, for he, and he alone, had been singled out by Chief Commander Yosef ben-Moshe to watch for the armies of Babylon, and if he saw anything, anything at all, he was to report it immediately.

Watching through dust, rain, and sleet, Michael had not once been intimidated by the thought of oncoming Babylon, because after overhearing an argument between Yosef ben-Moshe's war-trained daughter, Aridatha, and his war-trained commander Baruch ben-Zadok, he was confident the Fourth Man was going to burn Babylon and give Jerusalem the victory. Even now he wondered if the Fourth Man had already given Jerusalem the victory because when the fire signals from Lachish died out ten days ago, the outpost commander sent word that Nebuchadnezzar's armies were on the move. However, no spears, banners, or torches had yet surfaced, causing Michael to wonder if Nebuchadnezzar, quaking in his boots over the Fourth Man, had made a breakneck dash back to Babylon, leaving his armies choking in his dust.

Such happy thoughts always made him hungry and he was about to grab some cheese and olives, but thinking he saw something, he looked again. Was it a banner? Or perhaps a spearhead? Pacing back and forth as the soldiers did, his red hair tangled, his lips chapped, and apple-green eyes bloodshot, he searched the dust storm. As always, there was nothing. So chomping into his meal, he whispered, "We are waiting for you, Nebuchadnezzar. Or are you, King of Babylon, afraid of Jerusalem?"

Most of Jerusalem, feeling exactly like Michael ben-Ram, talked about Nebuchadnezzar as if he had nothing better to do than plot schemes against the City of David. Consequently, it might have been a bit humbling to know that Jerusalem was the last thing on his mind, his every nerve watching for his spies returning from Egypt, while simultaneously trying to calm his bucking warhorse. He certainly sympathized with the steed because his own blood was equally hot for battle, but moving armies required a plodding cadence. Arioch's cavalry and Nergal's charioteers were following at a brisk pace, but Gaspar's slow tribal levies and the even slower ox-carts laden with siege works were dragging behind. So turning his horse around, the king forced him to canter in the opposite direction, and soon the horse settled down.

Nebuchadnezzar, however, did not. He had been out of sorts since leaving Babylon, not because of the usual wartime setbacks, because there had been none. The entire campaign had been flawless: not one turned ankle, disengaged chariot wheel, or torn flag. Armor had arrived weeks before departure, warhorses and chariots delivered without delay, even the tribal levies had reached their deployment posts ahead of schedule. The weather had been perfect, the food abundant, and the battles won with relative ease. Considering all this, coupled with the fact he had not had one bad dream, one would have thought he would have been buoyant! Ecstatic! Rejoicing!

Instead, throughout the journey he had been ill-tempered and surly, challenging every commander with a raging tirade or a grueling silence, unable to eat or sleep. Not surprisingly, Crown Prince Gaspar seized the opportunity to promote himself, spreading the rumor his father was out of sorts because he was afraid of encountering the Fourth Man again.

Arioch was furious and would have gladly throttled the Crown Prince, but because Nebuchadnezzar had ordered hands-off, all he could do was glower. Then, gathering his commanders, he explained in his usual brusque manner that the king's dour mood was not because of the Fourth Man, but because of Egypt. By declaring Zedekiah's rebellion an act of war, Nebuchadnezzar had created an opportunity to place his finest armies in the Judean territory, hoping to lure Egypt north to defend it. If Pharaoh marched, Babylon's war chariots, cavalries, and archers would be in position to slaughter his armies, race across the border, and conquer the Nile. That, at least, had been the plan. But so far, not one Egyptian boot had tip-toed across Egyptian lines. No wonder the king was out of sorts. To come all this way with the greatest military might on earth only to waste it on an impoverished land instead of the Prince of the Nile was no cause for joy.

Dismissing the commanders, Arioch rode off in a foul mood. More than once, he had offered to lock up the Crown Prince and throw the key away, but Nebuchadnezzar had always ignored him. Moreover, as far as he could tell, the king also ignored Chenguang's reports about the Grand Preceptor Au Yang communicating secretly with Gaspar, sending him armor, horses, and weapons, and, most importantly, promising to support a coup against Nebuchadnezzar. What was he waiting for? It would be so easy to take down both Gaspar and Au Yang. Or did the king still think nothing could shake him?

Perhaps Arioch's frustration was a bit strident because he hated Gaspar and Au Yang, and could do nothing about it. Then again, perhaps he was out of sorts because it was he who was afraid of the Fourth Man. Moreover, sooner or later, he knew he was going to have to tell the king he should be afraid of him, too.

⸺⸙⸺

Michael ben-Ram rubbed his strained eyes and then looked back at the horizon. As usual, nothing was there, and because the wind had died and the sunlight was warming his back, he started to hum. Nothing particular, just one of the songs played in the park on Sabbath. Halfway through the happy melody, *Yields seed for the sower and bread for the eater*, he saw it. Only a flash far away, but it was there: the tip of a spearhead. Not visible to the normal eye, but to his exceptional eyesight a glowing beacon, exactly what he had been looking for. However, instead of whooping with delight, he did not utter a peep because he could not breathe. Furthermore, his knees were buckling, his head swimming, and his eyes welling with tears. If this was his reaction to the sight of a mere spearhead, he would surely explode and die at the sight of the entire Babylonian army.

Somewhere inside a voice spoke up, telling him to run to Chief Commander Yosef ben-Moshe. He was then supposed to stand on his ten-year-old legs and announce proudly, "They are coming." But Michael ben-Ram could not run because deeper inside, the voice of Jeremiah was echoing like thunder, crushing his confidence in Aridatha's Fourth Man with the prophetic words: "'I have determined to do this city harm and not good,' declares the Lord. 'It will be given into the hands of the King of Babylon and he will destroy it with fire.'"

The soldier next to him, the one who had given him the cheese and olives, looked at the shivering boy curiously. "What is it, Michael?"

Crumpling to the floor, Michael ben-Ram moaned, "They are coming."

29

It was the dead of night, black as the netherworld, and Arioch riding alongside Nebuchadnezzar wanted to turn back. However, the king had ordered him to accompany him to the Jerusalem wall, so with one hand clutching his sword and the other ready to grab his bow, he grumbled silently over the senseless risk. Yes, he might once again gallop across a burning bridge to follow Nebuchadnezzar. And yes, he might once again ride into a Chinese capital on Nebuchadnezzar's words nothing can shake me. But he was not so sure about himself, or his king, when it came to sauntering into the Fourth Man's territory: Jerusalem.

Even without the Fourth Man, Babylon's armies had just arrived on the outskirts of Jerusalem that morning, so it did not take wits to assume every Hebrew would be on full alert, ready to shoot anything that moved, especially the King of Babylon. Of course, Arioch understood the need for a last-minute reconnaissance of an unknown city laden with mysterious hazards, but every detail of the Jerusalem wall—its height, width, age, gates, stairwells, nooks, and crannies—had been mapped and studied by every Babylonian warrior until he could navigate it blindfolded. There was simply nothing else to know. So what was the King of Babylon looking for in such gloomy darkness?

Curiously, Nebuchadnezzar was having the same thoughts. Not about impending danger, because nothing could shake him. Instead, he was musing over the strange urgency that had drawn him out on this midnight ride. Starting with the first stones set by Shem to the great expansion of Solomon, he already knew every detail of the wall and its history. So what had lured him? What was he looking for that he did not already know?

"Arioch," he whispered.

"Yes, my lord?" Arioch readied to turn his horse around.

"Remember Shining One's great Babylonian epic?"

Arioch rolled his eyes. Of course, he remembered and it was not even close to *let's get out of here.*

"'I will ascend to the heights,'" Nebuchadnezzar breathed as if he could actually ascend into the unknown and unreachable heavens. "I will raise my throne above the stars, I will ascend above the...'"

"I know, I know..." Arioch groaned. "Nothing can shake you."

Nebuchadnezzar swung his horsewhip out so fast the night air jumped, but not Arioch. His face drawn, he was staring out so bleakly, Nebuchadnezzar did not have the heart to whiplash him. "Arioch, are you well?"

"Forgive me, my lord, but I do not think we should be riding this close to the wall."

"Why not? There is no one in sight."

It was true, not one human form could be seen. In fact, the wall with its gigantic stones rooted in antiquity and climbing into the night looked so ghostly, Arioch wondered if the Fourth Man had put the city to sleep and was now standing guard. "I cannot help thinking," he murmured, his voice as quiet as grass, "about King Sennacherib and Assyria a hundred years ago."

"Ancient history."

"Not ancient. Your grandfather was here building tents when Sennacherib's armies were wiped out overnight by plague. Miraculously!"

"Miraculously?" scoffed Nebuchadnezzar. "Arioch, it was rats."

"Yes, my lord," he mumbled, a bit ashamed for mentioning Assyria, because compared to the Fourth Man, rats and plagues were trifles. However, he had hoped that by mentioning the demise of Sennacherib's armies in the same breath with "miraculously," Nebuchadnezzar might have considered that those rats did not appear by ordinary means, and from there, perhaps his thoughts would have wafted to the Fourth Man.

"Arioch..."

"Yes, my lord?"

"I have the strongest sense..." The king paused to stare up at the Hebrew flags. Their Stars of David reminded him of something gentle and engaging. What was it? Unable to pinpoint it, he said, "I have the strongest sense when Jerusalem is gone, my dreams will be gone."

"My king!" Arioch whispered, motioning toward the turret ahead.

At the top of the tower stood a lone figure in a shock of moonlight, its robe and sash rippling in the breeze, its sword and bow lurking in the shadows. Was it a vision or was it real? A specter or flesh? How long had it been standing there watching them? Nebuchadnezzar started to call out to demand an accounting, but the moonlight disappeared and with it the lone figure. Even so, he kept staring, his mind flooded with images: the Three Hebrews living in his fiery furnace, the Fourth Man looking like a son of the gods, the Chinese word *yi* written in the dirt in front of Tin's seat, and a child with chestnut hair, her voice chirping, "Me? Why should I be afraid?" He even heard his own voice echoing, "Then, Aridatha, you and I will both remember the Fourth Man."

"If it pleases the king," implored Arioch, "replace King Zedekiah with a new king. A king who will keep your League of Mutual Assistance Treaty. Then we can leave Jerusalem as it is and…"

"Leave Jerusalem?"

"Yes, leave!"

The king stared at Arioch as if he had grown another head.

"King Nebuchadnezzar, you came here because of Egypt. But Egypt did not come out and fight. Now what are you going to do? Can Babylon's fire burn Jerusalem? Burn their Temple of Solomon? The Ark of the Covenant, too?"

"Babylon's fire can burn anything. And if I did not know you better, I would say you are afraid."

"I am afraid."

"You are not!"

"Not just for me. But for Babylon. And for you."

"Me?" Nebuchadnezzar objected, still searching the top of the wall, hoping the figure would reappear. "Why me?"

Sucking in a breath, Arioch braced himself, then blurted, "Because I believe in their God."

"You what?!"

"I said I believe in their…"

"Stop!" the king erupted, not wanting to hear it again. "You cannot believe in their God. You believe in Babylon's gods, Marduk and Ishtar. You believe in Shining One Son of Dawn, Prince of the Power of the…"

"Of course, I do."

"Then what are you talking about?"

"I do not know."

"Then stop talking!"

"King Nebuchadnezzar. When Daniel told you your dream and then interpreted it, I thought it clever magic. That was all: clever magic. But ever since the day the Fourth Man appeared in your fiery furnace…"

"Nonsense, that day never existed."

"I suppose the Fourth Man, whom we both saw with our own eyes, never existed either."

"All right," huffed the king, "If it makes you feel better, he exists."

"No, it does not make me feel better."

"Nor I," sighed Nebuchadnezzar. "But don't you see, Arioch? His very existence is why I must conquer Jerusalem: to prove Daniel's interpretation wrong. To prove Babylon crushes all kingdoms and will endure forever. Not some rock."

"But, my lord, consider the cost. You are alone in this. None of Babylon's gods, not even Shining One, have the power to help you. Not against the Fourth Man. You could lose everything."

"Lose everything?" the king exploded, his voice still a noiseless whisper. "Arioch, I lost everything on the day that Fourth Man trespassed into my kingdom killing my warriors and saving the very Hebrews who interpreted my dream. On that day, uninvited and unsolicited, he overruled my law in my own land. Right before my eyes! Right before everyone's eyes! It was outrageous. Uncalled for. Nevertheless, I have generously stayed away from his land, treating Judah and Jerusalem like any other nation but, Arioch," his voice dropped to a low growl, "they are not like any other nation."

Arioch was about to wholeheartedly agree, eager to tell the king about the fiery metal cages he saw that day, but their war-trained horses suddenly stepped back. Drawing their swords, they searched the darkness. When nothing stirred, not even the flags on the wall, Nebuchadnezzar ordered, "Come out. Come out where I can see you."

It was a long eerie moment before a lone figure stepped away from the wall. The same figure that was on the turret. But here, against the backdrop of Jerusalem's ancient stones, her rippling sash looked less ghostly, her sword less menacing.

"You should not have come," she said.

No longer a child's chirp, her voice pulsed warmly through the air, the Stars of David fluttering at her ankles just as gentle and engaging as before. Indeed, she was more beautiful than he had thought she would be, and it pleased him to say, "I know you."

"Papa calls you the servant of the Lord Almighty."

"Remind your father, I serve no one."

Her eyes flashed. "You have not changed."

"No, but you have." Dismounting, he stepped toward her. A gold filigree chain adorned her brow matching the chains woven through her seven braids hanging far below her waist. Her lips glistened, her skin beckoned, and her eyes, as dark as night, gleamed with that same steady inner light. "You have grown up."

"You said I would." Reaching out, she took his hand as she did when she was a girl, and instantly she was swimming in a happiness she had not known since that day.

Not so Nebuchadnezzar. The touch of her hand flooded him with an urgent right of possession. "You should not be here," he exclaimed. "What is your father thinking?"

"What are you talking about?"

"You are in danger. You must leave for Babylon at once."

"Babylon? Why should I go to Babylon? The Fourth Man is going to save us and burn you to the ground."

"Be reasonable."

"I am being reasonable. Reason dictates you are the one who should leave. That is why I came looking for you tonight."

"You? Came looking for me?" He pressed his other hand around hers.

"Someone had to warn you," she said a bit shrilly, for her childhood happiness was quickly melting into the heat of his hands, accompanied by a never-before-felt sensation of flying. So she yanked her hand away. "Obviously, you do not remember the Fourth Man."

"You still want to protect me, don't you, Aridatha? Like the day in the furnace arena."

"I did not protect you."

Her name warmed his tongue like a summer red wine, and wanting another taste, he said it again, "Aridatha."

"King Nebuchadnezzar, do you know what happened to King Sennacherib one hundred years ago? His armies surrounded Jerusalem—just as your armies did today—but they did not shoot one arrow over our wall. Do you know why?"

Arioch grunted his approval, his esteem for this young woman growing by the moment. But Nebuchadnezzar just stared at her, ringed in light, her fragrance like a meadow, her heart a resting place for the mighty. He remembered once thinking she was like a deer, more beautiful free than caged.

"King Nebuchadnezzar, did you hear me? Not one arrow over our wall because they all died," she announced pointedly. "Died overnight. From plague. Now they are gone. However, as you see, Jerusalem still stands."

"The Assyrians are gone because I destroyed them," he stated flatly. "You said you were going to marry Baruch ben-Zadok."

A sudden confusion caught her breath. How did he remember? Especially Baruch's name?

"Did you?" he queried.

"I did not come out here in the middle of the night to talk about me," she stammered, her cheeks burning. "I came to remind you about the Fourth Man."

"Did you marry him?"

Why did he want to know? What did it matter to him? "No, my lord, I did not."

"Why?"

Why? How many times had she asked herself the same question? Every time Baruch had asked her father for her hand, she had wondered why she kept putting him off with one excuse after another. So, shaking her head, she whispered more to herself than to the king, "I do not know why."

"I do," the king replied, stepping up to her.

Only inches apart, his scent of cedar and myrrh engulfed her, sending her heart hammering and thoughts spinning. Quickly, she turned to leave, but not quickly enough. He was already holding her in his arms, one hand clasping the back of her neck, the other tipping her face upward. She watched him lean in and rest his lips on hers, but she was not fooled. This was not an act of affection or love. He was trying to persuade her to go to Babylon, and determined not to be persuaded, she did not kiss back. However, she did not resist either.

At the touch of her lips, heat and ice shot through Nebuchadnezzar's veins with such force, his head spun. Certainly, this was not what he had intended. He had intended to overpower her, so she would come to Babylon. Instead, her warmth had rushed him so completely, he had had to jerk away. Nevertheless, the heat and ice were still there. So much so, both the king and the man knew that someday he would have to possess her, all of her: her heart, her soul and her flesh.

"You cannot stay here," he declared.

"Yes, I can," she replied with irritatingly clear eyes.

"Aridatha, tomorrow I am going to destroy Jerusalem."

"I am Jerusalem."

It hit him hard, reminding him of the moment in the tunnel when she said Jerusalem would be the victor of the final battle. Yes, she had grown up, but she had not changed, her shoulders thrown back, staring at him like a judge in a courtroom. "You may be Jerusalem, Aridatha, but never forget," his eyes turned treacherous, "I am Babylon."

She wondered if her crimson pouch still lay over his heart. Her good sense told her no, and with that, she said, "Until tomorrow." Without waiting for a response, she turned and disappeared into the shadows of the wall.

Arioch stared with admiration but King Nebuchadnezzar, even though his jaw was grinding, stared with satisfaction, for the mystery of his midnight ride to the Jerusalem wall had cleared. Aridatha had drawn him out and he was pleased, for she brought him good luck.

30

THE next morning hundreds of birds flew into Jerusalem trilling so happily everyone assumed the Lord Almighty had sent them as harbingers of the city's victory. No one even considered that similar choruses might be trilling over the Babylonian encampment. But there they were, just as noisy and just as cheerful amidst Marduk's banners and Ishtar's wreathes, brightening up the command post with lively melodies. However, unlike Jerusalem, Babylon did not notice. Too immersed in the last-minute preparations for war, even the mouthwatering aromas of roasting lamb made no impact on Nebuchadnezzar's commanders reviewing timelines and maps, his scribes packing up parchments and pens, and his tight-lipped warriors oiling their shields and swords. Tense, organized, and disciplined, the anticipation of a swift victory buzzed excitedly through the command post until someone shouted, "Is the king sleeping in this morning?"

No one actually froze, but Gaspar's familiar voice certainly shattered the unified focus on Nebuchadnezzar's war, throwing each man into a world of his own, wondering what to do. If one answered, "Yes, my prince, the king is sleeping in," he would be insulting the king. But to answer, "No, my prince, the king is not sleeping in," would contradict Gaspar and thereby insult him. Wouldn't you know? With only twenty minutes before mounting up for battle, Crown Prince Gaspar once again was rearing his ugly ambitions, forcing them to choose between the king and the heir, and it took each man's tactical prowess to know how to choose both. The safest route seemed to be silence in order to protect one's position with the king while respectfully turning to acknowledge Gaspar's presence.

But Gaspar knew how to win the men over, and slathering onions on his meat, he grinned, "Doesn't he always sleep late after one of his *nasty* dreams?"

He said *nasty* with such exaggerated fright, they could not help but chortle. Yes, Nebuchadnezzar's dreams had heightened his mystique, but their terrifying impact, whispered throughout the palace by the women he slept with, had reduced him to their own mortal level, pleasing them greatly. Besides, it was prudent to occasionally laugh at Gaspar's jokes because someday he would be king.

Arioch smoldered at the spectacle. The king's dreams were no laughing matter. Nebuchadnezzar feared them because they were indeed terrifying, revealing mysteries far greater than any ordinary man could handle, telling of future kingdoms and nations, powers and destructions. The fact he had been chosen to receive such revelations should have instilled awe, not mockery, especially from his own son. Oh, how he waited for the day when the king would give him the order to challenge Gaspar.

The thought of going sword to sword with the Crown Prince usually put him in a sprightly mood, but this morning nothing could dispel his anxiety over the hundreds of birds flying in to greet the dawn. He had never heard such jubilation in the feathered kingdom, and like Jerusalem, he was inclined to believe they were messengers announcing the coming of the Fourth Man. In fact, if he had not been in charge of the command post, he would have hurried to the royal tent to see if Aridatha's midnight visit to the wall had prompted the king to start packing.

But Nebuchadnezzar was not even close to packing. Whistling just as brightly as the birds overhead, he was sorting through bows, deciding which one to use for the day. He had the finest collection in the world, so taking his time, he admired the hardwood overlays of the cream-colored flat bow, the balance of the Chinese composite bow, and the grip of the smaller whalebone bow. They were all works of precision and beauty, yet he returned them for the bronze. Not as comely as the others, but its reliability was unparalleled. Yes, the bow of bronze would be the extension of his arm for today. Next, he considered the array of arrows set before him. Again, the finest collection in the world, but after Aridatha's admonition about Sennacherib's armies not shooting one arrow over the Jerusalem wall, he had decided to bring only one arrow. So with fingers tapping, he chose the one with the razor blade fletching.

Lastly, he turned to an alabaster box, opened it reverently, and gazed down at the royal pendant of Babylon seated on a small gold pillow. To him, the pendant was more than a crest or an emblem. It was his authority, his power, his glory: Babylon the Great, past, present, and future. So, when he reached to pick it up and his hand jerked and knocked it to the ground, he was mortified. Quickly lunging to retrieve it, he stumbled to the ground, his breath labored, his legs trembling, his hands stiff like boards. Everything was slowing down until sound became a drawn-out yowl and objects were buried in shadows. Leaping up, he rubbed his eyes, but that only made it worse, now everything was a blur. Why was he so stiff? Why was the room rising and falling? What was going on? What was happening? Then he knew…

"Plague!" he gasped.

Like the Assyrians a hundred years before, instant death to all his men unless Arioch ordered a full retreat now. But how could he order a retreat? It was still night. No, that was not right. The sun had just risen. He had seen its first rays. But why was it dark now? Rubbing his eyes again, he kept them closed and waited. Then popping them open, he glared out only to see darkness everywhere. Frantic, he waved his hand in front of his face, his very own hand, but he could not see it.

"No!" he commanded, shaking his head back and forth, blinking again and again. When light still did not appear, he pounded his sockets, proclaiming, "I cannot be blind. I will not be blind." To prove it, he stepped boldly toward the tent entrance, slammed into his cedar chest, and crashed to the ground. Looking frantically for light, searching desperately for form, he knew his quest was over. Babylon was lost.

"Gone!" he groaned. "Vanquished… By rats."

A great wind screeched in, driving in hundreds of bat-like creatures, real yet not real, phantoms swirling around him, diving into his hair, biting his legs, fastening onto his face, shrieking, "There is no plague!"

He tried to slap them away, but they kept flying in. Hordes attacking him, so he threw his arms over his head and cringed into a ball.

"Get up, you coward," they squealed. "There is no plague. Get up, you coward. There is no…"

"I am no coward," he objected. "I am Nebuchadnezzar!"

"Then get up and fight. There is no plague."

The bats nipped at his shaking hands, forcing them away from his face and onto the floor, pushing them toward his fallen glory: the royal pendant of Babylon. Latching onto it, he wrestled it over his head and placed it at his heart. "Nothing can shake me," he panted. "I will ascend to the heights. I will sit enthroned…"

Like magic, the bats retreated. But Nebuchadnezzar, shivering from sweats and chills, did not notice. Hanging onto to Shining One's epic, he just kept gasping, "I will ascend to the heights. I will sit enthroned on the mount of assembly…" As he spoke, the darkness brightened, and forms once again took shape. "I will raise my throne above the stars of God, I will raise my throne above…" With each word, he could see more: the sunlight streaming in… the tent entrance… his cedar chest… his bows and arrows. Could it be by speaking Shining One's words, he was breaking the power of the plague? Were Shining One's words setting him free?

"I will raise my throne above the stars of God!" he shouted, and sure enough, his blood ran warm again. Marveling at such power, he leapt to his feet, threw his shoulders back, and breathed in, "I will ascend!" He breathed out, "I will ascend!" Thus he breathed the words in and out until his heart, his lungs, his every sinew, and his every nerve were rekindled by the burning force of Babylon. Indeed, nothing could shake him, and grabbing his bow and one arrow, he marched out of his tent.

<hr />

Inside Jerusalem, sunbeams streamed in through Aridatha's open windows awakening the room with a festive mirth, the walls glittering with reds sparkling from the rubies on her sword hilt, blues from the sapphires on her veils, and greens from the emeralds on her tiaras. The cheerful display surrounded her, dancing from wall to wall, but she did not notice. Nor did she notice the jubilant bird songs chorusing over Jerusalem. In fact, since being held in Nebuchadnezzar's arms outside the wall in the middle of the night, she had not noticed anything except his fragrance of cedar and myrrh still sealed on her lips. Troubled by his kiss, she had not slept, not because she was thinking about his kiss, but because she was wondering why he jerked away. Had she not been attractive to him? Had she done something wrong? Of course, she did not care. Or perhaps it was because she had not returned his kiss? No, that would not cause a man, especially a king, to retreat.

As she wondered about his kiss, her thoughts drifted back to when she was three years old and Baruch was eight. Wanting to see the small circle, she had hurried alongside Baruch up the steep steps of the Jerusalem wall. When she could not keep pace, he had picked her up, and as the men of Jerusalem hurtled down the steps, they both declared they were not afraid because they trusted in the scrolls. Then she kissed him on the lips, and promised that whatever happened, she loved him. Not an hour later, Daniel, Hananiah, Mishael, and Azariah were captured by Babylon, she was almost dead, and Jeremiah had given her the crimson pouch.

But something more had happened that day, something that had changed her life. She did not know exactly when it happened, but over the years she had pinpointed it to either the moment she hit the wall and lost her words or the moment Jeremiah gave her the crimson pouch. Furthermore, she did not know what had happened. But, whatever it was, she had started to suspect it had kept her from marrying Baruch, and because she had not married Baruch, Nebuchadnezzar's kiss was on her lips.

Now, once again, she wanted to go to the top of the wall and see Babylon. More specifically, she wanted to see King Nebuchadnezzar. Did he really believe he could take on the Fourth Man and win? Or had he heeded her warning about King Sennacherib and ordered a retreat? As if answering her question, Babylon's horns blasted into the air, and she knew Nebuchadnezzar's armies, instead of retreating, were marching, which meant the King of Babylon would soon be riding toward the wall. Knowing it would be his final ride, everything in her wanted to be there, but her father had ordered her to stay in her room. So she faced a decision much like the one at Dura when her father sent her back to camp. Should she obey her father and never see the king again? Impossible. She had to see him. So, cinching on her blue army sash, she grabbed her weapons and sneaked out the back way.

As Aridatha ran toward her father's stables, Babylon's armies approached Jerusalem from all sides. Marching to the cadence of blaring horns, regiment after regiment filled the four horizons until the skyline looked like one vast iron shield encircling Jerusalem. It was such a terrifying spectacle, it took each Hebrew soldier's concentrated courage just to stand at attention. But stand they did, and if any needed to evacuate or throw up, he did it discreetly, then returned to his post. Finally, the horns stopped, the signal the city was surrounded, and for miles nothing could be heard except armor rattling, horses snorting, and flags flapping. However, when Nebuchadnezzar's commander Nergal raised his standard, even the armor, horses, and flags cringed into silence because the King of Babylon was cresting the olive mount.

As he came into view, the sun struck his royal pendant, shooting rays of scarlet, purple, and gold flashing over his armies. His men had never seen the pendant up close, but they knew it was a replica of the heavenly sign Kesith the Archer with its constellation Dahrach the Dragon. However, the Dragon on the pendant, instead of being an ordinary coiling serpent like in the constellation, had the wings of an eagle. Furthermore, instead of the Dragon being cast down by the Archer like in the constellation, the pendant had both the Archer and the Dragon ascending. This was the Great Seal of Babylon, and as it poured streams of light over her amassed armies, the men felt waves of power flooding through them. Power that came not from the pendant, but from Nebuchadnezzar. For he was the man in Shining One's epic, and in him, they were each part of the epic.

So Babylon's warriors, slowly and reverently, pounded their swords against their shields and hammered their spears against the ground until the sky was a wall of ringing iron and the ground a floor of shattering rock. With such force raging about them, they knew they were no longer simple men, but a great historic will being fulfilled through their king, and swept away by their destiny, they pounded faster and harder. Thus, with the sky rattling overhead and the earth quaking below, Aridatha galloped out of her father's stables and into the groves. From there, she raced across the flags, hoping to make it beyond the outdoor kitchens without being noticed. Even so, as she neared the ovens, she heard her mother cry, "Your father told you to stay in your room."

Pretending not to hear, she spurred her horse faster, but her mother chased after her, shouting, "Only the army is supposed to be on top of that wall."

"I am in the army," Aridatha shouted back.

"Aridatha!"

"What?" The daughter ground to a halt.

Grabbing her foot and holding her there, Zillah said, "You saw him last night, didn't you?"

"Who?" the daughter queried innocently.

"You are supposed to marry Baruch ben-Zadok."

Aridatha's heart pounded for the battlefield, not another quarrel with her mother about whom she was supposed to marry.

"Do you love him?" demanded Zillah.

"I have always loved Baruch."

"I am not talking about Baruch! I am talking about Nebuchadnezzar. Do you love him?"

Everything in her wanted to bolt, but instead she forced herself to quietly explain, "Nebuchadnezzar is papa's friend. I only…"

"Friend?!" shrieked Zillah. "He is a Babylonian! And you…" she sputtered furiously, "You are a Hebrew!"

"I know I am a Hebrew!" Aridatha shot back. "Probably more than you do!" She immediately regretted her anger. She and her mother had always been at odds, but perhaps it was her own fault. She had never really given herself to her mother. So she decided to bare her heart and, in a moment of rare tenderness, whispered, "Mother, don't you know? I am Jerusalem."

"Jerusalem?!" scoffed Zillah. "You?! What is that supposed to mean?"

The daughter smiled sadly. "Ask Nebuchadnezzar. He knows." Before her mother could object, she tugged her foot free and galloped out the gate.

31

KING Nebuchadnezzar raised his arm and a throat-dry hush filled the land. This was it. The King of Babylon was about to speak. What would he say? Would he give King Zedekiah a chance to recant, or would he demand his head? Would he boast against the God of Abraham, Isaac and Jacob as Sennacherib had done, or would he boast for his own gods? Whatever it was, both sides had to wait, because although his arm was raised, he did not speak. Instead, he scanned the top of the wall as if looking for something. Long silent moments turned into long silent minutes, and as his scowl tightened, both armies began to fidget. What was wrong? Everyone was in position and waiting. His scribes, their gauzy robes billowing in the breeze, were waiting to write his immortal words; his archers, in leather armor, black sashes, and close-cut beards, were waiting to shoot; his warriors waiting to kill. Then again, perhaps he was not scowling. Perhaps he was just reviewing his hour-long harangue blaming Jerusalem for the war. Or perhaps in all the excitement he had forgotten King Zedekiah's name and could not begin until he remembered it.

"King Zedekiah!" shouted the King of Babylon. "Show your face!"

So that was it. The King of Babylon was looking for the King of Jerusalem. Nothing to fret over. Once that was settled, the courtesies before war-making could proceed. But as the minutes dragged by and King Zedekiah still did not appear, all of Babylon took up the search, whispering earthy jokes about where Zedekiah might be, and although the Hebrews on the wall could not hear their actual words, their faces burned with shame.

"Zedekiah!" hurled again through the air. Followed again by "Show your face!"

Baruch ben-Zadok, his curly black hair shorn for war, remained at stalwart attention as he moved his eyes toward the top of the Tower of

David. That was where his king was supposed to be. They had been rehearsing it all week. As Jerusalem's warriors quick-marched to their positions along the top of the wall, Zedekiah in his leather armor had ascended the Tower of David to the highest platform and delivered oracles and speeches about how the Most High was going to save Jerusalem. But the Hebrew army had been in position for over two hours, and no one was yet standing on the Tower.

Suddenly, an even greater indignity fell upon Jerusalem: six Babylonian voices whispering, "Ze-de-KI-ah. Ze-de-KI-ah." Instantly, it grew from six to twenty voices, from twenty to a hundred, and within moments, thousands upon thousands of Babylonian warriors were gently sing-songing "Ze-de-KI-ah, Ze-de-KI-ah" while tinkling their thousands of iron swords against their thousands of iron shields.

Yosef ben-Moshe, unable to take it any longer, marched into the shadows under the steps of the Tower of David, grabbed Zedekiah, and said, "You started this. Now get up there."

Clinging to his two sons, just boys, Zedekiah's emerald eyes searched for an escape, but Yosef ben-Moshe was grinding his knuckles under his collar bone, forcing his attention back to him.

"Your armies must see you are not afraid."

"I did not know it would be like this."

"Move!"

Wearing magnificent silver-scale armor polished to shine like mirrors, black boots just as polished, and two double-edged swords in lavishly jeweled silver scabbards—all much too heavy and much too hot—King Zedekiah knew he was going to be sick, but there was no time because Yosef ben-Moshe, one hand gripping his neck, the other pressing against his back, was shoving him up the Tower steps. Stumbling onto the third stair, his armor clanging clumsily, he peered out. Jerusalem's roads, her fields, her meadows, her groves, her highlands, and valleys were gone, exchanged for miles and miles of armored men, waves and waves of gleaming swords, and the foul breath of Babylon stinking the skies.

Horrified, King Zedekiah could go no further.

"Is he out there?!" cried a female voice.

Recognizing the voice, Yosef ben-Moshe swung around to see his daughter sprinting toward them from the stairwell.

"Get back!" he ordered.

Instantly, Zedekiah started to retreat. "Not you," Yosef ben-Moshe growled, holding him on the steps.

Ignoring her father's command, Aridatha charged up the stairs taking two at a time to the top of the Tower of David.

During Jerusalem's glory days, the Tower had been dressed with a thousand shields belonging to Jerusalem's finest warriors. When the breeze was gentle, the shields would create a melodious hum, and when the wind kicked up, they would bang and clang so furiously, the city gloried in their song. But Jerusalem's glory soon faded, and one by one, the shields were taken away by Jerusalem's conquerors until the Tower was completely undressed and exposed. Today, however, a young maiden adorned it, the daughter of Yosef ben-Moshe.

Armed with a double-edged sword and the blue sash of Jerusalem's army, she searched through the tribal levies' flags, between the charioteers' banners, and deep into the cavalry's standards, until she found whom she was looking for. He was on horseback next to Arioch, looking exactly as she thought he would: a simple gold band for a crown, gold studs glittering through his hair, and full gold armor shaped to his regal form, dazzling in the sunlight.

"He is looking for you," she called down to Zedekiah.

The King of Jerusalem stared up at her as if she was mad. Of course, Nebuchadnezzar was looking for him. Who else would he be looking for? And who was she to tell him what one king was doing or the other? Furthermore, what right did she have to be so self-assured while he was facing the reality of Babylon? He had a good mind to order her to the whipping post, but he could not speak because his throat was choked with fear.

If Yosef ben-Moshe could have trusted Zedekiah to stay where he was, he would have marched to the top of the Tower, pulled his daughter down, and ordered her home. On the other hand, perhaps it was better he could not, for she had caught the attention of the entire Jerusalem army, drawing all eyes away from their pallid king.

"Throw a flag over the wall," she cried to the soldiers below, "so the King of Babylon can see the King of Jerusalem." Not knowing what to do, they did nothing. So Aridatha hurtled halfway down the steps, grabbed a flag, and returned to the top of the Tower.

"King Nebuchadnezzar," she shouted, waving the Star of David for all of Babylon and Jerusalem to see. "King Zedekiah is over here."

If they had not noticed her before, Babylon's armies certainly noticed her now, their jaws dropping at the sight of Jerusalem's ingenious introduction to their king. The impact was more startling than a thousand shields rattling on a tower, for not only was she beautiful, but she was fearless under that flag, reminding them of three other fearless Hebrews—Shadrach, Meshach, and Abedneggo—the ones who defied Nebuchadnezzar on the day that never existed.

"Over there," Arioch said, motioning to King Zedekiah's head barely visible at the bottom of the Tower. But Nebuchadnezzar like everyone else had forgotten Zedekiah, his attention fully on her, remembering the day he first met her and wondered if she was like other children: running loose, disobedient to their fathers, and recklessly in and out of people's affairs. Quickly, he learned she was not, but was a child of sense, her paths governed by destiny, each step placed purposely in and out of people's affairs. And now here she was again. Nothing planned, just following the path laid out before her, unable to even stop herself. And he, unable to stop himself, turned his horse in her direction, riding straight through his cavalry.

As the horsemen dodged out of his way, more than one infantryman and charioteer took the opportunity to break ranks in order to get a better view. King Nebuchadnezzar had started this war by calling out, "King Zedekiah, show your face." Now what was he going to say? Watching him steer his warhorse toward the vision on the Tower, all strained to hear.

Curiously, when Nebuchadnezzar squared off before her, he said nothing. Yet even in his silence, he seemed to be speaking to her, especially when he raised his one arrow high above his head, not as a threat, but for her to see.

In response, she raised her Star of David flag high above her head, not just for him, but for everyone to see. Then she shouted for everyone to hear, "Remember the Fourth Man!"

Of course, not everyone heard, so "What did she say?" whispered rapidly along the top of the wall and even faster through the ranks of Babylon, each query answered by "Remember the Fourth Man."

For long minutes, nothing but "Remember the Fourth Man... Remember the Fourth Man..." rippled far and wide, spreading like wildfire across the top of the wall and through Babylon's lines, until every man—king, soldier, Babylonian, and Hebrew—did remember. And although Nebuchadnezzar had declared the day never existed, he could see his armies had not quite believed him, because under the Hebrews' spontaneous roar, "Remember the Fourth Man," his men were actually stepping back.

Transfixed by the spectacle, he pondered the turnabout. By simply waving Jerusalem's flag and shouting, "Remember the Fourth Man," Aridatha had ignited confidence in Zedekiah's armies, which only moments before had been cringing in fear. But that was not all! Simultaneously, she had ignited alarm in his armies, which only moments before had been raging with power. On further thought, why should he be surprised? Hadn't she, just the night before, ignited both confidence and alarm in him with the touch of her hand and the taste of her lips?

"I will have her, Arioch," he declared. "I will have her for Babylon."

"Yes, my lord," his commander replied, wondering if Babylon would last the day. For he too was remembering the Fourth Man.

Nebuchadnezzar spotted the intruder first, a Hebrew warrior running up the stairs toward the top of the Tower.

"Who is that?" he demanded.

That was a tall, broad-shouldered young man bounding up the stairs with the ease of a leopard, exuding a strength and stature only found in Babylon's elite. So Arioch, with Nebuchadnezzar and Aridatha's midnight conversation still fresh in his mind, assumed it was Nebuchadnezzar's competition, and thus replied tactfully, "Some Hebrew warrior."

"Some Hebrew warrior?! It is Baruch ben-Zadok and you know it." Watching the young man argue with Aridatha and then grab her arm, Nebuchadnezzar's hand went to his dagger. But when the Hebrew tried to tug her down the steps and she refused to go, his grip slackened. In fact, his heart actually softened for the lad because if it was Baruch ben-Zadok, Aridatha's resistance proved he had no control over her, which was disconcerting to any man, especially a young man. But now his armies were watching the wrangle. Not only had Aridatha scattered his own thoughts and heartbeats in every direction, but his men's also, and he would not have it.

"Jerusalem!" he shouted.

His booming voice sent everyone's attention back to where it belonged: Nebuchadnezzar King of Babylon.

"Assyria never made it through the night!" he roared, his scribes writing furiously. "Babylon has! Assyria never shot one arrow over your wall. Babylon will."

"Shields!" shouted Yosef ben-Moshe.

"Come on, Ari," ordered Baruch.

But Aridatha, waiting to see the Fourth Man strike down the armies of Babylon, refused to go.

"Ari! You have to get off this tower now."

"Baruch," she chided, "King Sennacherib never shot one arrow over this wall."

King Nebuchadnezzar aimed his arrow with the razor blade fletching at a soldier not far from the Tower of David. All eyes followed the arrow's arc, watching it rise into the clear blue sky, hurtle down through the targeted soldier's wicker shield, and slice into his heart. It was Ishri's heart, Jerusalem's first casualty, and as he looked up to the heavens asking *why—why* Nebuchadnezzar had chosen him to kill and *why* the heavens had let him do it—Baruch pulled Aridatha down the steps and, pressing his body against hers, covered her against the onslaught of the arrows pelting down out of the sky.

32

AFTER shooting the first arrow into Jerusalem, Nebuchadnezzar returned to Babylon to do the work he loved most: building his kingdom. From constructing the Gulf Port to erecting bridges across the Euphrates to overseeing the restoration of the Lake, he completed one magnificent feat after another. Even so, nothing satisfied because he was squandering his finest warriors on the siege of Jerusalem instead of trouncing Egypt. Consequently, as the months dragged by and the tension grew, no one around him was safe. His royal engineer did not work fast enough, so he demoted him. His architect sneezed, so he had him whipped. And his baker, always so cheerful, always so busy, always so proud of his breads and sweets, did not bow low enough, resulting in a lifetime prison sentence.

Arioch soon sensed even he was not safe, so using the excuse his father needed help ruling the tribes, he scuttled up to the mountains for the first time in years to live with Soheil and his six sons. It took over a month before the tensions of Babylon fell from his shoulders, but when they did, he found himself strengthened by the peacefulness of the peaks, the arms of Soheil and, most of all, the hard-working pleasures of sheering the sheep and cultivating the land with his sons. Meanwhile, back in Babylon, Nebuchadnezzar, with no one else to yell at, raged at Daniel, Shadrach, Meshach, and Abedneggo, making impossible demands, reminding them of Pharaoh ordering the Israelites to make bricks without straw.

Finally, the long-awaited message arrived: Egypt was marching north to rescue Jerusalem. Instantly, all was well again. The King of Babylon signed royal pardons ordering everyone back to work and Arioch back to his side. Then singing, "I will ascend to the heights," at the top of his lungs, he galloped west to lead his armies against Egypt.

Receiving orders to abandon Jerusalem and head south, Babylon packed up and vacated Jerusalem so swiftly, the Hebrews did not know what to think. Was it a ruse to draw them out of the city? Or were Nebuchadnezzar's armies truly gone? More importantly, if they were gone, would they be coming back? Within hours, the news came. Babylon's armies were in full pursuit of Egypt, and because everyone knew Nebuchadnezzar would be fighting Pharaoh for years, it was determined Babylon would not be coming back. Hence, Jerusalem had won the war. Praise be to the God of Abraham, Isaac and Jacob, and praise be to King Zedekiah and all the prophets (except the traitor, Jeremiah) because they had been right. In fact, the entire city had been right, and after months of meagre rations, King Zedekiah proclaimed a week of celebration.

So, breaking open all the storehouses, Jerusalem ate, drank, sang, and danced. But most of all, she raised her cup to the heroes of the siege: children who moved food caches while Babylon's fireballs landed nearby, grandmothers who collected water for the sick, fathers who searched through flames for the lost, and the Adullamites who risked their lives sneaking into the Babylonian encampment to scavenge for weapons and food in order to arm and feed the city.

Michael ben-Ram loved hearing about the Adullamites. Named after the Three Mighty Men who risked their lives getting water for King David, he had wanted to be one. But how could he have been one when he was so young? Besides, no one knew who they were. Michael, along with everyone feasting at the Ophel storehouse, spent hours trying to guess the identities of the clandestine champions, all agreeing Baruch ben-Zadok was probably the leader, with his friends Eli and Reuben in second and third command. Michael had a hunch Aridatha was in the group too and was about to say so when a messenger approached and, slapping him cheerfully on the shoulder, told him to report to Chief Commander Yosef ben-Moshe at the king's stables.

Everyone was in such a congratulatory mood, Michael was hoping Yosef ben-Moshe was going to reward him for his job well done by inviting him to the king's victory banquet. So, scrubbing his ruddy face and pulling back his red hair, he practiced his bow to the king all the way to the stables. But Yosef ben-Moshe was not in a congratulatory mood, not even a congenial one, as he sorted out Jerusalem's finest horses for pasturing in the northern wastelands, his scar frowning, his white beard trimmed in severe angles. Shouting from amidst the horses, he ordered Michael to get back to the wall and watch for rain clouds, specifically toward the south, and if he saw anything, anything at all, he was to report it immediately. End of interview.

Michael stomped out onto the road. Only moments before he had envisioned himself as the most celebrated watchman at the king's victory banquet and now he was nothing, exiled to the top of the wall to ferret out rain clouds. What did rain clouds matter? Whether rain came or not, no one could do a thing about it. However, there was still a lot of celebrating going on on top of the wall, so breaking into a smile, he ran to his new job.

By the fourth week, the festivities had wound down, and the soldiers without a war to fight had gone home, leaving Michael alone and lonely. To keep himself from being too lonely, he had scheduled a different activity for each hour, and right now, it was time to dig into his knapsack. After the sparse rations during the siege, he had promised himself he would never go hungry again, and pulling out bread, curds, and dates, he ate until his stomach bulged. Then it was time to give his eyes a rest, but first he looked at the horizon.

The turbulence in the south had expanded. However, because of its yellow hue, he knew it was not rain, so stretching out under the sun, he began to hum the happy melody, *Yields seed for the sower and bread for the eater.* But instead of breaking into cheerful song, he broke into a clammy sweat because the last time he sang it, Babylon appeared. Terrified, he leapt to his feet, raced to the edge of the wall, and looked out.

The yellow stain was still growing, but that was not unusual. The south wind often kicked up large dust storms. Even so, he kept looking, all the while knowing he was being silly. Randomly singing a song did not mean Babylon's spears were going to reappear. Babylon had gone to Egypt, and everyone said Nebuchadnezzar would be fighting that war for years. Yet suddenly, there they were. The spears of Babylon. Rows and rows of twinkling specks rapidly budding into glittering splinters.

Now he understood Yosef ben-Moshe's strange command. Anticipating the possibility of Nebuchadnezzar's return, and not wanting to alarm the city by ordering a special watch, he had invented the rain cloud subterfuge. Indeed, his ploy had worked. Even Michael had been caught by surprise, his legs turning to water. However, this time he did not crumple to the floor. This time he charged down the steps, ran to Yosef ben-Moshe, and told him Babylon was returning.

Michael was correct. Babylon was returning, and just like the first time, Nebuchadnezzar was in a dour mood. Only this time it was because Pharaoh, upon hearing Nebuchadnezzar was leading the attack, had thrown all his legions into fortifying his borders. So Nebuchadnezzar, knowing he would need more troops to infiltrate such a prepared resistance, terminated his Egyptian campaign, and now his goal was simple: annihilate Jerusalem as soon as possible and go home.

"Arioch," he called out.

Arioch, hot, thirsty, and hungry, yet determined to never appear so, trotted up alongside.

"When we get to Jerusalem," the king said, opening a map, "I want battering rams here. Here. And here. Working day and night."

Usually armies waited until a city was low on flaming arrows and burning oil before positioning battering rams so close to the wall, and Arioch, convinced Jerusalem had spent the last weeks stocking up instead of depleting her storehouses, did not like the order. "You mean when we arrive?"

"What else would I mean?"

"But, King Nebuchadnezzar, day and night? The men are tired. They need sleep."

"Do I sleep?!"

Facing the king's hunted eyes, Arioch considered suggesting perhaps it was not Egypt but the Fourth Man who was interrupting his precious sleep. But too weary to argue, he replied, "Yes, my king, battering rams, day and night."

"And get those siege ramps built. I cannot have the wall falling apart with no way to get into the city."

Arioch also assumed Jerusalem's fighting spirit would be stronger than ever and, seeing catastrophe in the orders, answered disapprovingly, "As you speak, so be it, my king."

"When the wall does collapse," the king said, his voice far away, as if ascending into the heights, "I will be the first to ride in."

"My lord!" Arioch objected.

Nebuchadnezzar shot him a dagger glare. But this time Arioch did not concede. This time, the king's loyal commander glared right back.

33

JERUSALEM was not only stunned by Babylon's return, but overwhelmed by her new aggressive tactics. First came a host of archers shooting non-stop streams of flaming arrows over the wall. Under their protection, carts loaded with timber, ropes, dirt, hides, tools, and water rolled in, followed by swarms of engineers erecting siege ramps and battering rams as ordered by Nebuchadnezzar. At first, the daily call to put out the fires inside Jerusalem brought everyone together, like the days before Babylon went to Egypt. But with the storehouses almost empty and the dead littering the streets, survival became more important than putting out someone else's fire. Thus, Jerusalem turned inward. Men, hoarding what little they had, locked themselves and their families in safe dark places, while men who had nothing broke into those safe dark places and stole whatever the hoarders had. Women hid their babies until a time when they might need a desperate meal, while women who had no babies clawed through the walls searching for rats. But after a time, even the rat population disappeared.

Indeed, not all of Jerusalem's men and women took to their dens. The Adullamites still believed they could save the city by sneaking out into the Babylonian encampment and stealing whatever was needed, a risky venture but usually successful, because the vendors soon tired of chasing after one stolen onion only to return empty-handed. However, after Crown Prince Gaspar put a price on the thieves' heads, the chase became worthwhile and most were caught. To prove they were caught, Babylon sent them back to Jerusalem via catapult. In fact, one catapult was set apart specifically for the spying, thieving, murdering Hebrews. The Hebrew catapult was also Gaspar's idea, along with the expanded impalement yard where vultures tore the Jerusalemites apart.

"What a stink hole," griped Zorpo, covering his nose as he and Gaspar rode past the impaled Hebrews. "Arioch should have given you command of the cavalry."

"I like it here," replied the Crown Prince, his eyes fixed on the fourth Hebrew of the day launching into the air. "Zorpo, do you remember the ancient Babylonian saying…" Waiting until the Hebrew reached the top of his arc, he mimicked his father, crying out, "I will ascend to the heights!"

Exploding into laughter, they both reveled in the image of Nebuchadnezzar catapulting into the heights, his legs and arms flailing like the ridiculous Hebrew's. Wouldn't that be a satisfying way to bring down the King of Babylon? The thought was especially gratifying because Gaspar was getting very close to bringing him down. First, however, he had to return to Babylon before his father did. Once there, he would gather his armies—financed by Au Yang—and overthrow the capital. At the same time, his assassin here in Jerusalem would kill Nebuchadnezzar and his assassin in China would kill Au Yang. Hence, his assignment to the execution yard had been a stroke of good luck because if he had been assigned to the cavalry, he would have been obligated to stay in Jerusalem until the bitter end, whereas any clever excuse could get him relieved from the execution yard and ordered back to Babylon. So as the two patrolled the yard, they worked on clever excuses.

<hr />

Baruch ben-Zadok was putting out fires in the Fish District when Michael ben-Ram came running, telling him Eli and Reuben had been captured. Determined to save his last two friends, Baruch immediately sneaked out of the city, crawled inch by inch to the edge of the execution yard, and now lay hidden in the shadows of an abandoned vendor's cart. Gaspar and Zorpo were patrolling the area, not looking to the left or to the right as they turned away from the prisoners' wagon where twelve Adullamites, including Eli and Reuben, were roped together. The wagon was in full view, surrounded by fifty-yards of nothing, so Baruch calculated if he left now and dashed to the tar kilns, he could sprint the open fifty yards before Gaspar and Zorpo turned back. So, drawing his dagger, he made one last surveillance of the soldiers' camp nearby, the horse corrals beyond, the prisoners' wagon stranded in the open, and Gaspar and Zorpo still riding in the opposite direction. Ready to go, he felt a sudden rustling burst into the shadows behind him. Swinging around, he was about to strike, but it was Aridatha dressed as a tanner, her army leathers and daggers concealed underneath.

"What are you doing here?" he whispered angrily.

"I came to help."

"Your father ordered you to stay in the city."

"There they are," she said, raising her head to get a better view. "In the wagon."

"Put your head down. Gaspar is looking this way."

He was about to tell her the hated catapult commander had been identified as Nebuchadnezzar's son, the Crown Prince. But flattened side by side against the cool earth, he was more distracted by the threat of the father than the son. When Baruch was eight years old and Jeremiah spoke about Aridatha's exile to Babylon, he had regarded Babylon as the threat. So, when Yosef ben-Moshe took her to Dura, he was certain she would never return. Hence, when she did return, he thought the Babylonian threat was over. But a few days after her return, Yosef ben-Moshe called him aside, and confiding that Aridatha had not said a word to him about her private meeting with King Nebuchadnezzar, he asked Baruch if she had said anything to him.

Baruch was stunned. Yes, she had told him stories about riding alone in a foreign land, getting lost in Dura, and seeing Hananiah, Mishael, and Abedneggo living in fire with the Fourth Man, but nothing about Nebuchadnezzar. After that, every time he was with her, he waited for her to come forth, but she never did. Weeks turned into years, and her silence told him everything: Nebuchadnezzar was the threat. So, instead of talking about Gaspar or his captured friends or even Nebuchadnezzar, he decided to tread on ground he had always avoided. "Aridatha, why won't you marry me?"

"Baruch, what are you talking about?" she ruffled. "Eli and Reuben need you."

"I am waiting for the field to clear. So while I wait," he looked her in the eye, "answer me."

"I cannot marry you."

"Why?"

"Papa said no."

"You told him to say no."

"Why would I tell him that?"

"Indeed, why would you?"

Pointing to the Babylonian camp not far away, she said, "I could create a diversion by burning their tents. I will go first, give me ten seconds, then you go. Baruch, stop shaking your head. It will work."

"Tell me something, Ari."

Trying to hurry him along, she nodded hastily.

"Where is your crimson pouch?"

She was so blindsided by the two words, crimson pouch, she stared at him dumbfounded, her mind spinning. Year after year she had hoped he had forgotten about the pouch, and year after year when he said nothing, she had convinced herself he had.

"You gave it to him, didn't you? You gave it to King Nebuchadnezzar."

Suddenly sweltering, not from the army leathers underneath her tanner's tunic, but from guilt and confusion, she scrambled for an answer. "Baruch, I was ten years old."

"Why did you give it to him?"

"I wanted to tell you, but I knew you would be angry."

"Why did you give it to him?" he pressed.

What could she say? Her mind was numb, all her memories driven out by the crushing blows of starvation and war. So, struggling to reach into her past, to that day long ago, she found Nebuchadnezzar turning away from the tunnel and ordering her to stay in Babylon. She heard her own ten-year-old voice ring out brightly saying she was going to marry Baruch ben-Zadok when she grew up. The king stomped away. She chased after him, and offering him her crimson pouch, she said something, what was it? Oh, yes...

"I gave it to him to remember me by."

"Remember you by?! The King of Babylon? How stupid was that, Ari?"

"It was not stupid, Baruch," she shot back just as heatedly. "There was more to it. Much more."

"How much more?!" When she said nothing, he gently took her face, and with a voice low and commanding, he declared, "If there is nothing between you and Nebuchadnezzar, you will marry me."

Seeing panic flash into her eyes, he knew what he had known all along. He was never going to have her. Even though she had been living in Jerusalem all her life, her heart had been preparing for Babylon since the day Jeremiah said *when the Lord takes you into exile...* Baruch had heard every word, yet he had continued to deceive himself thinking he could have her whereas she, who had not heard one word, had continued to reject him. Not because she did not love him, but because unbeknownst to her, she was being obedient to the prophet. This, of course, made him love her all the more, and because of that love, he could never be this close to her again. So he said something, anything, just as long as it sounded lucid, and darted toward the kilns.

Dumbfounded, Aridatha watched him go. He had been so stiff telling her to return to the tunnel, as if he did not know her. His eyes, usually warm like the earth, had been cold. Why had he sounded so final, as if he never wanted to see her again? Didn't he know she loved him and hated Nebuchadnezzar? But if that was true, why hadn't she told him she loved him?

Suddenly, she saw Gaspar and Zorpo turning toward the prisoners' wagon. In minutes, Baruch would be seen and captured, and instead of twelve, thirteen Adullamites would die. So, slipping out from under the cart, she strode toward the Babylonian camp at the edge of the marketplace.

No one paid attention to the approaching tanner picking up a lighted torch and going behind the tents. Hence, no one saw Aridatha set fire to one tent, then another, and another.

"Fire!" yelled the cook.

Soldiers came running. Intent on dousing the flames of the first tent, they did not expect another tent to be on fire, or another, or another.

"Over there!" the cook shouted, pointing to the tanner.

Gaspar and Zorpo, still racking their brains for a foolproof excuse to get sent back to Babylon, looked up offhandedly. Tents were burning, soldiers scrambling, and a tanner throwing a torch into a tent was racing toward the stone corral.

"Your Hebrews are getting away!" shouted from behind.

Swinging around, Gaspar saw the prisoners' wagon emptying, the condemned Adullamites scattering across the field, and one lone rebel brandishing a dagger at him, yelling, "Come on, Gaspar! Both of you! Come and get me!"

It was Baruch ben-Zadok. Frantic for Aridatha's safety, he was challenging the commanders to chase after him in the hope they would forget the tanner. It worked. Enraged by the Hebrew's effrontery, they drew their swords and spurred their horses toward him.

At the same moment on the east mount, Nebuchadnezzar was reviewing Chenguang's latest report from Babylon. She and Tin had uncovered an assassination plot contrived by Gaspar against the Grand Preceptor Au Yang, and the Chinese assassin had been executed. In addition, Arioch had downed another assassin here in the Babylonian encampment, spending large amounts of gold—payments from the Crown Prince—and boasting about Gaspar's plans to assassinate Nebuchadnezzar.

It was the first good news since his Egyptian debacle, and basking in it, Nebuchadnezzar stared out at the siege zone. A magnificent sight! Power in the making! Thousands of engineers erecting battering rams and earthen ramps backed by thousands of archers shooting fire into Jerusalem. Poor old Sennacherib, unable to rouse one arrow over the massive stone wall, whereas he had been shooting forests over it for months and was well on his way to annihilating the city.

But what was that going on in the execution yard? Three, four, five plumes of smoke blackening his cheerful sky? Men running around like crazed ants?

"Who is in charge down there?" he demanded.

"Crown Prince Gaspar, my lord," responded from five different directions.

"Get me a horse," ordered the king.

34

Four Babylonian soldiers chased the tanner toward the stone corral, and just as they hoped, he clambered over the wall, dropped down, and disappeared amidst the horses. Now all they had to do was take the perimeter, wait for more soldiers to arrive, and flush him out.

Meanwhile, across the execution yard, Baruch ben-Zadok ran like the wind, leading Gaspar and Zorpo away from Aridatha. Pumping his legs as fast as he could, he knew the two commanders would soon be upon him, yet incredibly the distance between him and their horses remained the same. It reminded him of the prophet Elijah running ahead of Ahab's chariot. Had Elijah's legs burned like Baruch's were burning? Had his chest heaved just as uncontrollably? Baruch knew it was absurd to compare himself to the great prophet because he was neither great nor a prophet, so dismissing such thoughts, he just kept running, trying to save Aridatha.

However, before long, it no longer mattered because the commanders had stopped to stare at a lone rider inside the corral, no longer a tanner, but a young woman atop a sturdy black Barb. Dressed in army leathers and wrapped in sunlight, she herded and shouted the churning war horses to one end of the arena, and when it was cleared, she spurred to a gallop toward the opposite stone wall, obviously intending to jump.

"No, Ari," gasped Baruch. "The wall is too wide."

By now the entire Babylonian camp was staring, not because she would never make the jump, but because they recognized her as the maiden who had waved the flag on the Tower of David. Shouting, "Remember the Fourth Man," she had captivated both Babylon and Jerusalem's armies, and today she was just as captivating: stealing into their camp, burning their tents, and now riding toward a deadly jump. Deadly, because the corral had been built exceptionally high and wide so the horses could not be stolen. Quickly, the men laid bets on whether she would crash her horse into the wall or her horse would prudently jerk to a stop, sending her crashing into the wall. Since no one wagered she would actually make the jump, all bets were void because the long-haired rider sailed effortlessly over the top.

"Go, Ari," breathed Baruch, watching her gallop away. "Go."

Gaspar recognized her, too. Waving her flag defiantly on the first day of the siege, she had made a fool of Nebuchadnezzar and all of Babylon. Well, she was not going to make a fool of him. "Zorpo, round up the prisoners. She is mine."

Watching Gaspar thunder after Aridatha, Baruch knew he had to get to her first. But how? His legs had run their course, he was still gasping for breath, and Zorpo was charging straight at him. Still, he had one option: squaring off to meet the oncoming Babylonian. So quickly removing his dagger belt, he waited until Zorpo's horse was almost upon him, then raising his belt over his head, he swung it around and around while roaring at the top of his lungs. Depending on the proficiency of the rider, the horse would either gallop right over him or spook and rear back. Zorpo was an excellent rider but his horse resented his brutal mistreatment, so he reared back throwing Zorpo to the ground, giving Baruch the opportunity to lunge at him.

On the other side of the yard, Aridatha, galloping at full pace, saw Eli and Reuben darting into the shadows of the Jerusalem wall. Good, she thought, they will live to see another day. Now she had to find her way back to the wall, but the catapult commander was closing in fast; so fast, she could see tattoos on his forearms. Looking like daggers, they reminded her of something out of her past, instilling an even greater urgency to escape.

So, wrapping her arms around her horse's neck, she wheeled into the low-lying branches of an olive grove. Zigzagging in and out of the trees, her strength rapidly drained away. After months of willing herself to be strong against the onslaught of sword, famine, and plague, every breath was now an effort, her eyelids too heavy to keep open. Thus, with her cheek fastened to her horse's neck and her eyes closed in slumber, she soon found herself floating over a land of milk and honey, basking in the smell of baking bread, the taste of red wine, and the voices of the bride and bridegroom. Multitudes were streaming to their wedding banquet and Aridatha, yearning to be at the feast, let go of her horse and reached

up to them. Instantly, Rachel weeping for her children yanked her arms
down, her eyes jerked open, and she saw the tattooed commander careering out of the trees, charging straight at her. Drawing her dagger, she
aimed for his heart but when their horses crashed together, she lost her
balance and tumbled to the earth.

Gaspar jumped to the ground, yelling, "You are dead!"

Picking herself up, Aridatha scrambled to get away, but her heart was
not in it. Because for the first time in her life, death was more desirable
than living. To be set free from hunger and terror, disease and sorrow,
and, most especially, from watching and waiting for the Fourth Man
would be so much easier than… That was it! She had seen those tattoos
on the day she saw the Fourth Man. He was younger then, standing on
the royal dais and flexing his muscles defiantly at Nebuchadnezzar. It had
angered her then, and it still angered her. Why should she let such a man
kill her? So, drawing her other dagger, she swung around to face him.
"You will never kill me."

"Oh, no?" He raised his sword and dove at her.

Dodging to the side, she feinted a turn, slashed one dagger across
his arm, then thrust the other at his ribs, but he blocked it, punching
his palm into her face. Her head jerked back, her nose bled, and her eyes
stung, but worse, her daggers were gone. Too weak to hold onto them,
they had flown from her hands leaving her helpless as he lodged the
point of his sword against her neck. He ranted like a wild man, bellowing curses at her. Then, spitting out his triumphs and railing against the
King of Babylon, he raised his sword to kill her, when a whip, lashing
in from out of nowhere, wrapped around his neck and wrenched him
backward.

They were both so astonished, they just stared at each other, Aridatha watching dumbly as Gaspar clawed at the choking whip, his eyes
bulging.

"I want her alive!" rapped through the air.

Looking up, her mouth dropped. It was King Nebuchadnezzar.

"She is an enemy of Babylon," Gaspar garbled, still battling the
leather around his neck.

"I know my enemies, Gaspar."

"Get this thing off of me, father!"

"Father?" Aridatha gasped. Nebuchadnezzar was this man's father? Stunned, she stared at the father, then at the son, then at Arioch and Nergal galloping in, jumping from their horses, and wrestling Gaspar to the ground.

"Arioch!" the king shouted sharply. "He is the Crown Prince."

Obediently, yet clearly disgusted, the two commanders—Arioch kicking dust and Nergal biting down hard on his ever-present bronze toothpick—backed away, leaving Gaspar sitting in the dirt brushing off his boots.

"Gaspar, you do not seem happy here," the king said reassuringly.

Confident of his power over his father, Gaspar smirked at Arioch, then openly grunted his distaste for everything around him.

"So!" King Nebuchadnezzar said, again reassuringly. "I am sending you back to Babylon."

The Crown Prince immediately dropped his head. No one must see his bliss. His father had just handed him his dream, his chance to take the crown. Oh, how he wanted to jump on his horse and leave right now.

The king, slowly rewinding his whip as if creating a work of art, added quietly, "To Canal Prison."

He said it so quietly, Gaspar did not hear. But the words hung in the air until he did hear, and his face drained of color. "Canal Prison?" he sputtered.

"As I said, Gaspar, I know my enemies. Nergal, get him out of here."

Gaspar darted for the grove, but Arioch and Nergal cut him off and hauled him back to the horses. They were especially rough when they threw him over his saddle, his head hanging on one side, his legs the other.

"You will regret this, father!" the Crown Prince yelled as they roped his hands and feet under the horse's belly. "You think nothing can shake you? I will shake you!"

Watching Nergal gallop away with Gaspar, Aridatha knew her ordeal was over. The commander with the tattoos was gone and somehow—because of her swift horse or Rachel weeping or Nebuchadnezzar's whip or because of all three—she was still alive. Whatever it was, all she wanted to do was crumple to the ground and cry, but Nebuchadnezzar was striding toward her.

"Get away!" she shouted.

The King of Babylon was not used to taking orders, but Aridatha was shaking so violently, he stopped, giving her a moment to get her bearings and himself a moment to study her. One side of her face was swelling from Gaspar's blow, the other still wore the scar from Babylon's first visit to Jerusalem. Those kinds of injuries he understood, she had been hit and sometimes scars remained. What he did not understand and what angered him more than he thought possible was she was bone-thin, her eyes brilliant from hunger. What had ben-Moshe been thinking?

"I told you, get away!" she screamed, knowing she did not have to scream, not at him. But after months of fighting everything from sword to starvation, she was desperate to stay strong, and screaming was all she had left. How else was she going to control the hurt and disappointment welling up inside her? But why should she be hurt or disappointed? Jerusalem still stood and the Fourth Man was going to come. Yet because he had not come, she collapsed into groaning sobs.

The king wanted to go to her, to take her in his arms and soothe her, but he knew if he moved, she would bolt. So, reaching into his tunic, he pulled out something close to his heart.

"Aridatha," he coaxed softly.

It was a long time before she looked up, but when she did, she burst into more racking sobs. She did not know why she was heaving tears. It was only her crimson pouch hanging from his neck, exactly where she placed it so many years before, only now the leather was much suppler and its color a deeper red, as if he had been wearing it a long time.

"You see, I did remember you," he said softly, adding the words he asked that day. "Is it a curse or a blessing?"

"Are you out of your mind?" she screeched. "I hate you! It is a nightmare behind those walls."

"Then hate the Fourth Man," he replied indifferently. "Wasn't he the one who was supposed to save you?"

"He will," she retorted. "You know he will."

"My lord," Arioch interrupted.

A rider was fast approaching, the same warrior who had tried to tug Aridatha off the Tower, most probably Baruch ben-Zadok. Not wanting him anywhere near her, Nebuchadnezzar grabbed her and began to force her up onto his horse. But, holding her shrunken waist in his stern broad hands, he weakened. If she was going to step up onto his horse, he wanted her to do it willingly.

So, letting her go, he gently took her hand and said, "Aridatha, come to Babylon with me."

But she did not hear, because Baruch ben-Zadok was galloping in on Zorpo's horse, drawing his sword and jumping to the ground, ready to take on both men. It was wonderful, yet horrible because he could never win, not against Nebuchadnezzar and Arioch. She tried to run to him, but the king tightened his grip on her hand, so she cried out, "No, Baruch! He is Nebuchadnezzar King of Babylon."

Baruch stared at Jerusalem's mortal enemy holding Aridatha's hand and wearing her crimson pouch. Did he need any more reasons to kill him? With one stroke of his sword, the war would end and Aridatha would be his. His legs were ready to spring and his arms longed to thrust, but he did not move.

King Nebuchadnezzar was counting on Aridatha's suitor to raise his sword against him, giving him the opportunity to cut him down. But the young man just stood there, his jaw tight and eyes fierce, displaying the same powerful control he had seen so often in Yosef ben-Moshe, Daniel, and even Aridatha. But this was no time for a stalemate because one of his cavalry units was galloping toward them.

"Aridatha," he said, looking her in the eye, "you must leave Jerusalem now."

"I am not leaving."

"Ben-Zadok, tell her to come to Babylon." When the Hebrew said nothing, he added, "Or perhaps you want her to stay here and starve."

"If you are concerned about her starving, King Nebuchadnezzar, then return to Babylon and take your armies with you."

"Do not play games with me," the king barked. "You know she is mine. She took my hand when we saw the Fourth Man."

Baruch felt like a child again, wanting to pound his fists into Nebuchadnezzar's face as he had pounded them against Jeremiah's legs. But he was not a child. He was a man and he was a warrior. So, he stared blandly at the king.

"Do you also know she gave me this crimson pouch? I did not demand it. She gave it to me so I would remember her."

"Yes, I gave you the pouch," Aridatha shot back. "I also told you I was going to marry Baruch ben-Zadok when I grew up."

"But you did not marry him, did you?" the king countered. "Instead, on the first night of the siege, you came out to see me."

The blow hit so hard, Baruch could feign indifference no longer. He had often wondered where Aridatha had gone that night, but had protected himself by not asking. Now he knew, and with Nebuchadnezzar staring him in the face, he also knew Jeremiah's words were about to come true. Before she starved or burned or was stabbed to death in Jerusalem, Aridatha would be exiled to Babylon. Furthermore, if he was a true man and a true warrior, he would readily admit that the best way to be exiled would be under the king's protection. Thus, with his heart thundering so hard he could barely breathe, Baruch heard himself say, "The king is right, Ari. You must go. You will be safe in Babylon."

"Splendid!" pronounced Nebuchadnezzar.

"I am not going anywhere!" she screamed, glaring at one and then the other.

This was her second refusal to come to Babylon, and growing impatient, the king growled, "I will give you anything you want."

"I told you before, I already have everything I want. I am a Daughter of Zion!"

Anger shot through the king so fast, he wanted to slap her. Or better still, pull her body in close and show her what a real king could do. But his warriors were closing in fast, so he threw her onto Baruch's horse and bellowed, "Get her out of here."

Instantly, Baruch jumped behind her and galloped off.

"If you want to stay in Jerusalem," Nebuchadnezzar shouted after her, "then by all the gods fall with Jerusalem!"

"Fall with Jerusalem?" objected Arioch. "My king, you promised Yosef ben-Moshe you would protect her."

"Arioch!" Nebuchadnezzar stamped his foot. "You are a fool." Springing onto his horse, he threw the crimson pouch to the ground and charged away.

Arioch motioned the oncoming warriors to follow the king, but instead of enjoying the rare moment of quietude, he found himself chafing under Nebuchadnezzar's words. Indeed, the king had every right to call him anything he wanted, but he had never called him a fool. Was he a fool because he reminded him of his word to Yosef ben-Moshe? Or did the king's outburst have more to do with Aridatha's refusal to go to Babylon than Arioch's mere concern over a promise? Whatever it was, perhaps it had something to do with the crimson pouch.

Arioch had often seen the pouch settled at the king's heart, and curious to know what was in it, he picked it up, poked his finger inside, and pulled out... Why it was nothing but a scruff of dirt! No wonder Nebuchadnezzar felt the fool, riding around with nothing but dirt at his heart. So Arioch was about to throw it back to the ground, but reminding himself the pouch had been close to the king's heart for many years, he paused. Men often wore talismans around their necks, but why would Nebuchadnezzar? He did not need a talisman. He wore the royal pendant of Babylon. Stymied, he steadied his keen eyes on his king galloping back toward the command post, his braids flying out behind him, his broad back straight, his war horse swifter than eagles. He was a striking figure, his men separating and making a path before him: one lone man ruling the world, one lone voice commanding the nations, one lone vision leading to glory. Indeed, there was none beside him. He rode alone.

Thus, because Arioch was not a fool, he tucked the pouch into his pocket for a time when his king might need it again. Because no man could ride completely alone.

35

YOSEF ben-Moshe sat in the dust staring out at the burnt remains of his vast estate. Everything was gone except Zillah's statues of Sarah and Ruth. Thankfully, Baruch ben-Zadok and twelve-year-old Michael ben-Ram had saved his scrolls: Moses, Kings David and Solomon, and the Histories of the Judges. If those had gone up in smoke, he would have regretted it until the day he died. As for the rest of his fallen riches, he had no regrets. In fact, after eighteen months of siege, he was now convinced his pursuit of wealth had been rooted in folly rather than wisdom. Of course, his motive had been noble. He had wanted the Pillar of Salt Caravan so his family name would once again be esteemed in Jerusalem. But what was the value of an esteemed name in a city under the wrath of the Lord? Naturally, his missteps were clear now. Weren't all missteps clear in retrospect, especially when one was about to meet one's Maker?

Although he had no regrets about his wealth being reduced to ashes, he had a lifetime of regrets when it came to his beloved daughter, Aridatha. He had been a fool not forcing her to stay in Babylon when she was ten. After missing that opportunity, he should have sent her away when she was growing up or at least packed her off when the siege began. Instead, he convinced himself she would refuse to go, so he never ordered her to go. But facing his follies head on, he had to admit—to himself and to his God—it was not Aridatha who had stopped him, but his own secret unwillingness to believe Jerusalem was actually going to be destroyed.

However, after witnessing sword, famine, and plague destroy the world around him, he knew—again in retrospect—that Jeremiah's lament, "The Lord determined to tear down the wall around the Daughter of Zion," was not an abstract threat, but actual fact. Furthermore, it was a horrifying one, for it was the foundation to his daughter's future.

"Look what I have!"

Turning toward the gate, he saw Aridatha running into the court-yard holding three fat figs, and it angered him because he had ordered her never to go outside the city wall. "I want to talk to you."

"Papa, please," she implored, "you know we have to eat."

"It is not about the marketplace."

"In a moment," she called, eager to get the figs to her mother be-cause ever since the fire Zillah had been cooking in the rubble as if the kitchen and the food were still there.

"Come here!" he ordered. When she did not move, he spoke more gently, "You eat them."

"They are for mother."

"Baruch ben-Zadok brought fish and barley for your mother." It was a lie, but it was the only way to stop her from giving away her food.

It took some moments for Aridatha to realize the treasures in her hand were her own, and moving in semi-awe to the well that once watered the estate, she sat on the bench and ate for the first time in two days.

Staring at her, Yosef ben-Moshe could not believe this was his daugh-ter—the daughter of the great Yosef ben-Moshe—taking the tiniest of bites, then chewing and chewing until she eked out every thread of meat and every drop of juice. It was the same slow process for each conscien-tious nibble, and unable to watch any longer, he turned away. Truly, he had been a fool not sending her to Babylon. How selfish. How arrogant. But not anymore! From now on, she was going to eat, and she was going to eat the food of kings. He had a way out for her, and she was going to take it whether she liked it or not.

"What do you want to talk about?" she said, licking her fingers. "If it is about leaving with mother tonight, I told you I will not go."

"I know what you told me," he answered sharply. For days he had been trying to convince her to go with Zillah on King Zedekiah's planned escape, and each time she had refused.

"Give me your hand," he said.

Instinctively, she balked. Anticipating her resistance, he seized her hand and shoved a ring on her finger. "It is King Nebuchadnezzar's," he explained. "He gave it to me for saving his life."

"I know what it is and I do not want it."

"You will need it."

"Just because you have given up on the Fourth Man, papa, does not mean I have."

"I have not given up on him. In fact," he added remorsefully, "I see him more clearly every day. Someday, I hope you do too." Seeing she did not understand, he moved on, "I have something to tell you. Something you do not know."

"Is it mother?" she gasped. "Has something happened to her?"

"Your mother is fine," he answered gruffly, annoyed because Zillah's cunning had at last manipulated even Aridatha's heartstrings. "This is about your crimson pouch. The one you gave to King Nebuchadnezzar. Do you remember?"

The King of Babylon flashed into her mind. It had been over two months since she saw him wearing the pouch. Had her father found out about that day? If so, how? Who would have told him about her sneaking into the siege zone, burning the soldiers' tents, and fleeing from Gaspar? Certainly, not Baruch. "Yes, I remember," she answered guardedly. "I gave it to him when I was ten years old."

"Your mother and I never told you what Jeremiah said when he put it on you."

"Jeremiah?" she gasped, her heart flooding with sweet anticipation. "You mean he said something to me?" For the first time in years, she remembered seeing the tall man when she was one year old, kicking her feet to get to him, reaching her hands out to touch him. Then without warning, she thought of her mother pacing the burnt-out floors at night, tugging at her hair, and cursing the prophet, so she lashed out, "I do not care what Jeremiah said."

"'When the Lord carries you into exile to Babylon...'" he enunciated slowly, making sure she understood. "You are to build houses and settle down. You are to plant gardens and eat what they produce."

Of course, she understood. Each word springing on her like a trap: exile, Babylon, build, settle down, plant, eat...

"Papa," she laughed nervously, not knowing why she was laughing. "I know you want me to go to Nebuchadnezzar, but making up a story about Jeremiah and the Lord..." She kept laughing, high-pitched crazed laughter, tears rolling down her cheeks. "I guess I need to laugh every now and then, but making up a story about..." she chattered it again.

"It is not a story, Aridatha," he said with such chilling calm, her breath stopped. "You know as well as I do, the Lord has directed your path toward Babylon since you were a young girl."

"Not so!" she glowered, equally chilling. "If you believed the Lord was directing my path to Babylon, you would have made me stay in Babylon when I was ten!"

"I was waiting for the Lord to relent!" His jaw was so tight, he could barely speak. This was his daughter. Why did he have to fight her? Trying to calm himself, he continued, "But every time Baruch asked you to marry him and you said no, I knew the Lord had not relented."

"Are you telling me…" she almost shrieked, "I refused to marry Baruch ben-Zadok because of some words Jeremiah spoke over me when I was three years old? Words I did not even hear?"

"Do you have a better reason for refusing him?"

It was as if he had hit her in the stomach. How many times had she asked herself why she had not married Baruch ben-Zadok? How many times had she pinpointed it back to that day, the day Babylon almost killed her and Jeremiah gave her the crimson pouch? But of course, she had buried those thoughts. "I did not marry Baruch because I was waiting for the siege to end!" she blared back, then started to run.

But he grabbed her, making her face him. "If your mother would stop pretending to be insane, she would tell you. She was there and heard it all. That is why she has hated Jeremiah all these years. That is why she calls him a traitor."

"She is not pretending to be insane and he is a traitor!" she shouted, sounding exactly like her mother. "Everybody knows it."

"Silence," he commanded. "You will never call the prophet of God a traitor again." He knew he was hurting her, his grip harsh and his voice harsher, so he let her go. Then, trying to reach her heart, he said, "Aridatha, whatever happens, you must remember…" She turned and walked away. "Listen to me!" She stopped. "Jeremiah also said the Lord will bring us back. After seventy years, he will bring us back to rebuild Jerusalem."

Swinging around, she blasted, "Then why destroy it?!"

"You know why! We have followed our own ways—I have followed my own ways—and by doing so, Aridatha, we have rejected the Most High God, the Lord Almighty!"

"All these years," she seethed, "all these years, you have been teaching me to build and plant. Now I know why. But I will not build for Babylon, papa! I will not plant for Babylon! The Fourth Man is going destroy Babylon and save Jerusalem."

She looked so alone, so lost, so angry, everything in him wanted to recant and make her happy again. If only he could tell her the devastation surrounding her was a dream and God would never ultimately destroy Jerusalem because judgment was just a word, not an actual work of the Lord Almighty. But unwilling to lead her any further into his own folly, he said, "You will wear the ring. It will bring you safely to Nebuchadnezzar."

"I will not go to him, papa."

Studying her starving limbs, he remembered dressing her in her first tunic and riding her through the streets of Jerusalem. He recalled the years of training her, teaching her how to build and plant and fight so she would be ready for whatever lay ahead. He had taught her to love the scrolls and the Star of David. He had secured Nebuchadnezzar's promise to protect her, and just moments before, he had given her his ring. Now, facing the last days of Jerusalem, he had nothing more to give. From this day on, she would have to fight her battles without him. She would have to conquer Babylon or be conquered by Babylon.

"It is your fight now, Aridatha," he said. When she still did not look at him, he walked away.

"I hate Nebuchadnezzar!" she yelled as he disappeared out the gate. "I always have."

As if on cue, one of Nebuchadnezzar's battering rams jolted the city. The crash sounded like any other, but this time it was followed by a clamor of stone mangling against stone, the signal Jerusalem's ramparts were cracking.

36

WHEN Arioch heard the wall groan the first time, he froze. When he heard its second agonizing wail, he wanted to leave the command post to search for the Fourth Man, but Nebuchadnezzar was reviewing the final orders for the invasion of Jerusalem. So, stifling a worried sigh, he stayed where he was, responding to directives, revising attack routes, and recalculating intervals for the cavalry charge, all the while knowing Nebuchadnezzar's plans were futile. It was folly to go up against the Fourth Man! Perhaps he should have told the king, but on the day that never existed, he saw, like everyone else, the three Hebrew judges instead of dying in the fire, living in the fire. However, unlike everyone else, he saw his Babylonian warriors dead, but also alive.

That was the horror that had plagued him ever since. While staring at his Babylonian warriors dead on the ground, he had also seen the actual men being slammed into fiery metal cages. Surrounded by glowing metal bars, they had looked straight at him pleading for water. But even if he had had the water, he could not have given it to them because their cages were tumbling into cavernous mines deep inside the earth, leaving their dead bodies behind.

At first, he had refused to believe what his eyes had seen. In fact, he convinced himself that for those moments, he had gone mad. So, scanning the arena, he had searched for sanity, only to see the three Hebrews still walking and talking with the Fourth Man inside the fire. Equal madness! Everyone knew Shadrach, Meshach, and Abedneggo could not live in fire any more than his warriors could be dead on the ground and at the same time alive in fiery metal cages. Yet, the entire arena was watching, and the entire arena could not be mad. So he was forced to conclude that his men, although dead, were still alive, and it was because of the Fourth Man.

Thus, for the first time in his life, Arioch knew true fear. Not just for himself, but for his king. And, believing Nebuchadnezzar would be the

Fourth Man's next victim, he had tried to pull him away. But Nebuchadnezzar refused to leave, so Arioch planted his body in front of him so the flames would consume him instead of his king. But the flames never came. Nothing came except a little girl to hold Nebuchadnezzar's hand. Arioch could not believe it! Nine warriors who had obeyed the king's command, just as he would have done, were writhing in torment in the belly of the earth while Nebuchadnezzar, who had given the command, was having his hand held?

From then on, Arioch fumed over the injustice of it all. Furthermore, because it was unjust, he developed an irrational fear of fire because who could know when or where the Fourth Man and his fire were going to strike next? Telling himself his anxieties would soon wane, he threw himself into his work, continuing on as the mighty warrior he was, until the day he leapt for cover when a slave girl lit his oil lamp. That did it! He had to do something or he certainly would go mad.

So quick-marching to the Hall of Justice, he stormed into Shadrach's office, ordered everyone out except the Hebrew high judge, then ranted for over an hour, shouting and cursing against the God who locked obedient warriors into fiery pits while leaving Nebuchadnezzar feasting on lamb in the Southern Palace. He knew he was blithering because he repeated himself over and over, yelling it was wrong, growling it was unjust. What was Shadrach's God up to anyway? Whatever it was, it was wrong. What right did he have to come into Babylon? Whatever it was, it was unjust. Furthermore, what deadly mischief was Shadrach's God planning to do next? Whatever it was, it was unquestionably, indisputably and irrefutably wrong and unjust. Finally, pummeling his fists against Shadrach's desk, he demanded an accounting of the God of Abraham, Isaac and Jacob.

Shadrach said nothing for many minutes. Not because he did not know what to say, but because for the first time in his life, he felt compassion for a Babylonian, and it was taking some time to adjust to it. He had spent his life serving Babylon while being hated by Babylon which had not endeared him to her arrogant people. Yet, watching Babylon's chief commander throughout all his ravings actually fearing the God of Abraham, Isaac and Jacob, while knowing back home in Jerusalem the fear of God had been forgotten, he could not help liking the man.

So looking Arioch in the eye, he said, "The God of Abraham, Isaac and Jacob is not wrong and unjust. The God of Abraham, Isaac and Jacob is righteous and just."

Righteous and just. The words floated across the room like playful little clouds, and listening to them go round and round, Arioch dizzied, his knees gave way, and he tumbled to the floor. Shadrach, apparently too occupied with the provinces' annual budgets, did not seem to think it unusual for a Babylonian commander to be lying on his tiles. Similarly, Arioch was so shaken, he did not consider it odd to be flattened on them. In fact, the tiles were so cool and soothing, for the first time in weeks, he could actually think.

So Arioch thought. But no matter how hard he thought, using the knowledge he had employed to mount wars and conquer kingdoms, he could not grasp Shadrach's words because he knew a righteous and just God would never target obedient warriors and then ignore the king who gave the order. On the other hand, who else besides Daniel, Shadrach, Meshach, and Abedneggo had been able to tell Nebuchadnezzar his dream and interpret it? Who else besides Shadrach, Meshach, and Abedneggo had lived in fire? Not only had they lived in fire, but they had lived in fire with the Fourth Man! In other words, Shadrach had to be right. Besides, Arioch had nowhere else to go except back to his rage, which made even less sense. To rage at the Fourth Man who held fire, life, and death in his hands was not only foolish, but futile. Thus, Arioch accepted Shadrach's terms. The Hebrews' God was righteous and just.

From then on, Arioch wanted to know their God. The thought of walking and talking with the Fourth Man amidst roaring flames became to him an ever-increasing awesome prospect. But how could he, a Babylonian warrior, ever get close? He was not a king like Nebuchadnezzar or a Hebrew like Shadrach, Meshach, and Abedneggo. They all had been born into his favor, Arioch had not. Yet, he wanted that favor, resolving if he ever saw the Fourth Man again, he would ask for it. But now it was too late. Babylon was breaking through Jerusalem's wall, and in moments, they would all be incinerated by the Fourth Man's fire. So, looking up from the king's plans, Arioch whispered under his breath, "God of Heaven, I have tried to stop my king from destroying Jerusalem. When you send your Fourth Man to save Zion, please remember me."

It was a strange moment for Arioch, as if his heart and soul had been touched by an unexpected liberating light. Marveling at such freedom, he wanted to keep the moment alive and never let it go. But with the Jerusalem wall about to collapse, the faithful warrior turned back to his king.

37

As the sun dipped into the western horizon, Babylon's battering ram sank deeper into the Jerusalem wall. Hearing its grating cry, Yosef ben-Moshe knew he should be gathering his men for battle instead of carrying his wife through the smoky streets of Jerusalem. But Aridatha had run off, so the task of getting Zillah to the palace for King Zedekiah's escape had fallen upon him. He had tried to leave home earlier, but Zillah, possessing only one tunic because her clothes had burned in the fire, had insisted on changing it three times, trying to decide which one to wear for the king's twilight ride.

To an outsider, the haunting beauty would have appeared heartbreakingly insane as she flounced back and forth in the same ragged dress, prattling about her household and Jerusalem as if they were still intact. But Yosef ben-Moshe was not fooled. He knew Zillah, and he knew her well. Rather than losing her wits, she had been employing them with an even greater degree of cunning, carrying on as if nothing had changed in order to prove nothing had changed, and even more to the point, to prove she had been right about Jerusalem and Jeremiah wrong.

Now, trudging up the final hill to Zedekiah's palace, ben-Moshe hoped that after Zillah escaped from Jerusalem she might forget her resentments and once again—or maybe for the first time—be happy. Even so, his thoughts did not linger long on his wife, but on his daughter. That afternoon, after giving Aridatha Nebuchadnezzar's ring, their parting had been a bitter one. Even now, while hoping she would use the ring to get to Nebuchadnezzar, he knew she would not. As a child, she had seen the Fourth Man save Hebrews and destroy Babylonians, so how could she abandon what her eyes saw? She could not, or rather would not. So, she had probably gone to the top of the Tower of David to watch for the Fourth Man.

Envisioning her standing alone above the burning city, vainly awaiting rescue, shattered his soul. Because there would be no rescue. No comfort. No reprieve. If only he could run to her, take her in his arms and whisk her to safety. But as he told her that afternoon, it was her fight now, and in his heart, he knew she was ready. No matter what weapons Nebuchadnezzar used—words, sword, strength, even love—she would always be Aridatha of Jerusalem.

So, instead of shedding tears, his soul cried out proudly, "Aridatha, my daughter, may the Lord bless you and keep you; the Lord make His face shine upon you and be gracious to you; the Lord turn His face toward you and give you peace."

Yosef ben-Moshe was right. His daughter was standing alone on the top of the Tower of David on the very spot she had waved the Hebrew flag eighteen months before. Then she had been a vision of confident beauty. Now she was a skeleton of desperate will, scanning the heavens searching for the Fourth Man. Would he come as a man like in the fiery furnace, or as a whisper as he did with Elijah, or perhaps as the commander of the army of the Lord as he did with Joshua? Would he use fire to destroy Babylon? Plague? Sword? As her feverish thoughts gave her hope and her frantic eyes searched for the object of that hope, she suddenly realized everything was quiet, a peaceful quiet she had not heard in months. What was it? It took some moments to sort it out, then jerking around, she strained to see through the smoke toward the battering ram.

It had stopped!

Solomon's great wall had swallowed the iron-capped log, trapping it inside its ancient belly. From out of nowhere, Babylon's engineers scurried into position. Wrestling with ropes and winches, they pounded and tugged and cursed at the jammed log, but no matter what they tried, they could not pull it out. Heart in her throat, Aridatha watched Jerusalem's archers swarm to the top of the wall and shoot fire at the engineers. Knowing this must be the turnaround, she shouted the same confident cry of eighteen months before: "Remember the Fourth Man!" Of course, no one heard because everyone was shouting—or too busy to shout: Babylon's infantry dumping more and more water on the hides shielding the engineers, Jerusalem's soldiers shooting more and more arrows at Babylon… With fire sizzling all around and his engineers getting nowhere, Nergal called for twelve more teams of oxen, and within moments, the harnessed beasts pulled the iron-capped log out of the wall, dislocating two of Solomon's majestic stones.

Watching the two stones slowly emerge and teeter, Babylon gasped with relief while Jerusalem gaped in horror, both sides waiting for the stones to drop. But the see-sawing stones seemed unable to make up their minds. Should they slow down and settle back into the wall or teeter faster until they crashed to the earth below? On the other hand, perhaps they enjoyed taunting their audience. Whatever it was, it gave both camps a heightened sense of the reality of the Fourth Man, exacerbated by an angry rumbling coming from out of the firmament, a marching chant so all-encompassing Jerusalem turned from the teetering stones to watch it roiling in from the four corners of the sky. From the north, the east, the south, and the west, the furor galloped in, a tempest of conquering princes in fiery chariots led by fiery horses, all reaching the City of David at the same time, all exploding into one deafening crescendo, "The Lord determined to tear down the wall around the Daughter of Zion…"

They were the words Jeremiah had spoken, but he had never spoken them like this: living and active, slashing through the sky like a double-edged sword, crying out in anguish, "He did not withhold his hand from destroying…"

The words were especially deafening at the top of the Tower of David and Aridatha, not wanting to hear them, pressed her palms over her ears. But even with her ears covered, she knew they were the same voices she had heard in Nebuchadnezzar's furnace arena. This time, however, they were shouting a different message. So, holding her ears tighter, she screamed at the heavens, "I will not listen! The Fourth Man will come! Jerusalem's wall will stand!"

<hr />

Inside King Zedekiah's garden, Yosef ben-Moshe put Zillah on his fastest horse, then raced toward the doomed wall. Passing Jerusalem's warriors along the way, he ordered them to hurry to the gates and get the fires ready, but no one moved. Hence, he let his starving soldiers stay where they were. What else could he do? If he had taken a whip to them, they would not have noticed, for like everyone else, they were staring at

Jeremiah's words tearing apart the sky, judging the thoughts and attitudes of the heart.

The voices reminded Yosef ben-Moshe of the voices in the fiery furnace. However, on that day, their presence had given him hope. Today the only rational response was fear, a solemn fear he had never encountered, not even before battle. Still, he ignored it because the only way to handle fear was to ignore it and move on. But today the tremors in his bowels and the saliva foaming at his mouth refused to be ignored, and Yosef ben-Moshe knew why.

So wrenching to a stop, he planted his feet, raised his arms to the heavens, and shouted, "I admit it! Before heaven and earth, Jerusalem's battle is not against Babylon, but against your Word given to us through your Prophets. Instead of believing them, we—including myself—believed what we wanted to hear, believing the prophets who said, 'The Lord will do nothing. No harm will come to us. We will never see sword or famine.'"

Having made his grand confession, he was certain he would be all right and could move on. But the sickening chills were still there. In fact, they were worse, gnawing at him not only from the inside, but from the outside also. And no wonder! Both he and the Lord knew his fine-sounding words did not change a thing. Long ago, he had set his course to defend Jerusalem's wall against Babylon, and in doing so, he had set himself up against the rumbling lament overhead: "The Lord determined to tear down the walls around the Daughter of Zion."

But what could he do about it now? Let the wall fall without a fight? Quit being the commander of the Jerusalem army? Forsake his men who could not survive without him, so he could assuage his guilt at the final hour? No. He was their commander. This was his lot. This was his life. So trembling and sweating, Yosef ben-Moshe evacuated from both ends.

When he could stand upright again, he panted King David's prayer, the one he always prayed before battle: "Search me, O God, and know my heart. Test me and know my anxious thoughts. See if there is any offensive way in me and lead me in the way everlasting." Still, he felt no comfort, and why should he? The God of Abraham, Isaac and Jacob owed him nothing. So begging forgiveness for his offensive ways, he raced toward the battle, bellowing, "Lead me in the way everlasting!"

Reaching the corner turret, he caught a glimpse of the stones. They were no longer teetering. In fact, they looked as if they were sinking back into their ancient seats, and if that was true, he was witnessing the turn of the tide, the miracle Jerusalem had been praying for. Perhaps the Most High had even heard his prayer and, seeing how sincere he was and how sincere everyone was, had decided Jerusalem had been punished enough and, as Aridatha had been hoping, sent the Fourth Man to hold the wall together.

The good news spread, and before long, everyone in Jerusalem was clamoring up the steps to the top of the wall to watch the two motionless stones. Clutching their amulets of Ashtoreth the Queen of Heaven, much acclaimed for her comforting sweetness to anyone who prayed to her, and clinging to their pocketsize images of Baal who had proven trustworthy again and again, men, women, and children called out to the God of Abraham, Isaac and Jacob begging Him to return Solomon's stones to their rightful place, proving to the world that no one could destroy his city because it housed the Temple of Solomon which bore the Name of the Lord and contained the Ark of the Covenant.

Hence, the two massive stones became Jerusalem's rallying cry because in those stones lay the future of Jerusalem and God's Chosen People. Yes, the Lord had tested them, putting them through the horrific trial of the last eighteen months, but today was their day. They could feel it! The day Jerusalem was going to be saved. Moreover, as their fervor increased, their cries and petitions actually drowned out the heavenly choruses, until as if conceding to Jerusalem's will, they faded and drifted away. Upon their departure, cheers erupted because everyone knew their retreat was the sign the Lord had relented. However, midway through their cheers, their voices suddenly stopped, and a great silence fell upon the land. A silence not from themselves, but from outside themselves, as if a mighty hand was sweeping through the air scooping out not only sounds, but the strength of sound, the aftermath of sound, the comfort of sound, even the light of sound. Everything about sound was gone. Indeed, it was frightening in every way because without sound, it was impossible to hear, impossible to speak, impossible to move, even impossible to breathe.

And it lingered... and lingered... until all of Jerusalem and all of Babylon, locked in the absence of sound, not only remembered the

Fourth Man, but had the horrifying conviction he was amidst them, above them, below them, surrounding them and… angry at them! If one could have run to the hills and cried out to the mountains to cover him, he would have. But it was too late because it was then, with every thought, breath, and nerve attending, the two ancient stones bolted upward and, with a dying shriek that no one heard, spilled like rotting timber down the hillside. The upper portion of the wall was so surprised it held fast, suspended by its own consternation. But soon, with nowhere else to go, it too collapsed, plunging head over heels to the earth below and, with a booming crash, belched out great clouds of Jerusalem dirt.

Because the whole world knew no one could break through the Jerusalem wall, the whole world gasped in amazement at its great gaping wound. The whole world that is except Babylon. Babylon had neither the time nor the inclination to gasp. Instead, her well-fed warriors prepared for imminent invasion. By daybreak, they wanted be inside the city, looting, burning, killing, and destroying as rapidly as they could because the faster they destroyed, the sooner they could go home.

Staring at the wall's desolate hole, Nebuchadnezzar was a bit disappointed. Over the past weeks, he had been entertaining thoughts of the Fourth Man shooting flames out of the wall, and while his warriors battled their way into the inferno, he would gallop through the holocaust into victory. But instead, the stones had just fallen away, leaving a hole like any other hole in any other wall. No glory in that. Even so, watching the massive stones fall to the earth had ignited a visceral quickening he had not experienced before. Possibly because the stakes had never been so high. The Fourth Man had trespassed into his kingdom, and now with the wall breached, he was going to trespass into the Fourth Man's kingdom. Would the Fourth Man's fire annihilate Babylon or would Babylon's fire annihilate Jerusalem?

There was only one way to find out, and turning to his commanders, he raised his sword and shouted, "Ready the cavalry, archers, and tribal levies. Full on assault!"

38

"Go to the palace, Ari!"

Hearing Baruch's voice, Aridatha looked down from the Tower to see him motioning to his men, shouting, "Get to the breach or they will be marching into the city before daybreak!"

As if in a dream, she watched the soldiers pick up their wicker shields with more will than strength, then hurry toward the broken wall. She had grown up with them, working together in their fathers' olive groves, shearing their sheep, and treading their grapes. Even so, she could not remember those days. Not because the olive groves were burned, the sheep stalls empty, and the wine jars broken, but because her heart had deserted her. She could not pinpoint when it had fled or why it had abandoned her, but it was gone, taking with it everything good including memories, leaving her stranded in the timeless horrors of the siege: never-ending days and nights of crawling head to heel through narrow tunnels with those same young soldiers, hiding side by side in the Babylonian marketplace, and creeping one by one into enemy tents to steal meat and bread.

"Aridatha! Go to the palace!"

Baruch had been telling her all week to escape with King Zedekiah and her response had always been the same: she was going to stay in Jerusalem and wait for the Fourth Man. So she shouted back, "I am not leaving."

Baruch could not hear her, but he had a good idea what she was saying, so throwing his weapons down, he hurtled up the steps.

As he drew near, she yelled, "Do not start telling me about Moses and Jeremiah warning us about this. Do not tell me this is judgment."

"It is judgment," he declared starkly, leveling his angry eyes on hers. "Now get off this wall." When she did not move, he grabbed her arm and started pulling her toward the stairs.

"Let go of me, Baruch."

"Ari," he said, holding her arm tighter, "we have lost."

"Lost? Just because two stones fell to the ground? The Fourth Man can stop Babylon with or without our wall, Baruch."

"There is no Fourth Man!" he rasped, his voice hoarse from shouting through days and nights of smoke.

Whipping out her free arm, she slapped him. "No Fourth Man?! Even King Nebuchadnezzar knows there is a Fourth Man!"

"Then go to King Nebuchadnezzar!"

"Do not say that, Baruch!" she cried, slapping him over and over. "Do not ever say it! Ever!"

Wrapping his arms around her thrashing body, he whispered, "Aridatha, you must go to Babylon."

"Why?!" she cried, burying her face in his chest. "Why me?"

He had not held her this close since Reuben's wedding before the siege. Sneaking out into the night, they had kept their voices low, talking about a future with herds of goats, honey from their bees, and grapes from their vines. Her fragrance had been like a flowering field, just like her name, Aridatha, and he had wrapped his arms around her and held her close. He had wanted to kiss her; indeed, he had wanted to do more than that. But he did not kiss her or do anything more, not then or ever because always in the back of his mind, he wondered if she belonged to another.

Now, as she cried into his chest asking why she had to go to Babylon, he knew he had to tell her. "You must build houses, Ari. You must settle down, plant gardens, and eat what they produce."

"You are talking about Jeremiah. About the day he gave me the pouch."

"You know?"

"Papa told me this afternoon." Her bone-thin flesh was growing cold and she started to shiver. "I will not go, Baruch. I am staying with you."

"Listen to me, Ari."

"No!" she cried, struggling to get away. "I am staying with you!"

"Stop it and listen!"

Unable to break free, she went limp, staring blindly at the floor.

"You have had only a few hours to think about this. I have had years." He waited for her to look at him. When she did not, he continued, "Jeremiah gave you more than a pouch and Jerusalem dirt on that day. He gave you words, and whether you like it or not, they are your way out. You must go. You must live the life the Lord gave you."

Before she could object, he was gone, hurrying down the steps, grabbing up his weapons, and running toward the breach in the wall. She watched and waited for him to look back, but he did not look back. He simply disappeared into the smoke, gone, leaving her arms empty, her flesh cold, and her rage hotter than ever.

"I will not go!" she yelled. "I will not go to Babylon!" To prove it, she yanked Nebuchadnezzar's ring off her finger and threw it into the night. "I am staying in Jerusalem with you, Baruch! Either the Fourth Man will come and save us together or we will die together! Here! On Jerusalem soil!"

39

PREPARING to charge up the earthen ramp, Nebuchadnezzar checked and rechecked his daggers, swords, shield, and breastplate with a keen eye. But when he leaned down to readjust his leg armor, he was attacked, not by armor, but by something far more malevolent: the age-old foe, Doubt. Describing all the reasons why one was not going to succeed, Doubt was the first stage of retreat. So, jolting upright, he took a deep breath and whispered, "I will ascend!"

Thus composing himself, he looked out at the field only to see Doubt everywhere, creeping in like a thick fog. Deceptively innocent, it never came out and demanded what it was after, but veiled its treachery in simple questions. Even now he could see those questions seeping into his men's minds: "What if the Fourth Man is real? If he is real, why are you fighting for Babylon? Do you really think King Nebuchadnezzar can fight a god and win?"

Under such artful subtlety, his archers at the wall began to squirm, his tribal levies at Jerusalem's gates cringe, and his elite cavalry fidget. One moment, they had all been ramrod straight, strong and impenetrable; the next moment, their faces were wincing, chests sagging, and armor trembling. Even his horses, Babylon's finest fighting Barbs and Arabians, felt the pressure, laying their ears back and snorting uneasily. His own warhorse, usually calm as ice before battle, was so skittish Nebuchadnezzar again breathed "I will ascend," but to no avail. The agitation coming from all directions was too much, so he looked for Arioch. Arioch would calm his nerves. Where was he?

Searching the cavalry, he saw his commander under a cluster of torches, probably reviewing the intervals between each four-man charge up the ramp. From his cool piercing eyes to his swift barking orders, anyone could see he was not seized by this sudden hesitation, proving at least one man understood Nebuchadnezzar's Babylonian quest. Consequently, when Arioch spotted him and immediately signaled for him to stop the attack, he could not believe it.

Enough of doubt! The King of Babylon was the man in the epic, not the Fourth Man. Babylon was the glory of kingdoms, not Jerusalem. He, Nebuchadnezzar, was the head of gold, not some rock.

So, yanking his horse around, he ordered the charge and, without looking back, galloped up the ramp. Dumbfounded, the entire camp stared. Not only was their king racing fearlessly toward the Fourth Man, but he was also racing fearlessly toward a huge gap between the top of the ramp and the breached wall. It was one thing for a lone cavalryman to miss that jump, but for the King of Babylon to miss and go crashing down onto the rocks could mean injury and possible death. Or worse, historic humiliation. So, if their king was willing to risk it all, they were willing to risk it all. Thus, Babylon's armies, tribal levies, archers, and cavalries, forgetting their doubts, raised their swords and shouted, "BA-BY-LON!"

As soon as Nebuchadnezzar's horse hit the earthen ramp, Yosef ben-Moshe ordered his archers to shoot, a vain effort because Babylon's men and horses were dressed in bronze. So he shouted for fire, and Baruch ben-Zadok, with great satisfaction, threw burning torches into the straw at the breached entrance. With nowhere else to go, Nebuchadnezzar and his first wave of horsemen leapt over the gap, landed in the inferno, and the battle for Jerusalem began.

After eighteen months of siege, Baruch's friend Reuben was more than ready to fight Babylon. Slashing his oiled sword across booted legs, then grabbing the upper part of the severed limb, he pulled pain-shrieking warrior after pain-shrieking warrior off his horse and speared each in his exposed side. He never missed because he had been planning and practicing the maneuver for months, and nothing was going to stop him now. However, before long, his sleeve began to burn. Still, he fought on, desperate to spill Babylon's blood. But the more he fought, the hotter the flames glowed, and watching them lick up his arm, he panicked. Fire was not supposed to consume him! Fire was supposed to consume Babylon! Hananiah, Mishael, and Azariah's sleeves had not burned. Their hair had not singed. They had not smelled like smoke. So why was his sleeve burning, his hair searing, and the smell nauseating? Wasn't the Fourth Man going to save him?

If Baruch ben-Zadok had looked up, he would have seen Nebuchadnezzar almost upon him, smashing his way through horses, trampling
over men, ordering his cavalry to get down into the city and open the
gates. But Baruch, instead of looking up, was watching Reuben fighting
down the line, his wicker shield and sleeve on fire. He knew he should
forget about Reuben and keep fighting, but Reuben was his last living
friend. So, lunging through the horses, he grabbed the burning shield,
jammed it into a cavalryman's face, and pulled Reuben out of the horse's
path. At least now his friend could fight and die by the sword instead of
being burned and crushed to death.

Nebuchadnezzar had no such concerns because Nebuchadnezzar had no friends. He was the man in the great Babylonian epic. So,
thrusting his sword into every Hebrew in his path, he hacked his way
through armor and flesh with the same indomitable resolve he had employed at Carchemish against the Assyrians and Egyptians. Likewise, Yosef ben-Moshe used the same indomitable resolve he had employed at
Carchemish as he hacked his way through the Babylonians. So, with Nebuchadnezzar driving his horse toward the stairwell leading down into
the city and Yosef ben-Moshe stopping every horse before it reached the
stairwell, it was inevitable the two should meet and when they did, they
reared back, staring at each other.

Certainly, they were not surprised to see one another. Yet they
were shaken. Not because they were now enemies, and not because if
they fought each other, it would be to the death. In fact, both relished
the idea of going sword to sword against the best of enemies. So why
weren't their swords clanging back and forth in one epic row? What
was stopping them?

The answer was simple. A little girl. Ben-Moshe saw her looking up
at Nebuchadnezzar's gold image saying it looked like him, then adding
with a grin, "Except for the wings." Nebuchadnezzar saw her standing
in the tunnel offering him her crimson pouch, saying, "To remember
me by."

"Get out of my way," growled Nebuchadnezzar.

"You must protect her."

"Who are you to tell me what to do?"

"You gave me your word."

Nebuchadnezzar's warhorses were flying in on top of other warhorses, his foot soldiers were throwing down timbers to bridge the gap, and his warriors were clogging the stairwells, yet all he could think was Yosef ben-Moshe was not pleading but demanding, not bowing but threatening. And suddenly, he hated the man. Furthermore, he hated Daniel. He also hated his three judges, Shadrach, Meshach, and Abedneggo. Without a doubt, he hated Aridatha. In fact, he hated all Hebrews because their very existence defied Babylon. Thus, he was going to annihilate everyone in his path.

Nevertheless, when he raised his sword to strike down Jerusalem's Chief Commander, he could not do it. He had already seen Yosef ben-Moshe slumped on the ground, bloodied and half-dead because of an arrow meant for him. How could he plunge his sword into that same man? The answer was simple: he could not. So Nebuchadnezzar found a different target and, charging past Yosef ben-Moshe, slashed his sword into him.

40

AFTER Aridatha threw Nebuchadnezzar's ring into the night, she wandered through Jerusalem's empty streets. She had no idea where to go because she had no place to go. Her home was gone, the palace was being evacuated, and Baruch had ordered her off the wall. Furthermore, she was starting to realize wherever she did go, for the first time in her life she would be going alone. Always before, she had been with her father, her mother, or Baruch. Now her father was probably fighting his last battle, her mother would soon be escaping with King Zedekiah, and Baruch would fight to the death rather than be taken by Babylon. They were gone, and she was alone.

If only she could lie down and rest. But where? If she rested in the street, she would be beaten and robbed although she had nothing to take. If she crept into one of the remaining buildings, those inside would assume she was a prowler and attack her before she could explain. She had never considered she would have no place to go in her own city, and thus abandoned to the deserted streets, she wanted to give up. But, her father's words, "There is always a way out," would not let her give up.

Her father and Baruch believed Nebuchadnezzar was her way out, but there had to be another way. There had to be! Then she remembered: The Temple of Solomon. Why hadn't she thought of it before? She would wait for the Fourth Man there. Starting to feel alive again, she looked out to get her bearings and found she was not far from the Temple, for she was already approaching the Field of the Dying.

Only eighteen months before, the Field of the Dying had been called *Aridatha*, a Flowering Field, because long ago it had been a field of wildflowers. An ancient prophet had erected a stele in its center, and when he died, the king bought the field, dug out the wildflowers, and built a park of pomegranate tree mazes, red lily topiaries, monuments, and altars. Over the decades, each king had added to its tranquil yet profound beauty, planting more trees and gardens and building more monuments and altars until it became Jerusalem's favorite gathering place, especially on Sabbath, because on Sabbath there was nothing to do except go to the Temple and rest from work.

So, each week, all of Jerusalem crowded into Flowering Field to sit and stroll, laugh and play, eat and drink. Old men, watching wrestling matches under the teil trees, gambled on their favorite champions; women and children, dancing under the Ashtoreth poles, sang along with Jerusalem's popular musicians; and merchants and city workers, discussing the slow-turning wheels of the city authorities, reviewed the latest scandals. Then, at the end of the day, each family regrouped to promenade through the park, shop at the artisans' stalls, and head for home until the next Sabbath.

Not many knew about the prophet's stele in the center of the park because thick prickly acanthus and junipers had grown up around it. But now, after eighteen months of siege, everyone could see the stele because it was the only thing left. The food, wine, singing, and dancing were gone. The Ashtoreth poles and altars, gone. The flowers had fallen and the trees had withered. Even the name Flowering Field had faded away. Nothing remained except the dead, the dying, and the prophet's stele with its written message shining out like a beacon: *"All men are like grass and all their glory is like the flowers of the field. The grass withers and the flowers fall because the breath of the Lord blows on them. Surely the people are like grass. The grass withers and the flowers fall, but the Word of our God stands forever."*

Many times, Aridatha had sneaked into the Field to read the message, wondering what it meant and why it was important. But tonight she picked up her step, eager to get away from the stench and the corpse-eaters who prowled through the park at night searching for plunder. Even more importantly, she was eager to get to the Temple. Nevertheless, something turned her head, forcing her to look at a tall man moving from one dying wisp to another. Instantly, she recognized him, the traitor to all Jerusalem, and never wanting to see him again, she started to run. But whatever had turned her head to look at him tugged her back toward him. So, stepping into the Field, she crisscrossed her way over burned and shrunken bodies until she reached Jeremiah the prophet of God.

As the prophet lifted a feverish boy out of the grasp of his dead mother and wrapped him in a tattered blanket, the moonlight highlighted his face as if wanting Aridatha to see his scabbed flesh stretched taut over his bones. But she felt no pity. Everyone had suffered, not just him. Besides, wasn't it a little too late to be washing wounds and offering water to the dying when he could have prayed to the Lord—when Jerusalem begged him—so none of this would have happened?

Soon, he came upon two little girls, mere skeletons with wide frightened eyes, and taking them in his arms, he rocked them.

"Why?" moaned one of the skeletons.

Aridatha edged closer, wondering how he was going to explain this!

"In days to come," he answered, "the Lord will make a righteous Branch sprout from David's line."

As always, his answer was camouflaged in imagery which no one could dispute or disprove. Disgusted, Aridatha was about to challenge it, but seeing the girls' leaden eyes brighten, she held her tongue.

Looking toward the horizon, he continued, "He will do what is just and right in the land."

Watching the girls follow his gaze, Aridatha remembered when she was a little girl and followed his gaze toward the horizon. Even then he had spoken words she could not understand, words about Rachel weeping and mourning for her children.

"In those days Judah shall be delivered and Israel shall dwell secure," he said. Then, raising his voice for all to hear, he announced, "This is the name by which he will be called: The Lord Our Righteousness."

His words about Judah being delivered and Israel dwelling securely "in those days" angered her all the more. He was always proclaiming good news about the faraway future, but she wanted to hear something good about the present or else he should be quiet. Then she realized he was quiet. Everything was quiet. The painful groaning that had gripped the Field only moments before had been transformed into soft restful breathing. Evidently his words, "The Lord Our Righteousness," had brought some relief to their suffering. Even the little girls in his lap seemed comforted as they nestled their icy bodies into his chest. Then sighing peacefully, they closed their eyes and the anguish on their faces completely disappeared.

They were dead.

Aridatha had seen death a hundred times over during the past eighteen months, so she knew they were dead. However, she also knew they could not be dead because they were in the arms of the prophet. After all, she had looked dead in those same arms when she was a little girl, and her breath had returned. So she waited. But believing their small chests were rising up and down, did not make it so, and Aridatha panicked.

"Do something!" she cried.

When the prophet did nothing but weep, she broke into a rage, "You are responsible for this. For all of our sufferings and all of these deaths. You!" she screamed just as her mother had screamed at her father. At the time, she had hated her mother for it, but now like her mother, she gave way to her fury. "Death by fire, famine, and sword, isn't that what you said? You want Jerusalem destroyed!"

With the two little girls tucked next to his heart, the prophet reached out to Aridatha, trying to take her hand.

"No," she shrieked, leaping back. "You cannot have me anymore. I am no longer fooled by your traitorous words. That is what you are, Jeremiah, a traitor. A traitor to the God of Abraham, Isaac and Jacob. He would never destroy Jerusalem because it is the City of David, and he loves David!"

Her words blasted out of her so forcefully, she almost blacked out, and head spinning, she started to fall. But if she fell in the Field of the Dying, she might never rise again. So, hurtling through the darkness, she ran toward the gate.

If only she had waited and stayed with Jeremiah a few more moments, Aridatha might have seen the two little girls, their bodies still in his lap, being carried away by angels to Abraham's side.

⊶⊷⊶

Not far from the Field of the Dying, Jerusalem's wealthy remnant was in the king's garden, mounted up and ready to escape. However, no one could leave because the king had not yet arrived. After eighteen months of hanging onto hope that never came, these last hours of waiting had the shrunken noblemen and women of Jerusalem shaking to their bones, their horses just as anxious, jamming up and backing into one another. What was the king doing? Why was he taking so long?

Didn't he know every moment counted? Weren't they supposed to be halfway to the Arabah by now?

Suddenly, the sounds of hurried footsteps and muffled clanking approached through the darkness. At last, there he was, King Zedekiah, scrambling toward his horse, dragging two large bags filled with the last of the palace treasures: King Solomon's gold cups and chargers, his gold embroidered bedding, and King David's sword. Breathing a sigh of relief, the escapees watched for the signal to leave, but again they had to wait because Zedekiah's sons lagged behind. They too were hauling large clanking bags, stumbling and falling. So more minutes crawled by as four soldiers dismounted and rushed to help them. Meanwhile, the king reached his horse, but his hands were trembling so violently, it took him a teeth-grinding age to secure the bags. Once secured, still no one could leave because he had to search his pockets for the keys to the palace. Not until every key was painstakingly accounted for did he mount up and finally ride toward the garden gate.

Surrounded by shrouded faces and the ghostly backdrop of fire and smoke, Zillah jolted forward, her horse tiptoeing along with all the other tiptoeing silhouettes. In fact, everyone was tiptoeing so furtively, she soon started to titter. Were they going to tiptoe all night? In silence? Without one lantern burning? Unexpectedly, she hiccuped, and was so embarrassed, she tittered again. Then another hiccup. This time angry faces turned on her. She tried to be quiet, but who could stop hiccups? A sudden shriek of agony from the city ripped through the sky, and trying not to hiccup or titter, she belched out an explosive burp and burst into giggles.

From out of the darkness, a hand struck her across the face followed by a sharp *shut up*.

She could not believe it! No one had ever struck her! Now her beautiful nose was bleeding. If everyone was going to be so mean, she would go home. But Zillah did not go home. Instead, she shut up and tiptoed her horse forward.

41

Oɴ the first day of the siege, Aridatha believed the Fourth Man was going to destroy Babylon with a firestorm. Much to her surprise and disappointment, that did not happen. From then on, she awakened each morning believing the Fourth Man was going to do a marvelous miracle to stop Babylon on that particular day. Finally, the miracle came when Nebuchadnezzar's armies suddenly withdrew and went to Egypt. However, they soon returned, and as Jerusalem grew weaker and still nothing happened, Aridatha was forced to rethink her position, concluding the Fourth Man was going to come when Nebuchadnezzar broke through the wall. Only hours before, he did break through the wall, and still the Fourth Man had not come. So, as Aridatha raced out of the Field of the Dying toward the Temple of Solomon, she did not know what to think. Where was the Fourth Man? Why hadn't he come? What was he waiting for? Again, she wanted to give up, but she sensed if she could make it to the Temple, all would be well. Then, it dawned on her. Of course, all would be well at the Temple because that was where the Fourth Man would come. That had to be it! He must have been planning it all along, because the true and righteous battle should be at the Temple and for the Temple.

Ignited by visions of the fiery furnace and the glory of the Lord descending on the Temple of Solomon, her feet flew up the hill. Climbing over the gate, she hurtled through the smoke out into the abandoned courtyard, and her heart sank. Nothing about the Temple looked like the splendor of the fiery furnace or the glory of the Lord. Nothing about it looked as grand and powerful as King Nebuchadnezzar's towering gold statue, his temples, or his palaces. Nothing about it looked grand or powerful at all. It just looked old and drab and dreary. Quickly, she reminded herself, anything in the black of night without torchlights blazing and patriots singing would look old and drab and dreary. Still, because this was the Fourth Man's battlefield, she had expected something a bit more stirring, something like heavenly lights or winged cherubim or glorious music. The dwelling place of the Ark of the Covenant should look like a mighty fortress when Babylon arrived, not an abandoned building.

An abandoned building? How could she even think it? But wait! Rumors had been flying about Jeremiah sneaking the Ark of the Covenant out of the Temple in the middle of a moonless night and hiding it in the mountains. If that was true, then it would look like an abandoned building. But that could not be true. No one would allow a traitor to take the Ark of the Covenant away. In any case, the Fourth Man would soon be filling the Temple and it would look grand and powerful again.

So, turning round and round, she searched for the Fourth Man, scanning the Temple rooftop, its walls, the bronze Sea, and the two pillars, Jachin and Boaz. As she spun, she remembered spinning round and round when Red Beard hurled her through the air, only this time she did not see her mother, Baruch, or the swaying crimson pouch. This time she only saw smoke and ashes stinging her eyes and burning her lungs, until gasping and coughing, her knees gave way and she slumped to the ground.

She tried to push herself back onto her feet. Surely, after eighteen months of watching, she could watch one more hour. But her arms and legs kept buckling, and her eyes kept falling shut, until she and Baruch ben-Zadok were riding together on his horse across summer pasturelands. Flocks of goats dotted the hillsides, and anise, crushed by the horse's hooves, scented the air. With his chest warming her back and his voice warming her soul, they rode toward heavenly lights, winged cherubim, and glorious music. Not at all like the day when King Nebuchadnezzar threw her on Baruch's horse and ordered him to get her back to Jerusalem. That day, rushing to escape the oncoming Babylonian warriors, his body had been cold and stiff... cold and stiff...

Cold and stiff, Aridatha jolted awake. Her face was fixed to hard tiles, her every bone aching. Where was she? How long had she slept? Why was she so cold? Then she remembered. Babylon had broken through the wall during the night and she had come to the Temple where the Fourth Man was going to win the final victory. Everyone else must have known it too because she was surrounded by hundreds of Jerusalem's starving and wounded streaming into the courtyard, falling to their knees.

They were a pathetic, stinking lot, and Aridatha loved them all. They had not given up on the Fourth Man. They trusted what she had seen: three Hebrews living in fire while Babylon's warriors burned to death. Thus, inspired by their trust, their tears, and their suffering, she cried out, "Our God will save us!"

Immediately, the sunrise lit the Temple, haloing it with pillars of gold. No longer looking old and drab and dreary, the Temple of Solomon was a blinding radiance, a throne of majesty, and Jerusalem gasped in hopeful wonder. Was this the moment they had been waiting for?

Aridatha believed it was and, raising her arms to the heavens, shouted, "He is coming!"

Everyone knew Aridatha had seen the Fourth Man, therefore she must know what he looked like. So, although the Hebrews could not see him, they raised their arms and praised the God of Abraham, Isaac and Jacob, singing the song of the ages:

"Sh'ma Israel, Adonai Eloheynu, Adonai echad..."

But their voices, thin and frail, were soon drowned out by Babylon's horses charging through the city streets getting closer...

"... Baruch shem Kavod malchuto, Le'olam Va'ed."

... and closer.

⚬

As Jerusalem's remnant sang in the Temple courtyard, King Zedekiah, his army, and his hand-picked nobles charged across the Arabah in a scattered frenzy, fleeing the approaching Babylonian cavalry. Hebrew commanders shouted orders, Zedekiah's noblemen yelled curses, women shrieked, children cried, and in their midst, the King of Jerusalem raged at them all, demanding to know who had given them away.

Zillah, no longer counting on madness to support her, let out a bloodcurdling scream she hoped could be heard all the way back to Jerusalem, condemning her husband for sending her on this death ride. After that, she shouted, "Queen of Heaven, Mother of us all, save us. You who bring peace to the earth save your children." Pulling out a gold medallion hanging from her neck, she lifted the image of the Queen of Heaven to her lips, kissed it, and whispered, "Protect me."

Like magic, she no longer saw Babylon as the enemy, but Jerusalem. It was the City of David that had made her life miserable, burdening her with its heavy-handed, narrow-minded Laws, its one Temple, and one God, whereas Babylon... Babylon was tolerant of everything! With its thousands of temples honoring thousands of gods including Ishtar the Queen of Heaven, Babylon had room for all religions. Furthermore, Babylon did not frown on her astrology charts as her husband and Jeremiah did, but kept an assembly of stargazers studying the stars and their courses. Most importantly, Babylon was the wealthiest and most splendid city on earth.

So, if Zillah was the woman she thought she was, she could have it all. By using her husband's name because he saved Nebuchadnezzar's life and Aridatha's name because she was a favorite of Nebuchadnezzar, and by capitalizing on her own exceptional beauty, she could be the belle of Babylon. Thrilled by this unexpected turn of events, she wiped the dust from her face, rearranged the folds of her tunic, and waited demurely for her Babylonian conquerors.

42

At the ripe old age of twelve, Michael ben-Ram believed he had outgrown all his fears. After all, he had been the first to sight Babylon approaching—both times. Furthermore, over the past seven months, he had scavenged in the Babylonian marketplace with the Adullamites, fought on the wall, and witnessed untold deaths by fire, sword, starvation, and disease. Consequently, he was not fazed when a mere hundred Babylonian horsemen led by Babylon's chief commander, Arioch, galloped into the Temple courtyard. But as they thrust their spears into men holding families and slashed their swords at mothers and children trying to escape, he realized this was a slaughter his gifted eyesight was not prepared for. Nor was he prepared for the non-stop roar of Babylon's curses, Jerusalem's wailings, or the horses' squealings, objecting to their masters' villainous duties.

Trying to block it all out, he shut his tear-filled eyes and covered his ringing ears. But without sight and sound, he was instantly aware of the stench of urine, excrement, and disemboweled bodies, and before long, he was a frightened little boy again, wanting to run away and hide. But where could he go? Perhaps if he threw himself to the ground and covered his head, no one would see him. Why would anyone want to slaughter him anyway? What had he done to deserve such wrath?

Then he saw Aridatha. Crossing the battlefield to a fallen Hebrew soldier, she grabbed his bow, wheeled around, and shot a Babylonian warrior crashing toward her on horseback. Loading a second arrow, she turned and shot another warrior ready to spear a young girl. Riveted to her every move, the draw of her bowstring, the grim alertness in her eyes, and the Stars of David in her hem soaking up the blood of fallen Hebrews, Michael knew he would never run or hide again. Instead, like Aridatha, he was going to fight. So, wiping the tears from his eyes, he scrambled toward a dead Babylonian warrior and, picking up his iron sword, shouted, "For Jerusalem!"

"Michael!" blasted from behind.

Swinging around, Michael stared in awe at twenty Hebrew warriors galloping into the courtyard. Led by Yosef ben-Moshe carrying his dented Star of David shield and Baruch ben-Zadok carrying his sword and whip, they looked like twenty Samsons strengthened for their final triumph against the pillars of Dagon. Riding sleek fresh horses, the horses Yosef ben-Moshe had sent to pasture in the northern wastelands, Michael knew nothing was going to stop them.

"Get away from here!" yelled Yosef ben-Moshe.

Michael held up his sword. "I am going to fight."

"No! You are going to live. Now run."

Michael had no choice. Jerusalem's commander had given him an order. So, clinging to the magnificent Babylonian sword, he hurried to the perimeter of the courtyard.

As Yosef ben-Moshe's warriors rode headlong into battle, Baruch ben-Zadok held back to search for one man. He had been looking for him throughout the siege with no success, so he was probably dead or deployed to another front. However, if he was here, Baruch was going to find him and kill him. Studying every man on horseback, he finally came upon a red-bearded warrior with a larger-than-life chest hacking his sword through women and children. He was in the shadow of the bronze Sea, so it was difficult to tell if it was he, especially because his beard was lighter and chest flabbier. But that would make sense after so many years. Still, Baruch had to be sure.

Suddenly the warrior broke into a litany of curses, and Baruch's heart froze. The thick slobbering tongue had not changed. It was he, Red Beard, the Babylonian warrior who had hurled three-year-old Aridatha into the air to her near-death. Baruch's moment had finally come, and raising his sword, he yelled, "Lord, grant me vengeance!"

Amidst the din, Red Beard did not hear. Even if he had heard, he would not have turned because he was distracted by his arm cramping up. No surprise to him after power-driving his sword in and out of flesh since midnight. So with his horse weary, sword dull, and stomach empty, he took a moment to stretch his arm, and surprisingly, he saw a Hebrew on horseback charging toward him. On further examination, Hebrews were on horseback everywhere, like ants pressing in from all sides. But how could that be? Hadn't he and the entire Babylonian army worked all night annihilating every Hebrew and confiscating every horse? Apparently not. Oh, well, only a few more kills and it would be over.

"Come on, Jew!" he yelled.

Circling his sword overhead, Baruch yelled back, "From Baruch ben-Zadok!"

Red Beard was about to spur his horse toward him, but knowing intimidation was half the battle, he stayed where he was, bellowing curses and raising his bloodied sword high, creating the illusion he was a giant and therefore unbeatable. Unfortunately, after the strain of killing all night, his back, unable to take one more sudden movement, locked. To be arched upward like a flagstaff surprised Red Beard because nothing like it had ever happened to him. Hence, he was sure his back would loosen up because he needed it to thrust his sword into the oncoming Jew. But to his astonishment, his back did not loosen up. So the man who threw Aridatha into the arms of Jeremiah spent his last moments staring in terror at the man who loved her, galloping toward him, yelling, "For Aridatha!"

Baruch slashed his sword across Red Beard's neck, watched his eyes bulge and his cursing mouth fall silent.

On the other side of the courtyard, Aridatha hurried a wounded child to Michael ben-Ram. As Michael whisked the boy into the shade, he motioned to the bronze pillar Boaz, yelling something about Yosef ben-Moshe. Aridatha turned to see her father on horseback fighting two Babylonian cavalrymen. She had never seen him in battle before, and her heart leapt because he was unbeatable as he fought shield against sword and sword against shield, his two opponents floundering. She knew what he would do next: spur his horse into the weaker man causing him to lose his balance, then turn and crash into the stronger, a full circle and thrust. But before he made the circle, an arrow sank into his neck.

"No!" she cried, staring at the two warriors moving in for the kill, slashing toward his face and chopping against his legs. But Yosef ben-Moshe, no stranger to an arrow in his flesh, faced his enemies full on. Stabbing his sword into one and his shield into the other, he refused to drop until he brought both of them down with him.

"Papa!" she shrieked.

The word papa had been echoing throughout the courtyard all morning, but Arioch heard this cry because it was her cry. Swinging around, he scanned the field. There she was, racing toward blood-soaked Yosef ben-Moshe, unaware a Babylonian warrior was closing in from behind, his dagger raised to strike. Arioch ordered him to stop, but he did not hear. So galloping toward him, he continued to shout orders when a whip wrapped around the warrior's arm and jerked him away.

It was Baruch ben-Zadok at the other end of the whip, yelling, "Ari!"

Hearing his call, she looked everywhere, calling "Baruch" again and again. Finally, she saw him hurtling toward her with an arrow in his leg. Then came the horror: a horse's hoof flashed out, kicked him in the ribs, and pitched him backward.

"Baruch!" she cried, watching him crash to the earth and his body go limp. Gaping at Baruch, then at her father, trying to decide how to get to both of them at the same time, she was seized from behind. Terrified, she kicked and punched, trying to get out of the warrior's grip, when he jerked her around to face him. It was Arioch, his ice blue eyes commanding.

"No!" she yelled. "Papa needs me!"

"If I let you go, you will be dead before you get to him."

"I am not going to Nebuchadnezzar!"

"Aridatha, your father is dead. You belong to the king now."

"Baruch!" she screamed. But Baruch did not move. "Papa!" she cried. But Yosef ben-Moshe did not move. So, turning to the Temple, she shouted at the top of her lungs, "I know you are in there!"

"Aridatha!" Arioch blasted, tightening his grip until her wild eyes came back to his. "Come into the shade."

She had been fighting since daybreak, and before that, for a year and a half. A long time to fight, and suddenly she was tired. Certainly, a few moments in the shade could do her no harm. After that, she would fight again. So Aridatha of Jerusalem, her strength gone, let Babylon's Chief Commander bind her wrists and lead her into the shade.

43

Under the heat of the midday sun, the Temple built and dedicated by Solomon did nothing to help the Hebrew warriors on horseback fighting to the death. Likewise, the twelve bronze bulls supporting the bronze Sea did nothing to help the Hebrew children hiding under them. Nor did the two pillars, Jachin, meaning God establishes, and Boaz, meaning In Him is strength, do anything to help the Hebrew women swinging their bone-thin arms against horses and riders. Thus, abandoned to such pitilessness, the Hebrews no longer hoped for mercy from their God, but from Babylon.

Then, as if by some pre-ordained decree, everything came to a halt. Swords, daggers, and bows froze; cries, moans, and curses hushed. What had happened? What had caused this respite from the carnage, this welcome silence, this blessed moment to take a breath? Glancing from one to the other, the Hebrews wondered if it was over. Oh pray, God, let it be over, so they could rest. But the courtyard had not turned quiet so the Hebrews could rest. All was quiet because Nebuchadnezzar King of Babylon was riding in.

Aridatha stared numbly at his splendor. Dressed in gold armor and carrying a gold torch, he rode into the courtyard on a gold-shielded Barb draped in gold bells. Their tinkling was like a gentle bird song that would have delighted the senses elsewhere, but here it only mocked the mangled dead. Six warrior chiefs on snorting steeds rode behind him carrying signs and standards embellished with Babylon's gods Marduk and Ninmah, Kesith the Archer and Dahrach the Dragon. Each of their saddlebags was weighed down by six red-handled axes imported especially for the occasion from the savage Frank tribes living in the cold forests north of the Great Sea. His warriors on the ground, sweaty and bloody from the morning slaughter, quickly opened a path for their king, pitching bodies out of his way. But Aridatha knew none of this mattered to Nebuchadnezzar. Not the bells, the chiefs following behind, or the crushed bodies ahead. All that mattered to him was the Temple, his attention riveted to its height, width, and depth. And out of the three, she guessed his royal thoughts were most focused on its depth.

Indeed, Nebuchadnezzar's concentration was deep inside the Temple, all the way into the room called the Most Holy Place. Unlike Babylon's temples, the Temple of Solomon had no gods displayed outside or inside, not even a mummy ensconced in its inner rooms like the tombs of Egypt. Instead, the Most Holy Place housed one gilded acacia-wood box known as the Ark of the Covenant with two gilded olive-wood angels known as the cherubim of the Glory watching over it.

He had learned about the Temple of Solomon, the Ark of the Covenant, and the cherubim of the Glory from Daniel. But the Ark of the Covenant had intrigued him the most because of its curious importance. Once long ago when the Philistines captured the Ark of the Covenant, the Lord's hand weighed heavily upon their cities, bringing devastation and tumors. On another occasion, a man took hold of the Ark because the oxen pulling it had stumbled. For his irreverent act, the God of Abraham, Isaac and Jacob instantly struck him down. Being a king, Nebuchadnezzar understood immediate and deadly judgments over irreverent acts. What he could not understand was why a box without anything to identify its god, not a name or an image, should be so revered.

Daniel had explained the Ark of the Covenant was revered because it contained the Testimony spoken out of the fire by the Lord and written by the finger of God on two stone tablets. When the King of Babylon heard that the Lord had spoken out of the fire, he could not help thinking of the Fourth Man who also lived in fire. Then again, perhaps it was not two who lived in fire, but one. In other words, perhaps the Fourth Man and the Lord were one and the same. If that was true, then the Testimony in the Ark of the Covenant was the Testimony of the Fourth Man. Ever since, Nebuchadnezzar had wondered if the Fourth Man's display of power in his fiery furnace had been a warning. A sort of prelude to what might happen to him if he ever came against Jerusalem, the Temple of Solomon, the Ark of the Covenant overshadowed by the cherubim of the Glory, and, ultimately, his Testimony.

Indeed, it might have been a warning. On the other hand, it might have been a coincidence. Either way, Nebuchadnezzar had power too.

He was the man in Shining One's epic. He was Babylon, the glory of kingdoms. So he kept riding.

Loyal Arioch had to try one more time to stop his king, and galloping up beside him, he started to speak, but Nebuchadnezzar immediately cut him off.

"Get back, Arioch. You are not going with me."

"I do not want to go with you."

The words hit hard. Arioch had always wanted to go with him.

"I want you to stop," Arioch said so no one could hear. "Jerusalem is destroyed. That is all that matters."

"Nothing matters until their Temple is destroyed."

"King Nebuchadnezzar, mighty and great you are, but the Fourth Man lives in that Temple."

"Then he will have to find another place to live."

Grabbing the king's arm, Arioch jerked him to a stop. Their eyes met, both men breathing hard.

"Arioch. Remove your hand."

Tightening his grip, Arioch leaned in nose to nose. "Whatever you do, do not go into the Most Holy Place. If you do, do not touch the Ark of the Covenant."

"If you do not let go of me, I will have your head."

"Most importantly, do not try to burn the Ark of the Covenant. You tried to burn Shadrach, Meshach, and…"

Nebuchadnezzar smashed his torch handle into Arioch's wrist with such force, his hand splayed, releasing the king. Not until then did Arioch understand Nebuchadnezzar could not be stopped. So, bowing his head, he backed his horse away, leaving the king alone to clip-clop toward the entrance.

The King of Babylon rode regally, the picture of power and glory. He also rode slowly, not because he was tentative or afraid, but because he wanted to study the Temple he was about to enter. The building looked structurally sound, like any plain box with two simple pillars at the entrance. In fact, it was so plain and so simple, he was disappointed. If the God of Abraham, Isaac and Jacob had been his God, he would have used all his resources and ingenuity to build something unsurpassed for his dwelling place. Perhaps a ziggurat with gold fountains climbing along the outside tiers, or multiple circular towers with stairwells for the singers, or even a few hidden braziers for night lighting. Didn't these Hebrews have any imagination? He also would have maintained the edifice day and night, year in and year out. Yes, because of the siege, it was coated with ash, but the walls were stained, the steps cracked, and whole sections of the bronze pomegranates missing. In fact, the Temple was so rundown, it looked like an abandoned building eager to be burned to the ground. As if the very presence of Babylon had destroyed its will to live.

So, raising his torch high, he shouted confidently, "BA-BY-LON!!!"

Normally his armies would have responded, "BA-BY-LON!!!" Now, there was unified silence. Nebuchadnezzar hurled a disgusted scowl at Arioch, as if it was his fault. Then, whipping his horse into a furious gallop, he charged up the entrance steps and, bellowing BA-BY-LON, disappeared into the Temple of Solomon.

The moment he rode into the Temple, both the Hebrews and Babylonians froze in mortal fear. The Hebrews, because if they lost the Ark of the Covenant, what would be left? Without the presence of their God, they would be no different from any other kingdom, nation, or people, having nothing but themselves to rely on, nothing but themselves to live for, and nothing but themselves to glory in. So, as never before, they repented, hurrying through the commandments of the Lord, confessing each idol and blasphemy. They condemned their hatred of Jeremiah and their rejection of God's Word, acknowledging although their tongues had praised the Lord, their hearts had been far from Him. Not only did they say they were sorry for their past transgressions, but they made vows for their future, promising to keep the Law and hand it down to their children and children's children. Yes, Jerusalem was in flames and the City of David destroyed, but couldn't the Fourth Man still relent, saving the Temple and annihilating Babylon?

The Babylonians' fear ran much deeper, for unlike the Hebrews who were facing a mere identity crisis, they were facing extinction. Everyone knew man fought not only to survive, but to raise up his light forever. Everyone also knew Nebuchadnezzar had accomplished just that: fought and raised up Babylon's light to shine in the world forever. However, if the Fourth Man was in that Temple, he could extinguish Nebuchadnezzar's light with one fiery blast. Even closer to home, he could extinguish Nebuchadnezzar and his armies right now. What could be more horrific than that?!

So, the mighty warriors of Babylon, wondering if Nebuchadnezzar was going to enter the Most Holy Place, edged closer together. Would their king touch the Ark of the Covenant? Arioch had warned him not to, but from the way he had charged in, it looked as if he had every intention of doing so. Hopefully, the widespread rumor that Jeremiah removed the Ark of the Covenant from the Temple and hid it in the mountains was true. Yes, hopefully, the box was gone. Still, after long minutes with no sight or sound of their king, a sudden urge to urinate gripped more than one Babylonian warrior.

Arioch's nerves had tightened to the point of agony because it did not take this long to ride in and out of one small temple. Surely, the Fourth Man must have incinerated Nebuchadnezzar by now. Yet, there was no smoke. If there was, he knew it would not be from Nebuchadnezzar's torch, because if the Temple walls, ceilings, or floors were still gilded, the king would collect the gold for Babylon before torching the building. So what was going on? Why hadn't he returned? A new thought: what if Hebrew priests had been lying in wait inside the Temple? What if one had run a dagger through his heart? Arioch had never thought of an ambush. Then again, the Fourth Man did not have to use fire to destroy Nebuchadnezzar. He could use plague as he did with the Assyrians. Frustrated, Arioch could wait no longer, yet he had to. This was the king's battle, not his. Even so, if the king did not reappear soon, he planned to ride in and rescue him.

A muffled roar from inside the Temple, sounding very much like BA-BY-LON, exploded out of the entrance. Arioch wondered if it was King Nebuchadnezzar's last defiant cry. Whatever it was, it echoed on and on, and with all eyes fastened to the Temple, a discreet retreat would not have been noticed. Yet no one moved. Instead, both Hebrews and Babylonians stayed exactly where they were, to witness and bear witness.

Aridatha, still standing in the shade, also knew it did not take this long to ride in and out of the temple, so raising her bound hands, she shouted, "The Fourth Man has come and delivered us!"

It was the moment the Hebrews had been waiting for, and jumping up and down, they laughed and hugged and cried. Even Baruch, in a fog of pain, groaned words he had not dared to utter during the siege, words he and Aridatha had known since childhood, "Fire came down from heaven and the glory of the Lord…"

Arioch was frantic. He had to do something, and he started to charge toward the steps when he saw a wild man on horseback galloping inside the Temple, his torch held high.

Was it Nebuchadnezzar? Or was it his ghost riding inside the shadows? More likely, it was the Fourth Man coming out to annihilate them. But if it was the Fourth Man, why was he shouting Babylon so vigorously? Probably because he was angry at Babylon and calling her into account.

Thinking he was indeed calling them into account, the mighty warriors of Babylon stared down at their blood-caked hands. How many Hebrews had each slain that day? How many women? How many children? How many had begged for mercy? How many had called on the Name of the Lord for rescue? How many had screamed for the Fourth Man to save them? Thirty? Sixty? One hundred?

"I WILL ASCEND TO THE HEAVENS! I WILL SIT ENTHRONED ON THE MOUNT!" roared from inside the Temple.

Recognizing Shining One's words, words Nebuchadnezzar had spoken often, the men were so confounded, they started talking to themselves, low, frightened whispers blithering perhaps it was not the Fourth Man, but their king riding freely inside the Temple. Glancing from one to another, they cautiously suggested that maybe—just maybe—Nebuchadnezzar had won, and therefore, maybe—just maybe—he was more powerful than the Fourth Man.

One brave soul decided to test the waters and find out. So, quietly lifting his voice, he breathed, "Ba-by-lon." When nothing happened to him, a few more quavered, "Ba-by-lon." When still nothing happened, all together they ventured, "Ba-by-lon!"

"NOTHING CAN SHAKE ME!!!" thundered back at them, followed by Nebuchadnezzar riding out to the top of the stairs and stopping for all to see.

It was true! The man at the Temple entrance, looking like a pillar of gold with his torch held high, was not the Fourth Man, but King Nebuchadnezzar. He had taken on the Fourth Man in the Fourth Man's territory and won, overruling extinction and procuring Babylon's light forever.

"BA-BY-LON!!! BA-BY-LON!!! BA-BY-LON!!!" exploded back at him.

44

AFTER staring at the Temple of Solomon for over an hour, Aridatha no longer saw Nebuchadnezzar riding up and down the steps yelling, "I will ascend to the heavens; I will sit enthroned on the mount." Nor did she see the dozens of chiefs swinging their red-handled axes at the roots of the pillars, Jachin and Boaz. She had even lost sight of the thousands of warriors punching their swords into the sky chanting Babylon, because after a year and a half of waiting, all she could see was the absence of the Fourth Man.

Finally, she yelled at the Temple, "You did not come!"

"Quiet," ordered Arioch.

"I will not be quiet. The Fourth Man did not come. He did not listen to me."

"Aridatha, if the king hears you, he will kill you."

"Let him!" she bawled into his face. "He has killed everything else: Jerusalem, Baruch, my father." To prove it, she turned to her dead father across the courtyard and shrieked, "Pa-paaa!"

Arioch clapped his hand over her mouth, and she bit him to the bone. Instantly, his warrior reflexes struck her across the face, and she slumped deathlike into his arms. Aghast, he pressed his fingers to her pulse. After what seemed an eternity, he found life, weak but still there. Wondering if the king had seen her, he looked at the Temple. But Nebuchadnezzar, still shouting from the steps, saw nothing but his own victory. So, ducking behind the horses, Arioch considered his options or, more accurately, his lack of options. Yosef ben-Moshe, with an arrow lodged in his neck, was dead. Baruch ben-Zadok, with an arrow lodged in his leg, looked equally dead. The king had condemned her to fall with Jerusalem, so he could not take her to him. And if he let her go, some warrior would certainly ravage and kill her.

"You better get her out of here!" shouted from behind.

Arioch swung around to see his first commander, Nergal, riding in. "Here. You take her," he ordered, hoisting her up onto Nergal's horse.

"Me?!" he objected, spitting out his bronze toothpick. "What do you want me to do with her?"

"Put her with the slaves headed for hard labor in the capital."

"Hard labor?"

"The king will not look for her there."

"He will not have to. She will be dead."

"Not if we send her to Shadrach."

Nergal's eyes brightened. "The Hebrew high judge?"

"Yes, but hurry. If she starts yelling again and he hears…"

"May the gods reward you, commander."

Their eyes met. A rare occasion because their eyes never met, at least not to look into each other's souls. But in their decision to protect the Hebrew girl, they discovered they were bonded by more than just Babylon's glory, and for the moment, Arioch's face seemed less strained and Nergal's less sour.

Knowing Aridatha was on her way to food, shelter, and safety, Arioch turned to watch his king strutting before the beaten Hebrews, yelling, "Nothing can shake me." He was so animated, one might have thought he had vanquished Egypt instead of a subjugated city with no military or economic value. Clearly, the chanting, spear pounding, dancing, boasting, and laughter were not directed at his victory over Jerusalem, but his victory over the Fourth Man, and it weighed heavily on Arioch.

Throughout the siege, he, like Aridatha, had watched for the Fourth Man, even more so during last night's invasion. Where had he been during the siege and invasion of his city? Unlike Nebuchadnezzar's gods Marduk and Ishtar who never showed up anywhere, Arioch had seen the Fourth Man; thus he knew he would have had to be somewhere. And what about now? Where was he now? Was he nearby watching Nebuchadnezzar flaunting his victory, or was he inside the Temple standing beside the Ark of the Covenant, or had he gone back to Babylon to be with his faithful servants Daniel, Shadrach, Meshach, and Abedneggo? Wherever he was, could he see his opponent's laughter and his deserted city once so full of people?

More disturbing than *where* was he, was *why* had he gone through with it? *Why*, at Jerusalem's final desperate hour, hadn't he swooped in and saved his people, his city, and his Temple? Yes, Jerusalem's destruction was supposed to be an act of judgment by the God of Abraham, Isaac and Jacob, but Arioch was not born yesterday. He had lived amidst kings and gods since he was fifteen, so he knew no matter how angry they became with their subjects, they always used their power to win, thereby establishing their glory and name. They never used their power to lose, thereby establishing their opponent's glory and name. In this case, it had been obvious to everyone, except possibly Nebuchadnezzar, that the Fourth Man could destroy Babylon with his fire, and in doing so, establish his fearsome power before all history. Instead, he deliberately gave the victory to his opponent Nebuchadnezzar, thus deliberately taking the defeat, thus deliberately appearing impotent before all history. Why?

Wearied by such incongruities, Arioch turned back to Nebuchadnezzar's triumphant celebration. But he saw no triumph. Nor did he see Babylon as the majestic glory or Nebuchadnezzar as the light to the world. Instead, for the first time in his life, he saw Nebuchadnezzar as just another mortal and Babylon as just another nation, both to be judged by the same God who had just judged his own people justly and righteously.

Being judged justly and righteously by mortal kings was a fearsome prospect, but by the Fourth Man with his fiery metal cages? Indeed, that was too terrifying to consider, leaving Arioch almost wishing he was one of the dead. For after Nebuchadnezzar's so-called victory over the Fourth Man, what was the God of Abraham, Isaac and Jacob going to do to the mighty King of Babylon?

Lost in his thoughts, he did not see Nebuchadnezzar ride up until he was almost upon him, yelling he was leaving for his command post at Riblah. He then ordered Arioch to strip everything inside and outside of the Temple, and after that, burn it to the ground.

Folding his arms, Arioch shook his head.

Without a blink, Nebuchadnezzar turned to Nabuzaradan, chief of the guards, gave him the same orders, yanked his horse around, and galloped away.

On the tenth day of the fifth month, Daniel was in his Babylonian office arguing over road placement with his trans-Euphrates governors when his left shoulder cramped up and his words began to slur. No human messenger had come to report that the Temple of Solomon was in flames, yet gasping for breath and clinging to the table, he knew the Lord Almighty had fulfilled his word today: overthrowing Jerusalem without pity.

Unable to bear it, he hurried from the room. Running blindly through the corridors of Babylonian justice and power, he bumped into clerks, made wrong turns, slipped on tiles, and coming out into the fresh air, raced for home. Not until he was upstairs with the door locked and looking out the window toward Jerusalem, did he roar, "Sh'ma Israel, the Lord our God, the Lord is one." Still fighting for breath, he collapsed.

In those first moments, he tried to steady himself by remembering his boyhood in Jerusalem: walking down familiar streets, standing in the shadow of the Temple, eating the evening meal with his father. Usually, he could spend hours reliving his youth, but now, forsaken to live by the rivers of Babylon until the end of his days, he could only remember the morning he was taken captive, calling out to his friends, "We must keep the Word of the Lord."

He had not known why, amidst the Babylonian threat, he had shouted such a demand. Fourteen-year-old Mishael, wearing his silver armbands and gold rings, had been more practical, yelling they would all be killed. Furthermore, he had been right; Babylon had tried to kill them. But despite their fears of Babylon's brutalities, betrayals, and death sentences, the four had kept the Law and lived, nurturing the hope that one day they could all go home. Now there was no home to go to be-cause Jerusalem, without any threat of being thrown into fiery furnaces or lions' dens, had rejected the Law for her own laws and ways. Hence, the Lord had put a stop to it. Jerusalem was going to lay desolate. The land would receive her seventy years of Sabbath rests, while her children received hard labor.

Daniel was never going home again, and shivering uncontrollably on the floor, he groaned, "O Jerusalem, Jerusalem, if I forget you, may my right hand forget its skill."

45

Riblah

AFTER conquering Jerusalem, Nebuchadnezzar moved his prisoners to his command post at Riblah. There he shackled King Zedekiah to a chair and ordered him to watch the executions of the nobles who escaped with him to the Arabah. Because Zedekiah had taken refuge in his palace during the siege, he had not seen much of Jerusalem's violence, so within minutes he was tugging against his chains trying to break away. Finally, his stomach revolted.

"I said look!" commanded Nebuchadnezzar.

Zedekiah forced his emerald eyes to follow Nebuchadnezzar's finger to the center of the execution yard. There, amidst the carnage, his sons were being tied to posts. Horrified, he begged King Nebuchadnezzar to release them. But the King of Babylon just kept ordering him to look. So, hoping for a reprieve, King Zedekiah called out to his sons, telling them not to worry, everything was going to be all right. "Close your eyes!" he yelled. "Do not look around you! You are going to be fine!"

Arrows pelted into their bodies, blood appeared, and they slowly slumped.

Zedekiah stared in disbelief. "Not my sons!!!"

He tried to break loose, so he could run to them. But trapped in chains, he could do nothing. Nothing, but look. And looking from his dying sons to his dead noblemen and then back to his sons, he wondered why. Why had this happened to him?

Yes, he had wanted to be kingly, to make a name for himself like King David and King Solomon. So, yes, he had listened to his friends and rebelled against Babylon. And because of that one minor act, that one beautiful morning, that one thrilling order to tear down a few flags and spear a handful of Babylonians, Jerusalem had fallen?! The Temple of Solomon was gone?! His sons were dead?! How could that be? Any other king would have done the same, and after a few rebuffs, all would have been well again. But it had not worked that way for him. Truly, he had made a name for himself, a name no one would ever forget. But it was not a name to be forever coupled with King David or King Solomon, but forever coupled with the Fall of Jerusalem and the destruction of the Temple that bore the Name of the Lord and housed the Ark of the Covenant.

Jerusalem fallen. The Temple of Solomon gone. His sons dead.

"No!!!"

Suddenly, four rock-like hands unlocked his chains, but he was not going to let his body be hacked and sawed to death, so he gripped the chair. However, the two warriors, the size of Gog and Magog, had dislodged far superior specimens from far greater strongholds, so it was a trifle to loosen King Zedekiah's hold, drag him across the execution yard, and toss him at his dead son's feet.

Terrified, he leapt up to run, but they kicked him back into the dirt.

"Do not worry, Zedekiah," called Nebuchadnezzar. "You are not going to die."

Zedekiah jerked around to face the King of Babylon.

"You heard me. You will live."

King Zedekiah's head spun. Could it be true? After eighteen months and everyone dead, he was going to live?

"You are going to Babylon."

It was true! He was going to live! Jumping to his feet, he bowed before the King of Babylon, blessing and thanking him forever.

"But you will never see it," the king decreed, his voice harsh and angry. "Your sons will be the last thing you ever see."

Zedekiah had no idea what he was talking about. How could anyone go to Babylon and not see it? Then again, the statement sounded familiar. Didn't the prophet Jeremiah say he was going to Babylon while the prophet Ezekiel said he would never see it? Or was it the other way around? He could not remember, and at the moment, he did not care. He only wanted to hurry off the field and never look at death again. But when he started to trot away, the same two guards grabbed him and threw him to the ground.

"What are you doing?!" he cried. "Didn't you hear? I am going to live!" Kicking and flailing, he saw another warrior approaching with a two-pronged fiery poker. Seeing the two prongs, Nebuchadnezzar's last words crashed in on him, "Your sons will be the last thing you will ever see." And King Zedekiah finally understood that both the prophets, Jeremiah and Ezekiel, had been right.

Horrified, he wrestled against the warriors, but they controlled his body now, jerking his feet up behind him, pulling his arms back over a crossbeam, and tying his wrists to his ankles. Rock-like hands grabbed his head, wrenching it around to face his sons, limp and waxen, smeared with their own blood. King Zedekiah shrieked for mercy, begging to be shot with arrows like his sons and left to die, but the fiery prongs were upon him. Pressing in on his eyelids, they burned each layer of flesh until he could hear his eyeballs crackling, smell them burning, and taste them in his mouth. His body shook so violently it banged against the beam, and just as his heart was about to explode, the iron was yanked out. At least, he thought it was out. He did not know because he could not see. But the giants no longer held him, and his arms, legs, and head were free, so it had to be out.

Yet the pain, if possible, seemed worse. Then water struck his face, cold liquid burning into his blazing flesh, a new kind of torture sending him leaping from the ground, lunging forward and then backward in darkness. He reached for his eyes to rub and comfort them, but when he touched them, unendurable agony shot through his every nerve and King Zedekiah, with the image of his slaughtered sons seared into his mind forever, mercifully passed out.

⁓⊶⊷⁓

Later that night, Arioch and Nergal stood at attention in Nebuchadnezzar's royal bedroom. They had been standing for over an hour and Nebuchadnezzar still had not acknowledged them, apparently too preoccupied with pouring and gulping wine, rifling through documents, and pacing angrily. At first, Arioch stood at full attention ready to respond to all immediate orders. But as the minutes dragged on, although he stood at attention, he could not help contrasting the Nebuchadnezzar who had charged up and down the Temple steps boasting nothing could shake him, with the Nebuchadnezzar before him thrashing back and forth like a caged animal. On the Temple steps, he had been filled with a roaring vigor, possibly because he had just escaped the Fourth Man's wrath. Now his cheeks were drawn, shoulders hunched, and most significantly, his restless hunted look was back. All clear indicators that someone or something was shaking him.

But Arioch soon grew weary and a bit bored of thinking only of Nebuchadnezzar, Babylon's might, and the Egyptian enemy, so he let his thoughts wander up to the mountains to Soheil cooking over the fire at sunrise, his six sons working the fields in the heat of the day, and his father playing the drum at twilight, singing the songs of old. He knew he could never leave Nebuchadnezzar, but since the spectacle at the Temple of Solomon, it was comforting to know he had a life on the mountain. Not a long life if counted in actual days, but it was there, always waiting for him. Soheil had seen to that. Although they had been apart most of their married life, her love for him, even throughout his Chenguang years, had kept them together. More importantly, her love had kept his presence alive on the mountains—alive to his father and to his sons. Perhaps, he thought wistfully, he could get away from Babylon again someday. Perhaps soon and go home. Home... Strange, after living in Babylon all these years, he still thought of the mountains as home.

"I have not had one dream in the past eighteen months, Arioch!"

Startled, Arioch's warrior veneer remained stolid while his mind floundered. Had he missed something? Had the king been talking about dreams? He did not think so. At least he hoped not. "No, my king, I mean, yes, my king," he replied.

"You defied me, Arioch. You tried to stop me at the Temple. You thought I, Nebuchadnezzar, could not conquer Jerusalem. Furthermore, I ordered you to burn the Temple of Solomon and you refused!"

Arioch said nothing, galling him even more.

"I should execute you."

Arioch had always been willing to risk execution for the king's well-being, so he nodded.

"However," the king announced, slamming his wine cup down on the table, "execution is too simple. Instead," leaning into Arioch's face, he leered, "I strip you of your rank."

Both Arioch and Nergal knew it was a bluff because Arioch managed the king's armies and wars with a knowledge and vision surpassing any man alive. Consequently, they expected an immediate reversal reinstating him, followed by a jocular warning not to cross the king again. But Nebuchadnezzar had no intention of reversing his decision. He wanted to grind Arioch's superior attitude into the dirt, so he said, "From now on, you will command the captives."

Command the captives?! Arioch was stunned. Yes, he had always been willing to give up his life for his king, but to be relegated to moving condemned bodies from one work camp to another after moving the greatest armies on earth? Reduced to counting the living and the dead like cattle after counting the living and the dead for the honor and glory of Babylon? Excluded from the presence of the king and the royal court forever? It was a lifetime sentence of absolute degradation. The king knew it, Nergal knew it, Arioch knew it.

But Arioch also knew the king had the prerogative to decimate whomever he wanted, whenever he wanted, and however he wanted, thus he dutifully replied, "Yes, my king."

"You, Nergal, will be my new chief commander."

Three larger than life men filled the room, yet not one breathed. Nebuchadnezzar had just dropped Arioch into oblivion and promoted Nergal to the highest position in the land except for himself, but there was not one sound of joy or congratulations, disappointment or grievance. Nergal in his silence exuded rampant disapproval, Arioch in his silence unwavering loyalty, and Nebuchadnezzar just looked stunned.

"Get out," he seethed.

When the door closed, Nebuchadnezzar glared into his empty chalice. All the wine flowing through his veins had sobered him completely. On the other hand, how could he be sober when he could hear Daniel yelling at him? Daniel was not in Riblah, he was in Babylon. Yet, there he was floating in the dregs of his gold cup, bursting with youthful enthusiasm, shouting for all to hear, "The rock is a kingdom set up by the God of heaven. A kingdom that will crush the other kingdoms, bringing them to an end, but it will endure forever."

"I am the head of gold," Nebuchadnezzar hissed back, staring at his reflection hissing with him. "There can be no greater kingdom than mine."

"The God of Heaven," the voice whispered, causing him to lean in low to hear the words echoing round and round in the gleaming circle, "has made known to the king what will happen in the future... what will happen in the future... has made known to the king... what will happen in the..."

Nebuchadnezzar threw the chalice against the wall, marched to his desk and, pulling out ink and scrolls, started making lists for conquering Pharaoh.

PART III

THE TREE

46

Babylon

Six months later, Nebuchadnezzar sat up late reviewing his speech for his Victory-over-Jerusalem celebration. His spirits were especially high, because even though he had won the war, taken captives, and razed the city, the true transfer of power would come in the morning when the King of Babylon and the King of Jerusalem signed the tablets stating Jerusalem had been conquered and destroyed by King Nebuchadnezzar. Not until then would he be the official victor. Not until then would he be rid of the Fourth Man. Even so, he knew he was rid of him because as he had told Arioch, when Jerusalem was gone, his dreams would be gone. And, sure enough, they were gone. Since his return to Babylon, he had not had one dream, good or bad.

Now, with only eleven hours before the signing, he was ready for another refreshing night's sleep, and strolling out onto his palace rooftop, he laid down on his silk pillowed couch and gazed up at the stars. It was a clear moonless night, the stars so close he could almost touch them. So, stretching out his arm, he reached for his favorite sign *Kesith* the *Archer* with its constellations *Gnasor* the *Harp, Ara* the *Altar* and *Dahrach* the *Dragon*. It pleased him to think of himself as Kesith, because Kesith was *the gracious one coming forth*. It also pleased him to think of himself as Gnasor the Harp *ascending on eagle's wings* because he was destined to ascend, and how else could one ascend apart from eagle's wings? Furthermore, it pleased him to think of himself as Ara the Altar with its burning pyre telling the story of *finishing by fire* because he had finished the Fourth Man by fire when he burned his Temple bearing His Name. When he came to the third constellation, Dahrach the Dragon, he fell asleep.

It was a deep warm sleep, every limb relaxed as he stared out at a brilliant vertical shaft spinning wildly. Watching brown ribbons sail out of its top and gnarled tentacles thrust out of its base, he chuckled smugly. For, even in his sleep, he knew it was a tree. Of course, he was right. The ribbons soaring out of the top soon turned into branches stretching across the sky and the tentacles shooting out below transformed into roots sinking far and wide into the earth. Leaves, buds, blossoms, and fruits of all shapes and colors burst forth, creating a vast verdant canopy spreading over the land. Thousands of birds flew in, large and small, chittering and chattering as they nestled in the tree's branches while thousands of cattle, sheep, and horses grazed serenely in its shade. He had never seen such a wondrous world, all nurtured and protected by this one tree, and it pleased Nebuchadnezzar to think of himself as the tree.

All was bliss for a comfortable amount of time, then the birds and animals heard something unusual. Cocking their heads, they listened. Was it friend or foe? It was a long while before Nebuchadnezzar heard it, but when he did, he too cocked his head. Curiously, it sounded like an iron door rattling. Then came seven dull clanks—grinding, rusting, choking clanks—causing such alarm, the birds cried out, the livestock bleated, and the leaves cowered. After a long anxious wait, they all looked up, and there before them was an open door suspended in the heavens. On its threshold stood a heavenly messenger carrying seven massive chains and seven iron padlocks.

The messenger had the appearance of a man, but he was taller and stronger, so beautiful and radiant to the eye, the birds and animals, and even Nebuchadnezzar, marveled. He introduced himself as the holy Watcher and all the creatures, gazing in awe, wondered what incredible thing he was going to do next. Soon they found out. Swinging the chains over his head, he descended on stairs no one could see, declaring such frightening words of judgment, the birds took flight, the animals ran, and the leaves fled. Nebuchadnezzar would have gladly retreated with them, but a great weight pressed in on him, forcing him to stay and watch.

Within moments, an icy wind blasted in and, with one gust, cut the tree down.

Such a magnificent tree cut down?! Nebuchadnezzar was appalled! He wanted to run to it and push it back up, but the wind pounded him to the earth. Thus, pressed against the cold rocks and dying grasses, he watched helplessly as the holy Watcher wrapped the seven chains around the tree's stump, tighter and tighter until Nebuchadnezzar felt his own arms and legs, chest and belly being crushed. With more horrifying words, the heavenly messenger clamped one padlock onto each chain, locking the stump to the earth.

"No!" cried Nebuchadnezzar, leaping from his couch. "I will not have it! Not another dream! Not again! Not ever!"

Wild-eyed, he called for his magicians and sorcerers, and telling them every detail of the dream, he waited for their interpretation. They had none. So, throwing them out, he called for Daniel.

Daniel and Shadrach listened stone-faced to his narrative, each trying not to show his alarm. But Nebuchadnezzar sensed their uneasiness and, reassuring them, ordered them to tell him the meaning of his dream. So Daniel stated the meaning. A meaning no one liked. Especially Nebuchadnezzar.

"I am going to what?!" he protested. "Lose my kingdom?!"

Daniel's mind protested just as harshly, because if Nebuchadnezzar lost his kingdom, Gaspar would be king and murder every Jew in the land. "If only the dream applied to your enemies, my lord."

"Obviously, I am the tree," the king declared, his hands clenching and unclenching. "My greatness does reach to the sky and my dominion does extend to the ends of the earth. But I, Nebuchadnezzar, am going to live with animals?!" He marched to the mirror and, pointing to his reflection, commanded, "Look."

The two Hebrews moved their eyes to the chiseled image in the mirror.

When he was sure they had soaked up enough proof of his royal manhood, he challenged, "I, Nebuchadnezzar, am going to graze like cattle?! That is a lie, Daniel. An outright lie. I should have your head."

"My lord, the dream is true and the interpretation trustworthy."

Of course, Nebuchadnezzar knew the dream was true and the interpretation trustworthy, just as his head-of-gold dream had been true and Daniel's interpretation trustworthy. However, his dreams and Daniel's interpretations were only true and trustworthy as allegories and myths were true and trustworthy. In other words, everyone believed allegories and myths, but at the same time everyone knew they were false. The real truth—not allegory, myth, or dream—was that Babylon's ancients had appointed him, Nebuchadnezzar, to raise Babylon to its full glory, never to be destroyed, which meant he was not going to lose his kingdom!

"You are angry at me, Daniel, for destroying Jerusalem," he stated evenly, swords flashing in his eyes. "That is why you threaten me with a false interpretation of a meaningless dream. I will not hear another word. Not another word!"

Nergal, wishing he had never been appointed chief commander, wiped his sweaty palms on his leather tunic. He believed Daniel's interpretation, but with his slow thinking, he did not know what to do about it. Yes, he was capable of devising amazing war strategies if he had the time. And yes, with his sour face he could lead armies into victory. But he had never been mentally quick, especially about things not relating to war. Why else was he always gnawing his bronze toothpick? To hide his limitations! That narrow logic which never saw the grand picture, but instead had to line up every detail before he could plunge. As a boy, he had learned quickly if he kept grinding away at a dagger blade, stalk, or quill, his dull-witted silence would be interpreted as serious-minded thinking. Thus, the serious-minded thinker had promoted rapidly and most times, just like now, found himself completely out of his element. Oh, how he wished Arioch was still in command. Arioch understood both the grand picture and the smallest details. After hearing Daniel's interpretation, he would develop a plan to protect Nebuchadnezzar and his kingdom. On the other hand, perhaps Arioch was not needed, for Nebuchadnezzar was pointing out some very convincing proofs of his invincibility.

"Daniel, have you forgotten that the combined power of all the nations cannot match mine? Egypt is too lazy to fight. Since the Grand Guardian Li's chiefs assassinated the Grand Preceptor Au Yang, China has been my ally. My worst enemy, Gaspar, is locked in Canal Prison. I simply have no opponent from horizon to sky. If I did have an opponent, my capital is protected by my fortified walls, my armies, my mazes, and traps. The smallest thief could not slip into one of my sewers. So you see, even if I tried to lose my kingdom, I could not."

"Those who walk in pride, he is able to humble," murmured Shadrach.

"What?" demanded Nebuchadnezzar, the image of Yosef ben-Moshe jabbing his finger toward the heavens flaring before him, reminding him that Shadrach, about to be thrown into the fiery furnace, had been standing close by.

"Forgive me, my lord, I was thinking aloud."

"Well, stop thinking!" blasted the king.

Clearing his throat nervously, Nergal whispered to Daniel, "What can he do?"

Daniel launched into an earnest plea. "O king, be pleased to accept my advice. Renounce your sins by doing what is right. Stop your wickedness by being kind to the oppressed. Perhaps then your prosperity will continue."

The king however had found another solution and, looking quite pleased, sauntered to his wash basin. After several cooling splashes to his face followed by a brisk towel dry, he said, "Daniel, you said when I acknowledge Heaven rules, I will get my kingdom back. So *if* I lose my kingdom, which I am not going to do because nothing can shake me, but *if* I lose…"

Daniel cut him off, "My lord, you told me the holy Watcher decreed, 'Let him be drenched with the dew of heaven. Let him live with the animals. Let him be given the mind of an animal until seven times pass by for him.'"

"*If* I lose my kingdom…" Nebuchadnezzar repeated. "I will say Heaven rules and I will get my kingdom back."

Swept away by such profound reasoning, Nebuchadnezzar clapped his hands triumphantly, Nergal stared in awe, and the king's dog, Sagitta, thumped his tail cheerfully. But Daniel and Shadrach showed no enthusiasm at all. So Nebuchadnezzar King of Babylon leaned into their faces and growled, "I will say Heaven rules and I will get my kingdom back."

47

It was the last day of Babylon's month-long Victory-over-Jerusalem celebration and the city was dressed in a festive glow. By order of Nebuchadnezzar King of Babylon, all work had been cancelled, only feasting and dancing were allowed on the streets and canals, and above all, everyone was to be happy. Furthermore, everyone was happy. Except the king! Since his dream about the tree, his sleep had been haunted by such fearsome images, if he did not get rest soon, he knew he would go mad.

But the victory banquet had to go on, so standing in the midst of it, he glanced at the woman beside him. A confident beauty and eager to please, but did she really think those peacock feathers adorning her shoulders could seriously divert him? How absurd! Only one person had actually stopped his dreams: Yosef ben-Moshe. So, one sleepless night, he had considered finding the Hebrew and bringing him to Babylon. But assuming he would demand to bring his daughter, Nebuchadnezzar quickly squelched that idea.

"Your victory banquet is a great success, my king," smiled the feathered beauty.

"All my banquets are great successes," he rejoined, staring dryly at the sea of bejeweled noblemen eating and drinking from his royal table. It was a moderate celebration because he had not wanted to give too much importance to Jerusalem. Jerusalem was, and always would be, an afterthought. On the other hand, when Babylon conquered Egypt, he would order the entire country to celebrate for a year with banquets, hunting parties, parades...

"To the fall of Jerusalem," she purred, eyeing him seductively.

"To what?" he snapped.

"The fall of Jerusalem."

He had forgotten her name. And why not? She was no different from any other woman in the room. Lips, hair, tiara, tunic, all the same.

Her feathers were the only oddity and they annoyed him. Or perhaps it was she who annoyed him. Lately, all women annoyed him. All except one, and because he had resolved not to think about her, he let his mind drift back to Yosef ben-Moshe because thinking about the father helped him stay close to the one he resolved not to think about: a lone figure standing in a shock of moonlight, a vision waving the Hebrew flag on the Tower of David, a resting place for the mighty, a bone-thin defiance galloping away with Baruch ben-Zadok. Many nights, when looking up at the stars, he had found himself reveling in her image. Even now he was thinking about her! So jerking himself back to the moment, he blurted. "Do you believe dreams?"

"My lord?"

"Do you believe them? Can dreams tell the future?"

"My king," she smiled, her tongue skimming across her lips, "if no one can tell the future while awake in the daylight, how can anyone tell the future while asleep at night?"

Stunned, he stared at her. It was so simple, it was perfect. Why hadn't he thought of it before?! Everyone knew no one could tell the future while awake. So, how had he been conned into thinking he could see the future while sleeping?! Straightaway, all the weeks of fearsome images fell from his shoulders leaving him floating on air and laughing like a drunken man. Perhaps this was the female he had been looking for. Perhaps tonight in her arms, he would sleep, and leaning into her feathers, he whispered, "What was your name again?"

Before she could answer, a voice called out from behind.

Turning, he saw Arioch striding toward him. What a sight for sore eyes! Loyal Arioch! Throwing his arm around him, he exclaimed, "Where have you been?"

Arioch bowed stiffly, his hand moving into his chest pocket. Finding a small pouch, he wrapped his hand around it and pulled it out.

"Come, celebrate. Meet..." Nebuchadnezzar snapped his fingers at the beauty, trying to remember...

"Leila, my king."

"And her feathers," grinned Nebuchadnezzar. "You should hear what she has to say about dreams."

Arioch stared dumbly at their brimming wine cups and the hilarity surrounding them, a far cry from watching the misery of the Hebrew captives hiking across icy mountains and blistering plains. One captive in particular was especially on his mind, and if something was not done soon, she would be dead in less than a month. But the king was so light-hearted and in such a "let bygones be bygones" mood, he wondered if he should forget about her and try to win his commission back.

"Have you heard about my new plan to rebuild the Tower of the Seven Lights?"

"Yes, my lord," Arioch replied, shoving the crimson pouch back into his chest pocket.

"Never again will it be called the Tower of Babel! I forbid it! From now on, the generations will use its original name: the Tower of the Seven Lights." He felt so alive, so rejuvenated, so refreshed. Not only had the feathered female given him a clear picture of the folly of his dreams, but at the very same moment, as if ordained by the gods, Arioch had walked back into his life.

Arioch felt just as rejuvenated, chuckling along merrily with his king. For months, he had envisioned a moment like this, his past transgressions forgotten and Nebuchadnezzar taking him back into his good graces. Already he could see himself planning the invasion of Egypt, standing behind the throne, and eating at the royal table. All he had to do was never mention Jerusalem again. But could he, Arioch, forsake Aridatha's importance to his king just so he could walk in the halls of power? The answer was simple. First and foremost, he was loyal to his king, so coming to attention, he again reached into his chest pocket and wrapped his hand around Aridatha's crimson pouch.

"The Temple of the Seven Lights is riddled with mysteries, Arioch," the king beamed, scanning the room with rare animation. "No one knows why it was never finished. Probably waiting for me to come along and build it," he laughed.

But this time Arioch did not laugh. Instead, he pulled the crimson pouch from his pocket and murmured for the king's ears only, "She is here. In Babylon."

Staring down at the pouch, Nebuchadnezzar did not see Aridatha resurrecting before him, but Jerusalem. A complete frontal attack, stunning him into a stillness similar to the moment before combat when a man must decide between fighting through a war and living, or running from the war and surviving. Well, he was not going to fight or run! He had already conquered Jerusalem and that was that.

"She has been traveling with the captives these past six months."

"Captives?! Six months?!"

"It took me that long to get here, my lord."

"Has it taken you that long to take a bath? You stink."

Arioch knew he did not stink. As always, he had bathed with the royal soaps, anointed himself with the royal perfumes, and dressed himself in the royal robes before entering the king's presence. Nevertheless, he humbly replied, "Forgive me, my lord."

"Get out," the king growled, turning his full attention to his feathered companion.

But Arioch stepped between them, and expanding to his full height so the king could see nothing but the culmination of decades of hard-earned power in his sea-blue eyes, he whispered, "She will not talk to anyone. Not even Shadrach. Since the day Jerusalem fell, I have never seen her cry. You must speak to her, my lord."

"*I*? Must speak to *her*? Who are you to tell me what *I* must do?"

"She barely eats, barely sleeps. I believe she is willing herself to die, but I do not think she wants to die. Do you?"

"If you continue, I will have you hanged."

Grabbing the king's hand, Arioch slapped the pouch into it. "Your will be done. Hang me."

The pouch reminded Nebuchadnezzar of a child's hand slipping into his: a child of sense, her paths governed by destiny, each step placed purposely in and out of people's affairs. It also reminded him of the beautiful, young woman who had refused him more than once. Was he going to run from her or see her? This was the last day of his Victory-over-Jerusalem celebration, and if he did not see her, it would be the same as running. So, shoving the pouch into his belt, he marched toward the exit. However, before leaving, he turned and called out, "Arioch! Eat at my royal table. Next to my chair."

48

NEBUCHADNEZZAR arranged to meet her in his private office where the walls shimmered with his glory: the coat of bronze scale and the engraved silver sword given to him by Emperor Kuangwang, his leather armor inscribed with prayers to Marduk, the silk train he wore when all the nations bowed to him, his gold armor and red-handled axes from his victory over the Temple of Solomon, and shield after shield used in victory after victory. As he waited, he worked on his new project, the rebuilding of the Tower of the Seven Lights of the World. When Daniel suggested that the ruin known as the Temple of Tongues, also called the Tower of Babel, was probably the ruin of the Tower of the Seven Lights, Nebuchadnezzar immediately determined to rebuild it. Daniel, not surprisingly, objected because Daniel objected to anything he thought admirable. However, this time the Hebrew had been exceptionally adamant, telling him because the Tower had been an affront to God, he should leave it to the earth. But Daniel's opinions were not going to stop him from...

The door opened and a rush of warm air gusted in. It was probably her, but he kept working. Why should he look up? He did not need to watch her enter the room. Likewise, when the door closed and she started stepping toward him, he continued working. Why should he watch her feet cross the cold marble floor? However, it might be pertinent to know where she stopped: near his desk or far away. It might also be interesting to see if she was still beautiful. After defeat, probably not. Enough! Two times he had offered her a life in Babylon and both times she had refused. Now she meant nothing to him. He had only agreed to meet with her to prove he was not running away.

Moreover, he had more important things to do: calculating the months it would take to rebuild the Tower of the Seven Lights. But no matter how doggedly he stared at the figures, Daniel's argument kept broiling up inside him, insisting the Lord Almighty had been displeased by the Tower because Noah's descendants built the Tower in order to make a name for themselves and not be scattered over the earth. Consequently, the Lord confused their one language, making it impossible to finish the Tower, and he scattered them over the earth. To prove his point, Daniel had added—a bit triumphantly—the name Babylon had come from the word *bavel*, meaning to confuse or mix.

A soft rustling broke into his thoughts. Ah-hah, she was getting impatient. Good! Let her wait. Besides, if he told her about the Tower of the Seven Lights, she would probably agree with Daniel.

But Nebuchadnezzar had not agreed. He had reproached Daniel for ignoring Shining One's great Babylonian epic which declared—so eloquently—it was man's destiny to create all the languages of the world; hence, that was what had happened. In other words, there had been no confusion: *bavel*. Furthermore, the term *Babel* or *Babylon* came from the Akkadian *bab-ilu* meaning Gate of God, because the Tower of the Seven Lights with its planetary tiers led to the Gate of God. How could any god be affronted by that?

Then again, perhaps it was not her. Perhaps a clerk had entered with news about the chariot races, or Nergal had come with the treaty from Media. He needed to hear from them, so putting his pen down, he raised his eyes.

He was shocked. Yes, it was she: Aridatha of Jerusalem. But instead of a beauty, she was an apparition of horror: her flesh stretched over her bones, her tunic tattered, and her Star of David hem bloodstained. Why hadn't Arioch fed her? Why hadn't he bathed her or given her clothes? Not only that, he had bound her hands. What obscene purpose was to be found in that? Upon closer look, perhaps the answer lay in her defiant jaw and stony eyes. Clearly, he was well rid of her.

"Aridatha of Jerusalem," he announced brusquely.

He did not know what reaction he had expected, but he certainly had not expected jaw grinding silence. So, he decided to try again, only this time with something to break her insolent composure, something that would hurt. "Whatever happened to your Fourth Man?"

"There is no Fourth Man," she responded indifferently, everything about her completely detached.

"What did you say?"

"You heard me."

"Do not deny my victory. There is a Fourth Man. We both saw him. And I conquered him." When she still did nothing, he rose to his feet, marched over, and slapped her face.

She did not flinch. Not even a blink. Nothing about her revealed the heart he had once known. Nothing about her revealed anything except cold-blooded death, so he pulled out his dagger.

Stiffening, she readied for him to pierce her through. But he had no such intent. Instead, he cut the leather straps from her wrists, and letting them fall to the floor, he said, "You are free."

Again, there was no reaction. She was entirely unmoved, neither hot nor cold. Yet if he looked close enough, he could almost see her breath rising and falling with his. And if he looked long enough, he could almost see tears glistening within that curious light deep inside her eyes. The vision that had haunted him during the past six months rose up before him again. She was standing on the Tower of David waving the Hebrew flag, shouting, "Remember the Fourth Man," igniting alarm in Babylon's armies and confidence in Jerusalem's. Surely, that could not all be gone. Surely, there was still something inside her.

Quickly, he took her hands in his. "Aridatha, listen to me" he said, trying to reach her. "You can stop fighting now. The war is over."

Instantly, she spat on him.

Now it was his turn to be unmoved. Pulling out a handkerchief, fragrant with myrrh, he held it out to her. "Wipe it off."

She looked away.

His eyes narrowing, he scraped off her spittle, threw the handkerchief to the floor and, grabbing her limp body, yanked it in close and shook her. "You forget, woman, I have the power to destroy anything and everything."

"Not Jerusalem."

"I did destroy Jerusalem."

"I am Jerusalem! You have to destroy me to destroy her!"

So, that was it, the explanation for his strange reaction when he saw her pouch in Arioch's palm. Indeed, it had not been her, but Jerusalem resurrecting before him, and he was going to have to conquer it all over again. Not just the buildings, the kings, the priests, and the peoples, not just the city and its Temple, but her: the Daughter of Zion. What's more, looking at her clenched lips and contemptuous eyes, he was ready.

So, digging his fingers into her hair, he dragged her toward his desk. Fighting every step of the way, she twisted and turned, flailing her arms aimlessly yet in complete control, so when he least expected it, she reached for his dagger, pulled it free, and lunged at him. Quickly, he dodged to the side and, hitting her wrist, sent the blade to the floor. Straightaway, she raced to the red-handled axes hanging next to his gold armor and standards. She had recognized them the moment she walked in, used by Nebuchadnezzar's warriors to hack into the roots of the two pillars, Jachin and Boaz. Seizing one, she flung it at him.

Caught completely by surprise, not just because she had thrown it, but because she had such strength and alarming accuracy, he jumped back and watched it whiz by, slicing into his leather armor, bisecting his written prayers to Marduk. How dare she! Turning to admonish her, he was again caught by surprise, because she was hurtling toward him wielding another ax. In that moment, watching her cross the room swinging the ax randomly—high, to the side, high, to the other side, low, low, so he would not know from which direction she was going to strike—he wondered if she would really go through with it. Would she actually kill him?

Staring into her feral eyes, the answer was obvious. Yes! So, grabbing one of his standards, he whacked the ax out of her hands and, throwing her over his shoulder, marched her to his desk and slammed her down on top.

"I destroyed Jerusalem," he said, straddling her struggling waist. "And now..." he seethed, tugging her bloodstained Star of David hem up her legs, "I am going to destroy you."

"Jerusalem will rise again in seventy years," she screamed, flipping her body from side to side, sending scrolls, inks and pens flying. "But Babylon will be a wasteland forever."

Pressing his lips to hers, he growled down her throat, "Babylon will not be a wasteland. It will live forever."

"Because you say so?!" she shrieked, punching her bony fist into his neck.

Grabbing both wrists, he held her arms over her head. "Yes, because I say so. Because I am Babylon and there is none beside me."

Trapped under his sweltering armor and his fiery breath snarling, "Nothing can shake me," she finally grasped the war was over. During the past months, she had continued to fight because she had believed she would ultimately win. But now, trapped between the King of Babylon's lists and maps grinding into her back and the King of Babylon pressing down on top of her, she finally had to face the truth: she had lost. Worse than that, Jerusalem had lost. Furthermore, not only had Jerusalem lost, but the Temple of Solomon and the Ark of the Covenant were gone. Her father and Baruch ben-Zadok were gone. The sounds of joy and gladness, the voices of the bride and bridegroom, the sound of the millstones and the light of the lamp, gone. Everything was gone, and with everything gone, nothing mattered. So Aridatha stopped fighting, and with a voice as dead as her heart, she said, "Go ahead. You have destroyed everything anyway. You killed papa. Now destroy me."

It was no surprise to him he had destroyed everything. But to hear that her father was dead was like a spear driving into his soul. Yosef ben-Moshe—the man who saved his life and stopped his dreams—dead? No. It could not be. Yosef ben-Moshe was the only man he had ever confided in, telling him about the sky being a mask, the storehouses hidden behind it, the locks and chains flying out at him. He had never confided in any other man, certainly not Arioch. Arioch saw life too simply. But because of Yosef ben-Moshe's violent background etched into his forehead and seared around his neck, his command over both power and rest, and his steadfastness to his God, he had trusted him as an equal. And as an equal, he could not be dead!

"No," he proclaimed as if issuing an irrevocable royal edict. "It is not true."

"It is true!" she shouted, breaking into sobs. "That last day at the Temple."

"But he wore my ring!" he blasted, throwing himself off her, glaring angrily at a whole new world without Yosef ben-Moshe. "It cannot be. I do not believe it. Did you see him die? Did you actually see him?"

"Papa," she groaned, pulling her knees up to her chest.

King Nebuchadnezzar walked to the window, but he did not see his Great City. Instead, he saw Yosef ben-Moshe: his commander charging across the Carchemish plain in his war chariot; his rescuer with an arrow in his back, breathing, "The Lord is one;" his friend defending Shadrach,

Meshach, and Abedneggo over the roar of the fiery furnace; and lastly, against the flaming backdrop of the Jerusalem wall, his enemy demanding he protect Aridatha. Always demanding he protect her.

Turning, he looked at Yosef ben-Moshe's daughter curled up in a ball on his desk, her arms thinner than a child's, her tunic threadbare. She reminded him of a fawn shot through with many arrows, and determined she would never suffer again, he moved quietly over to her, lifted her in his arms, and pulled her close to his chest. "I will protect you, Aridatha. I will see nothing harms you. You are safe now."

He wanted to keep her in his arms, to have her always with him, not only because he was the king but because he was a man. But because he had promised to protect her, he planted her on her feet and walked from the room.

Aridatha stared numbly at the door closing behind him. She had just been given protection from the King of Babylon, a splendid prospect for anyone, but all she could think was her feet were cold. So, moving to the sunlight on the balcony, she looked out at Nebuchadnezzar's Great City stretching as far as the eye could see. His Euphrates ports with their colorful banners and shouting canal drivers were jammed with merchants and barges from all over the world. Procession Way, teeming with dignitaries arguing beard to beard, was being scrubbed by slaves from all over the world. Across the park, the Ishtar Citadel, with its gossamer streamers, was crowded with Nebuchadnezzar's harem of women from all over the world. From the greatest to the least, she could find the entire world here in his Great City, yet she could not find herself. Yes, her body was here, just like Nebuchadnezzar's other war trophies, but her heart...? Where was her heart?

Her feet could not get warm. In fact, nothing about her could get warm, so she turned to leave, but her stomach knotted up. At first she thought she was going to be sick. But how could she be sick when there was nothing in her stomach? Yet, there was something inside, trying to get out. Finally, she realized it was words. Familiar words. Words she did not want to hear, so she pressed her hands over her ears.

But the words were not coming from the outside, but from inside. For, whether she liked it or not, they had been planted in her when she was young, and they were rapidly growing to fruition, crying out, "This is what the Lord Almighty the God of Israel says to all He carries away into exile from Jerusalem to Babylon: build houses and settle down, plant gardens and eat what they produce."

"No!" she cried, lunging for Nebuchadnezzar's ash pot, dry-heaving once, twice, and again. "You cannot make me stay here. I will not build houses. I will not settle down. I will not plant gardens or eat what they produce."

49

THE first thing Arioch did when he arrived in Babylon was place Aridatha in Shadrach's household, ordering him to keep her out of sight and get her strong again. Shadrach had no trouble concealing her, but even with his influence as Baruch's older brother, he could not convince her to eat from his table, wash in the waters of hyssop, or sleep in her linen-canopied bed because she kept screaming she was a captive and was going to live like one: in hardship, poverty, and deprivation! So, Shadrach and his household watched helplessly as she wasted away, eating scraps for the dogs, washing with soap fragments meant for prisoners, and roaming the halls at night begging for news of loved ones. Then on a single day news came: her mother was alive. Without a moment to lose, Aridatha hurried to meet her, but the reunion was not a pleasant one.

Zillah had already been in Babylon five months, living in comfort and elegance. Upon capture, she had caught the attention of a Babylonian commander who had served under Yosef ben-Moshe at Carchemish. Knowing ben-Moshe had saved Nebuchadnezzar's life, the commander placed Zillah in a caravan of Babylonian dignitaries headed for the Great City. On the journey, she captivated one and all with her beauty and astrological intrigues, so by the time she arrived in Babylon, she was happily awarded an elegant home in the fashionable Ishtar Temple District. Since then she had worked hard to keep herself in the limelight, never mentioning her Jerusalem past while embracing everything Babylonian.

Thus, when Aridatha's emaciated form and her ever-present Stars of David hem appeared at her doorstep, she quickly pulled her inside, pressed her into a private room, and admonished her for looking like a penniless Jew in public! She then ordered her to clean up, put on the fashions of Babylon, and start eating from the finest tables in the land because it was her duty to enjoy the prosperity her father's name had provided for her. Aridatha refused the bath, the Babylonian clothes, and the lavish meal, declaring she would never exchange Jerusalem for Babylon. Then, giving her mother a doleful hug goodbye, she returned to Shadrach's.

Although she never received news about Baruch ben-Zadok, she convinced herself he was still alive. Probably one of the nameless thousands in the Babylonian work camps, and like those thousands probably half-dead, his bones breaking under Babylon's yoke, his flesh ripping under the lash. She also convinced herself his enslavement was her fault, because if she had married him, Arioch would have let her stay in Jerusalem, and they would still be together. Rent with guilt for being alive, she promised herself if she ever had the opportunity to marry Baruch again, she would seize it.

However, she renounced that promise when she was dry-heaving into Nebuchadnezzar's ash pot because Jeremiah's words, when the Lord carries you into exile from Jerusalem to Babylon, kept pounding inside her until she finally did listen to them, along with all his other words regarding Jerusalem. It was like hearing them for the first time, because for the first time, she saw he had been right: right about Jerusalem, right about her exile, right about everything. Hence, she had been wrong. Of course, being wrong was not so grievous. Anyone could be wrong about the future. But, in being wrong she had wronged so many: her father, when she threw his ring away; Baruch, when she slapped him over and over; Jeremiah, when she called him a traitor; and the Fourth Man, when she denied him before Nebuchadnezzar.

How could she ever face them again? Realizing she probably never would face them again, not even to beg forgiveness, she burst into tears—desolate, inconsolable tears—for she had rebelled against the word of the Lord and wreaked havoc all around. Now her loved ones were gone and she was alone in a foreign land.

Yet, even in her misery, she remembered her father had taught her there was always a way out, and indeed there was a way out. So, turning toward Jerusalem, she appealed to the God of Abraham, Isaac and Jacob, asking him to forgive her for not believing the words he had given his prophet, and for hurting and betraying so many; promising from then on, she would obey the prophet, which meant she would stay in Babylon, which meant she would not marry Baruch ben-Zadok.

Somewhere between her groaning and her prayer, she fell asleep, and when she awoke, the words, "build houses and settle down, plant gardens and eat what they produce," instead of causing grief, shone like a sunny path before her, her feet no longer cold and her heart pumping warmly.

Without a moment to lose, she ran to Shadrach's, ate from his table, bathed in the waters of hyssop, and slept in her linen-canopied bed. Over time, she became stronger and more beautiful than ever, her new life pleasant and settled. She even offered to assist in building houses and planting gardens, but Shadrach, following Arioch's orders, kept her cloistered, providing her with pens and inks so she could write down all the words she remembered from Yosef ben-Moshe's scrolls.

Then one morning, hours before dawn, she was unexpectedly awakened and ordered to meet the king on the palace rooftop. It had been eleven months since she had walked into his office purposed to kill him. Now she could hardly wait to see him again. But, before running to the palace rooftop, she must dress for a king. So, she sent her maidservants to the harem for anointing oils, her eunuchs to the palace for the royal hairdresser and jeweler, and her seamstress to the Chinese Village for embroidered silks. She even asked Shadrach to hurry to the Jewry to find a silk sheath with the Stars of David embroidered in the hem, preferably in pearls and gold. Not until she was satisfied that every fold of her tunic and jewel in her hair were set to perfection, did she appear before Shadrach. Staring at her, he mumbled something about how the king was going to be pleased, or more likely stupefied, and placing his hand on her brow, he blessed her and let her go.

In the dim light before dawn, Aridatha, dressed like a queen, rustled like a whisper down the garden trail toward Procession Way. Escorted by two guards wearing royal red uniforms and ivory-handled scimitars, the three turned onto the glazed brick road, then soundlessly hurried toward the palace rooftop stairwell. The guards at the stairwell, standing shoulder to shoulder blocking the entrance, opened a path for her, and as she placed her sandaled foot on the first gold step, they returned to their position, and she was alone.

She wanted to sprint up the stairs, taking two at a time, race out onto the rooftop, and rest her eyes on the king as she did the first time she saw him, with the joy and awe of a young girl. But instead of flying up the steps, she found herself ascending slowly in her royal robes, her head high, her step soft, her composure regal. She was so poised, she did not recognize herself. She had often seen noblewomen drift through rooms like untouchable statues as if they owned the world and all its beauty, and at that moment, she felt like one of them. Perhaps it was because she was ascending on gold steps to meet the mightiest king on earth. Then again, perhaps it was because she had changed. Perhaps she was grown up and regal. Whatever it was, it was brief because when she reached the top landing and saw the marvels before her, she stumbled over the threshold and gawked.

Towering fountains showered over rocks and ferns into pools of blue and yellow fish. Gold lampstands and swaying palms decked vast sitting rooms. Gold filigree cages of yellow song birds lined the jeweled pathways. Twenty-foot high bronze chimes rang a muted reminder of each quarter hour. A gold sun, a silver moon, and sapphire stars hung overhead. And in the center of it all, Nebuchadnezzar King of Babylon sat at his desk working, the man she thought she knew until now. For the splendor of his gold image at Dura was nothing compared to this!

This was a sanctum of riches and glory, a storehouse of subtle might, a feast for the eyes, a delight to the senses, and even more exciting, a glorious escape for the mind and soul with its hidden spouts spraying cooling mists, clusters of grapes dripping from arbors, oranges ripening on sculpted trees, giant silver swords rising up and down slicing at each other, life-size marble elephants and lions with moveable heads and legs standing at attention, mystical melodies fluttering like wings around the sky-high chimes, and jeweled star pictures floating in the air as if set in motion by invisible threads or more likely magic.

Surely, with one's mind and soul cavorting away into such enchantments, one's heart and strength must follow, and it sent her legs to trembling. For it was obvious this one man, Nebuchadnezzar King of Babylon, not only possessed the vision to create such realms, but the power to cast them into the world and, like a spell, draw all men to himself, to his cities and temples, to his wisdom and knowledge, to his ivory, silver, and gold. All men running happily to his feet, for who could resist him?

And what about her? Wasn't she running happily to his feet when she should be resisting his riches and delights, his might and glory? Shouldn't she be running away before it was too late and she was captured in his spell? But how could she run when Jeremiah, who had been right about everything, had told her to build and plant when she was exiled in Babylon? Still, as she stared out at King Nebuchadnezzar's celestial bodies and dreamlike works, she wondered how she could live immersed in such glory and wealth, yet remain Aridatha of Jerusalem.

As if on cue, a sunray broke through the horizon. Just one small gleam stretching across the landscape, yet it was bright enough to mock Nebuchadnezzar's little man-made sun which could only brighten his head. Simultaneously, Babylon's chimes rang the hour, but they did not summon the sun to rise, they only marked what was there: the passing of time already set in place. Relief washed over her like a cooling rain because she suddenly understood, just as the sun shone on Babylon and even served Babylon, it remained apart from it. And, just as time could be counted by Babylon and even serve Babylon, it marched on apart from it. In the same way, she could belong to Babylon, even serve Babylon, yet, like Daniel and Shadrach, remain apart from it. She even knew how she was going to do it. Shadrach's brother Baruch ben-Zadok had given her the answer long ago, when at the age of three, she asked, "Is the King of glory the Crown Prince of the small circle?"

Appalled, he had stomped his foot, declaring the King of glory was not a small circle or a crown prince! Then, he read from the scrolls, "The King of glory is the Lord strong and mighty, the Lord mighty in battle. The Lord Almighty, he is the King of glory."

Although his explanation seemed simple enough, the ideas were much too large for her to grasp. Furthermore, they still were, for she still did not really know who the King of glory was. However, she did know he was not Nebuchadnezzar. So, keeping her eyes fixed on the greater king, the King of glory, Aridatha walked like a queen toward the King of Babylon.

50

THE fragrance of royal perfume startled Nebuchadnezzar. Where had it come from? Certainly, not from Aridatha. Eleven months ago, she had reeked of starvation and death, and expecting the same defiant skeleton wearing the same stained and tattered clothes, he had anticipated the same stench. But if it was not Aridatha, who was it? He had given irrevocable orders not to allow anyone except her on his rooftop. Therefore, as ridiculous as it seemed, it had to be her. So, keeping his eyes on his work, he came directly to the point. "I will give you anything you want."

Uncomprehending, she said nothing.

Not looking up, he repeated the offer, reminding her he had made it twice before. "Remember?" he growled. When she still did not answer, he looked up and his jaw dropped.

Unlike eleven months ago, the woman before him was dressed in his finest silks and pearls, her form as bountiful as the harvest, her braids glittering with jewels, her lips like wine. Even so, he was not staring at them, but at the Stars of David laced protectively around her feet. Clearly, she had conceded to his authority by wearing his royal raiment, but just as clearly, she had not conceded her identity, filling him with pride. For if she had done so, she would have been like every other woman in Babylon, dull and spiritless.

"Well?!" he barked. "Or do you already have everything you want? Daughter of Zion."

He said Daughter of Zion with such mocking crispness, she quickly countered, "What do you think I want? I want to go home. To Jerusalem."

"Fine," he nodded and returned to his paperwork, his hands trembling.

Aridatha's knees almost gave way. What had happened? Why had she blurted she wanted to go home? The answer was simple: he had asked and she did want to go home. But he was not supposed to agree!

He was supposed to keep her in Babylon because Jeremiah said the Lord said... the Lord said... What did the Lord say?! Confounded by his unexpected offer and her unexpected reply, she could not remember. All she could think was he had not noticed the jewels she was wearing, the cassia and aloes perfuming her cloak, and the braids in her hair, all chosen to please him!

As Aridatha struggled over his lack of interest, Nebuchadnezzar fumed over her third rejection of Babylon for ramshackled Jerusalem. On the other hand, he admonished himself. Hadn't he already anticipated her answer? Hadn't he already prepared for her protection? So steadying his nerves, he added, "I have found Baruch ben-Zadok."

Her knees almost gave way again. "Alive?"

Reading from a list of Hebrew captives, he nodded. "Baruch ben-Zadok, Lebanon slave camp."

At the thought of Baruch in chains, his neck bloating, and ankles riddled with flesh-eating worms, she erupted, "How could you?"

"Bad leg, broken ribs, undernourished."

"Starved, you mean."

Throwing a bone to Sagitta, he exclaimed, "I am sending him back to Jerusalem with livestock, silver, and slaves."

"You would do that for him?" she gasped.

"No! I am doing it for you. So you can marry him. I am not sending you back to that wasteland alone."

This time her knees did give way and she landed with a thud on a hard marble bench.

"Do not worry," he sneered. "I will fatten him up to make the journey. He will be as healthy as an ox when you meet him."

"I am not worried about Baruch ben-Zadok," she mumbled. "I am worried about your dream."

He shot out of his chair so fast Sagitta barked with surprise. "Who told you?"

"I overheard Shadrach telling Arioch."

"Overheard?!" he blasted. "You eavesdropped!"

"They were in my room. I was feverish. They thought I was dying, but I heard every word."

"The dream was nothing."

Their eyes met, hers calling him to task. She was so beautiful, he wanted to grab her up in his arms and claim her. After all, he was king. Instead, he said briskly, "He will be waiting for you."

Baruch ben-Zadok. In Jerusalem. Waiting for her. How many times had she hoped to hear such a message? Now, it threw her into confusion. Her father had told her, she refused to marry Baruch because of Jeremiah's words. Moreover, eleven months ago when she resolved to submit to the prophet's words, her father's explanation made sense. But if she went back to Jerusalem now, before planting and building in Babylon… "Then why did I say no to him all those years?" she muttered.

King Nebuchadnezzar was about to tell her, it was because she had always belonged to him. But after her three rejections, he would never have her, not even if she begged him.

"Perhaps it is because I do not love him in that way," popped out of her mouth, shocking her. For she knew she loved Baruch.

It did not shock Nebuchadnezzar. He was positive she did not love him in that way or she would have married him years ago. "You will learn to love him."

"Learn to love him? What does that mean?"

"It means you will learn to love him."

"But if I stay here…"

"You said you wanted to go home," he snapped.

"I do," she snapped back.

"Then go," he commanded.

"Fine! I will!"

"Fine! Go!" To make it clear he had no regrets, and especially no need for reminders of her, he reached into his pocket, pulled out the crimson pouch, and held it out to her.

It was as if Jeremiah in all his power and pain had suddenly appeared before her, and it horrified her. "You still have it?"

"Of course, I still have it," he huffed. No need to tell her he had thrown it on the ground outside of Jerusalem and Arioch retrieved it. Besides, it did not matter; nothing mattered now except getting her out of Babylon. So he moved to put it on her, but she leapt off the bench and started to run. Grabbing her, he wrestled the leather cord over her head until the pouch banged against her nose and chin, bounced off three strands of pearls—his pearls—and settled at her heart.

She had not worn the pouch since she was ten years old. Furthermore, she had never expected to wear it again. But now, staring at it rising and falling with her every breath, she knew she had her answer. She was quiet for so long and so pleasantly absorbed, the king assumed she was thinking warm thoughts about him because he had kept the pouch.

So, he queried, "What is it?"

"When Jeremiah gave me this pouch," she whispered, more to herself than to him, "he said words over me I did not hear because I was half dead."

Warm thoughts about him because he had kept the pouch?! Hah! Throwing up his hands, he returned to his desk.

"He said, 'When the Lord takes you into exile from Jerusalem to Babylon...'"

Nebuchadnezzar swung around. "When the *Lord* takes *you*?!"

She nodded. "I am to build houses and settle down, plant gardens and eat what they produce."

King Nebuchadnezzar burst into a fury, pelting his fists up and down on his desk, yelling, "I do not want you here because of some prophet's words."

Having felt much the same way about being in Babylon because of "some prophet's words," she could not help smiling at his frustration. "King Nebuchadnezzar, whether you like it or not, that is why I am here. Besides, with Jerusalem dirt at my heart, I can be content anywhere, even here in Babylon."

He could not believe it! Instead of confessing her undying love and faithfulness to him, she, like Daniel, had wheedled her God through that crimson pouch into her decision to stay. "You will stay in Babylon because you want to live in Babylon and be with me. No other reason."

"When I was a little girl," she continued, as if he had not even spoken, "I asked papa why he fought for Babylon. He said sometimes everything in your life leads to a decision that does not make sense, is at odds with everything you are, and most people do not agree with, but you have to do it because somehow it is right. King Nebuchadnezzar, I could not go back to Jerusalem now. It would not be right."

"Aridatha, I determine what is right."

"I knew what you looked like before I saw you."

"Yes, yes, I am sure you did."

"I did! When I saw your gold statue, I knew it was you. Except for the wings."

"Do not mention those wings!" he seethed through clamped jaws. "I ordered them to make me look like I was *ascending*, not descending."

"When we saw the Fourth Man, I took your hand." Purposely, as she did when she was a girl, she put her hand in his. "Not to protect you, but because you were afraid."

At the touch of her hand, he knew he should immediately call his guards and order them to take her to Baruch ben-Zadok. But he could not. Regardless of her misguided reasons for staying, he wanted her. And if he wanted her, then he was going to have her.

So, taking her face in his palms, he leaned in and pressed his lips to hers. Unlike the night before the siege when she neither resisted nor responded, this time her lips were warm and welcoming. At first, he remained detached, determined to use his experience to excite her. But as he pulled her body into his, it was he, not her, who plunged into a rushing river, its current sucking him in and sweeping him away. Exhilarated by its rapids and wanting more, he steered her toward the couch, not the short hard marble one, but the full sofa with the creamy linen pillows. Nestling her into its soft downy warmth, he was about to wrap himself around her, when suddenly, and for no earthly reason, he leapt away, surprising them both.

Like a man thrown into icy waters, he stared out in shivering bewilderment, shambling back and forth. What had happened? Why his abrupt retreat? Perhaps Yosef ben-Moshe was calling out from the dead demanding he marry her. Or more irritatingly, the youthful manhood of Baruch ben-Zadok had come knocking, looming up to taunt his aging body. Whatever it was, he was certainly rattled, and to cover it, he blurted lamely, "For the last time, I was not afraid."

51

Alone on the palace rooftop, King Nebuchadnezzar and Aridatha of Jerusalem gazed out at Babylon. Without another word, Aridatha knew she belonged to him, and surrounded by his world of towering temples and palaces, she welcomed her new life. Jeremiah had said to build houses and plant gardens, and so she would. Using her influence with Nebuchadnezzar, she would build and plant for her people, strengthening them for the day they would leave Babylon and return to Jerusalem. Facing such a promising future, her mind raced with ideas, yet a frown soon creased her brow.

Seeing it, the king bristled. Had she changed her mind already?

"I was wondering... " she broached a bit cautiously.

He braced himself. If she was going to sweet-talk him into bringing that good-for-nothing Baruch ben-Zadok to Babylon, she would certainly get her wish. He would bring him directly, bind them together, and throw them into the lions' pit to be eaten alive.

"I was wondering," she repeated, still frowning, "about your dream."

"Is that all?" he laughed.

"Is that all?" she objected. "King Nebuchadnezzar, the holy Watcher said, 'Cut down the tree. Trim its branches. Strip off its fruit. Let the animals flee. But let the stump and its roots—bound in chains—remain.'"

"You had a fever and you remember all that?"

"They kept repeating it."

"Remind me to keep you away from those two gabblers" he reproved good-naturedly. Then, sweeping his hand across the vista before them, he announced, "It is mine, Aridatha. All mine."

"Yes, very nice," she nodded. "But Shadrach also said..."

"Nice?" he erupted. "Nice?! Aridatha, you are looking at fifty-three temples to our Babylonian gods, fifty-five chapels to Marduk, and one-hundred-and-eighty altars to Ishtar. Can you see the Ishtar Gate down Procession Way? I designed those bronze bulls and dragons myself."

"I know you did. They are beautiful."

"You know I designed them?" he queried, immensely pleased. "Who told you?"

"My lord," she persisted, "Shadrach told you the holy Watcher said, 'Let him be drenched with the dew of heaven. Let him live with the animals. Let his mind be changed from that of a man. Let him be given…'" she stopped.

"Go on," he said, folding his arms. "Let him be given what?"

"You know."

"Do I?" he challenged.

Looking up, she drilled her eyes into his. "Let him be given the mind of an animal."

"And you believe that?"

"Shadrach said…"

"Aridatha!" he exploded, stopping her in her tracks. "Look!" Grasping her head, he turned her to face the two massive walls surrounding his city. "Do you think anyone can get through or over those walls? Can you see how thick they are? I host chariot races on top of them every year."

"You are to be driven away from people!" she enunciated rabidly, her eyes wide and voice shrill. "To live with wild animals, eat grass like cattle, and be drenched with the dew of heaven! King Nebuchadnezzar, you are not listening!"

"I am telling you Babylon is safe."

"But what about you?"

Astounded, he studied her. Every nerve in her body was anxious for him. Actually frightened for him. What better proof of love? Without even knowing it, she loved him. He could see it in her eyes, feel it pouring from her heart, a tonic, a boost, a stimulant like no other, and suddenly on top of the world, he laughed a great royal laugh.

"King Nebuchadnezzar, this is no laughing matter."

Nodding in agreement, he put on his fiercest face. Even so, he could not hide his mirth when he queried, "Did Shadrach also tell Arioch that if anything happens to me, all I have to do is say Heaven rules?"

"Yes."

"So you see there is nothing to worry about." Slipping his arm around her waist, he very gently added, "Fear not, Daughter of Zion. *If* anything happens, I will simply say Heaven rules. Furthermore, Aridatha," he admonished charmingly, still relishing the taste of her name on his lips, "instead of listening to Shadrach, listen to me. For when I speak, the Euphrates moves, my deserts become fertile, my canals bring the cedars of Lebanon into Babylon…"

As he described his achievements and plans for the future, the morning sun crowned Babylon with such splendor, she could not help wondering how he was going to lose it all. Certainly, no enemy could break through such an impenetrable fortress, and the other two destroyers, plague and famine, instead of causing him to lose his kingdom, would only cause his subjects to need him more. Lastly and most baffling, what could possibly induce him, with his brilliant mind which had subdued nations and now ruled the earth, to leave people behind in order to go away and live with animals?

"Babylon," he breathed, glowing with satisfaction. Taking her arm, he escorted her onto his royal pathway. Following the blood-red marble trail, they circled under his celestial bodies, crossed over carved ebony bridges, and strolled through his forest of bronze chimes. Unlike when she arrived at dawn and was overwhelmed by the spectacle, she now saw each composition—whether it was a gold lampstand or filigree bird cage, a life-size marble elephant or engraved goblet—as the work of captives and slaves from all over the world, their souls and bodies crushed by sorrow and chains.

Nebuchadnezzar, of course, saw none of this. Citing his triumphs of the past and his certain triumphs of the future, it was not a moment for meditating on the contributions of captives and slaves, but a moment for basking in one's glory, even more so, a moment for basking in history. Perhaps he sensed it was such a moment. Perhaps he did not. Nevertheless, walking on his palace rooftop, he felt especially light-hearted, quite cheerful in fact as he listed his highways and roadways spanning the nations, his capitals in each nation, his wealth in gold and silver, cattle and sheep, and the bodies and souls of men. Then, as if to capture the essence of who he was and what he had done, he circled round and round, his arms outstretched toward his Great City, and with eyes gleaming, he said, "Is not this the great Babylon I built as the royal residence by my mighty power and for the glory of my majesty?"

As if roused by his words, a magnificent tree filled the sky. No eye could see it. But Sagitta knew something was there and, rising slowly, sniffed the air. Aridatha did not notice the dog's sudden wariness, nor did she hear the rumble of thunder coming from far above. However, she did hear something that sounded like chains rattling high in the sky. Approaching fast, their clamor soon trembled through the floor until it was shaking with such force, she and Sagitta were thrown off their feet, the young woman shrieking, the dog barking. Wind, hail, thunder, and lightning hurled down, and with lightning dancing around her, Aridatha ran for the stairwell.

"King Nebuchadnezzar!" she yelled, motioning to the landing. "We have to get off the roof!"

Turning, she saw the king standing exactly where she left him, next to his chimes and under his celestials, Sagitta tugging at his sleeve. She called again, but he did not move. So, covering her head with her arms, she hurried back to get him. But no matter how hard she pressed against the wind, she was no match for its strength. Yet she trudged on, pelted by hail and flying debris, tripping and stumbling into a pile of crumpled bird cages. The gold filigree was melting, actually melting, and staring in horror, she leapt away. Hands bleeding and hair whipping across her eyes, she jumped over fallen palms and zigzagged around broken benches trying to get to the king. "Run!" she shouted at the top of her lungs. "King Nebuchadnezzar! Get to the stairs! Get off the roof!"

Either he did not hear or he did not want to hear because he just kept standing there, staring upward, his braids flying out behind him, his royal cloak shredding in the hail, his sun and moon and stars shattering above, his chimes falling like timbers, his fountains, couches, and cushions ripping apart, his gold and silver melting like wax.

Suddenly a white radiance filled the heavens, blinding Aridatha to everything except a massive tree felled by the wind, leaving a jagged stump. Terrified, she watched its charred skeleton with its spider-like branches swirl away, spinning higher and higher, looking smaller and smaller, until it disappeared into the recesses of the stars and moon. When it was gone, the radiance withdrew, taking with it the wind, hail, thunder, and lightning.

And all was calm again.

52

HEART banging and teeth chattering, Aridatha stared at the aftermath. Nothing was left whole. The chimes were mangled, planets shattered, fountains crushed, and water was spurting everywhere. Fixing her eyes on a molten goblet, she thought she was going to be sick because the storm had liquefied all the gold and silver, yet it had done nothing to the wood or to her! Feeling like the helpless fish floundering amidst the rubble, its yellow gills gasping for breath, she cried out, "King Nebuchadnezzar, I think this was a warning!"

She expected one of his scoffing retorts, telling her not to worry because the Euphrates moved at his command, but he said nothing.

"Perhaps now you will listen to Daniel's interpretation of your dream!" Lunging for the fish, she grabbed it and, fumbling her way to the remnants of a pond, tossed it in. "Jerusalem did not listen to Jeremiah," she yelled, "and look what happened to Jerusalem!"

He still did not answer, but what could he say? She was right! Fish were flopping everywhere, stranded amidst melted lampstands, blood-red marble, and wet goose down, so she decided to save them all.

"The mind of an animal," she muttered, clumping here and lurching there, catching one and then another, dropping them into the pond. "The Most High can do it, too!" she shouted, knowing it was crazy trying to save all the fish, but she did not know what else to do. "Remember the Tower of Babel when the Lord went into the minds of men? Back then he confused their one language so no one could understand what the other was saying. Compared to that, the mind of an animal is child's play! Do you hear me? Child's play!"

It angered her that he did not respond, so she whipped around to confront him. But he was still standing in the same place, looking up. What was he looking at?

"King Nebuchadnezzar?" Perhaps the thunder had temporarily deafened him, so raising her voice, she called, "King Nebuchadnezzar?!"

He did not move, not even to look at Sagitta nudging his hand and whimpering, then scooting around to lick the other hand. Back and forth, the dog went, growing more and more agitated because the king did not respond. It was strange he made no effort to comfort the dog or at least shoo him away. Perhaps he was too distracted. He certainly looked uncharacteristically ragged after the wind and hail shredded his clothes and thrashed his hair. But something else was different. What was it? Then she realized Sagitta's persistence was not for himself, but for King Nebuchadnezzar. The animal was worried about him, trying to awaken his hands. Looking more carefully, she could see why. They were hanging limp, his arms were dangling, and his shoulders sagging.

It was a moment she would never forget. Her hands floating to her face and covering her mouth, her feet itching to run, her eyes lifting to the heavens. Was this it? With all his gold and silver melting around him, was this the beginning of the fulfillment of his dream? Was he, right now, going to lose his kingdom and be driven away to live with animals? If he was, was she going to fall into the hands of Gaspar? Was it her destiny to be killed by the Crown Prince who had already tried to kill her once before?

Not if she could help it! After all, hadn't King Nebuchadnezzar, less than an hour before, commanded her to return to Jerusalem and marry Baruch ben-Zadok? She had only agreed to stay in Babylon because he had pulled out the crimson pouch, as if pulling Jeremiah out to haunt her forever. But now, on further consideration, she had already fulfilled Jeremiah's prophecy. She had been exiled to Babylon, and while living at Shadrach's, she had offered to build houses and plant gardens which was almost the same as doing it. Thus, prophecy fulfilled, it was time to go home. So, hiking her Stars of David above her knees, she hurtled toward the rooftop stairwell, when Sagitta flew out before her and blocked her path.

"Get away," she ordered.

Hair standing on end, the dog bared his teeth, ready to attack if she moved one step further.

Forcing herself to be calm, she said firmly, "Sagitta… Go to the king…" The dog cocked his head, trying to understand. "Go. Go to the king."

Sagitta dashed away, then stopped and turned back, as if to say, "Aren't you coming?"

"I will be back," she reassured, knowing it was a lie.

Although the dog seemed to understand, he certainly did not agree, for he kept staring at her, willing her to come to the king. But after seeing the back of King Nebuchadnezzar's slumped shoulders and hanging head, she did not need to see any more. So again, she ran for the stairs, but again was stopped. This time not by Sagitta, but by the voice of her father repeating his last words to her: "It is your fight now, Aridatha." At the time, she thought he was speaking about the fight for Jerusalem, and accordingly, she fought long and hard at the Temple. But now, with Jerusalem and the Temple gone, why were his words beating so powerfully within her, even to the point of stopping her? Had her father meant something else, some other fight? She had no idea and no time to think about it. But one thing was certain: Yosef ben-Moshe would never scuttle back to Jerusalem without making sure Nebuchadnezzar was all right. So she hurried over to the king.

"King Nebuchadnezzar?" she ventured softly.

His eyes moved dully toward her, then rolled back into their sockets.

"Do you hear me?" she said a little louder. When he did not respond, she took his hand. "It is I, Aridatha."

His teeth were chattering, so perhaps he was in shock. After all, her own teeth had been chattering. But if it was just shock, why were his cheeks sunken and his jaw slack? "Are you all right?" she pronounced loudly.

When he still did not respond, she took hold of his shoulders, and jostling them gently, she awakened an unearthly groan. His chest heaved uncontrollably. Saliva spewed out. His body quaked. And his feet pounded up and down on the floor.

"King Nebuchadnezzar!" she cried, so frightened she had to press her fists against her chest to keep her heart from exploding. "What is it? Are you all right? Say something!"

Sudden noises from below distracted her. Hurrying to the edge of the roof, she looked down to see nobility and slaves staring at the scattered rubble fallen from the rooftop. Looking up, some started to point. Frantic, she swung around. The king was still stamping his feet. Not only that, he was snarling at his hands, opening and shutting them fiercely.

All she could think was she had to hide him. But how? What could she do? Finally, she grabbed his arm and tugged him toward the stairwell. "Hurry," she whispered, "We must find Arioch."

Yes, she would take him to Arioch. Then she would run away to Jerusalem.

53

"Insane?" challenged Gaspar, chomping through a steaming platter of shrimp. The idea was absurd. His father had too much willpower to let his mind be overcome by madness. "Are you sure?"

"Absolutely," Zorpo confirmed, taking Gaspar's sheathed swords and daggers from the wall and handing them to him. "Every physician has examined him and agreed. Your father, Nebuchadnezzar King of Babylon, is completely mad."

"It must be one of his schemes," Gaspar muttered. Pushing his meal away, he paced the length of his quarters, more like an administrative office, weapons cache, and drinking parlor than a prison cell. He was rarely in his cell, because after the first torturous month, he bribed the guards to give him the rooms behind the commissary. Then whenever the warden came, he threw off his princely clothes, hurried to his underground cubicle and, moaning miserably, writhed on the floor.

"I know!" he exclaimed, his eyes wild with intrigue. "He thinks I will use this opportunity to escape. Then anyone can kill me."

"Anyone can kill you anytime your father wants. In or out of prison. Trust me, it is no scheme."

As the news sank in, Gaspar started to feel alive again. He had almost given up his kingly ambitions. Now, without doing a thing, the throne was falling into his hands. "Where is he?"

"Nobody knows. But I did hear Nergal plans to take him away tonight."

"Do you know where?"

Zorpo nodded. "We have to hurry."

Only ten hours out of prison and Gaspar was galloping his warhorse through a warm windy night, racing toward the throne of Babylon. During his confinement, he had hoped for such a night, but never believed it would come, especially during those first weeks: days and nights in a lightless closet, his gut ravaged by pain where food and wine once reveled, his flesh bug-bitten and moldy, his toes curling at the rats—the only happy creatures in Canal Prison—scuttling from cell to cell. Immersed in such horrors, it did not take long to lose interest in everything, except escape. However, the only escape from Canal Prison was death. So, he decided to hang himself. But when he tightened his belt around his neck, he remembered his father's whip choking him, and flooded with indignation, he contrived a different escape. Not from prison, but from his cell.

Using a pittance of the gold he had received from the Grand Preceptor Au Yang—now happily dead and out of his way—he bribed the guards for new lodgings. He then ordered Zorpo to use another pittance of Au Yang's gold, horses, and weapons to get his men ready for the day he would fight Nebuchadnezzar and dethrone him. Now, to everyone's surprise, that day was here, and he and his warriors were galloping across the Babylonian plain under windblown torches, rapidly closing in on the insane king.

With only a mile to go, he motioned his archers to take the lead. They had prepared for this moment just as long as he had, and without one misstep, they formed into rows of six.

After a hideous morning of hearing every royal physician proclaim Nebuchadnezzar mad, Arioch ordered Nergal to keep Nebuchadnezzar's secret from leaving the room, a diplomatic way of saying execute all the royal physicians then and there. Nevertheless, the secret leaked out and Gaspar escaped. Now Nergal was making a wild dash across the Babylonian plain leading Nebuchadnezzar's elite cavalry with the king's chariot safely in its midst.

Seeing the Crown Prince closing in, he motioned the chariot to move into the lead. Eight pre-appointed warriors immediately surrounded it, and as they charged forward, Nergal signaled his cavalry to turn around. In a flash, they reversed their horses, but their eyes remained fixed on Nebuchadnezzar's chariot careering down the canal towpath, headed toward the King's Highway. The four white horses, a brilliant team racing together since they were young, ran like the wind, passing field after field of irrigated crops in a land that had been desert before Nebuchadnezzar brought water to it. The king's favorite chariot driver Sirius, the epitome of every chariot racer's dream with his legs and arms built like iron, drove the team seamlessly under the chariot's royal flags Kesith the Archer and Dahrach the Dragon, both snapping confidently for they had never known defeat. Nevertheless, with only eight warriors sent as protection, the lone cart battering along at top speed looked pathetically vulnerable.

With no time to lose, Nergal sped to the front of his men. Facing Gaspar's torches hurtling closer, he spit out his toothpick, called the charge, and he and Babylon's mightiest cavalry galloped back to stop the Crown Prince.

Gaspar knew if the king was truly crazy, he would not be returning with the cavalry, which meant he had probably gone on to the towpath, the fastest route to the King's Highway. He also knew his men could not defeat the elite army guarding the Highway, which meant he must stop the king before he reached it. So, ordering Zorpo and thirty of his finest swordsmen to fall to the rear, he waited for the battle to begin, then taking the direct route through the fields, he led them toward the towpath.

When Gaspar saw only eight warriors escorting the royal chariot, he could not believe Nergal's stupidity. Then, when his men hacked through them without losing a breath, he wondered at Arioch's stupidity for placing Nergal in charge. Then again, where was Arioch? Had he seized the moment to assemble Babylon's armies and take the throne for himself? Well, won't he be surprised when the Crown Prince, no longer in Canal Prison, comes parading into the throne room and kills him? Chuckling with satisfaction, Gaspar whipped his horse faster, steadily gaining ground until he was almost alongside the royal chariot.

Although it was the dead of night, he could see everything around him: Zorpo not far behind dueling with a cavalryman, the horses' manes slapping against their necks, a blanketed lump of a man inside the chariot, and Sirius grappling the chariot's reins, shouting to his team. Sirius must have known he was there, but like any true racer, he never looked

back, keeping his horses moving forward, always forward, faster and faster. Four horses against one, all had been galloping at full stride for miles,
and now with the King's Highway in sight, Sirius' team burst into an
even faster gallop. Gaspar's once-in-a-lifetime opportunity was edging
away and the Crown Prince's stomach dropped. Lashing his horse, he
tried to catch up, but hoof-beat by hoof-beat, Sirius was gaining the
lead. Frantic, Gaspar drew his spear and hurled it at the chariot driver.

It was a wild, misguided throw, but with the winds blowing and the
chariots bouncing, the spear hit its mark, cutting through Sirius' leather
armor and sinking into his back. The driver's arms flew up, the reins fell
free, and with nothing to hold onto, he reeled to the floorboards and
tumbled out onto the road. Coming alongside, Gaspar leapt into the
cart and, catching the tangled reins, tugged the team to a stop.

After the roar of pursuit and the panic of near-defeat, with dust
choking the air and the horses chafing under the grip of their new master, the Crown Prince was raging for battle. But when he saw the shrouded lump still on the floorboards, his black leather boot peeking out from
under the royal blanket, listing limply as if the owner was fast asleep, he
burst into guffawing laughter. His entire life he had prepared for this
day: a grueling fight to the death, sword against sword, dagger against
dagger, and sweat against sweat. The brute force of wills never giving up
until one choked the life out of the other. Instead, he was going to kill a
madman sleeping under a blanket. Indeed, it was laughable. Certainly,
anti-climactic.

"Well, father," he shouted to wake the lunatic up. "They say you
have gone mad." When the lump did nothing, he kicked the boot. "My
only regret," he sneered, "is that you will not know it is I, Gaspar, driving
my dagger into you."

When the lump still did nothing, he grabbed the blanket, and as he
pulled it away, Arioch sprang out from under it. Gaspar thought he was
seeing things! Certainly, Arioch's two blazing eyes and two gleaming daggers could not be lunging at him. He was so dumbfounded by the sight,
as if a leopard had unexpectedly sprung out from under the blanket, he
could not move, and in that eye-blink of time, he knew he had been
right: it had been a scheme! His father had discovered he had moved out
of his cell, pretended to go mad so he would escape, and then sent Arioch to kill him. But, as Arioch's two daggers rushed toward him, another

leopard soared into sight: Zorpo, jumping from his horse. Having grown suspicious of the effortless pursuit, Zorpo had anticipated a surprise, and crashing onto Arioch, they both fell to the floorboards.

Watching the two men wrestle off the cart onto the dirt, Gaspar came to life. Scrambling after them, he kicked Arioch's ribs over and over, yelling over and over, "Where is he?! Where is he?!"

Not until Arioch's ribs were broken and his face kicked in did Zorpo back off. Then they both shouted for an answer.

Without a wince or a groan, Arioch slowly turned his shattered body and looked up at Gaspar. Although his face was a bloody mix of torn flesh and broken bones, his sea-blue eyes were bright with triumph.

Seeing that triumph, Gaspar knew he had made a stupid and costly mistake thinking Arioch had put Nergal in charge of this escape. "I will find him," he seethed. "If it is the last thing I do."

Arioch cracked a nonexistent smile, for his jaw hung loose. "You have lost, Gaspar," he garbled. "You will never be king."

"I will be king!" he raged, and yanking Arioch's head back, he slashed his throat from ear to ear.

Pain screamed through Arioch's every nerve. The pain however did not matter, for the king was safe. To Arioch, that was all that had ever mattered: the king and his safety. Now, with his work finished, he faced death, yet he knew it was not complete death because always in the back of his mind were the nine Babylonian warriors incinerated outside of Nebuchadnezzar's blazing furnace. He had seen their dead bodies on the floor, but he had also seen the men alive, calling out to him from fiery metal cages dropping into the caverns of the earth. He had never lost his terror of those cages. So, choking on his blood, he looked to the heavens and asked if he could be allowed to escape the cages, and if he had to live in fire, let it be like Shadrach, Meshach, and Abedneggo... Let it be with the Fourth Man.

54

Far away on the opposite side of the province, a team of horses tugged a small cargo boat up the canal. The grey-haired horse driver, with rheumy eyes and a tired tattered cloak, had no idea his cargo was Nebuchadnezzar King of Babylon. All he knew was the young woman had paid him with trembling hands, her lips as pale as mountain snow. Throughout the journey she had maintained a quiet courage, but he had not traveled thousands of miles with nighttime passengers without learning a few things about human nature. He could tell, underneath her resolve to be brave lay a desperate heart. And why not? Her every kindness was rebuffed by her violent charge, and although the driver had long ago resolved not to get involved in the woes of his nighttime passengers, usually temporary woes due to carousing, brawling, and dallying, he could not help feeling sorry for her. He was even tempted to offer her a gulp of wine to calm her nerves and protect her from the nighttime dampness. But wine was illegal for drivers on Babylon's canals, so although he took a quick nip for himself, he did not risk it. Besides, she only had two more miles to go before she and her insane companion disembarked.

Inside the boat, Nebuchadnezzar, tied to the timbers, snarled at his ropes while Aridatha stared helplessly at a map she had never seen before. The charted waterways and pathways leading north to the Zagros Mountains were legible, but nothing—not one river, town, or fork in the road—was familiar to her. Looking from the map to the dogs, Arioch's Alcola and Nebuchadnezzar's Sagitta, she wondered what would happen if Arioch did not come. What would they eat? Arioch had packed the king's star maps, but no food; thrown in a sack of weapons, but no silver or gold. Without food or gold, she would be scavenging for scraps to eat, just as she had done during the siege, and it angered her. Why was she suddenly responsible for the king? Why hadn't some huge Babylonian guard been enlisted to take charge of him? What had Arioch been thinking?

Of course, the answer was simple. He had not been thinking because everything had happened so fast. After the physicians declared the king mad, Arioch had been calm and calculating as he plotted three different routes for sneaking Nebuchadnezzar out of the capital and hiding him. To insure concealment, he ordered everything about him to be unkingly: no guards to attract attention and no royal clothes, jewelry, or names. The only exceptions were his royal pendant and ring because they were his indisputable claim to the throne. Then, without warning, four messengers from four different parts of the city burst into the room with the same report: Gaspar had escaped from Canal Prison. Instantly, Arioch's calm, calculated plans were outdated, exchanged for quick improvised strategies for the inevitable war against the Crown Prince.

Without a moment to lose, he knocked out King Nebuchadnezzar, then threw him into a rickety covered wagon. Tying him to the slats, he commanded Nergal to prepare the cavalry for battle and Aridatha to put on the driver's sackcloth tunic and britches. Tossing the star maps, weapons, and dogs in with the king, he thrust a map into her hands and ordered her to follow it to the Zagros Mountains. When she questioned why he was sending her, he simply said not to worry, he would find her within the week, and she could go home to Jerusalem.

Now, after ten hours, Arioch still had not come. So, Aridatha forced herself to stop looking back and start planning for the next day. As she plotted where she would hide the king and hunt for food, she realized her hands were no longer trembling. Steady nerves were a welcome relief, but she did not understand it. After the explosive events of the day— the otherworldly wind on the palace rooftop, the quaking building, the brilliant flash of light, Nebuchadnezzar gone mad, and their hurried escape—she knew the simple act of water lapping against a boat could not have soothed her. Yet, there was a definite calm in the little skiff. What was it? Soon, she realized it was Nebuchadnezzar. No longer grinding his teeth and smashing his fists into the boat timbers, he was quiet and breathing effortlessly. He was sound asleep.

Looking at him so relaxed after raving uncontrollably all day, she thought of a sleeping child after a tantrum. Hopefully, like a child, when he awoke, his ravings would be over. Hopefully, the uproar on the palace rooftop and his madness were just warnings and not the fulfillment of the holy Watcher's words: "Let him be drenched with the dew of heaven, let him live with the animals. Let his mind be changed from that of a man and let him be given the mind of an animal."

But even if it was the fulfillment, as she approached the dock and a new day, she refused to be discouraged because her father had taught her there was always a way out, and King Nebuchadnezzar did have a way out. All he had to do was say Heaven rules, and he would get his kingdom back. Hence, there was no reason to be discouraged.

55

Zagros Mountains

WITH one end of the rope tied to Nebuchadnezzar's belt and the other to her waist, Aridatha tugged the king up a goat trail leading higher into the Zagros Mountains. Determined to reach the summit by nightfall, she had kept them hiking all day. She had not always been so dogged about moving on. In fact, the first months of their escape, she had taken her time so Arioch could reach them sooner. But after four months of looking back, she knew Arioch was not coming. No one was coming, except probably Gaspar. So now, urgency was in her every step, and so far, this day had gone well. Not once had Nebuchadnezzar laid down to sleep, tumbled into the crags on the other side of the path, run off to chase rabbits, or rooted around in the streams for frogs and fish.

"Aaarrrrggghhhh!!!" he shouted from behind, jerking the rope.

The sacks on her shoulders pitched to one side, and trying to right them, she lost her balance and skidded down the slope. Frantically grabbing for brush, she latched onto a spiny shrub, and with its thorns piercing into her palms, she stopped herself.

"I told you not to pull on the rope!"

"Aaarrrrggghhhh!!!" he yelled again.

After months of enduring his every ridiculous whim, she wanted to explode. Maybe if she screamed into his face, telling him he was insane and acting like a fool, he would be so ashamed or so humiliated, he would say Heaven rules. But she knew it was not in the King of Babylon's nature to be ashamed or humiliated. He would not even care. So, clawing her way back up to the trail, she simply said, "Come on."

But Nebuchadnezzar had found something more enjoyable to do than struggling up a mountain: listening to his voice echo off the peaks.

"Aaaarrrrggghhhh!!!" he roared again.

"My king," she pleaded, "we have to keep going. Please, just one more hour?"

Watching him leaping up and down as his voice banged off one peak, bounced off another, and then another, she knew it was hopeless. He would probably go on like this the rest of the afternoon. So, sinking to the ground, she plucked the thorns from her palm and licked the wounds, thinking how once long ago—in her lifetime before the siege—she would have enjoyed a moment like this, savoring the mountain peaks, the eagle's cry, and the rare isolation. But who could enjoy anything when each moment was locked inside the bellowings of a madman? Besides, the mountain peaks and rare isolation would soon be her enemies. Winter was coming, and with it, most likely starvation unless something changed.

Sagitta rumbled a low growl and Aridatha's eyes immediately went to the king. But the keen-eyed dog was not watching him. He was looking across the valley. It took her some moments to find his object, and when she did, her heart leapt. Coming down the mountain was a long line of men, women, and children, pack mules, goats, and sheep.

If she traded with them for supplies, she could get through the winter! But what could she trade? They would not want the king's star maps, her sackcloth clothes, or the crimson pouch. The weapons would be a valuable trade, but she would never give them up, not with the prospect of Gaspar suddenly appearing. Hopes sagging, she looked to the king for the answer. Even after four months, she still expected him to be the king, knowing practically everything and making decisions for the entire world. But all she saw was a wild man hopping up and down bawling to the mountains in the late afternoon sun, his royal pendant shooting out rays of purple, gold, and scarlet. His pendant! That was it! She could trade his pendant for years of supplies. Certainly, that would be all right, for he would still have his ring for identification.

So, waiting until he fell asleep, she carefully lifted off the pendant, then leaving Sagitta behind to guard, she and Alcola ran the distance to the caravan. There, in the dead of night, she found an ancient Tsiari tribesman, and telling him she found the pendant on the ground, she traded it for something far more valuable: goats, pack mules, pottery, tools, food, seeds, and grain.

56

A month later, Aridatha was building their new home, a wood hut sitting on a south ledge high in the Zagros Mountains. She had chosen the ledge because of the bubbling spring inside its small cave, its strategic view of the valleys below and, most importantly, its inaccessibility: one narrow trail coming down from the mountain above; for always in her mind was Gaspar. Even so, winter was her immediate concern. With the autumn temperatures dropping, the cave would be too small, too dark, and too miserably cold to live in all winter, so she had decided to build a hut. Day after day, she had been swinging her ax, but she had only felled two trees, and now, whacking the branches off their trunks, the ax was growing heavier, her arms weaker.

Finally, she glared up at Nebuchadnezzar. Sitting at the edge of a spur thirty feet above, he looked like a vulture basking in the sunlight. "If you do not come down and help me," she shouted, "the house will not be finished for winter."

He moved his eyes toward the stew simmering over her fire.

"Oh, no," she replied. "Nothing to eat until you work."

Jutting his chin out, he turned away.

If only she could get him to help! He could finish half the hut by dusk, because along with his insanity, he had received two other strange gifts: an otherworldly strength—able to lift boulders and timbers as if they were stones and twigs—and an uncanny command over the animals. If the livestock had been solely in her care, they would have run off seeking better pasture. But when Nebuchadnezzar called, using his royal roar that shattered the dawn, whether the mules and goats were in fertile fields or stone corrals, they came running.

"If you do not help, we will have to live in the cave." He always took a wide berth around the cave's gloomy threshold, growling at whatever might be lurking inside, so to make sure he understood, she marched over to its opening and shouted, "Do you want to live in this dark hole all winter?"

Within minutes, he was lumbering down the trail and stomping out onto the ledge, the two dogs circling him, tongues lolling and tails wagging. She showed him how to dig a hole and, putting the shovel into his hand, motioned for him to continue. Quickly, he dug the holes, threw the two logs in, shoveled in the dirt, and tamped it down. He went on to fell six more trees, hacking off their branches like Samson on the loose.

Trying to keep up, she measured and notched the trunks as fast as she could, harnessing them to the mule, and moving them to the frame. As she worked, she thought of her father teaching her how to build houses, telling her someday she might need such knowledge. Back then she did not have to fell the trees because the servants did the hard labor. Now, with the physical work weighing heavily upon her, she wanted to rest. But if she rested, the madman would surely stop. So, she pressed on, working until twilight when they could see no longer, and just as she had hoped, the walls were halfway up. Still, there was no time to rest because Nebuchadnezzar and the animals had to be fed.

When she finally did sit down to eat, the king was on his third helping and the dogs, lying at his feet, were halfway through their deer marrow. She would have liked to talk about her plans to build a smoke house or his plans for saying Heaven rules. She would have liked to talk about anything, even the weather, but he said nothing, more like one of the dogs than a king: his nose twitching, his beady eyes staring out into the night, his ears riveted to the sounds behind the wind.

Like every evening, he soon snarled. Whether the moon was bright or shadowed, the wind warm or chilly, the air damp or dry, he would raise his eyes to the heavens and from deep inside his chest rumble a low threatening growl, his teeth bared, his lips curled.

Both dogs were instantly alert, and Aridatha, equally alert, tried to divert him.

"My king," she spoke gently, "why don't we go hunting tomorrow? We need skins to double-line the house, don't you agree?" But it was like talking to stone with hands clenching and unclenching. "Or if you want, we can go to the river and you can catch some fish."

Hunched and leering, he slowly stood.

"King Nebuchadnezzar," she coaxed, hoping he would sit down, "you like to fish, remember? You always catch the biggest one. Standing in the water, you watch and wait. Then you throw your hands in and pull out…"

He dove for the ax!

She grabbed it first!

Not a clever tactic, because he yanked it from her hands with such force, she flew to the ground. The dogs eyed him cautiously, wondering what he was going to do next. Some nights he pounded the ax into the trees or threw it, other nights he ran for the edge of the ledge or jumped into the fire. Whatever he was going to do, they readied to dodge the ax or block his run.

Aridatha, however, had discovered another way to stop him, shouting, "Gaspar! Get Gaspar!"

Like any dog who turns when hearing the call for the hunt, he stopped and looked at her.

Pointing to the trail leading up the mountain, she yelled, "Get him!"

The dogs ran toward the stony path and Nebuchadnezzar, as if ignited, followed. Soon he would be up on the spur again, a silhouette of madness standing arms akimbo looking out at the horizon, his eyes watching… prowling… stalking…

Every night, when he finally settled down and went to sleep, the tension broke, and Aridatha, her nerves raw and stomach knotted, felt like falling to the earth and sobbing. But knowing tears would only sap her strength, she straightened her shoulders, took hold of her crimson pouch, and stubbornly declared, "With Jerusalem dirt at my heart, I can be content anywhere, even here in Babylon."

They were the same words she had spoken to Nebuchadnezzar on the palace rooftop. However, when she said anywhere, she had no idea it would mean the Zagros Mountains with an insane king. Even so, she knew the words were true, and lying down next to the fire, she went to sleep.

The first winter flew by faster than Aridatha expected. Once the house was built, she had dreaded the idea of being trapped inside all winter. But although the winds howled and the snow and ice came, they were followed by days and sometimes weeks of sunny arid skies. On rainy and snowy nights, Nebuchadnezzar slept by the hearth from sunset to sunrise, and in those quiet hours, she tanned skins, carved arrows, sharpened blades, and thought. More often than not, her thoughts settled on Gaspar. Had Arioch killed him or was Gaspar now King of Babylon? If he was king, was he content knowing his father might still be alive? Aridatha assured herself even if he was not content, there was no possible way he could find the king.

Nonetheless, to calm her uneasy heart, she thought about the day Nebuchadnezzar would say Heaven rules and get his kingdom back. Surely, he would say it soon, maybe tomorrow or even the next day. But if he did not say it soon, she must prepare for spring.

57

NEBUCHADNEZZAR did not say Heaven rules the next day... or the next... or even the next.

So Aridatha planted in spring, harvested in summer, hunted through the fall, and during the shortened days of winter, she tanned and spun. Soon, she no longer resembled the young Jerusalem beauty who learned to run a vast estate, manage servants, and catch a man in the royal family. Nor did she look like the starving wisp of a maiden who darted through the Babylonian marketplace stealing food during the siege of Jerusalem. Instead, after living two years in the rugged, austere Zagros, she was now just as rugged, her skin toughened by hot and icy winds, her hands strengthened from butchering goats and tanning hides, her shoulders broadened from building shelters and hauling game. However, she was no match for the mountains' austerity, wearing seed pod necklaces and bracelets, the Stars of David embroidered in her goatskin hems, agates braided in her hair, and her crimson pouch at her heart.

During those years, Nebuchadnezzar also began to reflect the mountainous terrain: grizzled and weatherworn, yet never disheveled. In fact, for him, grooming was a satisfying pastime, sitting for haircuts, proudly wearing new hides, washing in the river. Soon, his routine became as predictable as the seasons. Each morning, he and Sagitta left the spur and disappeared into the mountains. In the late afternoon, they reappeared, and the king hunkering down like a vulture on a throne waited for Aridatha to serve him supper. Afterward, she brought out an old gardener's bag containing three leather sacks of star maps and one purple silk sack. Then, sitting by the fire, she would read one of the maps aloud.

At first, she had been angry at Arioch for packing the star maps instead of food and gold, but as time passed, she was grateful for his foresight, because the maps were her one connection to man, especially Nebuchadnezzar, Daniel, and a stargazer named Tin. Not only that, reading the maps aloud calmed Nebuchadnezzar so completely, he stretched out by the fire and slept. Occasionally, he would snarl, clench his fists, or stomp away, but those outbursts became less and less until one night when, unexpectedly, he went wild.

She was reading a map from the purple silk sack with the Signs and Constellations embroidered in gold. Authored by the stargazer Tin, he said the Sign of Pisces—*Pisces Hori* (two large Fish bound together by the Band) meaning *the fishes of Him that cometh*—made special reference to Israel. At this point, Nebuchadnezzar yawned and closed his eyes, as did the dogs. But Aridatha, captivated by the mention of Israel, read on into the next section: the Conjunction of Jupiter and Saturn in the Sign of Pisces. There Tin postulated that special historical events occurred in Israel during such conjunctions. His calculations were long and tedious, but his conclusions spellbinding, revealing that the conjunction—Jupiter and Saturn in Pisces—had occurred at the Revelation to Adam, the birth of Enoch, the Revelation to Fohi, and the birth of Moses. Not only that, he had calculated for the future, noting there would be another conjunction within the next three decades.

She was so astonished by the prospect of a conjunction happening in her own lifetime and so intent on guessing what the special historical event for Israel might be, she did not see Nebuchadnezzar bolt upright and snarl. If she had, she probably would have stopped and he might have calmed down. But swept away by the grandeur of Tin's theory, her voice grew even more animated as she read his underlined calculation at the bottom of the page stating there would be three conjunctions of Jupiter and Saturn in Pisces in one year in six hundred years. Before the words left her mouth, Nebuchadnezzar snatched two torches out of the fire and, roaring at the heavens, sprinted toward her drying hides.

It had been a long time since he had taken the torches, but she knew what to do. "Gaspar!" she yelled. "Get Gaspar!"

The dogs ran toward the mountain trail, but Nebuchadnezzar kept his course, thrusting the fire into the hides.

"No!!!" she shrieked, leaping up and racing to him.

Seeing her coming, he brandished the torches at her, a clear warning to back off, and back off she did, staring helplessly as he shoved the flames into her sacks of grain. But when he turned and hurtled toward the hut, she jumped on his back and, wrapping her arms around his neck, tried to pull him down.

"King Nebuchadnezzar, please! Not the house! Get Gaspar!"

It was nothing to throw her off, and bellowing like a bull, he again charged toward the hut.

"Stop him!" she yelled to the dogs. Sagitta and Alcola raced ahead of the king and, grappling his arms in their jaws, pulled him to the ground. Flattened under their snarling bulk, he immediately calmed. What is more, he started to howl, an amiable dog pack howl.

Aridatha could not believe it! Here she was throwing her burning hides and grain into the water trough, and he was howling? Apparently, he had forgotten setting them on fire. For him, it was over, as if it had never happened. But it was not over. Her hides and grain were gone. It had happened, and she was not about to forget! So, marching over to him, she yanked the torches out of his hands, threw them into the fire, and yelled, "Say it!"

Sighing contentedly, he howled again.

"You heard me!" she screamed into his face. "Say it! Say Heaven rules, so we can leave this place and go home!"

He did not even snarl.

Outraged, she grabbed his shoulders and shook him. "You said you were going to ascend to the heights?!" She jerked his head to face the mountains. "Well, there are your heights! But you did not ascend them. I tugged you every step of the way up these mountains, so you could escape your enemies." Watching his lips tremble and his eyes widen like the grave, she knew at last she was shooting arrows that worked. "You said nothing could shake you?! You said you were going to say Heaven rules and get your kingdom back?!" she shrieked, her fury real, her scorn rabid. "But you cannot even speak! All you can do is snarl like a dog! A dog!!!"

He had no idea what she was saying, but he understood he was the object of her fury and, worse, her contempt. So, he leapt up and ran away.

Watching him scramble up the mountain, she yelled over and over: "Say it! Say Heaven rules!"

The first day, she did not care if he ever came back. When he did not appear the second day, she prepared his favorite deer stew, placed it out in the open, and watched from the hut. Still he did not return. Not even to steal it. The third day, Sagitta disappeared, and hoping the dog would bring him back, she again laid out a savory meal. But neither Sagitta nor Nebuchadnezzar returned. So, trying not to fear the worst, she left the ledge and went looking for him, climbing trail after trail, traversing the meadows and hiking the peaks, shouting, "King Nebuchadnezzar!!! King Nebuchadnezzar!!!"

58

AFTER running away, Nebuchadnezzar wandered for days. Abandoned to the wilds, he ate seeds and berries until Sagitta led him to the river. The river he understood, and splashing into the waters, he waded into a pool and planted his feet. Schools of minnows weaved in and out of his legs and sprightly bluegills hovered nearby, but just because he had the mind of an animal did not mean he was stupid. He knew a good meal when he saw one, and there it was: a lone trout slinking around the boulders, flicking its tail one way, then the other, getting closer... closer...

Nebuchadnezzar lunged, locked his hands under its belly, swooped the loner up, and hurled it onto the riverbank. Sagitta yapped from the shore and Nebuchadnezzar yapped back, both sounding like young pups all triumph and companionship. Flushed with his success, he returned to his task, but when he looked into the water, he saw a wild man. Furthermore, the closer Nebuchadnezzar moved his face to the water, the closer the crazed eyes, lank cheeks, and thick drooping lips moved toward him. So he punched the wild man in the face, splashing water everywhere, and the wild man disappeared. However, as soon as the water calmed, he was back again, uglier and angrier than ever, so Nebuchadnezzar tore out of the river and ran.

That night he was still running, scrambling up a rocky cliff with a club in one hand, his other hand pulling him higher. It was a moon-bright night, but he saw only darkness, a netherworld of colorless contour, a haunt for shades, a haven for silence, hushed and expectant, broken only by his panting and the worried murmurings of Sagitta pacing protectively alongside. The man and the dog went on like this for hours, a frantic climb, not just wanting to reach the top of the peaks, but higher. Thus, when Nebuchadnezzar reached the summit and found he could go no higher, he was stunned.

Far away, Aridatha hurried out of her house into the night. Her livestock were safely penned and Alcola, as always, was on guard. Still, she sensed imminent danger. Not for herself, but for Nebuchadnezzar. Looking up at the spur, she willed him to be there. But he was not there. He was not anywhere.

"King Nebuchadnezzar!" she called. "Come back to me. I beg you! King Nebuchadnezzar!"

The king was too far away to hear. Besides, he was throwing all his strength into trying to pull himself into the sky. Yes, his heart was galloping painfully from the climb and his shrunken stomach rumbling from hunger, but something was in the sky, something he had to have, and like a goat on its hind legs reaching for leaves too high, he reached and reached until his legs buckled. Even so, he would not stop. Huffing and wheezing, he jumped toward a star, trying to grab it. He jumped again, and when that did not work, he stepped up with one leg and then the other, as if climbing stairs, until unable to control his limbs any longer, he let out a desperate wail and collapsed. Rolling back and forth in the dirt, he moaned and groaned, pounding his fists and kicking his feet, when suddenly he saw it: the sky! Not just overhead but straight ahead, beyond the edge of the mountain.

Immediately, he raised his club and charged toward it. Sagitta barked a shrill demanding bark, warning him to stop. When the king kept running, he nipped at his heels. When he still kept running, the dog leapt on him, threw him to the ground, and ran away. Just as he wanted, the king chased after him. Sagitta was the finest of all war-trained dogs, so he had no difficulty dodging the king's club. Furthermore, he could thrust and parry too, charging forward and darting backward, luring the snarling king back toward the mountain trail. When Nebuchadnezzar realized the barking dog was trying to draw him away from the sky, he quit his pursuit, turned around, and sped toward the precipice.

Sagitta ran alongside, but just before hurtling off the edge, he sat. Not Nebuchadnezzar. Leaving solid ground behind, he pumped his legs and reached for the heights. But although he stretched his arms higher and spun his legs faster, he did not ascend. Instead, Nebuchadnezzar King of Babylon plunged into freefalling darkness.

59

THE next morning at the bottom of the precipice, a screeching racket echoed through the valley, irritating the king. Shivering with cold and wanting the noise to stop, he tried nuzzling into Sagitta, but he could not move. His mind did not recollect his nighttime leap into the air, plunging ninety feet, hammering against cliffs, bouncing off boulders, and crashing through trees, but his body remembered every blow and now screamed painfully. No bones were broken, but his ligaments and muscles were mightily bruised, so taking little sips of air, he opened a bleary eye and searched for the noise, echoing in the morning mist.

Looking at the sky first, always the sky first, his eyes targeted the sparrows flitting from tree to tree, the finches warbling in the branches, the swallows disappearing in and out of the fog, and lastly, the crow directly overhead, pacing back and forth on a stout limb screeching down at him. He was the culprit.

"Caw! Caw! Caw!" blared the crow.

So Nebuchadnezzar blared back, "Caw!"

It was a caw that shattered the dawn, and hearing it, four other crows careered in from hiding places throughout the valley. Swooping in and landing on the branch, they paced up and down with the other crow, all squawking insults at the king.

Outraged, Nebuchadnezzar leapt to his feet, and although dizzy and staggering from pain, he thundered, "Caw! Caw-caw! Caw!"

But the crows were not impressed. They were high in the branches and he was down on the earth, so flicking their tails, they each evacuated a large green and white response—splat and splat, and splat, splat, splat—down onto his shoulders.

All the birds in the trees thought it hilariously funny, laughing merrily at the man on the ground slapping off turds, waving his fists at the screeching crows, and caw-caw-cawing at everyone.

Suddenly, the man caught a glimpse of his arm. A horrifying moment because it was covered with a strange crust. Quickly, he hid his arm behind his back. Then, heart racing, he slowly brought it around and looked again. Horrors! It was still there! Not a crust, but a filmy bird down. Furiously, he scratched at the hatchling feathers trying to make them go away. But they would not go away because they were growing out of his skin, growing out of everywhere, his arms, legs, chest, and back: gossamer wisps of dark greens speckled with gold, feathery tufts of royal purple lined with shimmering silver, and glossy blacks spangled with yellows and reds. Captivated by the glittering colors, he touched them. They were soft and warm. So soft and so warm, instead of scratching at the feathery down, he plopped to the ground and started stroking it. Soon, his heart calmed, his eyelids grew heavy, and burying his head in the crook of his feathery arm, he fell asleep.

60

DURING Aridatha's third and fourth years on the mountain, she searched day and night for the king. Hearing wolves on the hunt, she imagined they were chasing after him ready to tear him to pieces. So, grabbing bow and torch, she ran out into the night, scrambled up trails, crawled through draws, even sneaked near their dens trying to find him, but she never did. When the spring floods came, she envisioned him being swept into the roiling waters. So, watching at the river day and night, she called out for him, ready to jump in and save him when he passed by, but he never passed by. Then, she got it into her head he might get it into his head to run off a cliff and plummet to his death. So, combing the bases of the cliffs, she searched for his broken body. But she never found it.

Arioch's huge dog Alcola searched along with her, but to Aridatha's surprise and frustration, she was not much help. At first, the dog seemed to understand, sniffing out and finding human footprints and waste. But each time it was in the vicinity of a herd of wild donkeys, and Aridatha, fearing the donkeys would kick Alcola to death, ordered her to stay away. From then on, the dog kept clear of the herd and, from then on, found fewer and fewer footprints and droppings.

Even if Aridatha had come upon Nebuchadnezzar, she probably would not have recognized him because he no longer looked like a man, but a feathered beast. Furthermore, he was rarely out in the open, but well-hidden in a herd of wild donkeys because the five crows who screeched at him on his first feathered day, for no earthly reason, took it upon themselves to lead him to the herd.

Although no one witnessed the little parade, it was a sight to behold. With one crow perched on each of Nebuchadnezzar's feathered shoulders, one flew ahead taking the lead while two swooped in from behind, tormenting him into taking each step. Sagitta ran ahead and woofed, then raced back and woofed again, trying to keep him moving. It was not as if the king did not want to go forward, there were just so many other delightful things to do: swatting insects, munching thyme, sniffing dung and, most enthralling, gazing at the streaks of gold glittering through his feathers whenever they caught the sun. With all these distractions, it took the entire day for the little group to reach its destination: the herd of wild donkeys. Naturally, the donkeys were wary of the unfamiliar bird-creature and huge dog lumbering toward them. But when the two strangers rolled on their backs to let the donkeys sniff them, a swift acceptance swept through the herd, and the donkeys had protected them ever since.

During those two years, Nebuchadnezzar fell into another predictable routine. With the crows never far off, he migrated with the donkeys to and from the seasonal grasses, grazing in the brush-filled crannies, the fragrant meadowed plateaus, and the forested valleys; watering in the high lakes, the mountain streams, and rivers. Now, because it was spring, he and Sagitta were with the donkeys on the high plateau grazing peacefully in the windy sunrise. As usual, the crows flew in to see how he was doing, slicing his teeth through the grasses and chewing heartily, then settling down for his dirt bath. They were especially proud of his dirt bath because they had taught it to him: loosening the topsoil with his iron-strong bird claws, rolling in the dirt—first one way then the other—then working the grit down through his feathers to sand the bugs and mites away. It was a pleasant respite and normally they would have joined in, but today they squawked at him, trying to get his attention. Even Sagitta pawed at his arm. But the king, cradled warmly in his dust bowl, was in a world of his own, rubbing, scrubbing, and scratching, a low contented growl reverberating through his chest, rubbing, scrubbing, and scratching until a giant snowflake smacked him on the nose.

Startled, he looked up. A snowstorm was blasting overhead, Sagitta was covered with white, and the crows were scolding. Worse, the donkeys were gone! Terrified, he jumped to his feet and waited for them to reappear. When they did not, he wailed the alarm, but no one came. So, he wailed louder. Again and again. Louder and louder. Still, no one came. Frantic, he darted here and backtracked there, his feathers frosting over with white, wailing and moaning, until Sagitta yipped. Staring down at the huge black form running up to him and then running off, Nebuchadnezzar quickly followed. Fluffing his feathers against the icy blast, he pumped his legs as fast as he could, staggering on until the dog led him safely back into the herd.

So, with the king covered with feathers and living in a pack of wild donkeys, it was understandable why Aridatha never found him. It was also understandable, after searching for two years, she came to the conclusion he was dead and it was time to go home. Yet strangely, the thought of going home was not as comforting as she had expected, because after being away from mankind for five years—one year traveling to the Zagros and four in the Zagros—she was now more familiar with the faces of the mountains than the faces of people. Even so, she knew she had to leave because staying alone in the wilderness could become a madness in itself. So, bit by bit, week by week, she bundled up the king's star maps and weapons. Then, on a single day, she packed all her clothes and food so she could leave the next morning. First, however, she wanted to say goodbye to the mountains. So, calling Alcola to her side, she headed up the trail.

She had envisioned her farewell to be a tearful one, because although her years on the mountain had been harsh, she was truly sad to leave. But even hiking through the beauty, the silence, and the wonders of the peaks, she could not conjure one poignant memory because if the king was truly dead, then he was not going to get his kingdom back. And, if he was not going to get his kingdom back, then Daniel and Shadrach had been wrong, which meant she had wasted the last five years of her life. Five years! Three slaving for a madman. Two searching for him. Wasted! Five horrible years! From there, her old grievance against Jeremiah rose up like a foul meal. She had not planted or built in Babylon! She had been a fugitive from Babylon, planting and building in the Zagros Mountains. In other words, Jeremiah had been wrong, too! She even railed at herself for believing she could be happy anywhere with a pouch of Jerusalem dirt hanging from her neck, a madness more bizarre than Nebuchadnezzar's because she, at least, was sane.

Angrier and angrier, her shoulders hunched and glowering at the earth, she stomped across spring pastures, thrashed through streams, and bolted up crags. What had Nebuchadnezzar said about the pouch? Yes, she remembered: "Will it bless or will it curse?" When she was ten, she did not know the answer, but she certainly knew it now: it was a curse! Furthermore, the only way to rid oneself of a curse was to rid oneself of the amulet. So, ripping the pouch from her neck, she threw it as far as she could, into a sky of snow.

Snow? It must have come in fast because everything around her was white. So white, she did not know where she was, which made her even angrier. Now she was lost because of Daniel, Shadrach, and Jeremiah! At least, faithful Alcola was at her side. Then again, Alcola was not at her side. Alcola was slinking away, angling toward a herd of wild donkeys silhouetted against the cliffs across the draw.

"Alcola, come!"

The dog stopped.

"I said come!"

Head hanging, the dog reluctantly shuffled back.

"I told you those donkeys will kick you to death if you..." Suddenly she saw what Alcola saw: two strange lumps off to the side of the herd. One looked like a large dog covered with snow, and as Alcola whimpered, Aridatha wondered if it was Sagitta. On the other hand, perhaps Alcola was whimpering because the other lump was...

No! It could not be! Not King Nebuchadnezzar! Not sitting out in the freezing snow! It was probably a boulder or a donkey's colt hunkered down. Whatever it was, she was not going to slog all that distance on her belly through snow just to find out. For two years she had climbed cliffs, traversed rivers, and crawled into gullies only to find boulders, thickets, or dead animals. But not anymore. She had to quit hoping and be sensible. It was not the king! Then again, Sagitta would not have stayed away from Alcola just to be with a herd of donkeys. Moreover, she had searched this long, so why stop now?

So, motioning for Alcola to stay, she ran to the draw. Scrambling down one side and clambering up the other, she flattened herself onto the ground and looked out. Even through the distance and the snow, it was clear the other lump was not a boulder or a donkey. Curious to know what it was, she inched slowly toward the herd when suddenly the lump jumped up. Horrified, she dove behind a tree. Then, heart hammering and knees shaking, she peered out.

It was a bird! A giant feathered creature, its wings outstretched like two billowing sails, its plumage trimmed with snow. But that was impossible. There were no birds six feet tall. Besides, everything was blurred, its back was to her, and the snow was in a flurry, so she had to be seeing things. It was probably a... a...

Suddenly, it took off running, running like the wind, springing into the air and leaping onto a donkey's back. Lifting its feathered wings to full extension, it flapped them up and down, then bellowing with a voice that shattered the dawn, it grabbed the donkey's mane and charged into the storm. The entire herd followed, their ears laid back, snorting and bucking, a thunderous stampede racing after it.

Any herd of wild donkeys galloping full speed inside swirling snow and silhouetted against a backdrop of craggy stone walls would be captivating, but with the magnificent feathered creature roaring the charge and Sagitta racing alongside, their presence was spellbinding. Advancing like the clouds and swifter than eagles, their hooves gobbled up the land getting closer and closer until they raced by, the feathered creature still in the lead, his plumed chest broad, his spangling arms pumping in stride, and his keen eyes darting here and there, first to the sky, always the sky first, watching, prowling, stalking...

"King Nebuchadnezzar!" she shouted, jumping up and running after him. "King Nebuchadnezzar!" Too late. He was gone, disappeared around the cliffs, and with him, the whole galloping herd, leaving a blast of snow closing in like a wall between her and them.

"King Nebuchadnezzar!" she yelled and yelled, but the wind yelled louder, drowning her out. So, once again, she lost him, but this time she laughed and skipped and cried tears of joy.

"Feathers!" she yelped. "Who would have guessed feathers?!" Not Daniel. Not Shadrach. Not Nebuchadnezzar. Certainly, not her! Indeed, all her worries about the king and all her plans to feed and protect him through the long cold winters had been groundless. For the God of Heaven had fed the King of Babylon with pastures to graze on and protected him with feathers.

"Feathers! What a sight! Feathers! What a sight!" she called over and over into the snow and up into the sky, still laughing, still skipping, still crying tears of joy. And, why not? A great weight had been lifted off her. For she now knew, without a doubt, Daniel and Shadrach had been right: Nebuchadnezzar would say Heaven rules and get his kingdom back. Furthermore, without a doubt, she knew she would build and plant in Babylon just as Jeremiah had said when he placed the crimson pouch on her.

"Oh, no!" she gasped, her hand going to her heart. "My pouch!"

Hurtling back across the draw, she ran to where she thought it would be, only to find a thick carpet of snow. "Alcola, quick. Find my pouch!"

Barking merrily, Alcola bounded over to a flurry of crocuses just peeking out, and there it was: her crimson pouch. Pulling it over her head, Aridatha could breathe again. She still had it! Jerusalem dirt! Looking through the snow toward the cliffs where Nebuchadnezzar and the donkeys had disappeared, she remembered putting it on him when she was ten years old. He had tapped his royal pendant proudly and said, "Babylon." She had tapped her pouch proudly, saying, "Jerusalem."

Tapping her pouch as she did then, she suddenly wondered what had happened to his pendant, and a chill gripped her heart.

━━◄◅▐▌▻►━━

But Aridatha did not need to worry. The royal pendant of Babylon was right where she left it: in the possession of the ancient Tsiari tribesman who in the dead of night had traded all he had for it. His name was Eli and he came from the house of Reuel, the father of Zipporah, the wife of Moses. Eli had sensed the distraught young woman had not found the pendant on the ground, but was in charge of its owner, the King of Babylon. For the secret of the king's dream had found its way out of the palace, onto a canal barge, through the forests, and into the mountains until some of the most unlikely men and women knew about it. Eli was one of those men. So, if King Nebuchadnezzar had been driven away from people and now had the mind of an animal, and if this young woman was in charge of him, he knew she would need everything he could supply. Thus, he had given her all he had.

Over the years, he had kept the pendant a secret, hidden inside his tunic so no one—not even his wife—knew about it. It warmed his heart to think, when the King of Babylon said Heaven rules, he could return the pendant to the king, and thus make her happy. He knew making her happy was a silly notion of a vain old man, but it was important to him because he had seen so much heartbreak in her eyes.

However, after six years, the ancient tribesman suddenly died, and his wife and sons for the first time saw his secret. Marveling at such rare good fortune, they kept the pendant hidden from the tribe, arguing for days about what to do with it. They knew if they tried to sell it, they might be accused of stealing it and promptly executed. On the other hand, if they dismantled it and sold it jewel by jewel, they would certainly fall under some Babylonian curse. So, after many contentious nights, they agreed to apply for a reward.

Thus, the eldest son of Eli, a strapping figure with oiled hair, traveled to the City of Babylon. It was weeks before he was allowed to enter Gaspar's throne room, and after exacting a promise for an exorbitant reward, he set the pendant before him.

"Didn't I tell you, Zorpo?" exclaimed Gaspar, putting the pendant on and moving to the mirror. "Didn't I tell you we would find him?"

"But this information is over six years old," the commander objected. "Besides, she would not give up the pendant unless he was dead."

"No," declared Gaspar. "If he was dead, I would know it."

So Zorpo paid the tribesman, then ordered him to make a map showing where his father, Eli, had traded his supplies for the pendant.

61

ARIDATHA's sixth spring in the Zagros was filled with tempestuous winds bringing in lightning and thunder followed by pelting rains, blizzards, and more rains. Cloudbursts flooded the ridges transforming the crags into muddy waterfalls, while hail shredded the meadows turning the land into an icy crust. The animals, their coats soaked by rain turned to ice, searched helplessly for a way out of the blinding storms, slogging through drifts until they dropped dead in their tracks. Aridatha, forced to stay in her hut because the ledge was buried under snow, worried about Nebuchadnezzar as never before, reminding herself repeatedly he was protected by his feathers and the herd of donkeys. Indeed, the donkeys, although they lost half their young and half their old, continued to shelter the wild feathered creature and his huge dog in the center of their pack, huddling around them day after day and night after night.

Then on a single day, the sun broke through, and after a month of storms, a week of tenderness fell upon the land, birds singing, blossoms dotting the hillsides, ferns unfolding in the crannies. Once again, the calves and colts, kids and lambs nursed hungrily while their mothers fed on bright green grasses. Once again, the donkeys, the crows, Nebuchadnezzar, and Sagitta grazed on mountain meadows in sunlit breezes. Then, at sunrise on the eighth day, as the shadows dallied in the grasses and the dew glistened on the webs, a noxious odor wound its way up into the fresh mountain air.

Recognizing it immediately, Sagitta rose on all fours and sniffed, not as he usually did with his ears catching the wind and his nose scanning the familiar fragrances, but with his ears cocked, his eyes narrow, and his black-rimmed mouth drawn down in a snarl.

Hearing his snarl, the crows chattered anxiously, wondering what was wrong. Nebuchadnezzar cawed for quiet, then shaking the dew from his feathers, he too sniffed the air. When he found nothing but a hint of smoke, he returned to his grazing. Sagitta, however, kept snarling. So, Nebuchadnezzar jumped to his feet and, arms akimbo, sniffed again. This time, he caught the noxious odor and his feathers bolted upright. Targeting the smoke, just one lazy stream rising up from the valley below, he took off running, Sagitta alongside.

———❦———

Aridatha had been up all night studying the stars. After being confined in her hut most of the spring, the clear moonless sky had lured her out. When she was a girl, her mother had instructed her in the stars and their courses, but whenever Aridatha had asked her questions, Zillah had scoffed at her prattling ways, telling her to keep quiet and listen. So, when Baruch read from the scrolls, she had looked to him for answers. Poor Baruch, only eight years old and she had expected him to know everything, thinking because he read from the scrolls, he knew what they meant when they said something like, "The heavens declare the glory of God; uttering forth speech day after day, displaying knowledge night after night."

Now she sought the answers for herself, searching the heavens, trying to hear the speech they uttered forth, hoping to find the knowledge they displayed. But like any stargazer, she only found wonder, and in her wonder, she had stayed up all night.

Consequently, she was fast asleep when her door flew open and Sagitta charged in. Jumping on her bed, the dog licked her face with his great lolling tongue, bounced away, nipped Alcola on the neck, and they both raced out the door before she even opened her eyes. Thinking it was Alcola, she nestled deeper into her blankets and was almost asleep when Nebuchadnezzar crashed in. Charging through the goats with his feathered legs and batting her grain baskets aside with his winged arms certainly opened her eyes. They widened even more when she saw his feathered hands because his fingernails were horrific bird claws, curved, thick, and tough, able to grab her swords and daggers, bow and quiver with the deftness of an eagle clasping its prey. Before she could blink, he was gone.

Bolting from her bed, she dashed out the door to call him back. But all she could see was a phantom shadow disappearing up the mountain trail. Or did she see it? Misty clouds were trailing across the morning sky, so perhaps she had imagined the shadow. Perhaps she had even imagined his visit. He and Sagitta were nowhere to be seen, so it must have been a dream. But, glancing back at her weapons, she knew he had come because half of them were gone.

But why weapons? Why not food?

Noticing the thread of smoke rising up from the valley floor, she had her answer.

Horrified, she hurtled inside, grabbed the other half of the weapons and, looking Alcola in the eye, said, "You must find them, girl. Find Sagitta and the king before Gaspar does."

62

With his animal mind fixed on his quarry, Nebuchadnezzar ran down shale paths at breakneck speed. Protected by his feathers, he crashed through nettle and hawthorn branches without a scratch. With his intense strength, he vaulted up and over boulders without losing stride. Sagitta stayed protectively alongside, but he would have preferred to throw the king to the ground and make him wait for Aridatha and Alcola. Unable to see them skirting around the salt rift behind, he knew they were there, and he knew his master needed them. But he also knew he could not divert Nebuchadnezzar away from the noxious odor, so the worried dog kept pace.

The odor was emanating from the far end of the valley where four Babylonian warriors and their guide waited for their midday meal. Handpicked and paid sacks of gold to find Nebuchadnezzar, they had been a proud group leaving Babylon alongside Gaspar and Zorpo. But after months of searching in vain, their high-mindedness had deteriorated to ribald jokes about the absurdity of eight grown men scouring the mountains looking for human excrement, footprints, and clothing just to find a king who was already dead. Because if he was not dead, he would have returned to Babylon and claimed the throne. On the other hand, if he was still alive and crazy, who cared where he lived? At this point, Clorvel, a huge hairy warrior, usually said something about the daggers tattooed on Gaspar's arms and where he could put them, resulting in coarse har-har's all around.

Naturally their banter stopped when Gaspar and Zorpo rode in, but the mirth in their eyes was hard to stifle. For who could not laugh at the two most powerful men in the world clip-clopping into camp dejected and weary after arguing all morning over which trail to take? Sometimes Gaspar would take the lead, but plagued by doubt, he would soon return to the starting point and let Zorpo take the lead. Other times they cast lots or came to blows. Whatever their tactics, they always returned to camp emptyhanded, until their quest became so absurd, the cook had to breathe in smoke just to keep himself from laughing. Oh, the tales he would have to tell when he returned to Babylon.

Aridatha, nearing the valley floor, could not see beyond the brush. Running through nettle that stung every part of her body and facing boulders too steep to climb, all she could see was Alcola trailblazing before her, stopping to wait, and then continuing on. Sweat poured off her palms, but her breath was steady and her strength strong, so scurrying around the boulders and leaping across the streams, she pushed herself harder, hoping to reach Nebuchadnezzar in time.

Like Aridatha, Nebuchadnezzar was also blinded by the landscape, but he did not need landmarks to guide him. With his animal mind, he was driven by his keen sense of smell, hurtling not toward the aroma of deer and onions braising over a fire, but the living prey next to it.

The camp cook always produced savory meals, so the men ate heartily as they watched the guide step gingerly over to Gaspar and ever-so-tactfully suggest they might have strayed a bit… not too much… but a bit off the tribesman's route.

"My father is here," seethed Gaspar, slapping the map out of the guide's hands. "In this valley. Close by."

"But if the king would just look at the map," implored the guide, picking up the scroll and dusting it off.

"Map?! I do not need a map! I can smell him!"

Smell him? Amused eyebrows shot up all around. If Nebuchadnezzar had gone crazy being king, his son was certainly following suit. But their eyebrows soon fell, distracted by a high-pitched yowl in the forest.

"What was that?" gasped the cook.

"Quiet!" ordered Gaspar.

Obediently, the cook slumped quietly to the earth. No one noticed the arrow in his back because all eyes were fastened to the eagle-like screechings bouncing off the trees. Suddenly, all was still, an eerie, sneaky stillness… Listening to it creep in around them, no one breathed. Then came a rustling noise pumping through the air, louder and louder… Closer and closer… Ending with a thump behind them. Swinging around, they stared at the cook on the ground and Clorvel sagging next to him, an arrow in each of their backs. As they gaped, a third arrow rustled in, sinking into the chest of another warrior.

"Weapons!" shouted Gaspar. "Circle the horses!"

Nebuchadnezzar's eyes honed in on his prey scuttling back and forth. One frantic screamer, unable to control his resisting horse and grab his weapons at the same time, was wide open, so he shot him.

"There!" Gaspar pointed into the trees.

In the distant shadows, a great hulking creature carrying a bow and wearing a sword stole through the mist, disappeared behind the trees, reappeared as a shadow within a shadow, then disappeared again. It was so ghostlike, if there had not been four very real arrows inside four very real men, one might have thought one was having a very real nightmare.

"It is a bear," whispered Zorpo, so the bear could not hear.

"Idiot!" the guide growled. "A bear cannot shoot arrows." As if to prove his point, he fell to the ground with an arrow in his chest.

"It has feathers," squeaked the only warrior left. "So it must be a bird."

"No," grinned Gaspar. "It is the king."

Aridatha sped along the river path following Alcola toward Nebuchadnezzar's high-pitched screechings. Although she had no idea what to expect when she got to him or what she was going to do, she knew she was ready to do anything. So, into the river she plunged, hurtling to the other side.

"Father!" Gaspar shouted into the forest.

Hearing the familiar voice chilled Aridatha to the bone, and knowing the king would rather die than hide from it, she forced her legs to move faster.

"I am King of Babylon now!"

Aridatha saw a flash in the trees. It was Nebuchadnezzar stepping out into the dappled sunlight raising his bow in one bird-clawed hand and an arrow in the other. He was a splendorous spectacle with his gold-feathered head and outspread wings glittering with reds, blues, and greens. He was also a perfect target.

"No," she breathed. "Hide."

"Babylon is mine!" yelled Gaspar. "And anyone who tries to shake me…" Safely tucked behind his horse, he laughed, "I, King of Babylon, destroy."

Nebuchadnezzar did not understand the words, but he understood the taunt, and throwing his bow down, he drew his sword. Seeing his father abandon his bow, Gaspar came out from behind his horse with his bow loaded and ready to shoot.

"Get back!" cried Aridatha, charging through the trees.

No one heard because Gaspar's two remaining men were yelling at him, ordering him to shoot the monster. Gaspar, however, had waited too long to hurry and bungle the shot. So, taking a deep breath, he steadied his arrow, and when he was sure he had a clear path to the king's heart, he released it. A perfect shot, skimming confidently toward its mark, when from out of nowhere, a young woman, wild and rugged like the mountains, leapt out of the forest onto the hulk.

Stunned, Gaspar stared at his arrow sinking into her back instead of the king's heart. Even then, she did not fall, but clung to him, making herself a shield between him and Gaspar.

"Run," she pleaded. "They will kill you. Run."

The feathered beast pulled her up into his arms, a warm and tender balm until he saw her blood dripping onto the forest floor. Frightened, he did not know what to do, and looking for the donkeys or the five crows, his eyes lit on the man exuding the noxious odor. Suddenly back on the scent, he tossed the wounded beauty to the ground, and raising his sword, he hurtled toward him.

Knowing a mad woman would not be propelling out of the trees a second time, Gaspar calmly aimed and shot again. But with uncanny prescience, Nebuchadnezzar shifted and the arrow sped by.

Staring at the feathered monster still alive and charging toward him, Gaspar recalled hearing about the time his father eluded death when Yosef ben-Moshe took the first arrow and Nebuchadnezzar stopped the second with his shield. The third arrow was never shot, but that was not going to happen today. Gaspar would wait until his father was so close he could not dodge it. However, when the usurper King of Babylon reached for his third arrow, it was not there. In the frenzy of circling the horses, he had grabbed only two. So he ordered Zorpo and his last remaining warrior to shoot.

Gladly the two men aimed, but the horses, panicked by the sight of the approaching bird-man with his barking dogs, reared up and blocked their vision. Before they could reposition, the dogs flew in. Alcola, leaping onto Zorpo, knocked him to the ground, and Sagitta, sinking his teeth into the warrior's neck, ripped it apart until he was dead.

With his men fallen, Gaspar stood alone against the oncoming beast. He was pleased to be alone. This was his fight, and after spending a lifetime working toward it, he, not Nebuchadnezzar, was going to walk away. So, drawing his sword, he set out running. All the forest creatures from the birds in the branches to the foxes on the ground locked their eyes on the two kings of Babylon, one feathered and one tattooed, racing toward each other, not for power, not for glory, not even for Babylon, but for death.

Zorpo had not worked his way up the ranks of Babylon to be slain by a dog. So, with Alcola's teeth slashing into his shoulder, he wrestled his dagger out of its sheath and stabbed her until she fell dead. He also had not come this far to have Gaspar die and Nebuchadnezzar recapture Babylon. So, pulling out his other dagger, he hurried toward the two kings clanging sword against sword. Seeing Zorpo sneaking up behind the king, Gaspar lunged to the right, then pressed forward, forcing the feathered hulk backward toward him. But when Zorpo raised his dagger, an explosion of pain hit him so hard, he lurched forward, his eyes blurred, and his dagger fell to the ground.

He could not comprehend it. Where had the sudden pain come from? Perhaps the dog had dislocated his shoulder, and turning to look, he saw an arrow in his back. Impossible! All his men were down. Besides, they would not shoot him. So, where had the arrow come from?

Then, he remembered.

Swinging around, he looked out. She was up on her knees, a bow in her hand and ready to shoot again. He even recognized her. She had waved the Hebrew flag on the Jerusalem wall, burnt his tents in the execution yard, and then escaped by jumping over a wall no horse could jump. Buckling from pain, he started to fall, but seeing her still upright with Gaspar's arrow in her back, he locked his knees. She was not going to get the better of him this time. For long moments, the two swayed in unison, back and forth, side to side, both refusing to drop. Finally, Zorpo's strength bled fully away, and he fell to the ground. Not until Aridatha was certain he was dead, did she allow herself the luxury of collapsing to the earth.

The two kings of Babylon fought on, swords banging, flesh burning, throats searing. Even so, neither was distressed. In fact, Gaspar was enjoying the combat, all his years of training finally paying off. So assured of his victory over his snorting opponent and so eager to get on with his kingship, he crouched low, spun around, and thrust his sword with lightning speed at Nebuchadnezzar's heart. However, the feathered creature simply caught Gaspar's arm in mid-swing, snapped his wrist in two, then wrapped his bird-clawed hands around his neck.

Gaspar could not believe this was happening to him. Once before, Nebuchadnezzar had grappled his wrist to the breaking point. Now he had broken it. Once before, he had wrapped a whip around his neck. Now giant bird claws were ripping his throat apart. But the pain in his wrist and the air gushing out of his gullet were irrelevant compared to the thought of not being King of Babylon. He had spent his life striving to dethrone his father, and just because he was drowning in his own blood did not mean he was going to give up now. He would live another day, just as he always had. Thus, tomorrow he would renew his quest to kill his father. Yes, that was what he was going to do, and believing he would actually awaken with the dawn and seize the kingdom, he died with a smile on his face.

The feathered hulk waited for the body with the noxious odor to go limp, then weary and hungry, he plopped onto the earth.

63

ARIDATHA's body lay deathlike on the forest floor, but her mind was as alert as ever as she stared at Nebuchadnezzar's royal plumage: his head crowned in a sweep of gold feathers, his back mantled in purple, his raven wings lined with shimmering reds, blues, and greens. If only she could reach out and touch them, feel their sunlit warmth and silky softness. But crippled by pain and quickly losing breath, she could only stare at the glorious wonder, far greater than all the wonders of Babylon, yet amazingly no one would ever see it. If the King of Babylon had been able to make feathers grow out of a man, he would have done it so the whole world could see and thus give him the glory. Yet, the Lord Almighty, the King of glory, had hidden Nebuchadnezzar's feathers from the world. Furthermore, they would remain hidden, because Nebuchadnezzar would not remember, and if he did, he would never say anything. She was dying, so she could never tell anyone about what she saw. Only the birds of the air and the animals of the land would be left as witnesses, and their voices were mute. Thus, the Lord Almighty, the King of glory, had deliberately hidden his glory from all the world. Why?

It was so amazing, so delightfully confounding, so opposite to everything King Nebuchadnezzar was, that even as she faced death, she wanted to laugh and sing forever. But all she could do, her eyes beaming with wonder, was whisper her lifelong question through racking pain and parched lips, "Who is this King of glory?"

Nebuchadnezzar, staring dully at his bloodied bird claws, did not hear, but Sagitta did and darted over to her. Hearing the dog whimper, the feathered creature looked. For long moments, he stared dumbly at the crumpled body, but when her hand lifted to pet the dog's glossy head, he too scrambled over and, pulling her in close, let out a mournful groan.

His crushing arms tore at her wound, but she refused to scream because it might frighten him. So, cringing with pain, she rasped, "My king, I beg you… Say it. Say Heaven rules."

It was as if he had not heard, clinging tighter and tighter as he rocked her back and forth, his eyes darting here and there, first to the sky, always to the sky first, watching, prowling, stalking.

So, that was that. She had come all this way only to be beaten, and closing her eyes, she sank into stillness.

Repulsed by the sensation of her stiffening limbs, Nebuchadnezzar threw her body off and jumped away. Now she lay twisted in the dirt, so he growled at her. Still she did not move, so he ran, but everywhere he ran, wide-eyed dead men stared up at him. Staring back at a glassy eyeball, he poked it with his huge bird claw, and a grey specter shot out of the body. Astounded, Nebuchadnezzar jumped back, warily sniffing its ashen air. Then, hopping to another eye, he poked it. This time a hairy banshee screeched out spewing a putrid yellow mist. Howling gleefully, Nebuchadnezzar darted from one dead man to another, poking all their eyes until all their ghosts and all their dank vapors were liberated. Then, springing onto a boulder, he extended his arms like a bird in flight and shrieked down at them, demanding they cringe before him.

Instead of cringing, they let out a unified howl and chased him. Dodging here and hopping there, Nebuchadnezzar looked like a giant vulture flapping amidst corpses, leaping over the campfire, hiding behind trees, tripping over arrows lodged in chests and backs, when without warning, he stopped to stare at one. Sensing he must do something, he sniffed the air, his eyes scanning the terrain. Then he saw it: the arrow in Aridatha's back. Quickly dashing over to her, he planted his foot on her back, grabbed the arrow, and wrenched it out.

When she still lay frozen with her arms and legs contorted, he raised his leg to kick her, but Sagitta charged in and bit him. So, he kicked the dog, and was about to kick him again, when his old cronies the five crows swooped in. Landing on Gaspar's chest, they pecked at the shiny royal pendant. Rat-a-tat-tat. Rat-a-tat-tat.

"Caw! Caw! Caw!" scolded Nebuchadnezzar, flapping his wings until they retreated into the trees. Grabbing the glittering bauble for himself, he tugged it over his gold head and, expanding his chest, strutted back and forth.

Oh, how the crows guffawed at the lumbering beast and his squawk-ings, acting as if he really was somebody. And the ghouls, how they mocked and cackled as they dove in, pulled out a feather here, and tugged a feather there. The beast stomped his feet and cawed at them, but they just laughed and laughed until King Nebuchadnezzar dropped to the ground, crossed his arms and legs, and stared out blankly.

Obviously, the game was over, so the crows flew away and the ghouls slipped back into their vessels, leaving Nebuchadnezzar alone, yet not alone, for the question, "Who is this King of glory," still rustled through the leaves. He had not heard Aridatha whisper it before, but he heard her now, as if her heart was calling out to his heart. But he did not want her heart mocking and laughing at him, so he stiffened even more.

However, unlike the crows and ghouls who had readily departed from his blank stare, the words did not. Instead, they floated closer, and without warning, a burnt tree stump hurled toward him.

"Caw! Caw! Caw!" he screeched, attacking the vision with his bird claws. Soon, it too faded away, but he could not shake the words, "Who is this King of glory?" Nor could he ignore the treacherous whisperings coming down from the sky, "Let him be given the mind of an animal until seven times pass by for him."

It was the voice of the holy Watcher, and if he could just get his hands on him, he would kill him, but instead he bolted upright, because he had formed a thought: "If I could just get my hands on him, I would kill him."

Astounded, he stopped breathing as he gingerly conceived another thought, "If I say Heaven rules, I will get my kingdom back."

Another thought immediately screeched, "Heaven rules?! If Heaven rules, then I do not rule. I, Nebuchadnezzar King of Babylon, will lose all my power and all my glory. I will lose everything I am!"

"Everything I am?" another thought scoffed roundly. "And what am I? A feathered beast with bird claws who cannot think or speak. Only a fool would choose the mind of an animal over the mind of a man."

Suddenly, a new horror! With words and thoughts swirling through his head, he was able to worry about losing them again. What if after one moment, two hours, or ten days, his words and thoughts were again taken away? What if he was given the mind of an animal for another seven years? What if he was given something worse? How could there be anything worse?! Oh, yes, there were things worse, many things, like a seven-times-hotter fiery furnace. Thus, with a fear he had never known gripping his heart and tearing at his lungs, he opened his mouth and gasped, "Heaven rules."

He was staggered! Shaken! Even transfixed, because the words shot right out of his mouth. Not cawings or squawkings or shriekings, but actual words. He could speak again! Speak and think! What more could a man want?

Yes, yes, he still had feathers and bird claws, but they were no cause for alarm because it could have been worse. Much worse. Besides, he could think again. Think about the past, the present, and the future. Think about kingdoms and glory. He could even think about his feathers and bird claws. Once where hair had been, he now had feathers, layer upon layer of brilliant color and protective plumage. Once where fingernails had been, he now had bird claws, tough and craggy for digging into the earth.

As he considered his quilled raiment and the fearsome power from where it came, he was suddenly transported into the highest House in the heavenly realms: the House with the Seven Hewn Pillars. It was the House he had read about in Shining One's great Babylonian epic, telling how Shining One surrounded it with his light-filled images, voices, and sounds. In fact, he surrounded it with himself: Shining One, Son of Dawn, Prince of the Power of the Air, so pleasing to the eye, so brilliant to the ear, and so desirable for gaining wisdom, that ever since the incident in the Garden of Eden, his images, voices, and sounds had successfully blocked the path to the House so no man could find his way in.

Yet curiously, he, Nebuchadnezzar, had entered and was now standing beside a table laden with the finest of foods and wines, enough to feed multitudes times multitudes, as if the feast would never run out but always be there for anyone who was hungry and thirsty. Wondering what else was in the House, he hurried from room to room gaping at the vast collections of rare and beautiful treasures, more profitable than gold or silver, more precious than rubies. A gentle breeze, reminiscent of the fragrance of apple blossoms, sparkled high up inside the domes, misting the rooms with an unchanging, everlasting light. Long life poured out from the right, riches and honor from the left, every way pleasant, each path peace. Then, there were the seven hewn pillars to stare at, those towering monoliths without blemish, the wellsprings to the earth's foundations, built to last! Utterly unlike any of Shining One's wonders which were always transforming and ever fleeting...

Suddenly, he raced to the window and looked out. Yes, Shining One's seraphic images, his luminous voices, and his multidimensional sounds were still there surrounding the House so no one from the other side could see it or find its entrance.

So, how had he found the entrance? What had he done? Or was this another one of his dreams? Because, as far as he knew, he had done nothing. Nothing, except mutter Heaven rules because he was so terrified something worse than losing his words and thoughts might happen to him. Anyone would have done the same. Yes, anyone would have cried out in a panic. But he was not *anyone*! No! He was Nebuchadnezzar King of Babylon! Even so, he had cried out in his panic, and here he was. Eating at a feast for multitudes, swathed in unchanging light, and overshadowed by seven hewn pillars, all in every way superior to anything Babylon or Shining One could ever offer.

Furthermore, he did not want to leave!

Instantly, something like a sword of light, a doubled-edged, flaming sword, opened his eyes, and he knew he was in Wisdom's House. Wisdom... Hadn't King Solomon prayed for wisdom? Was this the Wisdom he had prayed for? Because this was nothing like Shining One's great Babylonian epic. This was better. Indeed, this Wisdom was supreme. And he, Nebuchadnezzar, had done nothing, except...

Thus, Nebuchadnezzar said it again, only this time without fear. This time, he said it with all his heart, roaring with his voice that shattered the dawn, "Heaven rules!!!"

Roaring it over and over, he listened to the words clamber up the mountainsides and echo from peak to peak. But for King Nebuchadnezzar that was not high enough or far enough. So he kept roaring until he heard them ascend to the heights and soar out into the world.

"Heaven rules!!!... Heaven rules!!!... Heaven rules!!!"

Finally, reeling at the sound of his voice, the voice of a man, and marveling at his feathers and bird claws, the robes and weapons of the birds of the air, Nebuchadnezzar King of Babylon fell to his knees and wept.

As he wept, a ray of light shone down, hiding him in a sparkling mist. Inside the mist, hidden from all eyes, a gentle breeze passed over his feathers wafting them up through the trees one by one, as if each feather was being counted before soaring up into the sky. During that time, his hands were returned to the hands of a man, royal clothing was placed on his featherless skin, his mind was restored, and his heart and soul washed clean. He was not aware of any of this, because between tears and laughter, he was too absorbed in thinking about words and feathers and the Wisdom behind them.

But what was that sound? A quiet summons reaching out to him?

"My king…"

There it was again. Or was his madness returning?

"King Nebuchadnezzar?"

Slowly, he turned. Her wound was healed, her color restored, her hands reaching out to him. "Aridatha!" his voice pealed.

"Your feathers," she cried. "They are gone."

Racing to her, he pulled her in close. "You are alive. You have come back to me."

"What has happened?" she gasped. "You are speaking. Oh, my king, tell me what has happened."

Their eyes met. They both knew what had happened, and weeping together, their tears mingled.

64

THAT evening, standing on his spur high above Aridatha's ledge, Nebuchadnezzar King of Babylon was still thinking: thinking about the God of Heaven who had reached into his mind and made it the mind of an animal, then reclaimed it with a sanity purer than ever. This was not the first time he had reached into the minds of men. At the Tower of the Seven Lights, he had confused man's one language, so they could not understand each other. Of course, Nebuchadnezzar had scoffed at such a notion, declaring to Daniel that man created all the languages of the world. However, after living through a seven year demonstration of his own inability to create anything but screechings, cawings, and growlings, he knew man could not create, or even destroy, language. Perfectly clear today, but not seven years ago.

Similarly, he had once believed he possessed the ultimate power over all the kingdoms, nations, and peoples of the earth. After all, he was the head of gold. But, after losing everything in a single moment, he scoffed at his vanity. The Lord alone possessed the ultimate power over all the kingdoms, nations, and peoples. Again, perfectly clear today, and yet... not clear at all. For the Lord God—at least according to Daniel's interpretation of his dream—was going to give Babylon and all of Babylon's glory back to him, a power-reversal so incredible, so bewildering, and so awesome, he could not help exclaiming, "Who is this King of glory?"

As Nebuchadnezzar mused on getting his kingdom back, Aridatha, alone in her hut, stumbled about in a daze. Setting out a meal not meant for kings, she picked up an onion but did not know what to do with it. Moving to the goats, she grabbed her comb instead of the milking bucket. Stopping to look for something, she dropped berries on the floor and started to cry.

Naturally, she was grateful the king had finally said Heaven rules and was going to get his kingdom back. But what about her? What was she going to get back? Long ago, she had been Aridatha of Jerusalem, then the King of Babylon destroyed Jerusalem. Long ago, she had planned to build houses and plant gardens for her people, then Nebuchadnezzar lost his mind and Arioch ordered her to take him to the Zagros. Ever since, she had lived in the mountains, feeding, clothing, and warming herself in harsh isolation. Yet, with the stars to study, the animals for companionship, and the birds for song, the mountains had become her home. Now, once again, her home was being ripped out from under her, and she did not know what to do. If only the king would stay on the mountain a few more days, a week, perhaps even a month, at least until she could get her bearings.

Suddenly, the door opened and there he was! More magnificent than ever, his sane eyes light-filled, his braided hair shimmering, his shoulders upright and natural. He was the King of Babylon all over again, and she was terrified because he could crush her so easily by leaving her behind. So, turning away, she let the goats gather round him as he ate.

He ate quickly and heartily, three helpings, all in silence. Then, pushing his platter aside and wiping his mouth, he announced cheerfully, "We will leave at sunrise."

So! It was over. He had already forgotten her. And why not? What did she matter when he could return to Babylon and get his kingdom back?

"Aridatha," his voice was tender, more tender than she had ever heard. "You have not looked at me."

She wanted to look at him. To share his joy. But if she looked at him, she would burst into tears, and she could never let that happen.

"You have not eaten either."

Trying to accommodate, she picked up a rib, moved it to her lips, and dropped it back down.

He had never seen her like this: head down and arms wrapped stiffly around her waist. Clearly, she did not want to be near him, and all the reasons were written on her face. For unlike after the Fall of Jerusalem, when her pain appeared and disappeared just as quickly, now the story of her suffering was permanent: the creases in her brow, the guarded eyes, the rigid jaw. The fault was fully his. His arrogance, as cruel as any whip, had lashed at her relentlessly. But if she had not wanted to be near him, why had she stayed? Why had she searched for him through brutal winters and lonely summers when she could have gone back to Jerusalem and Baruch ben-Zadok?

Not many hours ago, he would have said she had stayed because of him, Nebuchadnezzar King of Babylon, and all his greatness and glory. Now he scoffed at such nonsense, for he knew she was made of finer mettle. She had stayed faithful to him, not because of him, but because of her faithfulness to Jeremiah's words when he put the crimson pouch on her. It was that faithfulness which made her more beautiful than ever. The harsh lines of sacrifice, the inner misery, the years of deprivation and hard labor, all told the story of a heart as steadfast as the sun and a soul as yielding as the moon, and unable to resist the sun or the moon, he took her calloused hands in his and raised her to her feet. If she did not want him, she would have to tell him now, because there would never be another woman like her or another moment like this when they were both so completely alone, and he without the responsibility of Babylon.

Aridatha tried to steady her trembling hands, pathetically vulnerable in his firm clasp, but how could she steady them when her entire body was still shaking at his death knell words, "We will leave at sunrise?" Her soul was shaking too, not because of his words, but because she knew he was offering her a new life, rich and full, right now. This was it, never again would they be so completely alone, and she without the responsibility of Jerusalem.

Jerusalem... Why had she thought of Jerusalem? Once and for all, she was no longer Aridatha of Jerusalem. She was Aridatha, exiled to Babylon, alone on top of the world with Nebuchadnezzar. The two had been mysteriously bonded since the day they saw the Fourth Man, and she placed her crimson pouch next to his royal pendant. They had discussed two cities, Babylon and Jerusalem, more than just cities, at war since the beginning and advancing toward one final war at the end: Babylon, glory of kingdoms, against Jerusalem, the Throne of the Lord. Since then, Nebuchadnezzar had lost his kingdom and Jerusalem had been destroyed. Yet they both knew Babylon and Jerusalem would go on, just like the bond between them would go on. But how would it go on? As man and woman, or as king and slave? This was the moment to settle the matter, and so she would. Tonight she would lie in his arms. Tonight she would rest in the power of Babylon.

Nebuchadnezzar knew she was still troubled by Jerusalem, which meant she would probably reject him and Babylon once again, and if she did, he would leave. But for the moment, as far as he was concerned, there was no Jerusalem or Babylon, only the loveliness of her long chestnut hair. Thus, burying his hand in her silky mane, he readied for her resistance, but she surprised him. Instead of resistance, he met a rush of warmth. So, wrapping his arm around her waist, he swayed her back and forth in a slow rhythmic dance, drawing her closer… and closer… until their bodies were almost touching. Then, cupping the back of her head in his hand, he leaned down to rest his lips on her lips, but meeting the light in her eyes, like a light at the end of a tunnel, instead of kissing her, he let her go.

"We will leave at sunrise," he rasped with renewed commitment, and hurrying out the door, he slammed it behind him. Then, like a boy capering under the summer sun, he spun out into the starry night with a leap in each step and delight in every breath because he knew he loved her. If he had not loved her, he would not have denied his desire for her or his royal right to have her. But when he saw that light in her eyes, he remembered his word to Yosef ben-Moshe, promising to protect her. And tonight, for the first time, he actually wanted to protect her, even at the cost of his own desire. Thus, he knew loved her!

It was so pleasant to love someone, so freeing and so strange, he did not want to yoke himself immediately to the burdens of Babylon or his plans for future conquests. Instead, he simply wanted to be a man: a man who had words, a man who could think, a man who could love, a man who had everything, yet at the moment, no responsibilities for anything. So, warm-hearted and carefree, he ran and he skipped and he rambled, drinking in everything about him: the silence of the towering mountains, the whisperings of the distant streams, the croaking of the frogs, and the swoosh of the great owl pulsing through the air.

Spotting the flying silhouette gliding toward the valley, its outstretched wings noble and its cry plaintive, Nebuchadnezzar once again thought about his feathers. What had become of them? Had they each been accounted for and then locked away in a storehouse in the sky? Or had they drifted on the wind into faraway lands? Perhaps a young lad had plucked one out of the twilight and, feeling its strength against his flesh, understood it was a token of a great miracle. Feathers. Who would have thought it? From there, his mind wandered to the five crows and the herd of wild donkeys. What were they doing tonight? Were they grazing in the brush-filled crannies on the mountainside, or on the fragrant meadowed plateaus, or in the forested valley below? Calling Sagitta, he ordered the dog to find them.

So, as Aridatha stood exactly where Nebuchadnezzar left her, stunned by his retreat and consequently even more worried about her future, Nebuchadnezzar and Sagitta were hiking higher up the mountain. The dog, with his white-tipped tail looking like a beacon in the darkness, led the king over grassy trails, rocky paths, and slippery creeks, ending up on a plateau where the herd grazed amidst boulders and wild herbs. The young donkeys—gangly and knock-kneed—slumbered in peaceful huddles, until Sagitta yipped. Hearing his familiar voice and seeing him running toward them, they bolted to their feet and, along with the mares, whinnied their delight to their returning friend. But when the dark form of a man approached, their ears jerked forward and their tails twitched, their broad noses sniffed and their mouths frowned. Three quick brays, harsh and loud, reported through the air, and the herd, young and old, took off running.

Watching them flee was a bittersweet moment for Nebuchadnezzar. Never before had he had such willing subjects as the herd of wild donkeys and tonight they did not even recognize him. There had been a curious freedom with them, a warm and settled trust. Now it was over. He had to go back, back to kingship, back to Babylon.

65

Babylon

HUNDREDS of elephants led the King's Parade down Procession Way, then came the lions roaring in gold cages, and the falcons dropping sweets from the sky. Next, the front guard dressed in royal regalia threw flashing swords in precision time interrupted by magicians suddenly appearing on the road, turning their staffs into snakes, their snakes into staffs, then running into the shrieking crowd. Hour after hour, the splendor increased. To the sound of the horns, the javelin guard; to the beat of the drums, the flaming whips; to the songs of the singers, the rising incense. Then, just as the crowd thought it had seen all the wonders of the world, the royal regiment appeared, and in its midst, standing in a gold chariot pulled by four white Barbs, was the wonder of them all, Nebuchadnezzar King of Babylon.

At the sight of him, the crowd went wild, cheering and dancing, throwing flowers and pitching rings, completely forgetting to bow quietly as they had been instructed, because since Nebuchadnezzar's return six months before, a gentle freedom had settled over the land. Not only had Gaspar's mass executions ended, but Nebuchadnezzar had cut his own ruinous taxes, raised food allotments in the labor camps, and even increased wages for the canal drivers. The list went on and on, and it was rumored it was now one of his favorite lists.

Nebuchadnezzar had certainly changed, and all of Babylon was rejoicing. All of Babylon was also talking, because someone must have caused the change, so it must have been the young woman with the Stars of David in her tunic hem. In fact, her adventures with the king on the Zagros—although no one knew a thing about them—were talked about throughout the land, because when they returned, the king immediately lodged her in the Ishtar Tower allowing no one to see her except her guards.

But who did the king think he was fooling? Everyone knew seclusion meant only one thing: the young woman was busily growing an heir and this pleased all of Babylon, because even though no one had seen or talked to her, everyone knew all about her. She was Aridatha of Jerusalem! As a girl, she had taken Nebuchadnezzar's hand when they saw the Fourth Man. As a young woman, she defied him before the armies of Babylon, waving the Hebrew flag on the Jerusalem wall, shouting, "Remember the Fourth Man." Then when the king went insane, the legendary commander Arioch chose her out of all Babylon's nobility and warriors to take him away and protect him. Without a moment to lose, she and the king fled to the Zagros Mountains and remained there for seven mysterious years. Finally, when the king was no longer mad and no longer the Nebuchadnezzar he once was, they returned to Babylon. It was the most extraordinary and exciting tale anyone had ever heard, and everyone wanted to meet her, and today might be the day because it was also well-known that after the King's Parade and Banquet, Nebuchadnezzar was going to bring her to his palace and marry her.

But where was she? Young and old strained to get a glimpse of her on the king's platform jammed with Nebuchadnezzar's four judges, Daniel, Shadrach, Meshach, and Abedneggo; Shadrach's Chief Prefect Michael ben-Ram; Aridatha's mother, the widow of the great commander Yosef ben-Moshe; three rows of Chinese dignitaries including the Grand Mentor Tin, the Grand Guardian Li, and sitting between them with her face veiled, Chenguang, famed for her heroic deeds: warning the four Hebrew judges of Gaspar's escape, moving Nebuchadnezzar's wives, concubines, and children to safety outside the city, and then in the dead of night, rescuing Arioch's body—impaled by Gaspar and hung in the Palace Square—sewing up his slashed neck, embalming his body, and sending it secretly to Soheil in the mountains. In the center, seated on jeweled couches with linen pillows, were Arioch's white-bearded father and beautiful widow, Soheil, flanked by their six strapping sons, all dressed in mountain colors, their stalwart presence looking much like an impregnable forest.

But where was Aridatha of Jerusalem?

Happily, she was still in the Ishtar Tower. After living on the mountain for so many years, she was uncomfortable around crowds, so the king had not summoned her. Besides, she had more important things to do: gardening and tending her goats in the morning followed by three hours of reading, studying, and writing. Then, as always in the afternoon, she returned to her garden and goats, and in the evening attended to her weaving and tanning.

At first, the king had taken a sharp stand against the garden and goats, telling her she must rest after her years of toil on the mountain. But when she countered that inactivity would drive her just as mad as he had been, he built her a vast secret annex to work in. Her reading material, a basket of scrolls from Shadrach's office, had arrived unexpectedly one day in the arms of Michael ben-Ram. Since then he had brought a basket each month, and during each visit, they had talked about their youth in Jerusalem, the great Yosef ben-Moshe, the Fourth Man, and the wondrous Temple of Solomon. She never questioned him about his eight years after the Fall of Jerusalem, because she did not want him to question her about her years on the mountain. They were the king's business, not hers or anyone else's. Thus content to talk about their Jerusalem past, the young man with the gifted eyesight and the young woman locked in the Ishtar Tower became friends.

Once she had started to thank King Nebuchadnezzar for sending the scrolls, but something held her back. He had never mentioned them to her, and Michael ben-Ram had never mentioned the king, so concluding they were Shadrach's secret, she had kept his secret. Now, after six months, she had a substantial collection of the writings of Moses, David, and the Prophets and was eager to get to them, but sudden cheers exploded from Procession Way. Unlike the shouts and applause that had waxed and waned throughout the morning, this ovation grew into a deafening roar. Assuming it was for the King of Babylon and determined to ignore it, she opened one of the scrolls. But no matter how fiercely she glared at the words, she could not drag her mind away from the king, because although she was in isolation, guarded by three mute eunuchs and waited upon by three mute dowagers, they had already told her through gestures and handwriting about her rumored marriage set for today. So, as cheers for the King of Babylon filled her room, thoughts of the King of Babylon filled her mind, taking her back to their journey out of the Zagros.

Alone, the king would have galloped nonstop to Babylon, but disturbed by her depleted strength, he traveled slowly, attentive to her every need. During the days, his words were few and at night, fewer still. When he did speak, he talked about his concerns for Babylon: was his kingdom still intact or had Egypt conquered his lands; had his judges and counselors escaped or had Gaspar slaughtered them; was his army decimated or could it fight a civil war if he met resistance? She had only one answer: he was going to get his kingdom back. And so it was. When they entered the city, not only was Babylon intact and most of his judges and counselors still alive, but the news of his coming had ignited such fear in his enemies, they had already fled.

At the end of each travel day, he demanded she rest while he managed the animals, hunted, and cooked. She was not surprised he was an excellent cook, for he did all things well. His stews and broths strengthened her bones, while the fruit of the land brightened her weary spirit. Then, as twilight stretched across the horizon, he stretched out on his back and watched the stars in silence. His stargazing reminded her of their first years on the mountaintop, but unlike the mountaintop, he could now think and talk. Indeed, she wished he would talk, because she was bursting with questions. What had it been like having feathers? Did he ever try to fly? How was the mind of an animal different? Had he known the lights in the sky were the sun and moon and stars? Or had he only known their warmth and luster? What was it like living with animals? What did he eat? Did he seek out carrion like Sagitta or grasses like the donkeys? Of course, she had other questions about other things, especially about his ride inside the Temple of Solomon. Had he gone into the Most Holy Place and seen the Ark of the Covenant and the cherubim of the Glory? More than anything—dare she even think it—had he, with his own hand, touched the Ark of the Covenant?

Yes, she was bursting with questions, but as her father would remind her, it was not her place to speak first or question the king. So, as he was silent, she was silent, and in her silence, she thought perhaps her questions were better left unasked. After all, he might go into a rage if she mentioned his feathers. Besides, what if he had forgotten his feathers, his bird claws, and everything else about the past seven years? On the other hand, if he did remember, perhaps he wanted to forget. As for her, it was probably better not to know what happened to the Ark of the Covenant. So, with a doleful sigh, she returned to her own concerns: worrying about her future.

Then, on a moon bright night eclipsed by fog, he suddenly asked if she remembered their stargazing nights on the mountaintop. Bursting into a smile, she was about to mention the star maps, but quickly remembering his fury—burning her hides and grain when she read Tin's calculations for three conjunctions of Saturn and Jupiter in Pisces in six hundred years—she held her tongue and simply nodded. He did not mention the stars again until their last night on the road, the night before they entered Babylon.

As usual, after eating, they were looking up at the sky, but unlike any other night, he talked. Perhaps it was because it was their last night together, or perhaps he just felt like talking. Whatever the reason, he talked about Arioch, wondering what had happened to him. After a penetrating silence, he reflected on the Fourth Man, wondering what had happened to him and wishing he could see him again. He talked about Shining One, wondering what was going to happen to him after standing on the Mount of God boasting *I will ascend to the heights,* relating it to the day he, Nebuchadnezzar, stood on the steps of the Temple of Solomon boasting *nothing can shake me,* then soon after, he lost everything. With a burst of energy, he started talking about the Temple of Solomon, comparing the ancient and future kingdoms of Babylon and Jerusalem, muttering something about the King of glory, and without warning, he ordered her to get out the star maps.

It was a moment she would never forget. After years of studying the maps on her own, she was finally going to study them with him. Thinking how wonderful it was going to be sitting side by side reading the notes together, she hurried to get the gardener's old bag. Pulling out the three leather sacks along with the purple silk sack, she excitedly explained how she had packed the maps according to their authors, but in midsentence, he cut her off telling her to stand away from the light and recite everything she knew from the Hebrew scrolls.

She was stunned. The scrolls had nothing to do with the stars, so why was he relegating her to a Hebrew lesson? Did he think the star maps were beyond her ken? Had he forgotten she had read them to him every night on the mountain when everything was beyond his ken? Watching him turn his undivided attention to the maps, she finally understood why he had not kissed her on the mountain, but instead had fled. It was so obvious, she admonished herself for not realizing it before.

Yes, he had been kind to her on the journey, but tomorrow they were entering Babylon, so from now on, he was through with her. He did not want her reading his star maps or talking to him about his stars. He did not even want her near him. So, stomping to the other side of the fire, she searched her memory for verses she had learned from papa when she was in the cradle and then recited them loudly and angrily.

"Before that!" he commanded.

"Before what?" she snapped.

"Before Abraham."

"I only know as far back as Abraham."

"What do you mean you only know...? What about Noah?"

"I know about Noah," she clipped curtly. "But not from the scrolls."

"You know about the Tower of the Seven Lights. I remember you saying something about..."

"Yes, I know about the Tower. I also know about Cain and Abel, but that was from papa."

"All right," he erupted, growing restless. "Start with Abraham."

Folding her arms and glaring at him, she started again with the verses she learned in the cradle. However, as she traveled step by step through each passage, then coursed through the books Baruch had read to her while she threw Jerusalem dirt in the air, she soon forgot about Nebuchadnezzar and his star maps because she was watching Abraham offering Isaac as a sacrifice, Isaac blessing Jacob, and Moses keeping the first Pesach. She listened to David singing his songs and Solomon praying for wisdom. She shuddered inside the thunderous voice of Isaiah, "who has believed our report," and crumpled before the tears of Jeremiah, "a voice is heard in Ramah." Journeying inside their words, she was once again living through the terrors of the Fall of Jerusalem, when from out of the corner of her eye, she saw the king's hand waving at her, trying to make her stop. But she did not want to stop. She had never spoken all the verses, passages, and books in one sitting, and she wanted to keep going. Still, the king kept shaking his head, telling her it was time for him to speak and her to listen. So, shutting her mouth, she sat down.

Now that he had quiet, Nebuchadnezzar held the star map closer to the firelight, and starting with the first of the Twelve Signs, *Bethulah* the Virgin, he read the names of the stars in the Sign as if telling a story: *Tsemech, Zavijaveh, Vindemiatrix, Comah, Asmeath, Nekkar...*

Aridatha understood the names: *The Branch, Gloriously Beautiful, the Son—or branch—who Cometh, the Desired, the Sin-offering, the Pierced...* But there were hundreds more in the Sign, and as he called out each one, it took all her wits to follow the strangest story she had ever heard, especially because without taking a breath, he moved on to the next Sign: *Mozanaim* the Scales. After the Scales, he kept going and going and going, reading each recorded star name in each of the Twelve Signs until finally, after two hours, he came to the last Sign, *Arieh* the Lion hunting down his prey, and read its star names: *Hydra, Minchar al Sugia, Al Ches, Minchar al Gorab...*

Aridatha understood its names too: *the Serpent he is abhorred, the Piercing of the Deceiver, the Cup, the Raven tearing to pieces...*

"Arieh, the Lion hunting down his prey," he repeated over and over. Then turning to her, he challenged, "Didn't you say Judah is a lion's cub and the scepter will not depart from Judah?"

"What?"

"You recited it. Don't you remember? Then from Jeremiah, you said, 'The Lord will roar from on high...' That would be like a lion's roar, would it not? Arieh the Lion hunting down his prey. Look here." He pointed to the Sign of Arieh, then to his written translation next to Tin's Chinese characters. "Tin wrote, 'The Lion of the tribe of Judah aroused for the rending of his prey.'" He paused, his concentration fierce, as if he was quickly searching through the hundreds of lists in his mind. Then, raising his eyes to the sky, he repeated, "...aroused for the rending of his prey."

She had no idea what he was talking about. Furthermore, she was so surprised he had not snarled at the name of Tin, she blurted, "You know Tin?"

"Of course, I know Tin. Now pay attention. You said..." He then proceeded to speak for five minutes, repeating long passages she had recited, finishing with the words of Jeremiah: "'...the Lord will roar from on high against all who live on the earth. Bringing charges against the nations. He will bring judgment on all mankind. Disaster is spreading from nation to nation, a mighty storm is rising from the ends of the earth.'"

"You remember all that?"

For a long moment, he just stared at her. "Aridatha," he chided, "I remember everything."

"Oh," she gulped.

"We can learn something from the names of the stars, Aridatha, because Tin said, the God of Heaven named the stars, which means…"

"I said that! I recited it from the scrolls." To prove it, she recited it again, "'He determines the number of the stars and calls them each by name.'"

"Stop interrupting." Their eyes met. She was gaining weight daily and her answers were livelier, a welcome relief after the days and nights of her troubled silence. "Which means," he enunciated pointedly, "the star names are not random, but filled with meaning and purpose. However, over the ages, most of the names have been distorted, so Tin took me to the oldest star map in the world, engraved by Noah. That map shows the original names of the stars and the pictures which were once in the sky. Noah would have known all about that, Aridatha," he said, his voice growing tutorial, as if teaching her a history lesson, "because Noah learned the star names from his grandfather, Methuselah, who learned them from Adam, who learned them from the Lord Almighty. Noah also lived six hundred years before the flood, so he probably saw the pictures in the sky. If he did not see them, Adam surely did."

This was not news to her. She had read all about it in Tin's star maps, and more captivated by Tin than Nebuchadnezzar's history lesson, she blurted, "Who is Tin?"

Calculating at least four forces coming together in his mind at once—the star names, the Hebrew scrolls, Tin's three conjunctions, and his own dreams—Nebuchadnezzar wanted to ignore her question and get to his point. But he could not. For indeed, who was Tin? An intriguing question. With only one answer. So, turning his eyes eastward, he smiled, "Tin is a man who knows how to wait."

It was the strangest description she had ever heard. Furthermore, he had said it with such admiration, yet frustration, she wanted to know more.

But Nebuchadnezzar had had enough of Tin and his waiting, and overcome by an urgent restlessness, he jumped up and began to pace as if the faster he moved, the faster he could get to his point. "So!" he pronounced, rubbing his hands together. "The Lord Almighty named the stars. Therefore, their story, if untainted, will be consistent with his word in the Hebrew scrolls. Next, what about the stars themselves? Daniel once said the sun, moon, and stars serve as signs to mark the seasons, days, and years. Tin said the conjunction of Jupiter and Saturn in Pisces was a sign that marked historical events for Israel. He also determined that three such conjunctions will occur in one year in six hundred years. Thus, using the star names and the Hebrew scrolls, could I not determine what special historical event it might be?"

"Jupiter? Saturn? Pisces?" she spluttered. "In six hundred years?"

"You heard me."

Of course, she heard him. But she was so taken aback, her mind was in a whirl. This was the man who set fire to her drying hides and sacks of grain because she read to him about these three conjunctions. Now he was calmly applying the star names and the scrolls to them? Still grappling for air, she mumbled, "I do not know, my king."

Sitting down, he offered her berries from his pocket. "Did Shadrach ever tell you I had a dream about a statue with a head of gold?"

Again she was caught off guard. Here they were sitting side by side, arms pressed together, their minds filled with the heavenly story of the stars and the written word of the prophets, and now he was moving on to dreams? "No, my lord, Shadrach never mentioned it."

"Daniel said, the dream was given to me to show me what will happen in days to come."

"Days to come?" she gasped, knowing full well he was aiming at the three conjunctions in six hundred years.

"Yes, Aridatha, days to come," he nodded, pleased to see she was out of her daze and understood his meaning. "In my dream, there was a towering statue made of clay, iron, bronze, silver, and gold. It was so magnificent, I could have stared at it all night. But a rock, cut out of a mountain not by human hands, with no beauty or majesty to attract anyone, not anyone," he paused, waiting for her to grasp just how nondescript this rock was, then continued, "smashed the statue's feet so completely, the entire statue shattered and blew away. Daniel said the rock is a kingdom that will crush the kingdoms of iron-and-clay, iron, bronze, silver, and gold and bring them to an end, but the rock will remain and last forever. I am one of those kingdoms, Aridatha. I am the kingdom of gold."

Staring at his face wrapped in the fire's glow, she saw a raging man yelling seven times hotter, an arrogant conqueror prancing up and down the steps of the Temple of Solomon, and a beast in all his plumage charging crazily at Gaspar. Certainly, there was no other man in history who was more qualified to be the kingdom of gold. But he was still talking, conjoining the knowledge of the stars, the word of the prophets, the calculations of Tin, and now his dream, so she listened, trying to catch up.

"I can easily match Jeremiah's words, 'Disaster spreading from nation to nation,' to the nations in my dream rising and falling until the rock crushes them. Furthermore, it would take at least six hundred years for those nations to rise and fall."

"But how can a rock crushing nations be a special event for Israel?"

"Aridatha," he scolded, "haven't you been listening? I told you, the rock is a kingdom." Her brow furrowed even more, so he tried again. "A kingdom must have a king. Furthermore, this kingdom is an everlasting kingdom, which means it must have an everlasting king." Seeing she still did not comprehend, he whispered, "Who is this King of glory?"

Her heart leapt! Her soul surged! Her mind reeled! But, even as she was overwhelmed by the thought of the King of glory and the surprise of Nebuchadnezzar speaking about him, she had to say, "I do not know who he is."

"You just told me."

"I never told you. I said, '*Who* is this King of glory?'"

"You said, 'The Lord strong and mighty, the Lord mighty in battle. *The Lord Almighty*, he is the King of glory.'"

"Of course, the Lord Almighty is the King of glory! But what does it mean? What does it have to do with a rock or Israel?"

"Don't you remember? You recited it tonight from the prophet Isaiah, the same words you said to me in the furnace arena. You said, 'This is what the Lord says—Israel's King and Redeemer, *the Lord Almighty*.'"

She could not believe it! He actually remembered what she said when she was ten years old? Indeed, he did remember everything, so he must remember his feathers and living with the animals. But he was glaring at her, trying to get her attention, so once more, she tried to follow his thoughts.

"Put them together, Aridatha. From King David, *the Lord Almighty* is the King of glory. From Isaiah, *the Lord Almighty* is Israel's King and Redeemer. So, that means *the Lord Almighty*..."

"... is the King of glory and Israel's King and Redeemer?"

"Precisely," he answered. "You know, Aridatha, sometimes you can be uncharacteristically dull-witted."

She had to smile, for he was talking to her with the same frank familiarity he had used with her father. But now his hands were clenching and unclenching.

"Tin believed..." He stopped, his face darkening. "He believed one conjunction of Jupiter and Saturn in Pisces marked a special historical event for Israel. Thus, three conjunctions in one year would be a monumental historical event for Israel. I never listened beyond that. I hated him for even thinking it. How dare he use the stars to give Israel such paramount acclamation?"

So that was why he set fire to her drying hides and sacks of grain, because Tin had given Israel special acclamation.

"But now... Now I cannot get the three conjunctions in one year out of my mind." His body was coiled as if ready to spring, his breath fast. "Don't you see, Aridatha, if Tin is right about a monumental event occurring in six hundred years, then my dream could be the answer. To have all those kingdoms instantly shattered would be a huge upheaval for the world, especially because the rock—a kingdom the God of heaven sets up—will remain and last forever. An everlasting kingdom, Aridatha, governed by an everlasting king: the King of glory, the Lord Almighty, Israel's King and Redeemer. A monumental historical event for Israel."

Indeed, it was exciting, more exciting than anything she could imagine. But what exactly was going to happen? How could anyone know? Six hundred years was a long way away. Almost forever. No, she would not let herself be swept in so easily. Furthermore, she did not know who Israel's King and Redeemer was, which meant she certainly did not know who the King of glory was. Thus, folding her arms, she repeated her lifelong question, "Who is this King of glory?"

Shaking his head at her obtuseness, Nebuchadnezzar pointed to the fire, a benign inferno settled close to the earth. When she looked at the flames, dancing like gold feathers against the backdrop of the cool night, and still did not understand, he said, "Arioch, how many men did we tie up and throw into that fire?"

Thunderstruck, Aridatha buckled. "You mean..." she choked, barely able to breathe, the shock so complete. "You mean the Fourth Man?! You think the Fourth Man is the King of glory?"

"Aridatha, I am the head of gold. The king of kings. There is no king greater than I am! Except one. He proved it when he overruled my judgment in my own city, living in my fire, saving his three faithful servants who did not bow to Babylon. Those three faithful servants, Aridatha, bowed to him instead of me, and they lived in fire."

"But you went on to destroy the Fourth Man's city! You destroyed Jerusalem, the Throne of the Lord!"

"Yes," scoffed Nebuchadnezzar, "I destroyed Jerusalem, the Throne of the Lord. But the prophet Jeremiah had already foretold that. More than once! I knew it, Jerusalem knew it, the whole world knew it. In other words, the Fourth Man handed it to me. Where is the glory in that?!"

Her heart pounded so hard and so fast, her ears were throbbing. "So you think he might come back? In six hundred years? The Fourth Man? As Israel's King and Redeemer?"

But, he was on his feet, facing the heavens, yelling, "Tell me! Yes, tell me! Could not these two events—the year of the three conjunctions and the shattering of the kingdoms by the rock—be one and the same event?!"

He waited. But there was no answer. Even so, he did not seem to mind, staring at the heavens, muttering, "What a day it will be, Aridatha. What a day! When the whole world sees what I saw in my dream: the coming of the rock." Then wistfully, even longingly, as if searching into the horizons of the future, he looked to the north, then to the east, the south, and the west, whispering, "Perhaps it will even be the fulfillment of the ages."

It was late when they finally went to bed alone in the wilderness, the king on one side of the glowing embers, Aridatha on the other. He went to sleep immediately, his breathing deep and steady. Aridatha, on the other hand, could not close her eyes. Not because she was thinking about the stars or their names or what was going to happen in six hundred years, but because she was worrying about more urgent matters: her future. Now that the king was finished with her, what was going to happen to her tomorrow, the next day, and the next?

66

THAT had been six months ago, and today if all of Babylon was correct, her worries about her future would be over. But first, there had to be the royal wedding, so her mute servants kept urging her to dress in one of the many gowns Nebuchadnezzar had provided: magnificent cloaks, tunics, and veils from all over the world made of the finest linens and silks, embroidered with peacocks, lions, and dragons. But no matter how much they cajoled, argued, and even threatened, she refused to dress, explaining with pen and ink that until she received an official summons, she would keep to her daily schedule.

Even so, she could not keep her schedule because as the shouts for the King of Babylon ebbed away, she was distracted by thoughts of Baruch ben-Zadok. She had been thinking about him more and more over the past months, and before starting her new life with the king, she wanted to say goodbye to the boy she once knew, the warrior he became, and the man she never knew. But how could she say good-bye to him when she did not know where he was? Had he returned to Jerusalem or was he still in a labor camp? Or—she knew she had to face it—was he dead?

Then, she remembered the small pile of letters from Shadrach, written in a bold hand on fine leather parchment. He had sent a letter each month with the basket of scrolls, and because he was Baruch's brother and because Baruch had taught her the scrolls, perhaps reading the letters from Shadrach would be a way of saying goodbye to Baruch. So, with a heart full of memories which had to be left behind, she opened the first letter, a powerful and poignant description of Daniel, Shadrach, Meshach, and Abedneggo hurrying the Hebrews out of the capital when Gaspar escaped from Canal Prison. After moving them to safety, the four Hebrews and a handful of Nebuchadnezzar's elite guard returned to the Southern Palace to collect Nebuchadnezzar's scrolls, parchments, and tablets, bagging every important document they could find. Without warning, Gaspar and his armies returned with Arioch's body. So, grabbing as many bags as they could, the small group clambered down the slaves' stairwell, slipped into a subterranean tunnel, and found their way to Nebuchadnezzar's huge underground hydraulic system.

There, protected by thick vaults and the scraping echoes of the nonstop buckets carrying water up through the shafts and returning empty, they and dozens of other Hebrews spent their seven underground years collecting the writings of Moses and the Prophets, the histories of the Hebrew judges and kings, the Songs of David, and the Wisdom of Solomon. Together they organized specific scrolls into one special book, meticulously copying the book over and over, so the Hebrew remnant would have hundreds of copies to take back to Jerusalem when they returned from their captivity in seventy years.

In each letter, he added more information about the scrolls in the book, telling where each had come from and how each had been painstakingly studied in order to establish its authenticity: whether the author had written from his own imagination or written the actual words of the Lord. Then, at the end of each letter, he suggested particular passages he thought would be of special interest to her.

With the first basket of scrolls, he suggested the account of Shadrach, Meshach, and Abedneggo living with the Fourth Man in Nebuchadnezzar's fire. Having been a witness, she quickly scanned the account to see if she was mentioned, but to her disappointment, she and her father had not been cited. After that, she read the account again and again, reliving each moment.

In contrast, the second letter suggested a long passage unknown to her, yet equally captivating, especially the part about the cherubim. It was 'In the Beginning' written by Moses, telling about God creating everything very good. This was news to her because she had always thought, although God created the good things, he had also created the bad, like suffering, sorrow, and death. But here she discovered in the beginning God created everything very good, and the bad things, like suffering, sorrow, and death, were the result of the first man, Adam, eating from the tree of the knowledge of good and evil. God had warned him if he ate from the tree, he would die, but he ate anyway. So to prevent him from eating from the Tree of Life and living forever knowing good and evil, the Lord God sent him out of the Garden of Eden, placing cherubim and a flaming sword to guard the way to the Tree of Life. It was the cherubim who excited her the most—those great angels of the Lord with four faces and four wings, their entire bodies full of eyes—because the cherubim also guarded the Ark of the Covenant. For days, she could think of nothing else but the Tree of Life and the Ark of the Covenant, wondering why both had to be guarded by the cherubim.

She did not want to read the next suggested passage, although it certainly reminded her of Baruch, but it also reminded her of the first time Babylon came. Eight year old Baruch was holding her in his arms and she was looking at the Temple, reciting the marvelous account of fire coming down from heaven and the glory of the Lord filling the Temple of Solomon. However, there was more to the passage: a warning about the Lord uprooting Israel and rejecting the Temple of Solomon if Israel abandoned his commands and served other gods. She had believed the Lord filled the Temple with his fire and glory, but because she had expected the Fourth Man to save Jerusalem and the Temple, she had not believed the warning. Thus, it was not an easy passage to visit.

Then a few days ago, Michael ben-Ram had arrived at her door, handed her a small scroll, told her it would be her last, and abruptly left. There was no basket, no letter, and no suggested reading because there was only one passage quoted in the scroll: the words Jeremiah had planted in her soul when she was three years old. "This is what the Lord says, 'A voice is heard in Ramah, mourning and great weeping, Rachel weeping for her children and refusing to be comforted, because her children are no more.'"

She had no idea how Shadrach had known these passages were important to her, kindling a new awareness of the Fourth Man, the cherubim, Jerusalem, Rachel weeping and, even more curiously, a new awareness of Aridatha of Jerusalem.

Aridatha of Jerusalem! That was it! That was why she had not yet dressed for her wedding. Not one of the Babylonian gowns had the Stars of David in its hem. So, hurrying to her cedar chest, she pulled out one of the goatskin tunics she made on the mountain. Meticulously cut, sewn, and embroidered, it was the finest tunic she had ever crafted, but she had never worn it. Now she knew why. It was her wedding dress. Slipping it on, she braided her hair, and remaining unadorned except for her crimson pouch and the Stars of David in her hem, she placed Shadrach's letters in a silver box, said a solemn *shalom* to Baruch ben-Zadok wherever he was, then stood in the middle of the four walls of her solitary confinement, waiting for the king's summons.

67

When the summons came, Aridatha was escorted down a bright outside colonnade leading toward the stables. Hoping this meant the king was preparing horses to take them away instead of putting her on exhibition before all Babylon, she breathed easier until her six royal guards led her into an empty hippodrome and, without giving any instructions, left her alone. At least she thought she was alone. But when her eyes adjusted to the shadows, she saw Nebuchadnezzar on the other side of the freshly raked field. Dressed as simply as she, wearing a plain linen tunic, a gold band for his crown, and the royal pendant of Babylon at his heart, he was more striking than ever.

He motioned for her to come to him, but she could not move. For as suddenly as floodwaters appear, she felt Babylon rising fast around her, and if she did not keep her feet fixed to the ground, she knew she would be swept away forever. Oh, to be a little girl again, trusting and innocent, able to run to him and meet him face to face. But she was not a little girl. She was a woman and he was a man, and today was the day.

Seeing the crimson pouch resting on her handmade tunic instead of on one of his Babylonian gowns struck Nebuchadnezzar with painful satisfaction, especially because he had watched her make the tunic. However, back then, her actions—tanning, cutting, sewing, dying the goat hair, twisting the strands, embroidering the Stars of David into the ankle hem—had meant nothing to him, because his nose had been honed in on the meat cooking over her fire. But now, with his mind restored, he appreciated her hours of dedicated toil, pouring her heart into each Star of David, and once again, he was pleased she had chosen David's star instead of Babylon's jewels to guard her feet.

"I am going to write it down," he called across the arena. "I am going to tell about my dream: the tree, the words of the holy Watcher, Daniel's interpretation, living with the animals, my feathers, acknowledging

Heaven rules... Everything! I am going to send it to all the peoples, nations, and languages living throughout the earth, telling them what the Most High God did for me."

His words rapped out like flashes of light, momentarily stunning her. For even though she understood the words, she could not grasp their content because certainly he did not mean he was going to officially record everything?! Officially proclaim he lived with animals and had feathers just so he could tell what the Most High God had done for him? Send it out for all the nations to read and all of history to probe? No, he would never do that. No king would ever do that.

"I will also say, 'Now I, Nebuchadnezzar King of Babylon, praise and exalt and glorify the King of heaven, because everything he does is right and all his ways are just.'"

Something was missing. Indeed, the message was true, declaring the King of heaven righteous and just. But he had made such proclamations before: praising the God of Shadrach, Meshach, and Abedneggo for sending his angel to save them from the fire. Yes, something was missing. She could not put her finger on it, but she knew if she heard it, then perhaps her feet could move toward him. But he was still talking, so staying where she was, she listened.

Going back to the day when he ordered all the nations to bow to his ninety-foot gold statue, he spoke about his glory and power, citing three days: the day the Fourth Man overruled his glory and power by trespassing into his fiery furnace, the day he thought he overruled the Fourth Man's glory and power by burning the Temple of Solomon, and that crucial morning on the palace rooftop when he declared he had built his royal residence to his glory and by his power. Then, with the words still on his lips, everything was taken away: his glory, power, kingdom, and most impressively his mind.

Pacing restlessly back and forth, he went on to recount his confusion after he was given the mind of an animal, his fear when he was alone, and his stiff neck when he was eating grass like the cattle. He talked about the endless days and nights bound by bronze to the ground and shackled by iron to the grasses without words or thoughts for comfort and companionship. How he had roamed and searched, run and hidden, slept and sat in the darkest gloom, battered by winds and ice and drenched with the dew of heaven until his hair grew like the feathers of an eagle and his nails like the claws of a bird. Then, through no strength or will of his own, a door of light was thrown open and everything—his glory, power, kingdom, and most impressively his mind—was returned to him. Thus, determined never to forget, and even more determined the world never forget, he pronounced the royal verdict, words he had heard from Yosef ben-Moshe and Shadrach, words he had spurned all his life, but from that day on would be his witness throughout all history.

"The final words of my edict will be…" He glared at her as if glaring at anyone who would ever dare defy him. "Those who walk in pride," he paused supposedly to clear his throat, but even from across the arena, she knew he had tears in his eyes, his face twisted not by the old familiar hunted look, but by a new torment, a painful seeking, a yearning that was groaning to get out. He tried to collect himself, blowing his nose and discreetly dabbing his cheeks, but it did no good. The tears could not be stopped. So, straightening to his full unshakable height, Nebuchadnezzar King of Babylon wept for all the world to hear, "Those who walk in pride, he is able to humble."

She could not run to him fast enough. Sprinting across the field like a deer, all grace and ease, she wanted to leap into his arms and hold onto him forever, to dance and sing and laugh. But when she reached his towering presence, instead of exploding with delight, she ground to a halt and, head hanging, stared at the floor. For even in the center of Babylon, her father's voice was there, rising up before her, saying, "Daughters of Jerusalem, do not awaken love before it so desires." Oh, well, she thought, she had waited this long for the king to take her in his arms and marry her, she could certainly wait a few more minutes.

Staring at her fallen face, Nebuchadnezzar turned away. When she did not come to him, he finished blowing his nose and wiping his cheeks, then announced, "You will be getting married now."

It was a strange way to declare their wedding, brusquely and with his back to her. "What is wrong?" she asked.

"Nothing is wrong." To prove it, he turned and met her eyes. "I will give you anything you want."

Later in life, she would marvel at her response. The King of Babylon was again offering her anything she wanted. She could have asked for Baruch ben-Zadok. She could have asked to go home to Jerusalem. She could have asked him to rebuild Jerusalem! But the Daughter of Zion could only think of one request. A request that overruled even the re-building of Jerusalem. So, she asked, "My king…"

"Anything," he breathed.

"I want to know…" Fear gripped her. Dare she go on? Weren't some things better left unknown? Yes, perhaps they were. But this was her moment, and if she did not seize it, she may never have another opportunity. So she spouted as fast as she could, "King Nebuchadnezzar, when you rode into the Temple of Solomon, did you see the Ark of the Covenant?"

She put her hands over her ears, not wanting to hear. Because if he had seen it, then Babylon burned it.

He, on the other hand, burst into laughter, delighted with her query, because instead of asking to go to Jerusalem, she had asked about something beyond herself, even beyond Jerusalem, going to the heart of the matter: the Ark of the Covenant and its existence.

"Did you see it?" she queried, still cringing.

"No."

"You mean it was not there?" she burst out excitedly. "You mean Jeremiah took it away and hid it in the mountains before the siege?"

"I do not know if it was there or not."

"But you said you did not see it."

"That is because I did not enter the Most Holy Place."

"You did not enter…"

"They would not let me."

"They?" she gasped, wondering who else was in the Temple that day. "Who?"

"I believe you call them the cherubim of the Glory."

"The cherubim of the Glory?!" she exclaimed, her whole body trembling at the thought of their four faces, four wings, and bodies full of eyes. "Did you see them?"

He shook his head.

"Then how do you know they were the cherubim of the…"

He sighed heavily. "It was a very bad day, Aridatha."

Their eyes met. Yes, perhaps some things were better left unknown. Perhaps the Ark of the Covenant had been inside the Most Holy Place and therefore burned by Babylon. On the other hand, perhaps Jeremiah had removed it and hidden it far away. Even more startling, perhaps it had been whisked to safety by the cherubim of the Glory. Whatever had happened, no one would ever know. Or would they?

"Come," barked Nebuchadnezzar so abruptly, she jumped.

Staring at him striding across the field marching swiftly toward their marriage, she had to run to catch up. Reaching a latticed portico, he stepped over to a cedar door, grabbed the silver latch, and his face grew pale. His breathing was shallow and erratic, his heartbeat loud and formidable, or was it her heartbeat, she did not know. However, she did know she was confused, her face probably just as pale, both staring at the thick silver latch in his hand, neither looking at the other.

Then, as if kicking himself into action, he jerked the latch and, throwing open the door, mumbled, "You will learn to love him."

She had no idea what he was talking about, but he looked so severe as he motioned her to the doorway, she wanted to turn back. Perhaps if he told her where they were going? But he would not look at her. So, stepping onto the threshold, she peered down a long dark corridor leading toward a distant sunny courtyard. Nothing unsettling about that until a man rode into the middle of the yard and stopped. She could not see his face, but she knew who it was, and her stomach lurched. Had the king gone mad again? Inviting Baruch ben-Zadok to their wedding? How could he do such a thing?!

In her tumult, she felt Nebuchadnezzar moving in behind her, saying something about Baruch ben-Zadok coming to Babylon to search for her, only to discover she was dead. Then Gaspar, hearing about Baruch's queries, ordered his warriors to hunt him down. But Baruch's brother, Shadrach, found him first, and ever since, he had lived and worked with Shadrach.

Aridatha spun around. "Baruch works for Shadrach?!"

The king nodded. "Almost five years now."

Immediately, her mind raced to the scrolls and how she had kept them a secret from the king. Nebuchadnezzar must have learned about them and, in his search for who sent them, found Baruch. Was he now going to punish Shadrach, Michael ben-Ram, and Baruch?

Nebuchadnezzar had lived with her long enough to read her thoughts, and enjoying her little turmoil, he nodded, "Yes, Aridatha, I know all about the scrolls. I also know Baruch ben-Zadok sent them to you."

"Baruch sent them?!" Her eyes widened in horror because now the king was going to execute Baruch or sentence him to Canal Prison. "No, no, no! I beg you, my king, do not punish him. I know I should have told you about the scrolls, but I thought Shadrach sent them. Surely, it was not such a grave trespass. Please do not punish any of them. I will do anything, anything you ask. I beg you, do not punish…"

Gently placing his finger to her lips, he said, "I ordered Baruch to send the scrolls to you."

"You ordered Baruch…" From head to toe, she felt numb. No, it was tingling. Or was it searing heat, then icy chills? She was definitely seeing double, two royal heads bobbing up and down before her, and she collapsed so quickly, he barely had time to catch her. Dead weight in his arms and gulping for air, Aridatha tried to understand, and with Nebuchadnezzar's help, the pieces fell together.

First, he reminded her that when she was ten years old, she told him she was going to marry Baruch ben-Zadok because they both loved the Hebrew scrolls. So, because he wanted to make restitution for all the years of wrongs he had forced upon her—even though he knew this would never be enough—he found Baruch and ordered him to send the scrolls to her. Suggesting different passages each month, Baruch had actually been speaking to her, reminding her about the Fourth Man, God's goodness, Jerusalem, and lastly, Rachel weeping. In doing this, Nebuchadnezzar had hoped she would remember her love for Baruch. Indeed, the king had succeeded, which was not surprising, for he did all things well. For Aridatha, without even knowing it, had learned to love Baruch all over again.

Meeting the king's eyes, she could see he had been planning this since their last night on the mountaintop when he did not kiss her, but instead had fled. Grateful to him, and grateful she had not awakened love before it so desired, she threw her arms around his neck and buried him in kisses. Yes, this was the day of her marriage, but not to the King of Babylon. Today, she would marry Baruch ben-Zadok.

Nebuchadnezzar, holding her long and tight, breathed in her fragrance for the last time. Then, hand in hand, they stepped into the shadowy corridor, reminiscent of that day long ago when they walked together from the furnace arena through the dark tunnel and out into the afternoon light.

On that day, Aridatha had given him her crimson pouch. In later years, while hiding under a vendor's cart in the middle of the siege zone, Baruch had reprimanded her for it, saying, "How stupid was that, Ari?" But now, knowing Baruch would not object, she again held out the pouch to the king.

"To remember me by," she whispered.

With a grateful heart, he bowed his head so she could put it on him.

After settling it safely next to his royal pendant, she said, "When I first gave this to you, you asked if it would bless or curse."

"You told me you did not know."

"There came a point in my life when I believed it was a curse."

"And now?"

"It has always been a blessing."

Nodding his agreement, his thoughts flashed back to the day when he threw the pouch to the ground and called Arioch a fool. But Arioch had not been a fool. Arioch had picked up the pouch, kept it in safekeeping, and returned it to him even after he had demoted him to the lowliest of ranks. Now, as Aridatha was walking out of his life, she was giving him the pouch again. Without a doubt, it was a blessing, and although it brought solace, something in his life was still missing. Up on the mountaintop when his mind, kingdom, power, and glory were restored and everything around him was so new, he thought he had found it. But before long, the old familiar restlessness had returned, and it was growing daily. Yes, he was King of Babylon, but what did it mean? Recently, he had even started questioning the purpose of having his mind and his kingdom restored. Furthermore, what was the purpose of his power and glory? He had hoped Aridatha would have provided the answer, perhaps even through the pouch. Instead, he was still at a loss, but there was no time to dwell on it because she was leaving, and he had one more thing to do.

So, taking her hand, he removed his royal ring and placed it on her finger. "From Nebuchadnezzar King of Babylon to Aridatha of Jerusalem, for saving the king's life."

"I had to," she smiled.

His breath caught. Something sounded familiar, but what? He could not remember. "What is it, Aridatha? You must tell me. Why did you have to save my life?"

"You know the answer, my king," she said, her voice warming his soul. "I saved your life because you are the servant of the Lord Almighty."

Of course! That was it! The answer he had been searching for: purpose! Purpose for his mind, his kingdom, his power, and his glory, striking him as the rock struck the statue, shattering his entire world. But this time, he wanted it shattered. No longer would he live to serve himself or Babylon, but to serve the Lord Almighty as his faithful servant.

"Yes, Aridatha," he replied, his heart hammering under the weight of the royal pendant and the crimson pouch laying side by side on his chest. "I, Nebuchadnezzar King of Babylon, am the servant of the Lord Almighty."

Instantly, the young girl who had taken his hand so many years before stepped aside making room for the woman, Aridatha of Jerusalem, to bow to the ground before Nebuchadnezzar, all his power, and all his glory, and say, "Oh, king, live forever."

Even bowed to the dirt, she looked as tall as she did on the Tower of David waving the Hebrew flag, in all her power and all her glory: the faithful servant.

"Aridatha, rise," he commanded.

Obediently, she stood, but she did not look him in the eye. So, lifting her chin, he said, "You and Baruch will not be going back to Jerusalem because it is too dangerous. Instead, you will live here in Babylon. You will build houses and plant gardens for your people. Finally, do you understand, you and I will never see each other again?"

Tears welling, she nodded.

"However, if on occasion, you do think back on our days together," his voice was exceedingly tender, his eyes gentle, "do not think of me. Instead, remember the wondrous things the Most High God did for me."

Before she could answer, they were surrounded by a presence much larger than themselves, the presence of two cities, as if reminding them Aridatha had not relinquished the Throne of the Lord for the glory of kingdoms, while King Nebuchadnezzar had relinquished the glory of kingdoms for the Throne of the Lord.

"I will not forget," she whispered.

"Nor will I."

The two had been mysteriously bonded since she was ten years old, when for some unknown reason, she gave him her crimson pouch, settling it at his heart next to the royal pendant of Babylon. Now, after all these years, their bond was complete, it was time for her to go. She tried to turn, but tears streaming down her cheeks, she could not move.

So, putting his hands on her shoulders, he turned her toward the light at the end of the tunnel, and said, "Go."

She ran the whole way, crying the whole way: through the corridor, out into the courtyard, hugging Baruch, even galloping away in his arms. But despite her tears and the king's lack of them, Nebuchadnezzar knew he would miss her far more than she would miss him. For she was going to Baruch ben-Zadok to live out her days immersed in the Hebrew scrolls, while he was left alone to rule Babylon. Yet strangely, he did not feel alone, because since the moment he conceded he was the servant of the Lord Almighty, something had changed inside him. It took him a while to grasp what it was, but when he did, he burst out laughing. In his resolve to serve the Lord as his faithful servant, he had found what he had been looking for all his life. Nebuchadnezzar King of Babylon had found rest.

EPILOGUE

NEBUCHADNEZZAR wrote his letter and sent it out to all the peoples, nations, and languages living throughout the earth. He ordered it to be read publically on the summer solstice so everyone would have enough sunlight to come together to hear what the Most High God had done for Nebuchadnezzar King of Babylon.

He chose Chenguang to take his letter to China. Escorted by Arioch's six sons, she rode safely and comfortably in the middle of a mile-long caravan laden with gifts from Nebuchadnezzar to the new emperor. After the letter was read throughout China, the Grand Mentor Tin copied it onto a tablet, and then he, Chenguang, and Arioch's six sons carried the letter and the tablet down into the earth. With his three-pronged hat teetering the entire way, the Grand Mentor led them through a maze of tunnels to a foyer with a marble chair looking like a judgment seat. Escorting them through one of the two matching gold doors, he continued down into the earth passing an altar with *yi* written on it, going beyond Fohi's star map room, and stopping at an ivory door with crowns carved into it. Unlocking the door, he led the group into a freshly-constructed room with one stalwart marble chair in its center, much like the chair in the foyer. There, on the seat, they placed Nebuchadnezzar's letter to the nations: the original parchment wrapped and sealed, and its copy written on the tablet. Then, after locking the ivory door, they spent the rest of the day marveling at all the other treasures in China's subterranean tunnels.

Nebuchadnezzar's letter did not reach Jerusalem until seventy years after the Fall of Jerusalem, when under the rule of Cyrus King of Persia, Hebrew caravans returned to the desolate city.

An old woman with the Stars of David in her hem had gone ahead of the caravan and was now climbing the rubble that had once been the city's wall. At her side was her three-year-old great-granddaughter, also wearing the Stars of David in the hem of her tunic. They were a good hiking match, for although the little girl clambered over the boulders and animal carcasses as quickly as she could, their massive height and cumbersome breadth slowed her down long enough for the old woman to keep up. But the great-grandmother's heart started to hammer, perhaps because of the steepness of the grade or the weight of the sacks on her back or the unexpected caress of Jerusalem dirt under her feet. Whatever the reason, she had to stop and set her burdens down: a sack of scrolls compiled and copied in an underground crypt in the northeast corner of Babylon's Southern Palace, ten copies of Nebuchadnezzar's letter, and a cluster of star maps wrapped tightly in a purple silk sack with the Signs and Constellations embroidered in gold.

As her ancient eyes scanned the wall's fallen stones, she remembered how once long ago, she had waved the Hebrew flag from the Tower of David, shouting to both Babylon and Jerusalem, "Remember the Fourth Man." She said nothing about it to the little girl because she knew her past was not important. What was important was the future, and looking at her great-granddaughter, she saw that future: the rebuilding of the Temple in obedience to the God of Abraham, Isaac and Jacob, the God who created everything very good.

Soon, she looked down at the Jerusalem dirt under her feet. How long had it been? How many years since holding a handful? Unable to resist, she hunkered down, her bones creaking, and clasping some of the ancient earth in her ancient hand, she stared at it. In fact, she stared so long, as old people often do, getting lost in their memories, even hearing voices as if they were really there—*Stop it, Ari, you are getting dirt in my face; I am not, Baruch, the dirt is going to heaven*—the little girl grew impatient. And why not? How could she know the wondrous thoughts rising up in the old woman's tired mind: the Fourth Man, taking Nebuchadnezzar's hand, giving him her crimson pouch, watching a feathered king and a herd of wild donkeys galloping in a whirlwind of snow, building and planting for her people, proofreading the scrolls year after year?

Sensing the child's impatience, the old woman let go of her memories, and taking hold of her great granddaughter's hand, she sifted the Jerusalem dirt into the child's palm. Then, pushing herself up off the ground, she picked up her bags and continued her ascent.

Now it was the little girl's turn to stare at the dirt, laden with ancient and future sorrows, yet armed with ancient and future strength. And just as old people get lost in their memories, she, like the very young, got lost in the moment and, for no reason in the world, threw the dirt into the air. So intent on watching it rise to the heavens, she barely heard her great-grandmother's narration, telling her about the day fire came down from heaven and the glory of the Lord filled the Temple. Yet, for the rest of her life, she would remember every word.

NOTES

Nebuchadnezzar did write down his account of his dream, telling about the tree, the words of the holy Watcher, Daniel's interpretation, living with the animals, eating grass like the cattle, his hair growing like eagles' feathers, and acknowledging Heaven rules. Today, 2,600 years later, his account continues to go out to all the peoples, nations, and languages living throughout the earth telling them about what the Most High God did for him. The King of Babylon's account is found in the Holy Scriptures, the Book of Daniel, Chapter Four.

―◁◁◁◁◁||)((||▷▷▷▷―

Cyrus King of Persia, as foretold by the prophet Isaiah, set the Israelites free seventy years after the Fall of Jerusalem, so they could return to Jerusalem to rebuild their temple. Johannes Kepler (1571-1631), calculating backwards,[1] showed that Cyrus King of Persia was born in the year of a conjunction of Saturn and Jupiter in the sign of Pisces. This was the conjunction Tin calculated would happen during Aridatha's lifetime. In this light, Cyrus' birth was a special historical event for Israel.

---

1   Bullinger, Ethelbert, The Witness of the Stars (Kregel Publications, Grand Rapids, Michigan, 1983)